THE SECRET OF RUBY'S LIGHTHOUSE

BOOKS BY KRISTIN HARPER

THE SECRET OF RUBY'S LIGHTHOUSE

KRISTIN HARPER

bookouture

Published by Bookouture in 2025

An imprint of Storyfire Ltd.
Carmelite House
50 Victoria Embankment
London EC4Y 0DZ

www.bookouture.com

The authorised representative in the EEA is Hachette Ireland
8 Castlecourt Centre
Dublin 15 D15 XTP3
Ireland
(email: info@hbgi.ie)

ISBN: 978-1-83618-102-6
eBook ISBN: 978-1-83618-101-9

For my nephews, as well as my nieces—
with happy memories of your early years,
especially at the beach

PROLOGUE

Sitting in the rocking chair by her bedroom window, Ruby watched the lighthouse swing its luminous beam across the twinkling sky. *Where has the time gone?* she lamented, as a tear slid down her cheek.

Forty-seven years. It had been forty-seven years—nearly half a century—since her friends Gordon and Sarah Sheffield had invited her to come to Dune Island with them. Yet Ruby could picture that summer as clearly as if it were yesterday...

She recalled the languorous afternoons she and Sarah had spent reading and soaking up the sun in the Adirondack chairs on the back lawn because Sarah had been too weak to walk to the beach. And she remembered the erratic *clack-clickety-clack-clack* of Gordon's old manual typewriter rising from the cottage as he worked on his latest novel.

Usually, reminiscing about her first summer on Dune Island made her smile, but tonight Ruby had a splitting headache, and she felt oddly anxious. She wrung her hands to stop her fingers from tingling. *Am I worried that Gordon would disapprove of what I'm about to do?* she asked herself. But that was silly. Gordon had died a long time ago, and even if he were still alive, he'd understand why it was necessary for her to share their secret, wouldn't he?

Of course, she had never breathed a word about it while Sarah was living. Although it had pained Ruby to deceive her, Sarah's health had already been too precarious: she couldn't have survived the additional stress. Not to mention, if Gordon and Ruby's secret had ever gotten out, it would have utterly destroyed his reputation, and she'd dreaded to imagine the unwelcome attention she would've received, too. Besides, there'd never been a compelling reason to reveal this part of the past to anyone else.

But now Sarah's grandson had come to Dune Island with his family, and it was clear he was struggling. Ruby dearly wished she could help him, but he seemed so wary of her. She couldn't be certain why this was, but she suspected he'd been influenced by his father's opinion of her and Gordon.

I promised Gordon I'd never disclose our secret to Sarah, but that doesn't mean I can't tell her grandson the truth, Ruby reminded herself. *If I come clean about the past, it might change his perspective. Perhaps he'll relax enough to appreciate the tranquillity of this beautiful place, which is what Sarah always wanted for her family...*

With renewed confidence that she was doing the right thing, Ruby leaned forward and tried to push herself up from the chair, but her arm wouldn't move. It felt lifeless and numb, almost as if it were detached from her body. She couldn't make sense of what was happening. Had her arm fallen asleep? Was she having a heart attack? Is that why her vision was growing dim?

Am I going to take my secret with me to the grave after all?

ONE

TWO WEEKS EARLIER

Springtime always filled Meg Carter with hope, but today, she was so deliriously happy she couldn't stop humming. It seemed almost too good to be true that she got to spend the next three months on Dune Island helping her great-aunt, Ruby, run her small, six-guest-room inn.

She pushed open the side window to wipe the exterior sill with a damp cloth. A moment later, a lazy breeze, redolent of freshly mown grass and sea spray roses, fluttered in, along with the strains of trilling birds and lapping waves.

I'm so giddy I almost feel like I'm falling in love, she thought, admiring the vibrant blue-green beryl hue of the water in the distance. *Except this is even better than falling in love because I know it won't end in heartache and bitter disappointment.*

In February, Meg's boyfriend of almost two-and-a-half years, Josh, had proposed marriage to her and she'd joyfully accepted. They'd announced their big news a few days later during Meg's fortieth birthday party, and their family members and friends had burst into cheers, thrilled for the couple.

One of Josh's buddies had clapped him on the back and

said, "Best decision you've ever made, but what took you so long to pop the question?"

"He needed to run out the clock," Josh's older brother, Patrick, had interjected. "Now that Meg's forty and officially old like the rest of us, he figures she's not gonna nag him about having a baby."

Meg had received the comment as a joke—a very crass joke, but over the years she'd learned to expect that kind of humor from Patrick.

What she *hadn't* expected, not in a million years, was that when she referenced the remark during a private conversation with Josh later that evening, she'd discover that his brother had been more right than wrong. Although Josh might not have intentionally "run out the clock," before proposing to Meg, he'd admittedly believed that she'd given up her desire to start a family.

"I figured you must be over it by now," he'd said, as if wanting children was a passing whim, or something to recover from, like the flu. "You have to admit it, Meg, your chances of getting pregnant at this age are relatively slim."

"Maybe, but it's not as if it's impossible. Besides, as I told you very early in our relationship, I'd *love* to adopt a child, whether I can get pregnant or not."

Meg had been so upset that she'd felt her heart quivering in her throat, and it had seemed the room was listing sharply, like a ship just before it capsizes. She'd gripped the back of the nearest chair and repeated, "I told you all of this, right from the beginning—and whenever we've discussed a future together. In fact, I specifically remember sitting here at this very table and sharing that my great-aunt, Ruby, was adopted and so was my best friend in elementary school. I told you those relationships shaped my views on adopting a child, and you said you'd be open to adoption, too."

"*Open* to it, yeah, meaning I hadn't decided one way or the other. But the last time we talked about this was way over a year ago. And for the past six months, almost every time you've watched your nephews for the weekend, you've griped about it." Josh had imitated Meg complaining, "*I'm not cut out for this. I'm too old to stay up all night with kids who eat their body weight in sugar during the day. How am I supposed to keep my eyes open at work tomorrow when—*"

Exasperated, Meg had cut him off. "Good grief, Josh, that's called *venting*. I didn't *literally* mean I'm too old to be a mom or that I'm not cut out to take care of children. I only said those things because my brother and sister-in-law haven't exactly developed healthy eating habits and consistent bedtimes for the boys. But in case you hadn't noticed, even if I *sometimes* complain about watching their kids, I always say yes whenever they ask me. Because no matter how difficult it can be, I still treasure being with my nephews and nurturing them and watching them grow."

"Really? That's sure not how you came across." Josh had seemed genuinely surprised.

Maybe Meg had grumbled about babysitting more than she'd realized, but that was beside the point. "Even so, I don't understand how you could make such a huge assumption about whether I'd changed my mind about starting a family based on a few minor comments about watching my brother's kids," she'd replied. "Besides, if *you'd* changed *your* mind about having children, why didn't you talk to me about it before you proposed?"

"I didn't think I *had* to talk to you about it—I thought we were on the same page," he'd claimed defensively. "But just so there's absolutely no confusion or miscommunication about the subject now, I'm telling you in very plain language that I've made up my mind. I don't want kids, period. I mean, c'mon, Meg. I'm already forty-two. Most people our age are preparing to be empty-nesters in a few years. We're too old to become first-time parents."

"Speak for yourself," she'd shot back. "Because *I've* made up *my* mind, too, and I'm not going to change it—not even by my *fiftieth* birthday."

After many, many quieter but equally intense discussions, the only agreement the pair could reach was that they needed to call off their engagement and break up entirely. The decision had left Meg feeling devastated because she'd truly loved Josh and had fervently wanted to start a family and spend her life with him. She'd genuinely believed he'd shared that desire, too. Yet she'd also felt infuriated that he hadn't been more forthcoming about something as significant as whether he wanted to have children or not.

Wasn't he ever *going to tell me he'd changed his mind?* Meg wondered sarcastically as she used the damp cloth to flick a cobweb—there were too many at the inn lately, but she'd soon fix that—from the upper corner of the window frame. *Or did he figure he'd just let his brother blurt it out at our wedding reception?*

Almost immediately, she reminded herself that obsessing over what had happened between her and Josh was only going to make her feel angry—or heartbroken—all over again. She'd already grieved their broken relationship for four months. As long as she had a choice in the matter, she wasn't going to let anything steal her enjoyment of her once-in-a-lifetime opportunity to spend the summer at the inn.

Growing up, Meg had loved visiting her great-aunt, Ruby, at the seaside so much that every year when she blew out her birthday candles, she'd make the same wish: *this* would be the summer she'd get to stay on Dune Island for the whole season. But her parents wouldn't allow her to visit Ruby alone for that amount of time when she was a young girl. And once she became an adult, Meg couldn't take such a long leave from work. So she'd mentally filed away her youthful dream, deeming it too unpractical to come true—at least, not until she retired—and she'd contented herself with visiting her great-aunt for a week or two every summer, which itself was a luxury.

However, in March, Ruby had contracted a respiratory virus that had landed her in the hospital. As a widow, she'd relied on a cousin who'd come from Pennsylvania and several local friends to help her as she'd recovered. Meg had also traveled from New Jersey to Massachusetts on as many weekends as she could to support her great-aunt. But considering Ruby's weakened condition, as time wore on Meg began to wonder if her great-aunt would be strong enough to open the inn for the summer season.

Then, in April, Meg had experienced a health scare of her own. She was at the university where she worked as the director of student events. She'd just finished finalizing the accommodations for the graduating class's commencement speaker when she'd experienced a prolonged episode of heart palpitations. Her chest hadn't hurt, but the unsettling sensation had been so pronounced and so persistent that Meg had wondered if it was leading up to something worse. She'd tried deep breathing exercises to calm herself, but she'd been so anxious that she'd hyperventilated instead, which had caused her to pass out and her coworkers to call 9-1-1.

In her distraught state, bounding toward the hospital in the back of the ambulance, all Meg could think was, *I'll be so mad if it turns out I'm having a heart attack from the stress of planning a celebration for twenty-two-year-olds who have their entire futures ahead of them!*

A myriad of medical tests had proved that Meg hadn't suffered a heart attack, nor was it a panic attack. Rather, she'd experienced a harmless arrhythmia, most likely caused by a combination of caffeine, dehydration, stress, and fatigue. The doctor had advised her to make lifestyle changes: cut back on coffee, drink more water, reduce her stress, and increase the amount of sleep she got.

Stepping out of the emergency department and into the dusky light of evening, Meg had been struck by an epiphany: her childhood birthday wish to spend the entire summer on Dune Island might have been impractical, but it was also a necessity. Both for her own sake, as well as for her great-aunt's. *Josh might be right. Maybe it's unrealistic to hold on to the hope of marrying a man I adore who wants to raise a family with me, but there's no reason to let my Dune Island dream pass me by,* she'd decided right then and there.

Now, as she peered out the window at the ocean's satiny sheen, she smiled and said aloud, "Talk about the best decision someone ever made... *This* is it."

"What did you say?" Ruby asked, shuffling into the room. She sank into the sofa opposite the large picture window, which offered a sweeping view of the long grassy meadow just beyond the inn's tidy back lawn. A meandering groove cutting through the gently sloping field eventually led to Misty Point Lighthouse, which stood like a proud sentinel on the sandy tip of land jutting into the sea.

"I was just expressing how happy I am to be here." Meg took a seat on the sofa, too, angling sideways so her great-aunt could hear her better. She noticed that Ruby was "wearing" two pairs of reading glasses. One was perched on top of her short, fluffy white hair, and the other hung from a green cord around her neck. She had a habit of subconsciously picking up whatever reading glasses happened to be lying around. It wouldn't have seemed at all unusual if she'd also had a pair perched on her nose, or an additional pair nested in her hair.

"I still can't believe you'll be staying with me for almost three months." Her great-aunt fondly patted Meg's bony knee. "How did you ever finagle that much time off work?"

"It was easy, because there are hardly any student events scheduled in the summertime. And I assured the administration that I'd thoroughly prepare the staff and interns to plan everything for the early autumn events during my absence." Meg gathered her heavy, cinnamon-colored hair from behind her neck and pulled it over the front of her right shoulder. "But mostly, I think they said yes because the school is so underendowed that this year they're practically begging staff to volunteer to take unpaid leaves."

"Oh, no, you won't be compensated for almost three months? I didn't realize that." Ruby pressed a hand to her cheek. "I might be able to pay you for helping me, if I let one of the seasonal housekeepers go. But which one? Ava needs the money because she's saving for college, and Chloe's a single mom. But maybe if the three of you rotated shifts—"

"I wouldn't *think* of putting either of them out of a job or accepting any money from you, Aunt Ruby!" Meg interrupted, wishing she hadn't let it slip that her leave was unpaid. "I promise, it's not a financial hardship for me to take this time off. Besides, *I* should be paying *you* for letting me stay here. I'm so lucky you have a room that hasn't been booked yet—but remember, we've agreed that I'll sleep on the pull-out sofa bed in the den whenever you get any additional reservations."

"I'll probably have at least one vacant room all summer this year. Sometimes two." Ruby furrowed her brow. "I'm afraid this is going to be an ongoing trend for the inn, now that there's a preponderance of luxury accommodations on the island."

A preponderance of luxury accommodations. Meg smiled at her great-aunt's word choice. As a lifelong avid reader, Ruby had an extensive vocabulary. Meg admired how she expressed herself, but some of her family members thought she sounded old-fashioned or overly formal. Meg's brother once teased Meg that whenever she visited Ruby, she assimilated their greataunt's vocabulary, the way some people acquire an accent after traveling abroad. To his disappointment, Meg had considered his observation a high compliment, and she'd thanked him.

Unfortunately, no matter how it was phrased, Meg knew

Ruby was right: dozens of hotels, resorts, and vacation properties were being built on the island by the minute. Some of the accommodations were more upscale than others, but virtually all of them offered standard modern amenities and conveniences, at the very least.

By comparison, the inn was a no-frills environment. Its Wi Fi and cell phone connections were intermittent, at best. Ruby didn't subscribe to cable or streaming services, and she only had one television, which was in the den, for guests to share. Although the guest rooms were sparkling clean and the beds were supremely comfortable, some of the other furnishings and décor were a bit outdated, and not all the rooms had ensuite bathrooms.

Ruby's approach to hosting had always been very casual, and it was more that way now that she was almost eighty. Although she warmly invited guests to make themselves at home, she didn't fuss over them. In the morning, there was a pot of coffee on in the kitchen, but Ruby didn't prepare meals or snacks for guests. Instead, she allowed them to use the kitchen and dining room, if needed, in addition to the outdoor gas grill. They were also welcome to spread out in the common areas, including the living room, den, and three-season porch, and to help themselves to any of the inn's books, board games, puzzles, and beach toys and equipment.

Although this lenient arrangement wasn't common in the 1990s, it was very well received, especially among parents with young children. It wasn't unusual for two or three generations of the same family to reserve all six of the guest rooms so they could vacation as a group.

One family summed up their experience by writing in the guestbook, "Thank you for giving us free run of the inn. It made us feel like we had a summer home of our very own! We loved rolling out of bed and ambling down the path to the beach, and the view of the water and lighthouse is as gorgeous at night as it is during the day. The Inn at Misty Point is truly special. There's no place like it on the island—or in the rest of the world!"

Despite her eloquence, Ruby herself couldn't have expressed the sentiment better, and Meg wholeheartedly agreed. Whatever the inn lacked in amenities and technology, it more than made up for in its one-of-a-kind location.

Dune Island was comprised of five towns, collectively referred to as Hope Haven, and Ruby's inn was located in the town called Benjamin's Manor. This quaint fishing village on the western side of the island was renowned for its historic sea captains' homes. It also boasted a busy cobblestone Main Street running alongside a small harbor, which was the site of another lighthouse, informally known as Sea Gull Light.

The inn, however, was the only residence on a remote peninsula called Misty Point, in the southernmost part of the town. Because this isolated stretch of land was surrounded by Hope Haven Sound on three sides, it afforded the inn magnificent water views from every room. Of course, magnificent water views and private waterfront properties were to be expected on an island. What made the inn's vista so extraordinary was its proximity to Misty Point Lighthouse, which was literally in the back yard. Because there was no public land access to Misty Point—although it was reachable by boat—it seemed as if the beach and the lighthouse belonged exclusively to the inn.

But as guests' expectations and needs changed over the years, not everyone appreciated Ruby's place as much as they used to. Earlier this spring, when Meg was updating the inn's website to reflect the current room rates, she noticed several complaints among the compliments in last year's reviews.

Guests had posted comments such as, "Awesome beach and spectacular sunsets exceeded our expectations but we were disappointed by the lack of creature comforts." And, "The location can't be beat (private beach, close-up views of Misty Point

Lighthouse), but the interior needs some TLC." Or, as someone else had sarcastically put it, "Don't know what I loved more; the weak coffee, bad Wi-Fi connection, or sharing a bathroom with other guests. *NOT*."

As the familiar saying went, you can't please everyone, so Meg tried to take the remarks with a grain of salt. But occasional negative reviews were one thing, consistently losing business was another. Now that her great-aunt had brought up the subject, Meg figured it was time to make a few suggestions about ways to improve guests' experiences at the inn.

"If you're concerned about people choosing other accommodations, maybe we could make a couple changes to the interior of the inn to accentuate its uniqueness?" she hinted.

"I'd love to," Ruby readily agreed. She coughed into the crook of her arm repeatedly before saying, "But I had to take out a loan to replace the windows and repair the roof and chimney two years ago. I'm still repaying it, so I don't have the budget to renovate—it's too late for that this season anyway—and honestly, I can't even afford new furniture right now."

"That's okay." Meg had suspected money was tight for her great-aunt lately. "I'm sure there must be other small improvements we could make that wouldn't involve purchasing—"

She was interrupted mid-sentence by the sharp *brrrng* of the landline, so she went into the kitchen to answer it. The caller requested to speak directly to Ruby, and after Meg brought the cordless phone to her, she left to make tea to soothe Ruby's throat.

Returning to the living room a few minutes later, she noticed her great-aunt's apprehensive expression, and Meg suspected the caller had canceled his reservation. She placed the cups on the coffee table and sat down beside Ruby. "Is something wrong?"

"No, no. Well, yes, I mean, there is. Or there was." Her nonsensical answer gave Meg pause. Ruby was silent a moment, staring off into the distance, and then she mumbled, "I just received word that Bradley died six months ago."

"Oh, no, I'm very sorry to hear that." Meg touched Ruby's arm, waiting for her to elaborate. When she didn't, Meg asked, "Was he a close friend of yours?"

"No, we'd only met a few times in passing, remember?" Ruby prompted, but Meg shook her head. "Really? You don't remember me talking about Bradley? Bradley Harris, my friend Sarah's son—and Gordon's stepson?"

"Ohh, *that* Bradley," Meg uttered, feeling dense. Her great-aunt had shared countless anecdotes about Gordon and Sarah Sheffield, an older couple who'd moved into the apartment above Ruby and her husband's in Pittsburgh when Ruby was in her early thirties. Sarah's son from a previous marriage, Bradley, had been away at college, so Ruby had barely known him. However, despite the age difference, she'd quickly grown close to both Sarah, a homemaker, and Gordon, a mystery novelist and part-time university instructor.

According to Ruby, shortly after she'd met the couple, Sarah was diagnosed with cancer and she underwent multiple surgeries and an extensive course of chemotherapy. That summer, the pair asked their younger neighbor to accompany them to Dune Island to help care for Sarah while Gordon was completing his latest book.

"They acted as if I was doing them a huge favor, but I knew *I* was the lucky one. Not only did I have the privilege of staying with two people I loved as if they were my own parents, but I'd never been anywhere as beautiful as Misty Point. Fortunately, my husband—your uncle Alan—didn't mind me being gone for several weeks, since he put in such long hours during the summer that we hardly got to see each other, anyway," Ruby had told Meg. "I was devastated when Alan and I moved out of the city and I lost touch with the Sheffields, but I never forgot how kind they were to me and how special they made me feel."

Apparently, they'd never forgotten Ruby's kindness to them, either, because after Gordon died in the late 1980s—Sarah had already passed on—he bequeathed the couple's summer home to Ruby. It was a timely gift for her to receive back then, as her husband also had recently died, leaving her with a steep mortgage and a car loan she was unable to pay. She moved from Pennsylvania to Dune Island and began renting out rooms, until she eventually converted the house into a full-fledged inn.

Although Gordon had given Ruby the main residence and the small plot of land immediately surrounding it, he'd left the rest of the sprawling Misty Point property to his stepson, Bradley. Bordering Ruby's back yard, his acreage included the vast meadow stretching to the lighthouse, as well as a tiny, barely habitable cottage tucked into a haphazard stand of pitch pines on the right-hand edge of the property. Even in its undeveloped state, Bradley's land was worth ten times as much as Ruby's was. Yet according to the snippets of information she had shared about Bradley, he'd never shown any interest in his inheritance.

"He only visited Dune Island once," Meg said quietly, thinking aloud.

"That's right—he came for a weekend that first summer I was here," Ruby answered, a faraway look in her eyes. "After Gordon died, I wrote to Bradley dozens of times, inviting him to stay at the inn as my personal guest whenever he wanted, but he never replied. I always hoped one day he'd change his mind about visiting. Now it's too late…"

Her eyes welled, so Meg gave her a side hug, even though she was a little surprised by her great-aunt's tearfulness, considering she'd hardly even known Bradley. Or was Ruby weepy because she'd felt rebuffed by him? "It was a very gracious invitation. I can't imagine why he never accepted it."

"Bradley didn't share his mother's and Gordon's love of the

seaside," replied Ruby with a sigh. "Supposedly, he detested the tacky sensation of salt on his skin."

Meg vaguely recalled her great-aunt mentioning this excuse for Bradley's absence in the past, but she'd never given it much thought until now. "That seems like a petty reason not to visit Dune Island on occasion, especially considering he owned property here. Very beautiful and valuable property. It seems like he would have at least come here to try to sell it, although I'm glad he didn't. It would've been awful if noisy neighbors had moved in!"

"There was never any danger of that happening—Gordon's Trust precluded Bradley from selling the land," Ruby said, dabbing her nose with a tissue. "Sarah wanted to be certain her grandchildren had an opportunity to enjoy Misty Point. Now that Bradley's deceased, the property belongs to his offspring."

As soon as the words were out of Ruby's mouth, an unpleasant possibility popped into Meg's mind: was there a conflict among Bradley's descendants about the estate? Is that why they'd contacted Ruby? Meg certainly hoped they weren't going to try to involve her in any of their legal disputes.

"If Bradley died six months ago, why did his family suddenly call you today?"

"That wasn't his family who called. It was the attorney for Gordon's Trust." Her great-aunt's reply made Meg's heart sink. Was her suspicion about Bradley's family accurate? Ruby continued, "He was calling to tell me that Bradley's son will be arriving next Thursday afternoon for a family vacation with his young children. They're going to stay in the cottage."

"In the *cottage*?" Meg's voice squeaked with disbelief. "Does the toilet in there even work? The water must have been shut off a long time ago. And what about the electricity?"

"That was part of the reason the attorney called. He didn't want me to worry that something was amiss if I noticed a plumber or an electrician poking around. He said Bradley's son arranged for repairs and for someone to clean the interior, too."

"If his son knows what condition the cottage is in, then he must know how tiny it is." Meg couldn't picture a family staying there, since the dwelling only had two rooms—a kitchen/living room combination and a bedroom—as well as a bathroom the size of a closet. "How many children does he have?"

"The attorney didn't say. He didn't tell me how long they'd be staying, either," Ruby said, coughing again. Meg noticed she looked paler than usual. "I realize it's cramped quarters, but unlike Bradley, they might be outdoorsy types. Perhaps they consider this an adventure."

Meg supposed she could be right, but the timing seemed fishy to her. "Bradley inherited the property more than thirty-five years ago. Even if he didn't enjoy the oceanside, why didn't his son or anyone from his family visit Dune Island before now?"

Ruby's profile clouded, and she lifted her shoulders in a shrug. As Meg followed her great-aunt's gaze out the window toward the lighthouse, a disturbing thought ran through her mind. *For as long as Aunt Ruby has owned the inn, all her guests, including me, have cut across Bradley's meadow to go directly to the lighthouse and the beach. What if his son decides he doesn't want anyone trespassing on his property? How will anyone get to the tip?*

She already knew the answer: they'd have to take "the long way around." Which meant that instead of walking across the back lawn and through the meadow, they'd start by hiking hundreds of yards toward the water on either side of Ruby's property. If they went to the shoreline on the right, they'd have to pick their way over rocky terrain until they reached the smooth, sandy stretch near the tip of the peninsula. If they went to the left, they'd be forced to slog through marshland for the first half of their trek. Both options were equally arduous, especially during high tide.

Easy access to Misty Point Beach is one of the most appealing aspects of the inn! Newcomers aren't going to be impressed if it's so difficult to get there. And Aunt Ruby's longtime guests are going to resent the inconvenience of walking all the way around, too, Meg worried. *Then the inn will receive terrible reviews and next year, there will be even more vacancies than there are this summer.*

She could almost hear Josh's voice asking, as he'd done on occasion, "Why are you jumping to the worst-case scenario?"

"It's an occupational hazard of being an event planner. I anticipate the worst-case scenario so I can prevent it from happening. Or so I can at least prepare a contingency plan in case it does happen," she'd say. "I hate being blindsided."

The answer seemed ironic to her in retrospect, considering she hadn't anticipated the worst-case scenario with Josh. She didn't want to make the same mistake with Bradley's son, but she didn't want to alarm her great-aunt by voicing her concern about the guests' beach access, either. Besides, Meg supposed she might be letting her fear get the best of her.

I haven't even met Bradley's son yet, she reminded herself. *Aunt Ruby held his grandmother in high esteem, so maybe he'll be just as kind and generous as Sarah was.*

As if reading Meg's mind, Ruby abruptly announced, "Regardless of what's kept Sarah's grandson away from Misty Point until now, it'll be a privilege to meet him and his family. I'm looking forward to giving them a very warm welcome."

Did her enthusiasm sound forced or was Meg imagining it? Either way, she wanted to be supportive of her great-aunt. So, despite her misgivings about the situation, she promised she'd do her best to welcome them, too.

I'll add it to my summer goals, she thought drolly. *Along with, "figure out an inexpensive way to give the inn a fresh new* vibe," "complete a deep spring cleaning before the guests arrive," and "rest, relax, and be ready to start dating again by the time I return home."

"Thank you, dear. Knowing I can count on your help really puts my mind at ease," Ruby said, but a frown puckered her brows and tugged at her mouth. Her mind certainly didn't *seem* at ease.

Is she sad because Bradley died, or is something else upsetting her, too? Meg wondered, but she didn't want to make Ruby feel worse by drawing attention to how distressed she appeared. Instead, she leaned forward, lifted a cup from the coffee table, and handed it to her great-aunt before taking the other cup for herself.

The two women settled back against the sofa cushions and sipped their tea without speaking as they stared out the window. In the distance, the ocean was as dazzling and the sky was as brilliant as ever. But the attorney's news had cast a pall over the afternoon and no matter what she told herself, Meg couldn't shake the feeling that her summer wasn't going to go according to plan.

TWO

"I've been considering inexpensive ways we could give the inn a mini makeover, and I think I've got a good idea," Meg excitedly told Ruby.

The previous evening, she had tossed and turned until midnight, worrying about Bradley's son coming to visit and stressing out about how his presence might affect the guests' enjoyment of Misty Point. Finally, she'd reminded herself that her mental energy was better spent concentrating on what she *could* control, and she'd come up with a plan to enhance the inn's interior that she hoped her great-aunt would like.

"Instead of purchasing anything new, maybe we could focus on downsizing," she suggested.

"What do you think I should eliminate?"

Ruby's brows were knit, so Meg proceeded carefully. She remembered how reluctant her mother had been to scale down her belongings when they'd moved to a smaller house after her divorce from Meg's dad.

"I'm not suggesting you throw anything out if you're not ready to let it go yet," she clarified. "But maybe I could box up a few of the extra dishes and utensils in the kitchen and store them in the attic or garage for the season. Because even if all the guests happen to cook at the same time, they won't need four sets of measuring spoons or five vegetable peelers."

Ruby chuckled with noticeable relief. "I don't have *that* many."

"Okay, that's an exaggeration. But you do have multiples, which makes the drawers and cupboards seem messy. It's unusual for an inn to allow guests to use the kitchen to prepare meals, and I think people appreciate this amenity, especially if they're on a budget and can't afford to eat out every night. But if they have to rummage through the clutter to find what they need, they might get frustrated. So the next time they come to Dune Island, instead of staying here, they might splurge and stay somewhere that has on-site dining."

Ruby nodded slowly. "All right, we can downsize the kitchen drawers and cabinets."

Aware that her great-aunt wouldn't be so easily persuaded about the next suggestion, Meg rose and crossed the room to illustrate her point. Standing in front of the floor-to-ceiling bookcases on each side of the fireplace, she stretched her arms to the side, gesturing. "Some of these—"

Ruby didn't let her finish. "My books? You want me to dispose of my books?" She couldn't have looked more appalled if Meg had suggested she get rid of her closest friends. "What will the guests read in the evenings or on dreary days?"

"Most people use e-readers now, or else they bring their own books with them when they travel." Noticing her great-aunt's crestfallen expression, Meg added, "But you're right, there are always a handful of people who really appreciate browsing through your collection, especially the books about Dune Island. So we won't box up all of them. And you don't have to *get rid* of any, either, Aunt Ruby. You could donate the ones you definitely don't want, put some into storage for the summer, and keep some on the shelves. But right now, these are packed in here so tightly it's almost impossible to take one down. Look..."

Meg made a show of trying to wiggle a book free from the crowded shelf, using two fingers to tilt it toward her. When it wouldn't budge, she gripped its spine and attempted to rock it up and down, to no effect. Finally, using both hands, she gave it a hard yank, and it flew from the shelf, along with two other books, which fell to the floor with a powdery clap. Almost on cue, Ruby sneezed.

"That's another problem with having this many old books—they collect dust, and potentially dust mites, too..." Meg bent to retrieve the fallen novels and stacked them sideways atop of the other books on the shelf before turning to face her great-aunt.

"But reading preferences vary so much from person to person and..." Ruby stopped speaking mid-sentence to dab her eyes with a tissue. Meg was pretty sure, although not positive, that her eyes were only watering; that she wasn't crying at the thought of putting away her books. "... I want the guests to have a wide selection of choices."

"Right. We could still offer books from all the genres you own, but we'd arrange them like they do in a library. For instance, I could put ten to twelve mysteries on this shelf."

"Only ten or twelve? But I own at least one hundred or one hundred and fifty mysteries!"

Meg suppressed a giggle. "Okay, we'll keep fifteen or twenty, then. But I think guests feel overwhelmed when they see so many books. It's more enticing if you only offer a handful. And decreasing the number of books would allow the beauty of these built-in shelves to really shine. The room will feel lighter. Fresher."

Ruby's eyes were darting from the bookcase on one side of the fireplace to the bookcase on the other side, so Meg paused to allow her time to imagine the arrangement she'd suggested. Then she paced over to the big picture window opposite the sofa. Facing the beach and lighthouse, the window ran almost the entire length of the wall. Beneath it was a wide, window seat with cushions that were once navy but had faded in the sunlight to baby blue. Under the window seat was a long, built-in, two-tier bookcase. Meg pointed at it.

"I could reorganize your children's books and put them on these shelves, here, where the kids will see them as soon as they enter the room."

Ruby's expression brightened considerably. As a young girl who'd lived in half a dozen foster homes, she'd relied on books for comfort and even for companionship. So as an adult, she became a strong advocate of children's literacy. Over the years, she must have purchased more than three hundred books for the little ones to read at the inn. She'd reserved two bookcases in the den solely for children's literature, because that's where the board games were kept. But the kids preferred sitting on the window seat in the living room, where they could see the lighthouse better, so it made more sense to house their books there, too.

"What a terrific idea. I wonder why I didn't think of it sooner," Ruby said, and Meg had to bite her lip to keep from giggling. Organizational skills were not among her great-aunt's strengths. "But I don't want to add more work to your to-do list."

"It won't seem like work. Unless I'm under pressure planning an event at the university, organizing is a form of relaxation for me," Meg insisted, hoping her great-aunt would allow her to undertake this project alone. Ruby still looked a little peaked and Meg didn't want her to overexert herself. "So, it's okay to condense your collection?"

"Yes, in here and in the den." A frown crimped the skin on Ruby's forehead again as she instructed, "But please don't remove any of the books in my bedroom."

Ever since Meg was a child, she'd known and respected how special her great-aunt's personal collection was. On occasion,

Ruby had shared one of the treasured volumes she kept in her bedroom, but only with her express permission. "I wouldn't dream of touching your books or suggesting you downsize your personal collection," Meg assured her.

"Good. Because I want to leave the shelves in my bedroom *exactly* as they are," Ruby reiterated so emphatically she began coughing, and Meg offered to bring her a glass of lemon water with honey in it.

In the kitchen, she set the cutting board on the counter by the window and gazed past the dense bunches of white daisies and the proliferation of orange, bespeckled tiger lilies to the breeze-rumpled blueness of Hope Haven Sound. Funny, how such a beautiful view could make even the most mundane task, like slicing fruit or washing dishes, seem like a privilege, a cause for celebration.

Yet the last part of her conversation with Ruby had left Meg feeling troubled. *I know she trusts me, so why did she emphasize that her books are off-limits?* she thought. *It's not like her to be that stern. Did I come on too strong about downsizing the common areas, and now she feels overly protective about her personal space?*

Meg finished fixing the lemon water and carried it into the living room, intending to double check with Ruby about whether she was truly comfortable making the changes Meg had suggested. As she crossed the threshold, she was surprised to find her great-aunt standing near the bookcase to the right of the fireplace, an open volume in hand.

"You're right about getting rid of some of these books. I don't know why I've kept this autobiography for so long when I never did care for it. It's time to donate it to the library." She snapped the book shut and gave Meg a complacent smile. "There, that wasn't so difficult."

One down, only a thousand more to go, Meg thought, tongue-in-cheek. *But on the plus side, maybe I'll be so busy with this project I won't have time to worry about Bradley's son arriving soon...*

Whittling away at Ruby's collection of books took even longer than Meg expected. Her great-aunt reluctantly agreed that Meg could do all the physical work of packing and transporting the books. But Ruby understandably wanted to have the final word about which to store, which to give away, and which to reshelve. These decisions did not come quickly.

As a visual aid, Meg had labeled an area of the living room floor for each of the three categories. Ideally, her process was to remove a book from the shelf and announce its author and title so Ruby could tell her which section of the floor to place it on. However, her great-aunt frequently asked Meg to hand her the book. She'd leaf through its pages, often reading an entire chapter or two before making up her mind, only to change it a few minutes later.

After working on the project together for several afternoons, the women had only made their way through a quarter of the bookcases in the living room, and they hadn't begun to downsize any of the bookcases in the den. Even more discouraging, the "reshelve" section of books was disproportionately large compared to the "store" and "donate" sections, which was the opposite of Meg's intended result.

"Looks like we're about to hit our max for the 'reshelve' category," she warned. "If you want to add anything else to this section, you might need to move a few of these books to the 'store' category, first."

Her great-aunt ruefully clucked her tongue. "It's like choosing which of my children to turn out in the cold."

"Your children are hardly going to freeze," Meg assured her with a chuckle. "They'll either find nice, cozy homes in the library, or I'll store them in air-tight containers in the garage.

They should be toasty warm since the temperature and humidity are the same out there as they are in here."

Unfortunately, that's because the inn doesn't have air conditioning, she silently added, aware that this was one of the "creature comforts" most guests expected in their vacation accommodations. A lively onshore breeze usually kept the inn comfortable, but on the dog days of summer, when the humidity rose and the air was as heavy as a sodden wool blanket, not even the fans in each room provided adequate relief. While guests could cool themselves with a dip in the Sound or by taking an icy outdoor shower during the daytime, the nights could feel unbearable in a heatwave.

There's no sense worrying about that right now. I need to focus on the improvements I can help Aunt Ruby make, instead of those she can't afford, Meg reminded herself.

"Looks like I'll need to hold our book club meeting on the porch this afternoon instead of in here," Ruby remarked, surveying the orderly but space-consuming arrangement of books and bins on the floor throughout the room.

For as long as Meg could recall, her great-aunt had hosted a bimonthly book club at the inn. "But today is only Tuesday. I thought your club meets on Wednesdays?"

"Usually we do, but tomorrow Henry's having cataract surgery, so we're meeting today, since it's his turn to lead the discussion." Ruby licked her finger and flipped a page of the biography she'd been perusing for the past ten minutes. "I meant to tell you we'd changed our schedule, but it must have slipped my mind."

Meg wasn't surprised that her aunt had forgotten to mention it. "She's either got her head in the clouds or her nose in a book," was how Meg's father had often described Ruby when he was alive. She was his aunt by marriage, not by blood, and Meg often felt like his side of the family was overly critical of her. But in this case, he'd made a fair point: Ruby could be a little absent-minded.

Meg recalled numerous times when she'd visited the inn as a teenager, Ruby would slide supper into the oven and then wander off to read. She'd become so absorbed in her book that she'd forget all about the food cooking until the smoke detectors began screaming and a silvery, eye-watering haze emanated from the oven.

Ruby even shared a running joke with Meg. "When I'm old and gray, and my doctor says I'm becoming forgetful, be sure to tell him I've always been this way, won't you?"

The quip made Meg smile, despite her frustration that the project was moving along so slowly, and now it would be further delayed by the book club meeting.

I've only got ten days before guests arrive and I still haven't finished giving all the rooms upstairs a deep cleaning, so we really need to get moving on this, she thought, and almost immediately, she could feel her heart pattering a little quicker.

Realizing she needed a break, Meg volunteered to make turkey and cranberry wraps for lunch.

"Sounds tasty," Ruby answered, not glancing up from the paperback romance she was reading. Meg noticed the heavy biography she'd been looking through a minute ago was still open in her lap. Clearly, she hadn't determined what pile to put it in yet.

At this rate, we'll never finish, thought Meg as she side-stepped a mountain of "store" books on her way into the kitchen. But her deep affection for her great-aunt far outweighed any minor annoyance about their lack of progress.

During the two or three years of bickering preceding her parents' divorce, Meg had often visited Ruby for her winter and spring high school breaks, as well as for a week or two each summer. She'd found such solace in the seascape, and her great-aunt's easy-going mannerisms were a welcome relief from the intense friction in her own home. Often on rainy days, Ruby and Meg would lounge at opposite ends of the living room sofa without feeling any need to speak, so engrossed in their books that they didn't even notice that the tide had come in and was on its way out again.

Ruby was the one who'd taught Meg to love books but loving the ocean had come as naturally to her as breathing. Whenever she let too much time pass without a stroll out to the beach, she felt claustrophobic, as if she were suffocating. So, as she spread homemade cranberry sauce on the flatbread, Meg decided she'd head out to the beach during the book club meeting. *I know I've still got a lot to accomplish upstairs, but I do my best thinking when I'm walking and it'll be time well spent if I come up with a way to expedite our downsizing project.*

Padding barefoot along the winding rut through the gently sloping meadow, Meg took care not to brush her ankles against any poison ivy vines or to trip on the woody roots that occasionally crept onto the pathway. As she passed the cottage to her right, she thought about how odd it was going to seem for it to be occupied.

As far as she knew, the last time anyone had been inside the cottage was over fifteen years ago, when it was used for storing the groundskeeper's equipment. Until then, lawn services were paid for by Gordon's Trust, but the funds had long since been depleted, which was why a large portion of the land was overgrown with beach grass and wild roses.

They might be considered an invasive plant species, but they smell heavenly. Meg stopped to inhale deeply and slowly exhale again before journeying onward. Less than an eighth of a mile ahead, near the tip of the flat, sandy neck of land, Misty Point Lighthouse was waiting for her.

Every summer when she was a girl, Meg used to take a tour

of the navigational landmark, and she still retained various facts she'd learned about it. Such as that the 57-foot round, cast-iron tower was erected in 1878, replacing the wooden one that had previously stood in its place. There used to be a keeper's house next to it, but it burned down after a lightning strike in the mid-1970s. Since the lighthouse had been automated by then, the decision was made not to rebuild the keeper's quarters, so the lighthouse stood alone.

Because of its remote location, Misty Point Lighthouse wasn't the best-known lighthouse on the island, nor was it the most photographed or painted. But since it was the most familiar to Meg, it was the most special, as well as the prettiest. She loved the sight of the tower's clean, crisp colors—white on the lower two-thirds, red on the upper, and topped with a black cap—against the ever-changing backdrop of sea and sky.

During the night, when its windows glowed from within and its silvery ray cut through the darkness like a sword, Meg found the lighthouse to be just as striking.

"Hello, beautiful," she greeted it as she approached, assuming no one was nearby to hear her talking aloud.

She circled halfway around it, to where two wooden benches faced the water. Meg hesitated as she considered which direction to walk. She chose to amble along the beach on the northern side of the peninsula first, but after circling back to the tip, she continued beyond it, to the beach on the southern side.

The warm sun on her back relaxed Meg's shoulder muscles, and the nippy water put a spring in her step. The longer she walked, the more limber she felt, both in body and mind. As expected, she consequently came up with a solution to speed along the library project.

Instead of asking Aunt Ruby what she wants to do with each book, I'll name a genre and she can list the first ten books that come to mind in each category. Then I'll pull those books from the shelves, set them aside, and pack up all the remaining books to store for now, she thought. *It'll be quicker and easier than going through the books one by one. And she won't feel like she's being pushed to make too many decisions, because we won't be giving any books away. They'll all still be here, just not on the shelves.*

As she headed back toward the tip a second time, Meg noticed a small boat had anchored in the shallows. She recognized the older man wading ashore with an armful of short wooden stakes; he'd been the lighthouse tour guide for as long as she could remember.

"Hi, Lou! Are you here to make sure the light's plugged in?" she teased, referring to the joke he'd told her about his lighthouse-keeping duties when she was so young she'd actually believed him.

"Sure am," he answered with a broad grin, revealing a gold crown cuspid tooth. "I'm also here to mark where I want the crew to install the seasonal dock. Only a couple of weeks before we start ferrying folks here for the tour, so everything's got to be shipshape. They say the island is going to host a record number of visitors this summer. Some members of the Lighthouse Society think we should offer a third tour day, instead of just two."

Considering how many vacancies there are at the inn, I never would have guessed the island is expected be so crowded this year, Meg said to herself before replying aloud to Lou.

"An extra tour day? How do you feel about that?" she asked, aware that he was a volunteer who wasn't compensated for his time.

"Well, it's a moot point since the Society won't be able to pass a formal vote in time," Lou answered. "But personally, I would have loved it. Leading these tours is the highlight of my year. There's nothing like introducing newcomers to Misty Point and the lighthouse, telling them about its history and watching them fall in love with this place. Welcoming returning visitors never gets old, either. Especially families who've been coming here for generations. I'm sure Ruby feels the same way about her guests."

"Yes, she does," Meg acknowledged. *Even though there aren't quite as many of them as there used to be.* "I guess I'd better get back to the inn to help her finish getting it shipshape, too."

Lou shifted the stakes he was holding to one arm and saluted her with the other. "Aye, aye. See you around, Meg—and don't forget to tell Ruby's guests about the tours. Space on the pontoon boat is limited, but I'm always happy to accommodate walk-ins by land."

"Thanks, Lou. I'll do that."

Meg tromped back past the lighthouse and through the meadow. As she neared the inn, she noticed one of the participants in Ruby's book club making his way toward the expansive, crushed-shell parking area for guests. Because she'd been acquainted with him for years, Meg called, "Bye, Henry. I hope your cataract surgery goes smoothly tomorrow!"

"I'm sure it'll be over in the blink of an eye," he joked, raising the crook of his cane in a farewell wave before continuing toward his car.

Meg rinsed the sand from her feet in the outdoor shower, and then left a trail of wet prints across the patio tiles because she'd forgotten to leave a towel out. She reached the porch stairs just as another book club member, Betty, was coming down them. Meg greeted her and moved aside, waiting at the bottom for her to pass. Instead, Betty planted herself in front of Meg and grasped her arm.

Her eyes dancing, she declared, "You'll never guess what I have to tell you." She didn't wait for Meg to reply before blurting out, "My grandson, Hunter, is coming to visit me in August!"

After the last book club meeting at the inn, Betty had grilled Meg about her personal life, including her relationship status. Then she'd dropped not-so-subtle hints about her grandson, who was also single. Because Betty had mentioned he lived off island, in New Hampshire, Meg had thought she was safe from her matchmaking efforts, but apparently, she'd underestimated her.

Playing dumb, Meg responded, "How wonderful. You must really be looking forward to seeing him."

"Yes, I am. He's such a sweetie. Helps me with the yard work, and whatever else I need. He's very smart, too, a high school chemistry teacher. It's hard to believe he's not seeing anyone, but he's still single, never been married. Did I tell you that?"

Only half a dozen times. Meg politely replied, "Yes, I think you mentioned it."

"I'll have to bring him by to meet you. I bet the two of you have a lot in common, with both of you being educators and all."

Meg laughed in spite of herself. "I'm not an educator, Betty. I don't teach. I plan events for students at a university."

"Close enough. You'll hit it off right away, I just know you will. He's a real catch. He's about your height and he's got blue eyes. That's another thing you have in common."

I hardly think matching eye color is an indicator of compatibility. "Thanks for thinking of me, but I'm not interested in dating anyone right now. I—"

Before Meg could finish, Betty was distracted by a muffled buzzing sound. She ducked her head to rummage through the depths of her oversize purse.

"That must be my husband. I'm supposed to pick him up at the dentist. He's probably wondering where I am." She fished out her phone. Pressing it to her ear, she wiggled her fingers in a goodbye wave and scurried down the path to the parking area.

As interfering as Betty sometimes was, Meg trusted that she

had good intentions. And she'd always be grateful that when her great-aunt was recovering from the respiratory virus earlier that spring, Betty had brought Ruby homemade soup every other day for three weeks.

But of her great-aunt's local friends, Meg was most fond of Alice, who opened the porch door just as Meg reached the top landing of the stairs. "Hi, Alice. Are you leaving? Didn't Aunt Ruby mention we saved enough strawberry rhubarb crisp for the three of us to enjoy after your book club meeting?"

"She did, but unfortunately, I can't stay. Now that school's out for the summer, my husband and I are watching our grands while my son's working. Leaving the children with my husband for more than an hour is always a risk—I never know what kind of mess I'll find when I get home!" She affably rolled her eyes before darting down the stairs.

Meg wiped her feet on the lighthouse-themed doormat, and entered the inn, half-expecting to find Ruby retrieving the dessert from the refrigerator. But her great-aunt was in the living room, leaning back against the sofa with her eyes closed, her fingers interlaced across her abdomen and a damp rectangle of cloth on her forehead.

Her coloring is off, Meg fretted, studying her great-aunt's appearance.

Ruby must have sensed her presence in the doorway. Without opening her eyes, she said, "I'm not asleep, I'm just resting. You can come in if you want."

Meg wove her way through the tall columns of "reshelve" books, and gingerly lowered herself onto the sofa. "Are you ill?"

"Just a little bit of a tension headache. A few of our members had a heated discussion about the book Joan proposed we read for next month's meeting."

"Why? Does it contain controversial subject matter?"

"No." Ruby opened her eyes and removed the compress from her forehead. "Because it's a *cook*book."

Meg burst into laughter and then, remembering her great-aunt's headache, she asked in a quiet voice, "She wasn't serious, was she?"

"*Quite* serious. The cookbook is written by a celebrity, and apparently he includes a vignette from his childhood with every recipe, so Joan insisted it could loosely be considered a memoir," Ruby explained to her great-niece's amusement. "As you can imagine, not everyone shared her perspective."

Meg giggled. "Did the group eventually come to an agreement?"

"It was more of a compromise than an agreement... The opposing members said they'd make a one-time exception and discuss the vignettes in the celebrity's cookbook, if Joan prepares his famous Black Forest gateau to serve us."

"I guess that's a win-win," said Meg with a laugh. "I just hope the chef's writing is as palatable as his baking."

"Gordon used to quote an old saying that everyone has at least one good book in them, one good story to tell. So, you never know. Maybe these vignettes will be a masterpiece." The color was returning to Ruby's cheeks and she was smiling, as she usually did when she talked about her old friend.

She continued, "On the topic of cooking, I'd like to invite Sarah's grandson and his family for dinner when they arrive on Misty Point in a couple of days. They'll likely be tired from traveling and they'll appreciate having a homecooked meal here, rather than running out to a crowded restaurant or trying to cook in that tiny oven on their first day. What do you think?"

Honestly, although Meg thought it was a very kind invitation, the idea made her uneasy. *We don't even know if this person is truly only coming to Dune Island for a vacation, or if his visit might somehow affect the inn's business*, she felt like saying.

But she'd already promised her great-aunt that she'd help welcome Bradley's son and his family to Dune Island, and Meg could see that Ruby was too fatigued to host them by herself. So, she replied, "That sounds wonderful. If you'd like, I can make spaghetti and meatballs. I've never known a child who doesn't eat pasta."

"Are you sure it won't be too much trouble?"

"Not at all. I'm happy to do it and hosting Bradley's son and his family will be a nice way to get to know them," Meg answered, even though her stomach tensed with a growing sense of apprehension.

THREE

"I admit, I was skeptical. But now I see what you meant about the entire room feeling lighter and bigger," remarked Ruby on Thursday afternoon when she surveyed the results of their completed downsizing project in the living room.

"The luxurious tone of the wood stands out now, too. And since the books aren't packed in like sardines, there's finally a need for your fancy bookends," Meg said, referring to the eclectic assortment that friends and family members had gifted Ruby over the years.

"But *that's* not a bookend, is it?" Ruby scrunched up her face and pointed to a bookcase on the side wall near the window, making Meg smile. As nonchalant as her great-aunt was about most things, she was a purist about her bookcases, and her greatest pet peeve was when someone included vases or photos—or worse yet, knick-knacks—on the shelves.

So Meg explained, "I thought it would be helpful to include a pair of binoculars on the shelf of books about Dune Island wildlife, so they'd be handy for guests to use. And I've included a butterfly net, a magnifying glass, and a flashlight on the children's shelves, to accompany their stories. But if you don't want them there, I can remove them."

To Meg's surprise, Ruby clasped her hands beneath her chin. "No, leave them just where they are. That's an ingenious idea." Her exclamation triggered a coughing jag.

Meg didn't want to smother her with concern, but she couldn't help commenting, "It sounds like your cough is hanging on."

"It's probably only seasonal allergies, but I'll check with my physician. I have an appointment with him on July first." She rubbed her eyes. "Just seeing all the hard work you've done has made *me* tired. I think I'll go upstairs for a brief interlude."

Inwardly chuckling at her aunt's old-fashioned phrase, Meg said, "In that case, I'm going to sneak in a quick walk before Sarah's grandson arrives with his family."

Earlier that morning, after lugging the final bin of books to the detached garage, formerly a carriage house, Meg had made meatballs and homemade sauce, so all she'd need to do to prepare dinner would be to make the pasta and toss a salad. *Oh —I can't forget to grate some parmesan, too*, she realized, adding it to the checklist in her brain.

As she walked along the beach, the air vibrated with a low, menacing rumble. Yesterday's sunset had painted broad bands of orange and gold across the horizon, but today the sky was white, a blank canvas. She didn't see storm clouds in any direction, but Meg knew how quickly the unstable air could spawn a storm, so she kept a brisk pace and only walked along the northern curve of the beach before turning back toward the inn.

Head down, she wound her way through the meadow. Meg had almost reached the stand of pitch pines near the cottage when something caught her attention from the corner of her eye. She stopped and scanned the area, but she didn't see anything out of the ordinary.

She took a few more steps and there it was again, a flash of movement. At first, she thought it must have been a bird, but then her eyes homed in on the little fair-haired boy hiding behind a tree. He appeared to be about four years old, and his body was so thin that the trunk would have obscured him entirely, if he hadn't drawn attention to his presence by tipping his head sideways to peek at her. As soon as his enormous eyes met hers, he ducked behind the tree again.

Realizing that Bradley's son and his family must have arrived while she was on the beach, Meg called extra loudly, "Hello."

She hoped one of the boy's parents would hear her and come outside. Firstly, because she assumed that the child had been taught not to talk to strangers without his mom or dad present. Secondly, because although she wanted to extend Ruby's dinner invitation, she was reluctant to intrude on the family by knocking on their door when they'd just arrived.

Unfortunately, her greeting seemed to go unheard by anyone other than the boy. Once again, he tilted his head to one side and peered at her from beneath his fine, straight bangs. When their eyes met, he blinked twice. Then he dashed toward the back of the cottage, nimbly avoiding the random array of pitch pine trees with such speed that the blue fabric tied around his chest flew out behind him.

So that's *what I saw—he's wearing some sort of costume,* Meg thought as another rumble of thunder shook the air. *I'd better go introduce myself and invite them to dinner now. Otherwise, I might have to come back in the rain.*

Just then, a girl with a mop of bright coppery curls and a fierce expression flung open the screen door and allowed it to slam behind her.

"Cody Bradley Harris, you'd better not be—" she shouted as she trudged into the yard. But when she noticed Meg, she stopped yelling mid-sentence. "Oh! Hi. Where did you come from?"

"The beach," Meg answered, pointing toward the lighthouse.

"Did you see my brother there? We're never-ever-*ever* supposed to wander off to the beach by ourselves."

"No. I didn't see anyone." Lowering her voice, Meg told her, "I think your brother might be hiding on the other side of the cottage."

The girl, who appeared as robust as her brother was scrawny, held her hand sideways, even with her chest. "Was he about this tall, with light-colored hair and brown eyes?"

"Yes, that sounds like him."

The child blew the air from her pudgy cheeks. "That's okay, then. We're allowed to play around the cottage by ourselves. Anywhere there's pine needles is safe territory." She pushed at the plush, golden carpet of dried needles with the toe of her purple sneaker, before squinting up at Meg. "What's your name?"

"It's Meg. I'm your next-door neighbor. I live right over there in that inn," she said to assure the child she wasn't a stranger—not that the chatty little girl seemed to have any reservations about talking to her. "What's *your* name?"

"Abigail. I don't like to be called Abbey but if you forget, that's okay. Sometimes my teacher did that by accident, but I didn't get mad. My brother's name is Cody. He usually won't talk to you if you ask him anything. Don't take it personally." Her response struck Meg as comical, yet also as a little bit precocious, since the girl couldn't have been more than six or seven years old. "Do you have any children?"

Startled by her inquisitiveness, and hypersensitive about the topic, Meg's shoulders tensed up and she succinctly answered, "Nope."

"Aw, I wish a girl lived next door to me. I never had a girl for a neighbor, only boys."

Realizing she'd been mistaken about Abigail's intention in

asking the question, Meg softened her stance. "In a few days, there will be guests coming to the inn. Maybe one of them will be a girl your age." Her remark put a smile on the child's freckled face, and Meg noticed one of her top incisors was missing, and one was half-grown in. She grinned back at her. "I'd like to speak to your parents. Are they inside the cottage?"

"No. Mommy's in heaven," Abigail stated, as matter-of-factly as if she'd said that her mother was at the grocery store. Meg barely had a chance to absorb what she'd heard before Abigail added, "And Dad's getting his suitcase out of the car... Oh! Here he comes."

Meg turned to see a husky, square-shouldered man, who appeared slightly taller than she was, and about the same age, striding toward them. Casually dressed in jeans and a long-sleeved, fitted heather-gray T-shirt, he was pulling a large piece of wheeled luggage across the soft, uneven ground.

His daughter excitedly beckoned to him. "Daddy, come meet this lady. She lives in that inn and she said some girls are going to stay there who are six-going-on-seven, too, and I can play with them."

That's not exactly what I said, thought Meg. Noticing the hint of a grimace on the man's face, she wondered if he was annoyed at her because it wasn't Meg's place to give his child permission to play with guests at the inn. Or was he scowling because he was tired from a long trip?

She took a step toward him, asking, "Can I give you a hand?"

"I've got it, thanks." He gestured over his shoulder with his thumb. "Is it okay that I parked in the lot next to the inn? I didn't see a separate driveway for the cottage."

"That's because there isn't one. So yes, you're welcome to park in the guest lot. Even when the inn is full, we have plenty of room." She waited until he came to a stop in front of her before introducing herself. "I'm Meg Carter. I'm staying at the inn for the summer—the proprietor, Ruby Berton, is my great-aunt."

"Simon Harris," he said, and as he enveloped her fingers in a warm, strong handshake Meg noticed that although he was sandy-haired, like his son, his eyes were vivid green, like his daughter's. For some reason, this observation caught Meg off guard. "Sounds like you've met Abigail. My son Cody is around here someplace, too."

"He's hiding behind our little house," Abigail piped up. "I'll go get him."

But Cody must have been spying on them from behind the cottage drainpipe, because he suddenly emerged from around the corner of the house and charged pell-mell toward Simon, nearly buckling his legs as he grabbed onto them from behind.

"Hey, Cody, be careful. You almost knocked Daddy over," Abigail reprimanded him.

Simon released the suitcase handle and put his hand on Cody's head, guiding him forward. "Say hello to Meg."

Stroking the ends of the blue fuzzy fabric knotted around his chest, Cody wouldn't look up at her, so Meg squatted beside him. "Hello, Cody. You're so good at hiding among the trees that at first I thought you were a squirrel."

"Hi." His whisper was barely audible and he was clearly uncomfortable talking to her, so Meg stood up to address Simon.

"Do you need help with the rest of your luggage?"

"No, thanks. This is the last of what I'm bringing in today." He grasped the handle of his suitcase again, as if he wanted to start rolling it to the cottage. "We drove from Delaware, so it's been a long couple of days. We'll unload the rest of our stuff tomorrow."

Driving that far alone with two young children couldn't have been easy, Meg thought. "You must be beat. I'll get out of your way so you can settle in. But my aunt Ruby and I would love it if you'd join us for dinner. We're having spaghetti and meatballs, although if your children don't like that, I can make chicken tenders or PB&J sandwiches—unless they're allergic to peanuts, of course."

"We *luh-uh-ove* spaghetti and meatballs, don't we, Cody?" Abigail interjected and her brother nodded his agreement.

"That's a, uh, nice invitation but we were planning to go to the boardwalk for supper," Simon replied, before addressing his children. "Afterward, we're getting ice cream at that shop I showed you online, the one with the funny name, remember?"

Trying not to feel a little bit offended that Simon obviously didn't want to accept her invitation even though his children obviously did, Meg said, "You must mean Bleeckers. Their name might sound funny, but the Bleecker family has owned the shop for well over half a century and you won't find better ice cream anywhere in the state—maybe not even on the east coast."

"Hear that, guys? The best ice cream in the state," Simon repeated. "Don't you want to go to Bleeckers?"

"We can go there tomorrow. Cody and I want to eat spaghetti at the inn with Meg," insisted Abigail. If her brother objected to her speaking for both of them, he didn't show it. "Please, Daddy?"

Meg couldn't think of a way out of this awkward situation and apparently Simon couldn't, either, because he gave in.

"All right," he agreed, a look of resignation on his face. "What time do you want us to come by?"

"Five-thirty." Meg figured the earlier they ate dinner, the earlier their guests could leave, which Simon undoubtedly would appreciate.

Because Ruby had appeared more fatigued than usual, Meg let her sleep until she'd finished dinner preparations. It seemed risky to serve a messy meal like spaghetti to children in the formal dining room, so Meg set the table in the kitchen, and then she chopped vegetables for salad.

As she worked, she thought about how heartbreaking it was that Abigail and Cody had lost their mother at such a young age. Meg felt sorry for Simon, too. *He looks like he might be a couple years older than I am. I wonder how long he and his wife had been married—assuming they were married—before she passed away.* Judging from Abigail's calm and accepting manner when she'd said her mother was in heaven, Meg figured that the woman must have died a while ago. *It seems like Abigail might be too young to remember her clearly, which means Cody doesn't remember her, either.*

What about Simon, had enough time passed that he'd come to terms with his wife's death, if that was even possible after someone lost their spouse? Maybe the grimace he'd worn when they'd met wasn't because he was annoyed or tired; maybe it was grief pinching his face into a scowl. *That might be why he was reluctant to accept our invitation to dinner. He might feel too lost to socialize without his wife.*

It also occurred to Meg that perhaps the reason Simon hadn't brought his family to Dune Island earlier was because his wife had been too ill to travel. *Or maybe they traditionally vacationed somewhere else, but now Simon wants to avoid painful memories so he's brought his children to a new, peaceful location.*

While she felt a little guilty that she'd been wary of the widowed father's intentions before she'd even met him, there was something off-putting about Simon's behavior that still gave Meg pause. She couldn't completely dismiss her worry that he wouldn't allow guests to cut across his meadow, or that he had an ulterior motive for being here.

Hopefully, I'll get a better sense of him over dinner, she thought. *In any case, I'd like to help get his children's vacation off to a great start.*

She sliced and buttered a loaf of Italian bread so it would be ready to warm in the oven when the guests arrived, and then she hurried upstairs to exchange her T-shirt for a blouse, before waking her great-aunt.

Meg gently knocked on the door twice, with no response, so she tentatively cracked it open. The bed was empty, but when Meg peeked around the door, she saw Ruby crouching down near a small bookcase.

Although she had no interest in reading novels that were excessively violent in nature, and she didn't generally like dystopian fiction, Ruby's taste in literature was eclectic, and she was always open to recommendations. But she especially enjoyed historical fiction and mysteries, as well as virtually any book featuring an ocean setting. She'd generously shared books from her collections in the living room and den, and she never cared if a guest acquired one of her books, whether accidentally or on purpose.

"If they're enjoying it enough to read it, then that's all that matters," she'd say.

However, she only loaned out the books from the bookcase in her bedroom on rare occasion. This collection included all eight books written by Gordon Sheffield. Meg didn't share her great-aunt's affinity for mysteries, but she'd read three or four of his books the year she'd turned eighteen primarily because she'd felt so honored that Ruby had granted her permission to borrow them.

Her bedroom bookcase also contained two "picture books" from Ruby's youth, a Bible, and numerous signed copies from her favorite authors who'd visited Dune Island to give readings, as well as early editions of a few classics. A few of the books were lying on the floor beside Ruby, and she was pulling another from the shelf.

"I don't think you'll have time to read before dinner," Meg

teased, causing her great-aunt to flinch and nearly topple backward. "Sorry, I didn't mean to startle you."

"I'm fine. I just didn't realize you were behind me." She hurriedly began wedging the books back into place on the shelves. Meg bent down to help but Ruby shooed her hands away. "I can manage, thank you. Do you know if Bradley's son arrived with his family yet?"

"Yes, a little while ago." Meg described Abigail and Cody to her, and she told Ruby what she'd discovered about Simon being a widower, too. Ruby was very dismayed to hear such sad news and Meg didn't want to make her great-aunt feel worse by mentioning how reluctant Simon seemed to be to join them for their evening meal. So she told her, "He said how nice it was of us to invite them for dinner—they're coming at five thirty."

"That's wonderful. I'm so pleased!" she exclaimed.

The only person more pleased was Abigail. After introductions were made and Ruby ushered everyone into the living room, the little girl breathlessly gushed, "This is awesome. I really like your inn. We can see everything from here. Our cottage looks like a playhouse. Are we allowed to sit on that bench near the window?"

"Of course."

"Shoes first, please," Simon instructed his children, so Abigail slipped hers off and then unfastened Cody's for him, too.

The two of them climbed onto the window seat and knelt on the cushions, as Abigail pointed out the obvious to Cody. "Look, a path through the grass. There's the lighthouse. That's the beach. And those are three—no, four, no *seven*—seagulls."

Their excitement was so infectious that Meg didn't mind at all when they pressed their palms and noses against the picture window that she'd taken such care to wash. *It's too bad that Simon doesn't show a little enthusiasm, too, especially since Aunt Ruby is so delighted that he's here, but I can understand why he doesn't.* She wished she could stay in the living room to facilitate the conversation, but she had to prepare the pasta.

Fortunately, it only took a few minutes to put the finishing touches on their meal. Meg returned to the living room just as Ruby was saying, "You'll have to forgive me for staring, but your eyes remind me of Sarah's—she had such arresting eyes. 'All that's best of dark and bright,' is how Gordon used to describe them. Those weren't his original words, of course—he was quoting a poem by Lord Byron."

"Hmm." Simon acknowledged her remark with a sound, but he didn't say anything in reply. Was he annoyed because Ruby had compared him to a woman?

Meg quickly invited everyone into the kitchen, and Abigail squealed when she noticed the lighthouse-shaped salt-and-pepper shakers on the table. "They're so cute, and they're red and white, just like the one on the beach."

Simon was equally pleased to see the booster seat Meg had set on one of the chairs. "That's a relief—I forgot to bring Cody's with us to Massachusetts."

"No problem. We often have guests who need a little boost," Meg replied.

Her great-aunt chimed in, "Meg always thinks of everything. It's what makes her so effective at her job and so helpful to me here at the inn."

"What do you do for work?" asked Simon.

"I'm a student event planner at a university in New Jersey, where I live—I'm only here for the summer. What about you, what do you do?"

"I'm a carpenter. I specialize in restoration and remodeling," he told her before leaning over to quietly address his son. "Aren't you forgetting something?"

The boy tipped his head sideways, as if he didn't understand, so Abigail patted her chest, hinting, "It's something you're not supposed to wear at the table."

Cody's face fell, but he obediently unknotted the fraying piece of blue fabric from his chest and hung it over the back of his chair.

He looked so forlorn that Meg tried to cheer him up by saying, "I've heard that all superheroes take off their capes when they eat. Otherwise, they might spill things like spaghetti sauce on them."

"It's not a cape," Abigail informed her. "It used to be his blankie but then it got shredded in the washing machine so Grandma made it into a scarf. But a scarf is a choking hazard, so he wears it around his middle instead of his neck. Kind of like a high belt, except it's not for holding up his pants. It's just so he doesn't lose it. But Daddy doesn't want him to wear it at the table because it isn't good manners."

"That makes sense to me," Meg said, trying not to laugh. She noticed Ruby was fighting a smile, too.

The children practically dove headlong into their food, with Cody eating twice as much spaghetti as his sister and nearly as many meatballs as his father. While they dined, Ruby inquired about their trip from Delaware, and Abigail responded with a very long, very animated account of the contest they'd held to see who could spot the most animals along the way, and a story about the children's first-ever ferry excursion.

Cody was either too shy or too busy eating to contribute to the conversation, and Simon rarely spoke, either, except to interject quiet reminders to his children to use their napkins or to be careful not to knock over their milk glasses. Meg couldn't tell whether he was deliberately being reticent or if he simply didn't want to interrupt his daughter's enthusiastic reply to Ruby's question. But at least he squeezed in a compliment about the meal, which she appreciated.

As they were eating, the room grew increasingly dim and by the time Meg served gelato for dessert, the inky, swollen clouds had released a barrage of heavy raindrops.

"It's a good thing we didn't go to the boardwalk for supper," commented Abigail when she heard the rain pelting the window. "Cody hates lightning and thunder."

No sooner were the words out of her mouth than a triple flash lit the sky, followed by a resounding boom that rattled the windows. Cody slid beneath the table so quickly that Meg didn't notice he was under there until he stretched his arm up to yank his blankie from the back of the chair.

"What did I tell you?" Abigail remarked smugly in between spoonsful of gelato.

Simon leaned sideways to speak to his son. "Cody, it's okay. We're safe inside this inn. Please come sit with us. I'll turn your chair so you're not facing the window."

"I'll still hear it," whimpered Cody. It was his longest and loudest sentence so far, yet it was barely audible.

"You can cover your ears with your hands. Come sit with us," repeated Simon in a firmer voice, just before another clap of thunder reverberated across the water.

"I don't want to," Cody whisper-howled. "I want to stay down here. And I want Abigail to stay down here with me, too."

His sister started to slide beneath the table but Simon said, "No, Abigail."

He slowly up righted himself. He was red-faced, which might have been caused by leaning over, but Meg sensed Simon was also embarrassed by his children's behavior, even though there wasn't any need for him to be. "Meg and Ms. Ruby invited us here to eat *with* them, not to eat under their table."

Meg didn't know quite what to do. She didn't want to contradict Simon or interfere, but she also understood why Cody preferred being under the table instead of surrounded by windows. She caught her great-aunt's eye and gave her a helpless shrug.

Thankfully, Ruby spoke up. "Your father's right, we do prefer our guests to sit at the table with us. But if your dad agrees, we adults will take our dessert to the living room, and you two may make yourselves cozy under the table. There are some books on the shelves beneath the window seat that you might like. There's a flashlight you may use, too."

"Can we, Dad?" pleaded Abigail. "I'll practice reading to Cody and we can pretend we're in a cave."

"Okay, but only until the storm passes. Then you both need to come out from under there."

After the little girl had selected several books, Meg brought her two lighthouse-embroidered cushions from the children-sized rocking chairs in the den, and she joined her brother beneath the table. The adults retreated to the living room, where Meg hoped they'd be able to watch the fearsome storm advancing across the Sound. But the sky was too dark and the wind pushed thick sheets of torrential rain against the picture window, blurring their view.

"I thought we'd be able to see the lighthouse in action, but it's being outshone by the lightning," Meg remarked.

They chatted for a while about the weather, always a safe subject, before moving on to more personal topics. In addition to sharing recommendations for places to eat and sights to see on the island, Meg and Ruby expressed condolences about Simon's father's passing. They also told Simon a little bit about their lives and asked him about his.

Meg swallowed a gasp when he shared that his wife had been killed in an automobile accident a little under two years ago. She noticed the flicker of pain in his eyes when he said her name—*Beth*—but he didn't linger on the topic. He also told them his parents were divorced, and he didn't have any siblings. Meg was surprised to discover that he lived in Hickory Falls, Delaware, a very affluent town less than ninety minutes from where she lived in New Jersey. But what shocked Ruby was when he told them that he and his children were planning to stay in the cottage until the end of August.

"You're going to spend the entire summer in that little cottage?" Ruby sounded aghast. "It's not even furnished!"

"We brought camping cots and an assortment of essential furniture. We'll be fine. As you can see, my children are comfortable curling up anywhere," Simon said wryly.

"Yes, but what about you? You're far too big to sleep on a cot all summer," Ruby remarked to Meg's embarrassment. She knew her great-aunt didn't mean it the way it sounded, but since Simon was a little on the stocky side, her remark might have offended him. "I wish I'd known you were coming. I could've reserved a room for your family. But we'll have vacancies throughout the summer and you're more than welcome to stay with us when the occasion arises, no charge."

Simon held up his hands in protest. "Thanks, but I'll be fine, really. We're looking forward to spending a very simple, very quiet summer in the cottage."

It almost sounds like he's saying he doesn't want us to bother him while he's here, thought Meg. But maybe, like Ruby, he didn't mean anything offensive by his remark.

Her great-aunt shook her head, but she conceded. "If you change your mind, just let us know. And if you need a bigger, better equipped kitchen, you're welcome to use the inn's anytime. It's first come, first serve around here, so no need for advance warning."

"I'll remember that, thanks," Simon said, although Meg doubted he'd take Ruby up on her offer.

When she'd first met him near the cottage, she'd thought Simon was handsome, in an understated, slightly weather-beaten kind of way. Soft, yet strong, he probably gave incredible bear hugs—and even Ruby had noticed his "arresting" eyes. But now what struck Meg most was how stiff his posture was, as if it was literally paining him to engage in conversation.

In the lengthy pause that followed, she noticed the rain was letting up and there hadn't been a lightning flash in a while. *The storm is moving out*, she thought, but she didn't want to say it in case it seemed as if she was hinting it was time for Simon and his children to leave.

Ruby broke the silence, asking him, "Do you know what your grandfather used to call the cottage?"

"Gordon wasn't my grandfather." There was an edge to Simon's voice. "Technically, we weren't related to him and my dad didn't really consider him to be a father figure."

Ruby appeared stung. "You're right, I'm sorry. I misspoke. I shouldn't have called him your grandfather." She fell quiet again, dropping the subject.

Protective of her great-aunt's feelings, Meg pressed her to continue. "You were going to tell us Gordon's name for the cottage, Aunt Ruby."

"He called it 'The Writing Pad,'" she answered. "It was a pun, you see, because in the seventies, people often referred to their apartments or to small houses as their *pads*. And because Gordon retreated to the cottage to write his novels."

Simon noticeably cringed at Ruby's anecdote, which Meg thought was a bit rude even if Gordon's pun was awfully corny. So she overcompensated for his response by gushing, "*The Writing Pad*. That's very clever."

"Yes, well, he was good with words—of course, as a writer, he had to be." Ruby's comment was almost as inane as Meg's. She rambled on, "Gordon found the southwest view from the cottage to be very inspiring, but Sarah preferred the view from up here, where she could see Hope Haven Sound from all angles."

Simon restlessly shifted in his chair, showing little interest in Ruby's recollections. His aloofness surprised Meg, but he looked drained. Was he too wiped out to carry on a conversation?

Oblivious, Ruby continued, "The inn had originally been a farmhouse, you see, and it was nearly as ramshackle as the cottage, but your grandmother loved the scenery so much she couldn't have cared less that the interior was drafty and run-down. Besides, it was all they could afford—they'd rented it dirt cheap from one of Gordon's colleagues. However, by the time the property went up for sale a few years later, they had enough money to purchase and renovate it. After that, they summered here every year until Sarah passed away. They always hoped your father would enjoy Misty Point as much as they did, but apparently, he wasn't as enamored of the oceanside as they were."

"No, he wasn't," Simon flatly agreed, disappointing Meg. She had hoped he'd offer additional insight into why his father had never been interested in returning to the island. A more credible reason than that he was bothered by the stickiness of salt on his skin.

"I wonder why he didn't like it here," she hinted boldly.

Simon's glance flickered toward Ruby, and they briefly locked eyes before he looked down at his knees again. "He had his reasons," he answered with a shrug.

What did he mean by that? Meg noticed a pink blush spreading across her great-aunt's cheeks, as if Simon's comment had embarrassed her. Was he implying that Bradley hadn't ever returned to Dune Island because of *Ruby*? Meg couldn't imagine why Bradley would have born such a serious grudge against her, unless... unless he resented it that she had inherited Gordon and Sarah's summer home.

Maybe, like his father, Simon also feels it's unfair that Ruby inherited the inn, and that's why he's acting so standoffish toward her? Meg recognized she was only surmising, but the mere possibility made her want to defend her great-aunt, and she was tempted to ask if Simon knew *why* Gordon had bequeathed the inn to Ruby. *Perhaps he isn't aware of how fond Gordon was of her and how much he appreciated her help when Sarah was ill,* she thought.

But her great-aunt had always downplayed her role in caring for Sarah while her friend was recovering from cancer. Ruby would've loathed it if anyone sang her praises for doing something she'd considered an honor and privilege. So Meg bit the inside of her cheek and kept her questions to herself.

Ruby, however, graciously addressed Simon, saying, "Even though your father didn't frequent Misty Point, Gordon and Sarah would be very pleased that you and your children are here now. I hope this is the first of many happy Dune Island summers for you for years to come."

"So do I." Meg playfully raised her water glass, as if making a toast. "The first of many."

Simon averted his gaze toward the window and licked his lips before looking at her and Ruby again. "I'm afraid this will be our *only* Dune Island summer," he intoned with such gravity that for a split second, Meg had the dreadful feeling he was about to say he was dying. Instead, he told them, "I'm selling the property to a developer. They're going to build a resort on the land."

FOUR

Meg's jaw dropped. She looked at Ruby, but she, too, was speechless, and the blush that had brightened her complexion only a moment ago had now completely drained from her cheeks.

I can't believe this is happening, Meg thought. *A resort will ruin everything about Misty Point that makes it so unique. And surely it will block the view from here and put Aunt Ruby's inn —an inn which has been operating here for close to forty years— out of business. Then what will she do?*

It occurred to Meg that this was why Simon had been so reluctant to accept their dinner invitation. *He probably figured if he kept his distance, and didn't get to know us at all, he wouldn't feel as guilty about developing the property. And here the two of us are, naively welcoming him with open arms...*

Simon squirmed and ran a hand through his hair, making it stand on end. "I, uh, I didn't mean to drop a bombshell on you like this, but I figure it's better to have it out in the open now, instead of waiting until the surveyors and architects start poking around—although that won't happen until much later in the summer or early autumn. There are still a lot of details we've got to work out before I sign off on the sale."

"Yes, you're right, it is much better to have advance notice. I'm glad you told me," said Ruby.

If Meg didn't know her so well, she might have thought her great-aunt's reply was meant to be flippant, but she recognized that Ruby was genuinely being courteous in the face of this *bombshell*, as Simon had accurately called it.

Meg, on the other hand, was unable to disguise how upset she felt, and she didn't mince words. "The land you've inherited is exceptionally valuable, so I'm sure you're going to make a killing from the sale," she began.

"Meg!" Ruby sounded appalled, but Meg was unapologetic.

So was Simon. He looked her in the eye and readily admitted, "Yes. It's a very lucrative deal. My family's going to benefit greatly from it."

I can understand why a windfall like that will be wonderful for him, Meg admitted to herself. *But unfortunately, his gain is Misty Point's loss.*

He continued, "I've put a lot of research and consideration into this deal. It might seem like a small consolation, but I intend to include a clause in the contract requiring the resort owner to grant the inn's guests easy access to the beach."

"I'm relieved to hear that," Ruby said. "Thank you."

It seemed ironic to Meg that beach access had been her primary concern when she'd first heard of Simon's visit. A whole resort was a far worse problem. It seemed as if Simon had considered the smaller details, yet he was missing the big picture—and so was Meg's great-aunt, which was even more upsetting to Meg. *Don't you get it, Aunt Ruby? He's being considerate now because he's going to need something from you later, like passage through your property for the builders. Builders who are going to wreck Misty Point and put you out of business!* She crossed her arms against her chest, holding herself back from expressing what was in her heart.

"You're welcome," Simon replied to Ruby. "As you're aware, no one in my family has used this land for decades. It's time for us to pass it on so other people can enjoy it, but I'll do whatever I can to minimize the disruptions to you and your guests."

"How very altruistic of you," Meg muttered beneath her breath.

"Meg." Her great-aunt put a finger to her lips. "Shh."

It irked Meg that once again Ruby was hushing her, as if she were a child, but then she realized the reason for her warning: Abigail was in the doorway, rubbing her eyes. The spaghetti sauce stain on her cheeks exactly matched the color of her springy locks, and something about her innocence made Meg loosen her fists and uncross her arms.

"Daddy, you said to come out from under the table when the storm was over, but Cody fell asleep."

Groaning a little, Simon rose from his chair. "It's time for us to leave, so please go wake him up and help him put on his sneakers."

Why doesn't he just let Cody sleep and carry him back to the cottage? Meg inwardly challenged Simon's instructions, but Abigail dutifully retrieved both pairs of shoes and shuffled into the kitchen.

Wisely avoiding eye contact with Meg, Simon addressed Ruby in a low voice. "I told Cody and Abigail we came to Misty Point because I'm on a working vacation—that I'll be advising someone on a building project," he said. "They're aware that their great-grandmother stayed on Dune Island a long time ago. But they don't know anything about your relationship with Gordon and Sarah, or that I've inherited property here. I'd like to keep it that way."

Yeah, because you wouldn't want your children to discover

that you're a sellout, Meg silently scoffed, too distraught to care if she was being unfairly critical.

"I understand. We won't mention anything about it to them," Ruby answered.

They accompanied Simon and the children to the porch door, where Abigail oohed and aahed when the lighthouse flashed white against the drizzly sky, but Cody was too drowsy to lift his head to look at it.

"Thank you for dinner." Simon prompted his children, "It was delicious, wasn't it?"

"Mm-hmm. 'Specially dessert," said Abigail.

"We're so glad you came. Don't forget, you're welcome to use the kitchen or to take refuge here any time," Ruby reminded Simon. "We lock the doors from ten p.m. to seven a.m. but the code is 1-9-7-8, the year I first visited Dune Island."

"Good night, Abigail. Night-night, Cody," Meg said as they started down the steps. She tossed an impersonal "bye" in Simon's direction, but she turned and went into the kitchen without waiting for his response.

She noisily began collecting the dirty dishes from the table, and when Ruby entered the room, Meg burst out, "Simon has so much gall! I can't believe that after you were so welcoming to him and so accommodating of his children, he'd casually dump earthshattering news like that on you over dessert!"

"I didn't mind. I appreciated it that he was forthcoming," Ruby insisted. "And I wouldn't say he had a casual attitude. Judging from his demeanor, I think it was agonizing for him to deliver that news."

"I'd be *glad* if it was agonizing for him—at least that would mean he has a conscience," Meg ranted. "But apparently he cares about money a lot more than he cares about people."

"That's a bit harsh, isn't it?"

Not half as harsh as him wrecking Misty Point and destroying your livelihood, thought Meg. She didn't want to alarm her great-aunt by blatantly pointing out that the resort was going to ruin the inn's business, yet she couldn't fathom how Ruby could seem so dispassionate about it. Maybe the reality hadn't sunk in yet? "Aren't you angry that Simon's going to sell the property to a developer?" she asked.

"Angry? No, I'm not angry." Ruby calmly loaded plates into the dishwasher. "I am very disappointed, though, because I know it's not what Gordon and especially Sarah would have chosen for their family. And it's not what the lighthouse society would choose for our community, either. But mostly, I feel sorry for Simon. I don't think he realizes the value of what he's giving up."

"S-*sorry* for him?" sputtered Meg, unable to believe her ears. "He's going to make a bazillion dollars from selling his property!"

"Yes, I'm sure he'll receive a grand sum of money. But you must have noticed how forlorn he is. It's obvious he's carrying the weight of the world on his shoulders. Sarah always said that Dune Island was the remedy for whatever ailed a person, yet Simon doesn't seem to recognize how much he and the children might benefit from having a special place like Misty Point to visit," Ruby explained. "However, it's his property now, so it's up to him to do whatever he wishes to do with it."

Frustrated that her great-aunt seemed unconcerned about her *own* welfare, Meg tried a more direct approach. "There's a good chance that having a resort next door will put a big dent in your business. And you said you still need to repay the loan you took out to install new windows. If the inn can't generate enough income to cover your bills and expenses, what will you do?"

Ruby clicked the door to the dishwasher shut and pressed the button before answering. "I don't know, Meg. A lot could happen between now and then. This is only the beginning of the story. We don't know how the rest of it will unfold."

For as long as Meg could remember, whenever she told Ruby how worried she was about something, her great-aunt would reply with a variation on this metaphor. She'd say things like, *Hang in there for another chapter.* And, *There might be a plot twist up ahead that you never saw coming.* Or, *You're not the author of this story, so you don't get to decide how it ends.* Her sayings had always comforted Meg and helped her release her desire to control an outcome.

Tonight, however, she felt like urging her great-aunt, *This isn't fiction, Aunt Ruby, it's reality. The resort is going to put you out of business! You can't just passively watch this happen—you either need to prevent it or to make a contingency plan!*

But because she could see the exhaustion weighing down Ruby's features, Meg conceded, "Yeah, you're right. After all, Simon mentioned he hasn't finalized the deal yet."

Her tone lacked conviction, but Ruby cheered, "That's the spirit! For all we know, he'll end up falling in love with Misty Point and decide that he and the children will return to the cottage every year. Although if that's what happens, I hope he buys a proper bed. I don't know how he's going to sleep on a cot all summer..."

You're worrying about all the wrong things and the wrong people. Anticipating that Ruby might try to twist Simon's arm to stay at the inn whenever a vacancy arose, Meg replied, "As you said, he's probably the outdoorsy type. Besides, cots nowadays are a lot sturdier and more comfortable than the kind you're picturing. He'll probably sleep like a baby." *Thinking of all the money he's going to make,* she silently added.

"Speaking of which..." Ruby yawned and patted her mouth. "I think it's time to retire for the evening, don't you?"

"Not quite. There's a big glob of spaghetti sauce beneath Cody's chair, and I want to mop it up before it crusts over. It'll only take me a minute—you go on upstairs."

After she'd finished cleaning up the spill, Meg put away the cushions and books the children had used. *What a fat lot of good it did to downsize Aunt Ruby's bookcases*, she silently grumbled. *We could renovate this inn from the basement to the attic and it still wouldn't be able to compete with the resort Simon's developer is going to build.*

Meg circled the living room, turning off the lamps so she could appreciate the full effect of the lighthouse's radiance. Settling onto the window seat, she noticed the cottage was dark and she figured Simon and the children had already gone to bed.

Cody was practically sleepwalking, she thought, picturing how the boy looked when Abigail, such a little mother hen, had led him down the porch stairs. Meg couldn't help giggling to herself as she reflected on Abigail's explanation of Cody's "cape." *They're both sweet, humorous children—they must take after their mother's side of the family.*

As soon as the thought struck her, Meg felt remorseful. Abigail and Cody had been through so much, and so had Simon. *He's still going through it, because he has to raise his children without their mother*, she realized. *I don't know what his relationship with his father was like, but he recently lost him, too.*

It was difficult for Meg to separate her empathy for Simon from her anger about his decision, since both emotions seemed justified. But she acknowledged that Ruby had been right: she was judging Simon too harshly.

I guess it's not fair to say he cares a lot more about money than about people, considering he's going to ensure that Aunt Ruby's guests have direct access to the beach. The only problem was, once the resort was operational, Ruby likely wouldn't *have* any guests at the inn.

A realization dawned on Meg: she hadn't had the opportunity to explain to Simon in detail just how detrimental a resort would be for Ruby's business or for the community. She thought he would've connected the dots by himself, but perhaps he hadn't. *Maybe if I spell it out for him in detail, he'll under-stand how disastrous it will be for Aunt Ruby if this land is developed. And perhaps Lou could give him a sense of how much it means to visitors—and to the islanders—to preserve the beau-tiful setting surrounding Misty Point Lighthouse.*

She wasn't as optimistic as her great-aunt was: Meg didn't expect Simon to change his mind about selling the property, but perhaps there was another option that would appeal to him. *Maybe he'd be open to selling his estate to a wealthy individual, like a celebrity or a politician who wants an isolated summer home. Or maybe a historical society would be interested in buying the property because of its proximity to the lighthouse...*

Even though she'd hardly begun to brainstorm the possibili-ties, Meg resolved that the first step of her plan would be to speak candidly with Simon when her great-aunt wasn't around. Hopeful that the situation wasn't as bleak as she'd first thought it was, Meg tiptoed upstairs to bed.

Over the next week, as she was washing the windows in the three-season porch, or polishing the woodwork in an upstairs bedroom, Meg occasionally spotted Simon and his children tramping through the meadow on their way back and forth to the beach. The three of them were difficult to miss, partly because they were the only other people currently inhabiting Misty Point, and partly because Simon's height, Abigail's curls, and Cody's blankie-cape made them very conspicuous.

On Wednesday, as Meg and Ruby were sipping sun tea in the living room, they were entertained by the sight of Abigail skipping along the path, while Cody charged toward the light-house so fast a collision seemed inevitable. But at the last second, he adroitly veered away from the small, square cement platform supporting the navigational tower, circled around it, and then raced back to his sister, only to spin around and dash toward the lighthouse again, just as swiftly as he'd sprinted there the first time. Meanwhile, Simon lagged a considerable distance behind both children, with a towel looped around his neck, a purple beach bag in one hand and a blue one in the other.

"They certainly seem to be enjoying themselves. You should go take a dip, too," suggested Ruby.

"Mm, I think I will." The temperature was in the 80s and Meg had been cleaning so vigorously that she'd worked up quite a sweat. And even though she knew she wouldn't get the opportunity to speak to Simon alone, she hoped to give him a warm greeting to make up for her chilly farewell the other evening. "First I want to finish polishing the furniture in Room 4 so I won't have to do it when I come back."

"Leave that to me," Ruby said. "I'm not completely feeble."

"I know you're not. But you still have that cough, and you don't want to aggravate your throat by stirring up dust. I'll be done in a jiffy."

However, as she was polishing, Meg noticed the blades of the pedestal fan provided for the room were coated with dust. By the time she found a screwdriver, took the fan apart, cleaned the blades and then assembled the fan again, over an hour had passed.

She reached the lighthouse just as Simon and the children were coming off the beach. Cody stopped to poke at something in the sand with a piece of driftwood, and his father came to a halt, too, but Abigail bounded toward her.

"Hi, Meg," she exclaimed, droplets flying from her curls.

"Hi, Abigail. How was the water?"

"It was *great*. I dunked my head all the way under and I didn't even plug my nose," she proudly reported.

"Atta girl!" cheered Meg, raising a fist in the air.

"Do you like my swimsuit? The bottom looks like a skirt,

but it's got shorts underneath. They're purple, see?" She inched up the hem to show Meg.

"It's very sporty *and* very pretty, which is a winning combination," Meg commented, as Cody seemed to materialize out of nowhere. "Hi, Cody. Did you go swimming, too?"

"He only went in up to his knees."

Meg squatted down beside him, hoping he'd answer for himself, instead of letting Abigail answer for him. "Was that because you didn't want to get your blankie wet?"

"It's 'cause he doesn't know how to swim," his sister said, and Cody thrust out his lower lip and looked away.

"I'll bet you're going to learn this summer, though. And then, you'll be able to swim as fast as you run, right Cody?" asked Meg.

He stopped pouting to peek at her from beneath his sun-streaked bangs and whispered, "Right."

The little boy took off to circumnavigate the lighthouse just as Simon reached them. Meg stood up, giving him a cheery hello and a winsome smile. To her relief, he returned her greeting with an equal amount of enthusiasm.

Noticing his hair was dry and he was wearing a T-shirt, but his swimming trunks and legs were wet, Meg remarked, "Beautiful afternoon. Did you go in the water?"

"Only up to his belly-button." His daughter tattled, "He forgot to wear sunscreen and he said he didn't want his white tummy to get sunburned, so he had to leave his T-shirt on."

Meg struggled to keep a poker face, but Simon was less amused. "Abigail, remember what I told you about allowing people to answer questions and to speak for themselves?"

"Sorry." The little girl's shoulders slumped pitifully.

Meg understood why Abigail needed to learn not to speak for other people, but it was probably a hard habit to break, as she'd obviously been speaking on Cody's behalf for a long time. She also sensed that after gaining approval for her swimming skills and attire, the little girl was embarrassed that her father had admonished her in front of Meg.

Keeping her tone light, Meg questioned, "Okay then, Simon, would *you* like to tell me why you only went into the water up to your belly button?"

He jerked his chin back, but then a smile crept across his lips and he sheepishly repeated verbatim what Abigail had just said. "Because I forgot to wear sunscreen, and I didn't want my white tummy to get sunburned so I had to leave my T-shirt on."

Abigail tilted her damp head upward, looking at her dad with wide-eyed surprise. When he winked at her, she burst into giggles and threw her arms around his waist. Meg was so charmed that she almost felt like hugging Simon, too.

"That's a good reason," she said, nodding. "Although it's such a scorcher today that if it had been me, I wouldn't have cared if my T-shirt got wet—I would've gone swimming with it on."

"Daddy only has one clean shirt left, and he—oops." Abigail, who must have realized she was answering for her father again, stopped mid-sentence and cupped both hands over her mouth, while Cody buzzed through the middle of their huddle. In a blink, he buzzed back toward the lighthouse again. His sister traipsed after him, leaving the adults alone, so Meg took advantage of the chance to apologize.

"I'm glad we've crossed paths because I wanted to say I'm sorry I had such a... a strong reaction to your news the other evening," she began.

"It's all right. I know it came as a shock," Simon replied, but he was distracted by his children, who'd stopped running circles around the lighthouse and were heading toward the meadow. He whistled sharply through his fingers and when they looked his way, he hollered for them not to go any farther.

"We weren't going to leave without you. We just needed a head start," shouted Abigail.

"*I'm* the one who needs a head start," Simon good-naturedly complained to Meg. "I can't keep up with them."

"It's no wonder. Cody's like a hummingbird—his legs move so fast they're a blur. Zip-zip, he's here. Zip-zip, he's gone."

"That's the only reason I'm glad he ties his blankie around his chest. It creates a drag, slows him down." He grinned and Meg smiled, too.

"Ah, I see. It's all about aerodynamics."

"Yup," he agreed, passing by her. "I have to take every advantage I can get."

She said goodbye and watched him amble toward where his children were waiting. Funny, how dad jokes had been so embarrassing coming from her father when she was growing up, but were endearing coming from Simon just now. Or did his humor only seem endearing because it was such a sharp contrast to how unsociable he'd been on Thursday?

Either way, Meg was glad that they were on better terms now. *It'll make it easier to approach him later about whether he'd consider selling his property to someone other than a developer.*

She turned and strode toward the beach, where she peeled her T-shirt over her head, dropped it on the warm sand, and then wiggled out of her shorts. Her swimsuit was pale lavender, and as she waded into waist-deep water, it occurred to her that it was a few shades lighter than Abigail's swimsuit, and that they both had a similar shade of hair.

I wonder if Simon's wife was a redhead, too. Or was she dirty-blond, like Cody is? The random thought made Meg remember how Josh had always said he'd loved her thick, wavy locks. Out of the blue, she was struck with such intense yearning that she nearly doubled over from the acuteness of the emotion, and tears sprang to her eyes.

Deep down, Meg realized she wasn't still mourning the dissolution of her relationship with Josh as much as she was mourning the disintegration of her dream to start a family with him. And she intuitively recognized that this particular moment of intense sadness was triggered by watching Abigail and Cody with their father.

As crushing as it was that she didn't have her longed-for family yet, Meg imagined it was far worse for Simon's children to have lost their mother, and for Simon to have lost his wife. *I can still hold on to hope, but they'll never get Beth back again.* Her empathy for them eclipsed her personal sorrow, and Meg dried her eyes with the back of her wrist.

Okay, that's the very last time. No more tears about what happened—or what didn't *happen—with Josh. We don't have a future together, so I* really *need to leave our relationship in the past,* she resolved as she drew a full, deep breath, steepled her hands, and plunged forward into the cool, revitalizing water.

FIVE

Shortly after noon on Thursday, the day before the inn's first guests were scheduled to arrive, Ruby poked her head into Room 6, where Meg was wiping out the dresser drawers.

"I'm popping out to Gibson's market for peaches," she announced. When Ruby bought peaches, it could only mean one thing: she was going to make a peach pie. It was one of her rare culinary specialties. Sarah had given her the recipe and taught her how to make a perfectly flaky crust, and just thinking about the delectable aroma of it baking made Meg's mouth water. "Is there anything else I should purchase while I'm there?"

"No, we've got plenty of groceries." When Meg glanced up and saw the dark shadows beneath Ruby's eyes, she quickly added, "But I do need a few personal items. If you'd like, I can go get them now, and I'll pick up the peaches while I'm in town."

"I don't want to disrupt your work when you're already doing so much for me."

"It's fine. I've got everything here under control," Meg assured her, even though this morning someone had made a last-minute reservation for the weekend. The only available room was the one Meg had been staying in, so she'd hastily moved out. She had stashed her personal belongings in a storage closet, but she still needed to clean the guest room and change the bedding, in addition to the multitude of other chores she hoped to complete.

"If you're sure you can manage, I'd really appreciate it. I'm a bit tired," Ruby admitted, "I must seem terribly lazy to you, but while you're gone, I'm going to rest a spell."

"Rest as many spells as you'd like," Meg teased affectionately. "I'm happy to help. That's why I'm here. But I don't think you're lazy at all—you're recovering from an illness."

At least, I think *she's recovering*, Meg fretted as she hustled down the porch stairs a few minutes later. *But I'll be relieved when she sees her doctor tomorrow and he evaluates her cough and low energy...*

Ruby's nap must have refreshed her because when Meg returned an hour later, her great-aunt was rolling the dough. "Did I ever tell you what a disaster my first pie crust was?" she asked, a smile on her lips and a dusting of flour across her cheek.

Although Meg had heard the story many times, she questioned, "It was tough, right?"

"That's putting it mildly. We could barely cut it with a steak knife! I felt awful about how it turned out because I knew that Sarah and Gordon were on a tight budget, just like I was. We couldn't allow all those ingredients to go to waste, so we spooned out the filling and served it to Gordon in a bowl. He ate it for dessert three nights in a row and never once complained."

Meg chuckled, glad that her great-aunt's memories had put the sparkle back in her eyes. Even though she had a dozen tasks she needed to accomplish, she prompted Ruby to tell the rest of the story, asking, "By the end of the summer, you mastered the crust-making technique, didn't you?"

"Yes, although that wasn't to my credit. It was because of Sarah. As frail as she was, she patiently instructed me every week until I finally got it right. She was always so encouraging, and Gordon was, too. I wasn't a scholar, like he was, but he used to listen to my opinions and ideas, and he had a way of making me feel... *extraordinary*." A funny look crossed Ruby's face. She sighed and said, "I was very fortunate to have both of them in my life."

"They were fortunate to have you, too." Meg planted a kiss on her great-aunt's floury cheek before leaving to complete her chores. "And so am I."

The pie looked and smelled delectable. After it cooled, Ruby suggested that Meg should take a break and bring three slices to the cottage for Simon and his children so they could eat it after their supper. "Be sure to tell him I baked it using Sarah's recipe."

It smelled so enticing that as she carried the dish to the cottage, Meg was tempted to keep walking toward the beach to eat a piece of the dessert on a bench near the lighthouse. It would be like when she was a girl and her parents would buy a rare treat of saltwater taffy or peanut butter fudge from a shop on the boardwalk. Meg's brother would always gobble up his candy on the drive home, and later he'd pester Meg to share hers with him. So she'd sneak away to savor it around the curve of the lighthouse where he couldn't see her from the inn.

It's no wonder both of his sons have a sweet tooth—they're just like he was! Meg chuckled with affection, yet at the same time, she felt a tiny twinge of wistfulness because she wished *she* had children and her brother could joke about which of her habits they imitated, too.

Approaching the pitch pine trees, she pushed the longing from her mind and listened for voices coming from the cottage. Although she'd spotted Simon and his kids returning from the beach earlier that afternoon, she didn't hear anyone speaking. Had they gone back for another swim? Meg balled her fingers into a fist but before she knocked on the door, it swung open and Simon tiptoed out.

"Hi," he whispered, grinning. He jabbed a thumb over his shoulder. "The kids are out cold."

"The ocean air and sunshine had that effect on me when I was their age, too," Meg said softly, following him to the side of the cottage where they could speak without whispering. "My aunt thought that you, Abigail, and Cody might enjoy a slice of pie after supper. She wanted me to tell you she baked it using your grandmother's recipe."

Meg extended the plate to Simon, who hesitated before taking it from her. Didn't he like peaches? Was one of the children allergic? She was so thrown off by his reluctance to accept the dessert that she found herself repeating the entire story about Ruby's first pie-making attempt. She ended by saying, "Don't worry, though, this crust will be delicious."

"Thank you," he mumbled blandly, staring at it.

"You're welcome." An awkward, extended silence followed, so Meg said, "I guess I'd better let you enjoy your downtime before the children wake up."

"That's okay, no need to run off on my account," Simon unexpectedly objected, his eyes glistening in the sunlight as they met hers again. "It's nice having a woman to talk to. An adult, I mean, instead of just my children. Not that I don't love talking to them, but you know..."

Although she thought his bumbling remarks were kind of charming, Meg rescued Simon from his obvious embarrassment. "I'm glad I get a chance to chat with you, too. I've been so preoccupied with preparing the inn for opening day that sometimes I forget to take a break."

She told him about a few of her remaining projects, and then Simon turned the discussion to Abigail and Cody's most recent beach discoveries, the water temperature, and surf size. He also raved about how much he and the children enjoyed being able to see the lighthouse from their beds at night.

"For some reason, I thought the light might keep the kids awake, but then I realized it doesn't illuminate the room—it mostly just illuminates itself," he said. "Watching it is so mesmerizing that I think it actually puts Cody and Abigail to sleep, instead of keeping them up. It makes me more tranquil, too."

Meg smiled, pleased that he felt the same way about the lighthouse as she did. Because their conversation was flowing smoothly and Cody and Abigail weren't there to overhear it, she seized the opportunity to bring up the subject of his plans for the estate. In what she hoped was an interested, non-confrontational tone, she asked, "So, have you made any more progress with the developer?"

"Not yet, no. The kids and I are still settling in."

"Yeah, that's understandable. So, um, I realize I was awfully prickly the other night when you told us you're selling the property—" Meg started to say, but Simon cut her off.

"You've already apologized. It's water over the dam."

"Thanks, but I'd like you to understand *why* I was upset. As you can guess, this area is a special place to so many people—and I don't just mean to the guests at the inn, either. The vacationers and residents who visit by boat love it, too. Dune Islanders are very proud of Misty Point Lighthouse and its isolated, pristine setting," Meg explained. "Obviously, this place is extra special to me because my great-aunt lives here. I've visited her every summer of my life and most of my favorite memories are of times I've spent on Dune Island."

Meg unexpectedly choked up. She had to clear her throat before continuing. "Lately, I've been concerned about my great-aunt's financial situation. She wouldn't want me to tell you this, but it's been difficult for the inn to compete with other lodging on the island. So, when I heard you're going to allow a developer to build a resort in her backyard, I immediately panicked about how she'll be able to keep her business afloat—no pun intended." Meg laughed nervously, but Simon didn't crack a smile.

"As I've said, I'll try to minimize the disruptions to her and the inn," he earnestly replied.

"Yes, and that's very thoughtful of you. My aunt really appreciates it, and I do, too, even if I didn't show it the other night." She paused, carefully choosing her next words. "I recognize that the property is yours and you're entitled to do anything you want with it. So I'm not trying to take advantage of your thoughtfulness or to tell you what to do with your inheritance. But given that you're still in the early phases of negotiating, I figured it was worth asking if there's any chance you'd consider selling the estate to an individual or to a preservation society, instead of to a developer?"

Now that her question was finally out in the open, Meg felt a rush of hopefulness, followed by a wave of trepidation. She held her breath, waiting for his answer.

"I *did* consider those options, but the process would be slower and the deal would be less profitable than what I can make with the developer," he replied frankly. "And while I regret that the resort will affect Ruby's business, she's had Misty Point all to herself for nearly forty years. So now it seems fair that my family's getting a turn to benefit from this property, too."

Meg was confused by his implication. "You're almost making it sound as if my aunt somehow prevented your family from enjoying Misty Point, but that couldn't be further from the truth. For *decades* she invited your father to stay at the inn, but he never accepted."

Simon opened his mouth to respond, but then he pressed his lips together and eyed the plate in his hands. "I've got to go in. Please tell Ruby I appreciate the dessert," he said, brusquely dismissing Meg.

Dumbfounded by the abrupt change in his attitude, she barely managed to retort, "Yup, will do."

As soon as she entered the kitchen where her great aunt was arranging daisies in a vase, Ruby asked, "What did Simon and the children say when you delivered the pie?"

"The children were napping, but Simon appreciated it," she answered and then she quickly ducked into the bathroom to splash the hot blush of anger from her cheeks.

I tried to be as polite and respectful to Simon as I could. If he wasn't open to talking about selling his land to a private home-owner, then that's all he had to say. He didn't need to shut down our conversation so rudely, Meg groused to herself as she retrieved a set of fresh sheets from the linen closet. *And I don't get his remark about Aunt Ruby having Misty Point all to herself. This is the second time it's seemed as if he's blaming her for the fact his father never returned to Dune Island.*

Nor did she understand how Simon could be so friendly one minute, yet turn completely uncommunicative two seconds later. It was infuriating, and Meg's annoyance at him sparked a burst of energy, which she funneled into her remaining housekeeping projects. By suppertime, she'd accomplished nearly everything on her indoor to-do list and the inn was thoroughly organized and shining from floor to ceiling. But she'd somehow forgotten about the outdoor preparations. She still needed to wipe down the patio furniture and sweep the tiles. She also planned to retrieve the Adirondack chairs from the garage, arrange them on the back lawn, and wipe the dust and webs from them, too.

As they were eating, Ruby suggested, "We should include a gentle reminder in the 'helpful hints' list to let our guests know there's a family staying in the cottage this summer, so no one disturbs Simon and the children."

Ruby had always kept a list of "helpful hints" posted in each room. The document included emergency contact numbers, instructions about how to use the landline and fire extinguishers, and information about the kitchen and the laundry room, among other useful tips. The list was meant to be helpful, not prohibitive, because as Ruby often said, she didn't want guests to feel scolded; she wanted them to feel welcome to make themselves at home.

"Okay. I'll add it to the doc when I get the chance," Meg agreed.

"If you have too many other things to do, I can amend the list," Ruby offered. "I don't know how to fix it on the computer, but I can pencil it in on the printed copies."

"No, I'll do it," Meg asserted. Usually she appreciated Ruby's breezy attitude, which complemented her own methodical tendencies. But this evening she felt agitated that her great-aunt had waited until the last minute to suggest making a change to the document, which Meg had already posted in all the rooms. It also made her cringe to picture Ruby scribbling the extra info on the bottom of the paper sheets. *If we're going to do something as outdated as providing printed instructions instead of using an app, the least we can do is be sure the documents are neatly typed.*

To add to Meg's frustration, Ruby then said, "I forgot to tell Simon that he's welcome to use the laundry room at the inn. I imagine the children must have a heap of dirty clothes by now. We should mention it to him tomorrow, before the guests need to use the machines." Of course, by *we* she'd meant Meg, and Simon was the last person she wanted to see.

But again, she agreed she'd take care of it. As soon as they finished eating their meal, Meg hopped up and began clearing the table.

"Shall I slice two pieces of pie?" asked Ruby.

Meg patted her tummy. "Thanks, but I'm too full for dessert right now."

"Then at least join me for tea out on the porch. I want to tell you a story about Gordon, Sarah, and me."

You want to take a walk down memory lane now, *when I still have hours of work to do before bedtime?* Meg was exasperated, but she suggested as patiently as she could, "Maybe it's better if we wait until later? Right now, my mind is going in a hundred different directions. I really want to hear what you have to say, but I'm afraid I won't be able to concentrate because I'll be worried about the final projects I need to wrap up this evening."

"Oh, right. What was I thinking? I'm sorry," Ruby said so contritely that Meg felt guilty. "Of course we can wait until later to talk."

"Great," she replied. "Knowing I can look forward to pie and a chat when I'm done will motivate me to zoom through the last of my chores."

Ruby insisted on cleaning up in the kitchen, so Meg went outside and swept the patio. After wiping down the tables, chairs, and loungers, she began taking the Adirondack chairs out of the garage. Usually, the two high school football players Ruby hired to mow the lawn also transported the chairs at the start of the season, but either she'd forgotten to ask them or they'd forgotten to do it. Meg figured she could handle the task by herself, but the large pieces of wooden furniture were heavier and more cumbersome than she'd anticipated.

I'm athletic, too, but I might be in over my head, she reluctantly admitted to herself when she was forced to set the first chair down halfway to her destination to rest her arms. As she stood there, catching her breath, she thought, *I can't wait until next week, when Chloe and Ava begin working. Then I'll have more time to spend visiting with Aunt Ruby and taking walks on the beach. I want to catch up on my reading, too—I haven't even cracked a book since I've been here...*

After situating three chairs in their customary spot on the lawn, Meg was so sweaty and thirsty that she decided she'd wait until the following day to move the other five chairs.

It was nearly dusk when she went indoors and she was about to fill the kettle for tea, but she remembered she hadn't updated the helpful hints document yet. Although Meg made the changes quickly, there was a glitch with the printer and she spent almost half an hour fiddling with the antiquated equipment before she could print out the revised list.

Her work completed, she flicked on the hall light and headed upstairs, expecting to find her great-aunt reading in her bedroom. Instead, Ruby was sitting in the rocking chair by the window, with the lights turned off. "I'm sorry I took so long. Are you ready for pie and tea?" she asked.

"It's a little late for me to eat anything, but help yourself to a nice, big slice."

Meg hesitated, wavering. "It's tempting, but I think I'll wait until tomorrow and enjoy it for breakfast. Seems like a good way to kick off our first day of hosting guests. Besides, I really want to hear your story before you get too sleepy to tell it to me."

She pulled up a chair, and for several moments, they watched in silence as the twirling lighthouse lens sprayed white light across the charcoal sky. When Ruby finally began to speak, her voice was unusually somber and low. "The story I'm going to tell you is one I've never shared with anyone before now. A secret of mine, really."

"It's a *secret*?" Meg had assumed Ruby was going to recount one of the memories she'd already shared dozens of times.

"Yes, a rather delicate one." Her great-aunt massaged her forehead, partially obscuring her face. "Which is why I'm at a bit of a loss about how to begin..."

As intrigued as she was, Meg softly suggested, "There's no hurry, so take your time. But if you're too uncomfortable, please don't feel pressured to tell me it."

Ruby hesitated, as if she was weighing her decision, before saying, "No, I can't keep it to myself any longer, not when so much is at stake. And you've been such a supportive, devoted niece that I want you to hear it, first, before I tell Simon."

"Simon?" Meg's voice squeaked with disbelief. "Why would you tell *him*?"

"Because it indirectly involves his grandmother. And I believe what I have to say could have a significant bearing on his life."

A significant bearing on his life? Meg hardly dared to hope Ruby's expression meant what she thought it meant. "Do you think it might change his mind about selling the property?"

"Among other things, yes," she answered.

If she'd had any idea that her great-aunt's story was potentially so consequential, Meg would've dropped everything to listen to her earlier. Now she was on the edge of her seat, barely able to contain her curiosity as she waited for Ruby to elaborate.

But the next thing Ruby said was, "Before I begin, do you have any acetaminophen? I'm getting a headache."

"Oh, no, not another one," clucked Meg. She wondered if she should suggest that they postpone their conversation until the morning when Ruby was feeling better, but selfishly, she was dying to hear her great-aunt's secret. "I just bought a bottle in town today. I'll go get it."

"Thank you, dear. Meanwhile, I promise I'll collect my thoughts—no one likes an overly slow beginning to a story."

Chuckling, Meg hurried downstairs. It took several minutes to locate her purse, which she'd hung by its strap on the back of a kitchen chair. She'd nearly emptied all of its contents onto the table before remembering she'd put the medication in the storage closet with her other personal belongings. She retrieved the pill bottle, filled a glass with water, and returned to her great-aunt's bedroom, where Ruby was sitting at an odd angle in the rocker.

"These should help. They're extra strength." She extended the tablets but her great-aunt didn't make any move to accept them. "Aunt Ruby? What's wrong?"

"The light...the light," she groaned and at first Meg thought she was saying the light from the hallway was bothering her eyes. But as Meg turned to shut the door, Ruby grabbed hold of her wrist. In a halting voice, she said, "The light... house... holds... the... key."

"The lighthouse holds the key?" Meg repeated, bewildered. "I don't understand. The lighthouse holds the key to *what*?"

"My... shecret." Apparently aware she'd slurred the word, Ruby tried again. "She-cret."

She slapped her knee in frustration, and the room was bright enough for Meg to see Ruby's eyes going wide. No, only *one* eye went wide; her other lid and brow were drooping. One corner of her mouth tugged downward, too, and her arm dangled limply at her side.

Meg suddenly recognized why her great-aunt looked—and sounded—so different. Her stomach somersaulted and a surge of adrenaline spiked her heartrate, but she managed to stay calm. She set down the pill bottle and water glass, and then tucked a pillow in between Ruby's torso and the arm of the rocker so she wouldn't topple sideways.

"Don't move, okay? I'll be right back," she assured her. Everything seemed to be happening in slow motion and yet all at once as Meg raced to the kitchen, grabbed the landline, dialed 9-1-1, and uttered, "I think my great-aunt is having a stroke."

Rushing back upstairs with the phone pressed to her ear, she answered the dispatcher's questions and then she tenderly wrapped her arm around her great-aunt's left shoulder.

"It's possible you're having a stroke, Aunt Ruby. That's why your face and arm might feel strange and why you're having trouble communicating. I know it's frustrating and scary, but an ambulance is coming and you're going to be okay. Everything's going to be okay. You're going to be okay," Meg said, as if repeating the words would make them true.

SIX

Meg sat in the hospital parking lot with her car windows rolled down, too distraught to drive back to the inn.

"I should have known something serious was wrong," she lamented into her phone, after telling her mother what had happened. "The whole time I've been here, Aunt Ruby's had a nagging cough and she's been very fatigued. She didn't seem to be recovering well from the respiratory virus she'd had this spring, and I was so worried about her relapsing that I never saw her stroke coming."

"How could you have seen it coming? You're not a doctor," her mother replied. "Plus Ruby's physician has been following up with her regularly and even he didn't think she was at risk for a stroke—otherwise, he would've ordered tests or prescribed her something."

"But you don't understand," Meg protested. "You don't know..."

"What don't I know, honey? Hmm? You can tell me."

Her mother's prompting was so caring and quiet that suddenly all the guilt Meg had been holding in came pouring out in a flood of tears and words. "Last night Aunt Ruby wanted to have a sit-down with me after supper and I-I-I put her off because I still had things to do to get the inn ready for the guests coming today."

It barely crossed her mind to mention to her mother what Ruby had wanted to talk about before she'd become unwell. Something about a secret, and the lighthouse? Meg's recollection was hazy at the moment; besides, worrying about whatever Ruby had wanted to say paled in significance compared to her worries about her great-aunt's health.

With a hiccup-y sob, she continued, "I didn't go into her bedroom until after nine o'clock. Maybe if I had taken the time to chat with her sooner, she would have mentioned she'd had a headache. Maybe I would've known that—"

Now her mother spoke over her, drowning out her daughter's voice. "I want you to stop that right now, Meg. This is *not* your fault. As your mother, I'm sorry you've had to experience this alone, because it's obviously been very traumatizing. But for Ruby's sake, I'm glad you were there. If you hadn't been with her and acted so quickly when she had the stroke, she might not have made it."

"She *still* might not make it, Mom." Meg shivered, despite the heat. "Even though she's getting medication now and she's at the hospital, statistically, the odds are high that she'll have another stroke."

"The doctors told you *that*?"

"No. I looked it up online," admitted Meg. "But they did say she's got a long road ahead of her."

"Right. And by that I assume they mean she's going to have an extended recovery period. So you need to pace yourself physically and emotionally. If you don't, you'll wind up getting sick or breaking down and then you won't be any help to your aunt at all," her mother sensibly advised her. "I know Ruby has a cousin in Pennsylvania, but is there anyone locally who can give you a hand with the inn?"

"I've already spoken to her closest friend on the island." Before rushing out the door to follow the ambulance, Meg had the presence of mind to grab Ruby's purse, which contained her great-aunt's medical insurance card, as well as a small address book that listed phone numbers of her friends and a few distant relatives. "Her name is Alice and she's going to cover for me while I'm at the hospital this week. Some other members of Aunt Ruby's book club might be willing to help, too. And she's always said that the housekeepers, Ava and Chloe, go above and beyond to keep things running smoothly at the inn."

"Good. You know you can call me for emotional support any time, day or night. You can call your brother, too."

"I know. Thanks, Mom."

Next, she phoned Ruby's cousin, Linda, who lived in Pennsylvania. Meg had already called her twice, but she'd promised to give her one more update, even though she didn't have much new information to report.

"Ruby still can't speak or move her arm, which is what the doctors said they expected at this point," she told Linda. "She's resting right now, so I'm going to run back to the inn for a few hours to greet the guests, and then I'll come back to the hospital this evening. Her care team should know more by then and I'll call you again, if you'd like."

"Yes, please do." Linda kindly reminded her to drive carefully. "It can be difficult to concentrate on the road after something upsetting like this happens."

Meg promised she'd be cautious, but after they'd said goodbye, instead of pressing the car's ignition button, she scrolled through her contacts list on her phone, trying to decide which of her friends to call for an additional boost of moral support before she headed back to the inn.

Her best friend was scheduled to go on vacation on Saturday, and Meg didn't want to tell her bad news right before her trip. Her other two closest confidantes both worked at the university. Because Meg had taken "unofficial medical leave," for the summer, the dean had asked her to limit her social contact with staff members—just for the sake of appearances. A lot of Meg's other acquaintances were mutual friends with Josh, who'd had mixed reactions to their breakup, so she didn't feel comfortable confiding in them.

However, she stopped scrolling when she came to Josh's name, which she still hadn't deleted from her contacts. With her thumb hovering over the call button, she hesitated. Meg hadn't spoken to him since they'd broken up. But he knew how much she loved her great-aunt and he'd always had a way of helping her rein in her worries. She pressed the button.

The call immediately rolled into voice mail, and hearing his greeting unexpectedly made her feel even more emotional. Her voice quavered as she left a message. "Hi, Josh. It's Meg. I, um, I know we haven't talked since... a long time ago, and maybe I shouldn't be calling. But I'm on Dune Island and my aunt Ruby just had a stroke. She's stable now, but she's not exactly out of the woods. So I thought I'd call you because, well, I miss the way you used to tell me not to catastrophize."

She'd meant it as a sort of joke, but after saying it she realized he might take it as a jab at him. So she clarified, "I mean, it was always kind of comforting and I guess I sort of need something like that. But you don't have to call me back—my cell phone doesn't work at the inn. Anyway, I know this message is all about me, but I hope *you're* doing well. Bye, Josh."

As she drove to the inn, Meg asked herself, *Why did I leave a message? When I got his voice mail, why didn't I just hang up? He's going to think I'm pitiful. Or worse, he'll be miffed that I told him something so serious because he'll feel obligated to return my call even if he doesn't want to talk to me.* But there was nothing she could do about it now.

. . .

Pulling into the parking area beside the inn, Meg was relieved that the only other vehicle in the lot was Simon's minivan. She turned off the ignition and glanced at her phone: 3:08. Less than an hour until guests were allowed to check in.

Meg closed her eyes to mentally review her plan of action. *First, I'll give the inn a quick once-over, and straighten anything that's out of place. Then, I'll type a note to post so guests will know where to find their keys or how to reach me, in case I need to return to the hospital before everyone arrives and I can't greet them in person. The last thing I'll do is take a super-quick shower.*

She got out of the car and hurried toward the porch. She was almost within an arm's length of the stairs when she noticed Simon cutting across the back lawn. Cody and Abigail weren't with him.

"Hi, Meg," he said softly as he approached. "I saw the ambulance last night so I thought I'd check to see if everyone's okay?"

"Not really, no. My aunt Ruby had a stroke." Meg answered tersely, without looking directly at him. This was partly because she was in a rush and partly because she was still miffed at him. But mostly it was because every time she'd told anyone on the phone that Ruby had suffered a stroke, Meg's eyes had welled with tears. She didn't want that happening in front of Simon.

"Uff." He sounded as if someone had knocked the air out of him. "I'm really sorry to hear that. So she's in the local hospital?"

"Yes." Meg nodded and took a step away from him, toward the stairs. "In the intensive care unit."

"Wow. Is there... anything I can do to help?"

"No, thanks." She placed a hand on the railing. "I've got guests coming soon, so I need to go." Then she scuttled up the stairs and through the porch door.

Within half an hour, Meg had tidied the inn and printed

welcome letters for the guests. She grabbed a towel from the linen closet and made a beeline for Ruby's room to use her shower, but she came to a halt when she noticed her great-aunt's rocking chair pushed against the wall.

Oh, yeah, that's right, the EMT had to move it so he could maneuver the stretcher out of the room, Meg recalled. As she turned the chair so it faced the window again, she caught sight of the lighthouse. In the bright afternoon sun, its beacon faded to a faint blink of light, and as Meg paused to watch it, Ruby's cryptic words sprang to mind. *The lighthouse holds the key.*

Meg had absolutely no idea what she'd meant by that; she wasn't even confident that Ruby herself knew. *The stroke must have been affecting her thought process to some degree—otherwise, why wouldn't she have told me her secret outright, instead of giving me such a puzzling hint?* On the other hand, it wasn't as if Ruby had been speaking complete gibberish, so Meg was reluctant to dismiss her great-aunt's baffling clue, even if she couldn't decipher it.

The only way to understand for certain what her great-aunt may have meant was to ask her. And since Ruby wasn't in any condition to answer, Meg turned from the window and put the question out of her mind.

Never had Meg appreciated her great-aunt's lackadaisical approach to innkeeping as much as she appreciated it at the beginning of that summer. Because she wasn't expected to dote on the guests—and because either Chloe or Ava were always onsite in the morning and early afternoon—Meg had no qualms about spending most of her time at the hospital.

It was difficult seeing Ruby lying in bed, half of her face fixed in what appeared to be an expression of enduring sadness. Meg was deeply troubled to know that her right arm was virtually immobile, and she'd lost most of the strength in her right leg. But what she imagined was most challenging for her great-aunt was her inability to speak. Although Ruby could generally comprehend what people said, she couldn't find or pronounce the words she needed to express herself.

So Meg tried to entertain her great-aunt with quiet, simple anecdotes about the inn's guests, or she'd repeat well-wishes from Linda, Alice, and her fellow book club members. On the occasions when it seemed Ruby needed something, Meg would ask her *yes* and *no* questions, and her great-aunt would reply with a thumbs-up or thumbs-down. Or else she'd point to an object or draw a shape in the air.

This process reminded Meg of playing twenty questions or charades, and her great-aunt often became very agitated and gave up before Meg zeroed in on what Ruby meant to express. Meg never took offense at her great-aunt's obvious impatience with her. But for Ruby's sake, it broke Meg's heart to realize that her normally laid-back, mild-mannered aunt was so frustrated.

One evening, after fifteen minutes of trying to figure out what Ruby's hand motions meant, Meg apologized, "I'm sorry, I just can't understand what you're trying to tell me." Then, despite her best efforts not to, Meg began to weep. Covering her face with her arm, she confessed the regret that had continued to weigh on her heart, even after she'd spoken to her mother about it. "And I'm sorry—truly sorry—that I was so uptight about getting the inn ready the other evening. Maybe if I hadn't been obsessed with cleaning the lawn furniture, or if I had chatted with you after supper, I could have done something sooner. Maybe—"

Ruby interrupted her by smacking her left hand against the bed guard rail. When Meg lowered her arm from her face, her great-aunt vigorously wagged a finger at her and then made a thumbs-down sign, gestures Meg understood perfectly the very first time.

"Okay, I won't say another word about it," she agreed, chuckling through her tears.

Although Hope Haven Hospital provided outstanding short-term care for its patients, Dune Island only had one long-term skilled nursing and rehab center, and it was filled. So, Ruby's cousin, Linda, secured a spot for her at a facility that accepted her insurance. Located in Pennsylvania, it had an excellent reputation and Linda lived nearby, which meant she could see Ruby daily.

Meg knew that this was the best arrangement for her great-aunt, but she still wished that Ruby were staying in Hope Haven. *How will I ever get away to visit her?* she wondered as she drove back to the inn.

Rolling into the parking area, she noticed that once again, the only vehicle there was Simon's minivan. In the distance, the flat ocean melded with the tarnished sky. *No wonder none of the guests stuck around here this evening—it's too overcast to watch the sunset,* Meg thought.

Grateful for the solitude, she slipped off her sandals and sauntered through the grass to sit in one of the Adirondack chairs. It was the evening before Ruby was scheduled to be discharged from the hospital, and Meg felt almost as apprehensive as she did on the evening her great-aunt had been admitted.

She lowered her lids, trying to block out her worries, but she kept picturing how vulnerable Ruby appeared lying in the hospital bed. *If I'm not there, who will bring her tissues or raise her bed?* Meg fretted, a single tear trickling down her cheek. *How will she tell the staff if she's in pain?*

Suddenly, she felt a small, soft hand on her arm and she opened her eyes. Abigail was standing in front of her, hugging a plate against her tummy. Sitting up straighter, Meg sniffed and quickly blotted the dampness from her face.

"Hi, Meg. Daddy said I could bring your plate to you if I carried it very carefully. And he said to give you this, too." She slid her hand in between the plate and her stomach and produced a folded piece of paper. "It's a note."

"I see that. Thank you." She unfolded it and read what he'd written:

Meg,

I hope Ruby is doing better and that you're all right, too? My offer still stands if there's anything I can do to help.

Thank you for the pie. It was just peachy!

Simon

She smiled weakly at his pun and asked Abigail, "Could you please give your dad a message from me? Tell him I said he's welcome."

"Okay." The little girl handed her the plate, but instead of leaving, she slid onto the chair closest to Meg. Her legs were too short for the slanted, oversize seat so her feet stuck out straight in front of her. "Were you crying because Ms. Ruby is sick?"

Startled, Meg answered honestly. "Yes, that's why I was a little weepy... So I guess your daddy must have told you that Ms. Ruby is in the hospital?

"Yeah, 'cause me and Cody woke up one night when there was a siren. Then we saw an ambulance in the parking lot, and ambulances take people to hospitals." Abigail wiggled her feet, bouncing her sandals against each other, before comforting Meg, "You shouldn't be too sad. Everybody in the hospital doesn't always die and go to heaven like Mommy did."

Her words hit Meg right in the breastbone. "You're—you're right about that."

"Sometimes they get all better and they come home very soon," Abigail said knowingly, nodding her head. "My daddy came home in three days."

"Your daddy was in the hospital?"

"Mm-hmm, when the truck crashed into Mommy's car."

I didn't realize Simon was in the auto accident that killed his wife—that's awful! thought Meg. "I'm glad he got all better and came home, but you must have really missed him while he was in the hospital?"

"Mmm, maybe, I don't remember. But Grandma said I didn't cry at night, only Cody did, so we all slept in her bed." She flicked an ant crawling across the arm of her chair and sent it sailing to the grass. "Sometimes when people are in the hospital, they only get medium-better. If that happens, then they go to a special apartment in Phoenix."

Meg wasn't following her. "A special apartment in Phoenix?"

"Mm-hmm, it's for grandmas and grandpas who have holes in their rememories, and they forget how to put on their clothes and what your name is and they get lost a lot. But even if they're very far away and you miss them, it's better because their brother and sister can visit them all the time and they don't have to fly on an airplane anymore," Abigail explained.

Her grandmother must have some form of dementia. She probably moved to a facility that's closer to her family, Meg deduced. "A special apartment in Phoenix sounds nice. It's very sunny and warm there."

"Yeah, that's what Daddy told me. Is Ms. Ruby going to a special apartment when she gets out of the hospital?"

"I guess she is, in a way. But it's not in Phoenix and it's not because she has holes in her memories. It's because she had a... she had a kind of injury in her brain. So she's going to a place where they know a lot about the kind of injury she had and they'll help her get better so she can come back home."

"In a few days?"

"No. It will probably be a long time before she's well enough to come home."

"When she is, can you tell me so I can make a sign that says *welcome home, Ms. Ruby*? I'll draw a picture of the lighthouse on it."

Her upbeat outlook about Ruby's return made Meg feel more optimistic, too. Even though she doubted Simon and the children would still be on Dune Island when Ruby returned, she said, "She'd love a sign like that."

"Abigail!" Simon was standing on the front steps of the cottage. He scooped his arm through the air, beckoning her home.

"Uh-oh, I gotta go." She wiggled her way off the end of the chair. "Bye, Meg."

As Abigail skipped toward the cottage, her father lifted his hand in a silent greeting to Meg. Recognizing that he was making an effort to be more cordial and knowing that her great-aunt would want Meg to make an effort, too, she returned his wave.

And then, because of her affection for his darling, redheaded daughter, Meg also smiled and called, "Have a good night, Simon!"

SEVEN

Meg arrived at the hospital at 8:30, right on the dot. She wanted to make the most of every minute with Ruby before they had to say goodbye. But there was a flurry of activity surrounding her great-aunt's departure, and they only had a few moments alone before the nurse told them it was almost time for Ruby to leave.

"I brought two pairs of reading glasses and a few books for you," Meg told her. "I know you might not be ready to read for a while, so I also brought you a gift. It's an e-reader and I've paired it with these earbuds, so you can listen to audio books on it. I've downloaded a whole bunch that I think you might like. The staff should be able to set it up so you can listen to it, but I've included instructions, too, in case they don't know how to use it. Is it okay if I add these things to your travel bag?"

Meg had ordered the e-reader online earlier in the week, and when she'd returned to the inn the previous evening, she was delighted to discover it had been delivered. She'd stayed up past midnight setting it up and meticulously selecting books she thought her great-aunt might enjoy. She hadn't known if Ruby would listen to the audio books or not, since she'd always been a visual reader. So she was delighted when Ruby answered her with a thumbs-up, the signal she used to indicate *yes*, because she still had difficulty pronouncing the word. Meg slid the e-reader and instructions into the overnight bag, zipped it shut, and took a seat beside her great-aunt's bed.

Trying to keep her tone light, Meg began her goodbye. "That was sure some week you've had, Aunt Ruby. I know it's been grueling, but you're doing really well. The rehab center is excellent, so you'll be in very good hands. Linda's going to meet you there today, to help you get settled in. I hope to visit you in a few weeks, and—"

Her aunt interrupted with a loud, "No."

"You don't want me to visit in a few weeks? You want me to come sooner than that?"

"No."

"You want me to come *later* than that?" Meg asked and Ruby signaled *yes*. After a few more questions, she realized her great-aunt didn't want her to travel to Pennsylvania to visit her at all, although she indicated that she'd like her to call on occasion. At first Meg felt hurt, but then she said, "Oh, is it because you don't want me to be away from the inn?"

Ruby gave her a thumbs-up. Then she pointed a finger at herself and slowly made the okay sign. When Meg cocked her head to the side, trying to figure out what she meant, her great-aunt repeated the gesture.

"Oh, I get it. You're saying you'll be okay, and I know you will, but I wish you'd let me visit you," Meg argued.

"No," Ruby said, simultaneously giving a thumbs-down and bobbing her hand for emphasis. She waited a moment and then she pointed to Meg and made the okay sign again.

"Yes, I'll be okay, too," she agreed. "And so will the inn. I don't want you to give it a second thought while you're recovering. You know me—I'll run a tight ship."

"No." Ruby pointed to Meg again and then slowly walked her fingers over the sheet.

"You want me to go away?"

"No. No." Ruby's frustration was obvious. She repeated her actions, but this time, after walking her fingers along the bed, she mimed small waves in the air. Then she duplicated the sequence two more times.

"All right, I get it, you don't have to nag," Meg teased, managing a smile. "I promise I'll take breaks to go for walks on the beach."

Her response elicited a high-five from Ruby, which caused Meg to laugh outright, since it was so unlike her great-aunt to make that gesture.

But a few minutes later, as the driver rolled Ruby's stretcher backward into the medical transport vehicle, the lump in Meg's throat rendered her almost unable to speak. At the last moment, she called, "I love you, Aunt Ruby. I'll see you soon."

Her great-aunt lifted her left hand, tilting it in front of her face. But because she couldn't move one side of her mouth, by the time Meg understood that she was blowing a kiss, the driver had closed the doors, and Ruby had disappeared from sight.

After purchasing food in town, Meg loitered in her car in the grocery store parking lot, numbly watching the passersby. It seemed as if the island had quadrupled its population overnight; the sidewalks were bustling with people dressed in shorts and T-shirts, sundresses or swimwear. Virtually all of them were smiling, and their expressions seemed to proclaim, *Summer is here and so are we!*

But Ruby's departure left Meg feeling as if her heart had been hollowed out with a lathe. Just as she was debating calling her mother, her phone vibrated and Josh's name blinked on the screen. This was the fourth time he'd tried to return Meg's call, but she'd been so embarrassed by the voice mail she'd left him or so consumed by what was happening with Ruby that she hadn't answered any of his previous attempts. But Josh clearly wasn't going to stop trying to reach her until he spoke directly to Meg, and she knew it wasn't fair to keep ignoring his calls.

She took a deep breath and pressed the phone to her ear. "Hi, Josh," she greeted him in a falsely sunny voice, but he knew her too well.

"Hey, there. I've been worried about you. Are you okay, Meg-aret?"

His deliberate mispronunciation of her name was an old joke between them. Shortly after they started seeing each other, Josh sent Meg a handwritten note in the mail, telling her how happy he was that they'd met. She appreciated the sentiment and the old-fashioned delivery, but she couldn't help teasing him because he'd incorrectly addressed the envelope to *Megan Carter*, since he hadn't known her full first name was actually *Margaret*.

"Who's Megan Carter—and should I be jealous that you're writing her romantic notes like this?" Meg had ribbed him.

Josh was mortified at his error; he said he'd never heard of the name *Meg* being used as an abbreviation for *Margaret*. After that, in private he'd sometimes call her *Meg-aret* as a term of affection, a way to make her smile, or an intimate flirtation.

Now, because she was already on the brink of tears, it made her break down to hear Josh use his familiar, private nickname for her in such a tender voice. "No. I'm not okay," she wept.

Then she delved into a recap of everything that had happened, starting with the night Ruby had the stroke. She ended by telling him that her great-aunt had just departed for the rehab center.

"Rationally, I know she's going to be fine, but I can't stop worrying about her. I keep wondering if it would've been better if she'd gone to a facility in Hyannis, or southern Massachusetts, so I could've looked in on her more often." Meg blotted her cheeks and ruefully added, "Even if that's not what she wants me to do."

"She told you that?"

"Not in so many words, no. Not in *any* words, actually," Meg clarified, chuckling at the memory. "But yeah, she communicated that she doesn't want me to visit her while she's away. She knows I'll need to keep an eye on things at the inn, even though the place kind of runs itself. And she was insistent that I should go for walks on the beach."

"Sounds like good advice," Josh remarked. He paused before cautiously asking, "Can I give you my two cents, too?"

"Sure, go ahead," Meg said, even though she anticipated he'd hint that she was being pessimistic or overly emotional.

"You were in a life-or-death situation when your great-aunt had the stroke, and you've been with her a lot while she's been in the hospital. So you've seen her at her most vulnerable. It's no wonder you're concerned that you can't check in on her every day—you're probably experiencing some sort of separation anxiety or post-traumatic stress," he said, with a depth of understanding and compassion that surprised Meg, even if it didn't allay her worries about her great-aunt.

"Yeah, I guess. But I wish I could stop feeling this way."

"You will, eventually. Once Ruby gets settled in at the rehab center and her cousin meets the staff in person, you'll feel a lot more comfortable about the care she's receiving there," he suggested. "But for right now, you probably need a nap. Knowing you like I do, I'm guessing you've hardly slept at all this week. Then, after your nap, you might try going for a walk on the beach, like Ruby told you to do. If you still feel anxious after that—although I doubt you will—you can always make a list."

"A list of what?"

"Things you need to do at the inn? Questions you want to ask Ruby's care team? Alternative facilities in case you still have qualms? I don't know. My point is that you always seem to breathe easier after you've made a list."

Meg chuckled at the accuracy of his observation about her. "That's sort of an ironic suggestion, considering that a big part of the reason I came to Dune Island for the summer was because my to-do lists were making me breathe *harder*, not easier."

"Then make it a short list."

She cracked up. "I think you might be onto something there... Anyway, thanks for listening to me. It's been really helpful to talk through everything that happened. But enough about me. How about you? What's going on in your world?"

"Well, as you know, it's baseball season. So Patrick and I caught a game in the city the other night," he replied, and Meg could hear voices in the background. She hadn't realized he'd called her from the office; usually he worked from home. "Ugh, sorry, Meg, I've got to deliver a presentation in a couple minutes. Can I call you back another time?"

"You don't have to do that." She didn't want Josh to feel like he had to check in on her, and she didn't want to start to depend on him emotionally, either. "I really appreciate it that you listened to my meltdown, but I think you're right—after I've had a good nap and a long walk, I'll feel a lot better."

"I know you will, but I'd really like to talk some more." His tone was suddenly serious, and she couldn't tell if that was because other people were nearby or if something had happened recently that was upsetting him.

Regretful that she'd been so self-focused, Meg said, "Sure, I would, too. Call whenever you'd like."

. . .

While Ruby was in the hospital, Meg had been sleeping on the sofa bed in the den. She hadn't been able to bring herself to use her great-aunt's room because she wasn't ready to admit that Ruby wasn't returning soon. But in the den during the wee hours, it seemed as if she could hear every creaky door and floorboard, as well as every snore and cough overhead.

Now that Ruby had left for the rehab center, however, Meg accepted that it was sensible for her to move into her great-aunt's room for the duration of her absence. Years ago, Ruby used to occupy the bedroom downstairs, but she'd permanently moved to the second floor to make the first floor room available for guests with disabilities.

As Meg carried fresh linens upstairs to Ruby's bedroom, it occurred to her that when her great-aunt returned to the inn, she herself might need a room with modifications such as grip bars in the bathroom, or a door wide enough for wheelchair access.

Even if she regains enough balance and strength to walk unassisted again, it seems like it would be risky for her to go up and down the stairs several times a day, thought Meg. *Then what will she do? It's not as if she can cancel all the reservations for the downstairs bedroom so she can use it, but she doesn't have the funds for a stairlift...*

Meg had been so consumed with Ruby's day-to-day challenges at the hospital that she hadn't fully considered the long-term challenges her great-aunt would face after rehabilitation. But now Meg's mind was spinning so fast she doubted she'd be able to slow it down enough to take a nap, even though she was beyond exhausted. So when she'd finished making the bed and transferring her belongings from the storage closet to Ruby's room, she changed into shorts and a T-shirt and headed out to the beach.

Halfway across the meadow, she paused to take in the view. In the distance, the sky and sea were a competition of blues, and spiky tufts of verdant beach grass bent to tickle the sun-blanched sand, as the white, red, and black lighthouse looked on.

This. This is exactly what I need, thought Meg, her mood lifting. When she reached the tip, she scanned the beach in each direction: she saw two families, including Simon's, to the right, but the left side of the peninsula was deserted. Since she needed to ease back into being social again, she walked to the left, first. Then she circled back and continued to the right, stopping to greet a young couple who was staying at the inn with their son, Mason.

A little farther down the beach, Mason was making a sandcastle with Cody and Abigail on the water's edge. As she approached, Meg exclaimed, "Ooh, I like your moat."

"Watch out," warned Mason. "It has alligators in it to keep the bad guys away."

"And it has sharks," whispered Cody.

At the same time, Abigail answered, "It's not a moat. It's a swimming pool for the princess."

"She'd better swim fast or the alligators and sharks are going to eat her," Mason taunted.

"No problem," retorted Abigail, smoothing the castle wall with the back of a small plastic shovel. "She used to be on a search and rescue team in the Coast Guard before she became a princess."

Silently cheering at the little girl's sassy comeback, Meg took an exaggerated step to bypass the moat and joined Simon where he was standing on drier sand above the high tide line. After exchanging hellos, he asked in a low voice, "How's Ruby?"

"Okay, thanks. She was doing well enough to be transferred to a rehab center this morning, so I guess that's progress."

"Yeah, it is." Tracing a semi-circle in the sand with his big toe, he asked, "Is the rehab facility on Dune Island?"

"No. It's in Pennsylvania. It's got an excellent reputation, and she has a cousin living nearby." Meg repeated the same concern she'd shared with Josh, saying, "But I wish she were closer so I could look in on her every day. Or at least every week."

"I can understand that... I had a lot of anxiety when we made the decision that my mother should move from near where I live in Delaware to an assisted living facility in Arizona about a year ago. She was exhibiting the early symptoms of Alzheimer's and it wasn't safe for her to live alone," he said. Meg didn't let on that Abigail had already told her as much. "It was clear to everyone that I... I had my hands full, so it wasn't really an option for my mom to live with me. Her sister and brother live in the Phoenix area, and they wanted her to be closer to them, so that's where she went."

Although he didn't say it, Meg recognized a note of guilt in his voice. "The separation must be difficult, though. Your mother's a lot farther away from you than my great-aunt is from me. Are you able to visit her?"

"Yeah, I fly out there every four or five months. Which isn't as often as I'd like, but I sleep better at night knowing that my aunt and uncle live right down the road from her. They're both retired, so one of them visits my mom every day. Sometimes they go on outings, or she even stays overnight at their homes. The staff at the facility give her lots of support, too." With a reassuring smile, he added, "So, ultimately, when I consider the big picture, I know the move was in her best interest."

Because he'd recently been through a situation that was similar to Meg's, it was encouraging to hear Simon's perspective. His outlook on his mother's relocation inspired Meg to focus on the big picture, too: not only was Ruby getting excellent care at the rehab center, but her arrangement was temporary. Eventually, she'd return home.

"I think this move will benefit my aunt Ruby, too," she acknowledged.

"That doesn't necessarily mean it's easy, especially the first few days after saying goodbye. It'll get better, though." Simon squinted at the horizon, before admitting with a rueful chuckle, "And then it'll get worse again. It's a mixed bag—sadness, doubt, anxiety, relief... There are a lot of ups and downs."

"Mmm, it isn't a linear process," Meg mumbled, quoting what Ruby's care team had frequently said about her great-aunt's recovery.

Simon suddenly called to his son, who was standing in knee-deep water, splashing his belly to rinse sand from it. "Hey, Cody, you know the rules. If you're going to do that, you've got to take your blankie off. Otherwise, it'll get wet, and then it's going to smell like seaweed."

"Oh, that reminds me," said Meg, as Cody abandoned his rinsing technique and trotted back to rejoin Abigail and Mason. "You're welcome to use the washer and dryer at the inn."

"Thanks, but we can go to a laundromat in town. I figure it'll be a good indoor activity for a rainy day."

"Smart thinking—too bad half the island has that same idea." Meg said with a laugh. "Trust me. Do your laundry at the inn."

"You're sure? I don't want to put anyone out."

"It won't be an issue. The only caveat is that you can't use the machines until after noon. The laundry room is reserved in the morning so the housekeeping staff can wash the linens. I'll let them know you'll be dropping in some time. Their names are Chloe and Ava."

"Yeah, Chloe came by the cottage to introduce herself the other day."

Somehow, that didn't surprise Meg. The young, vivacious woman had a history of being very outspoken to guests—especially to male guests—about her desire to be in a relationship.

Although Ruby tended to overlook what she considered to be a "little foible," last year she'd been forced to address Chloe's behavior after a guest complained that she'd been flirting with the guest's husband.

It's kind of nervy for Chloe to wander over to Simon's cottage since she knows we've asked guests not to disturb his family, but maybe she thought our request didn't apply to her because she's a staff member, not a guest, thought Meg. *Besides, Simon doesn't seem bothered by it.*

"Good, I'm glad you've met Chloe," she said. "Ava's a lot more reserved—she's a high school student—but either of them will be happy to help if you have questions about how to operate the machines or whatever."

"Thanks, this is actually perfect timing. I've got an important meeting in town in a couple days and I've already worn all my clothes at least once, so I'm starting to smell a little like something from the marsh," he admitted.

"In that case, I'm *very* glad it works out for you," Meg joked.

But inwardly, she was dismayed to hear that Simon had an important meeting in town. As she walked back to the inn, she thought, *He's probably going to speak to the developer or a lawyer or realtor about selling his land. Which means I need to try to persuade him to reconsider his options while there's still time.*

The question was, *how?* He hadn't been open to talking to her the last time she'd broached the subject. But Meg wasn't going to give up that easily. *We're on friendlier terms now, so if we continue in this direction, he might be willing to engage in another conversation about selling to an individual or a preservation society.*

She figured it would help her case if she could come up with a compelling way to show Simon how special Misty Point was to Dune Island's residents and visitors, as well as to her and Ruby. *I suppose I could ask the inn's guests to tell him how*

much they love the isolation and unspoiled beauty of this location, she thought. *Chloe might be willing to mention how important the inn has been to her, too, since Aunt Ruby has always
allowed her to bring her children to work, and most seasonal
employers don't offer that kind of flexibility. And I'm sure once
Lou and the Lighthouse Society find out about the resort, they'll
speak up, as well.*

However, Meg recognized the potential for her plan to
backfire: if the residents or visitors laid it on too thick, no matter
how genuine their comments were, Simon might dismiss them.
Worse, he might feel resentful or defensive, as if he were being
put on the spot by virtual strangers, and Meg honestly wouldn't
blame him for that.

*It's too bad I can't appeal to his sense of appreciation for his
family's ties to the property,* she thought. *But how can I do that
when his father, Bradley, had absolutely no regard for Misty
Point, and Simon had never met his grandmother, Sarah, who'd
loved it here?*

Meg's mind flashed to the conversation she'd had with her
great-aunt just before she'd left the room to bring her some
medication. *Aunt Ruby was hopeful that the story she wanted to
share with Simon and me would change his mind about selling
the property. If only I had taken the time to listen to her earlier
that evening, I'd be able to tell Simon her secret now,* she
thought wistfully.

Meg estimated it could be several months before her great-
aunt could communicate well enough to tell even a condensed
version of her story. By then, it would be too late, as Simon
undoubtedly would've already finalized the deal with the
developer.

It briefly occurred to Meg that if she asked her great-aunt a
series of yes-or-no questions, she might be able to glean more
info about Ruby's secret. But just as quickly, she rejected the
idea. Her great-aunt was already frustrated enough about trying

to communicate about her daily needs. Meg didn't want to upset her further.

It's going to take all of Aunt Ruby's emotional and physical energy to recover from the stroke, she thought. *I promised I'd take care of the inn so she could focus solely on her health, and somehow, I'm going to take care of this problem by myself, too.*

EIGHT

After several reassuring phone calls from Ruby's cousin, Meg was growing increasingly comfortable about her great-aunt's relocation to the facility in Pennsylvania, and the therapies she was receiving.

"They went easy on her at first, but now they're really giving her a workout," Linda reported. "Six hours of exercises a day!—I bring my knitting or my puzzle books to do while she's sleeping or down at the rehab gym. The staff never minds how long I stay and sometimes they bring me lunch or dinner on the sly."

Meg chuckled. "You deserve at least that much! It's a huge relief to know you're there, keeping an eye out for Aunt Ruby."

"Like I said, I enjoy visiting my cousin, even if I don't get to talk to her as much as I want. Not that we could have a heart-to-heart conversation anyway, since she can hardly speak and I can hardly hear," joked Linda. "But it's peaceful at the center and being here gives me a sense of purpose. I didn't realize how isolated I've been."

I guess Pennsylvania really was the best place for Aunt Ruby, for more than one reason, thought Meg. As usual, she reminded Linda to reach out if Ruby wanted to talk to her on the phone. "No pressure, of course. I don't want to frustrate her. Meanwhile, please let her know I've called and everything at the inn is going well. We've had some knockout sunsets. Just... you'll be sure to tell me if there's an emergency or Ruby takes a turn or anything like that?"

"Of course, I'd call and tell you if there was any reason for concern. But don't you worry about a thing—Ruby has a whole team of people looking after her here. She'll probably be ready for a video call with you sooner rather than later. In the meantime, you just focus on doing what you need to do there to keep the inn running while she's away."

Keeping the inn running while Aunt Ruby's away isn't a problem, thought Meg after she'd said goodbye and hung up the cordless phone. *It's keeping the inn running* next *summer that's worrying me.*

As she began washing a pile of dirty pots and pans a guest had left in the kitchen sink, Meg's thoughts turned to the words her great-aunt had said to her before she'd completely lost her ability to speak. What could she have meant by them? Meg mumbled the phrase to herself, "The lighthouse holds the key... to my secret."

"You have a *secret*?" someone asked in a high-pitched voice.

Meg spun around to see a little girl and a little boy standing side by side in the doorway. The boy was sucking a purple ice pop, but the girl must have finished hers because she had purple juice on her chin and down the front of her shirt. Meg immediately recognized them: Madison and Addison, Chloe's twins, whose nicknames were Maddie and Sonny. But before Meg could say hello, Chloe came bustling down the hall.

"Hey, you guys, what did I tell you? No ice pops inside the inn. I don't want to have to mop the floor again. Scoot outside— and don't touch anything on your way out." The children scampered away and Chloe apologized to Meg. "Sorry about that. I never let them eat anything that melts inside the inn unsupervised. They must have snuck by me."

"It's fine," Meg assured her.

"Why are you doing the dishes? That's *my* job." Chloe crossed the room and tried to take the dish cloth from Meg's hand.

"It's just a couple pots and pans, I'll finish up here. If you're all done with the rest of the rooms, you should take off. It's a great beach day."

"Nah, I'm going to hang around for a few more minutes to see if Simon comes back from wherever he took his kids. I told Maddie and Sonny about Cody and Abigail, and they've been itching to meet them." Chloe pulled a dish towel from the drawer to dry the pan Meg had just rinsed.

"Oh, I see." Meg was taken aback by Chloe's comment, although she couldn't exactly put a finger on why it was unsettling. "I'm sure Abigail will be thrilled. She's wanted to make friends with a girl her age."

"Yeah, Maddie will be happy, too. I just hope that Addison is a good influence on Cody, instead of vice versa. I don't want my son wearing a scarf around his chest, especially not in the middle of the summer." She laughed, so Meg wasn't sure how seriously she meant it. "Hey, did you know that Simon's selling his property to a developer? They're going to build a resort and spa."

"He told you that?" Meg was surprised that he'd disclosed his plans to Chloe.

"No, my cousin did. He works for a builder who intends to compete for the bid. This is going to be one of the biggest construction projects starting up in Benjamin's Manor this autumn—everyone on my cousin's crew was talking about it at the Cove on the Fourth."

I missed the Fourth of July celebration! Meg realized. Every year, there was an impressive fireworks display at Beach Plum

Cove in Lucinda's Hamlet. Locals and visitors alike came in droves to enjoy the celebration and eat free ice cream from Bleeckers. But this year, Meg had been so absorbed in what had been happening with Ruby, that she'd lost all track of time.

"Well, the word might be out among builders, but Simon doesn't want his children to know anything about this project, so please don't mention it around them."

"How about Ruby? Does she know?"

"Yes."

"Was she really upset when she found out?"

Meg couldn't tell whether Chloe was genuinely concerned or if she was just fishing for info because she liked to gossip, so she answered cautiously. "No, not really. Obviously, she has bigger things on her mind right now."

"Yeah. That's another reason it's probably time for everyone to move on."

"What do you mean?"

"Well, Ava's going away to school, so who knows if she'll be back next summer. And I plan to get a job at the resort as soon as it opens, so I don't know how much longer I'll be here, either. This is probably the perfect time for Ruby to retire, especially since she's in such poor health."

"She's going to get better," Meg exclaimed defensively. "And she can't afford to retire, not if she wants to continue to live here—which she *does*. So right now, she doesn't have any plans to 'move on,' but I'm surprised to hear you say you'd want to go work at the resort." Actually, Meg wasn't that surprised; Chloe was rarely subtle about her intentions.

"Unfortunately, I need to go where the money is—and the tips are usually crazy-good at a resort," she explained. "The only reason I've stayed at Ruby's so long is that she lets me bring the kiddos to work whenever I want. But my mom is planning to semi-retire in a month, so going forward, childcare won't be an issue."

"Sounds like it might be a good opportunity for you," said Meg, faking enthusiasm, even though she thought Chloe was getting ahead of herself. Even if Ruby's inn lost business due to construction, it probably would take close to two years before the resort was up and running, so where would Chloe work in the meantime? Meg understood why she needed and wanted to earn more money, but she was sorry to hear that Ruby would lose such an excellent employee, especially because she'd always been so supportive of Chloe. "I'm sure my great-aunt will be disappointed, though. I know how much she values you."

"Yeah. I feel kinda disloyal, but being a single mom, I gotta do what I gotta do," she said with a sigh. "Too bad Simon doesn't plan on hanging around Dune Island after the deal goes through."

"Why is that?" asked Meg, even though she felt like she knew what Chloe would say.

"Are you kidding me? That guy is loaded. Don't tell anyone I did this, but I looked him up online. You should see his house. It's like, twice as big as the inn. Which makes it kind of ironic that he's staying in a tiny little shack all summer."

She paused to noisily stack a silver pot and lid among the others in the bottom of the cupboard. Then she stood up straight again. "But the nice thing is, he doesn't act snooty like most of the wealthy summer people. And yeah, he's a lot older than I am and he's kinda paunchy—I usually like my guys to have six-pack abs—but at least he's got some serious guns on him," she babbled. "And it's a bonus that he wouldn't be scared off because of my kids. Mostly though, like I said, his appeal is that he's mega rich."

"Nice," said Meg, sarcastically referring to the way Chloe had assessed Simon, but the younger woman misunderstood.

"Yeah. Too bad I can't move my kids out of state because of my ex. But you never know. The island always needs more carpenters. Maybe Simon will change his mind and he'll move *his* kids here."

"Maybe," said Meg flatly.

Chloe suddenly leaned over the sink and pushed the window open wider. "Hey, you two, knock it off before you poke each other's eyeballs out!" she shouted at her children, who were brandishing long sticks at each other on the side lawn. They paused to look her way, but then they raised the sticks at each other again. Hanging the dish towel on its hook, Chloe said to Meg, "I can't wait around for Simon any longer. I've got to get going."

After Chloe left, Meg started to go upstairs but she felt something sticky on the newel post: a purple handprint. There were two more purple marks on the balustrades. Sighing, she retrieved a rag from the bin in the laundry room, wet it, and returned to wipe away the ice pop juice.

Meg didn't mind the mess; she understood how challenging it must be for Chloe to work while also trying to watch Maddie and Sonny. And although Meg would never express herself as blatantly as Chloe did, she fully understood why she wanted to be in a relationship again. Meg only wished the young woman hadn't set her sights on Simon.

It's not as if I'm interested in him or anything. But I was still entertaining the possibility of asking Chloe to tell him how much she'd regret it if Aunt Ruby lost her business, Meg thought. *I guess I'd better cross that idea off my list.*

Once again, she was filled with regret that she hadn't taken the time to listen to Ruby's story—to her *secret*—when her great-aunt first wanted to tell it to her. Meg had a hunch that Ruby's disclosure would be far more compelling to Simon than anything anyone else could say to try to persuade him not to develop his property.

She considered calling her mother, thinking, *Mom might be able to shed some light on Aunt Ruby's life that would give me a better sense of what her secret might be.* But since Ruby had married into her father's side of the family, Meg doubted her mother would have any insider's knowledge. And even though she trusted her mom not to repeat anything Meg told her, Meg felt very protective of Ruby's privacy.

Aunt Ruby only mentioned she wanted to share her secret with me and Simon—not with anyone else, she recalled. *So unless I have explicit permission from her, I don't think I should let anyone know she even mentioned having a secret in the first place.*

Which meant Meg was completely on her own to try to figure out what Ruby had intended to tell her. No, not *completely* on her own. Her great-aunt had given her a hint: "The lighthouse holds the key."

Granted, she didn't know whether Ruby had been completely coherent or utterly confused when she'd uttered the phrase. But since it was all she had to go on, Meg resolved to try her best to make sense of her great-aunt's riddle.

Managing reservations, interacting with guests, helping tidy the inn and grounds, and chatting with Linda on the phone kept Meg busier than she'd thought it would. However, just as she'd promised her great-aunt she'd do, Meg made a point of taking daily walks to the beach, where she'd swim, lounge, or watch the sunset. But whether she was working or relaxing, her great-aunt's mysterious statement was never far from her thoughts.

Knowing how Aunt Ruby thinks and speaks, she probably didn't mean the lighthouse holds a literal key to her secret—she must have meant it holds a figurative key, she ruminated on Wednesday afternoon as she picked up stray pieces of a board game in the den. *I'll bet she was trying to tell me that the lighthouse is central to her story.*

With that in mind, Meg decided the next time she needed

to run an errand, she'd stop at the museum in Port Newcomb to check out the nautical exhibit. *I'm sure I've forgotten a lot of facts about the lighthouse since I was young, so maybe seeing the display will spark new insights about Aunt Ruby's clue. I should join one of Lou's tours again, too—and even if I come up empty-handed, the view from the lantern room is worth the trip!*

Her scheming was interrupted by a mewling sound in a room nearby. As she walked down the hall and stepped into the living room to investigate, Simon entered it from the opposite end.

He was leading his son by the hand: Cody hid his eyes behind his other arm. Fat tears rolled down the lower half of his face, and bounced off his chin, wetting his shirt. He sucked his lower lip in and out, and his chest jumped as he gasped with sobs.

Alarmed, Meg rushed forward. "What's wrong?"

"He'll be okay," Simon assured her, which seemed to make his son bawl even harder. "Do you care if I check the washer and dryer? I used the machines earlier this afternoon and I think I might have left Cody's blankie behind."

"Of course I don't mind. Let me know if you need help." As she moved aside to let them pass, Meg spied Abigail in the yard, obviously combing the grass for the blankie. From her higher vantage point, Meg scanned the yard, too, as well as the meadow, but she didn't see a hint of the blue fabric anywhere.

A few moments later, the father and son emerged from the laundry room. Meg's heart sank when she saw that Cody's little torso was still heaving up and down with his cries. "No luck?"

"Not yet, but we'll find it," Simon answered optimistically, but his expression was bleak. "It's got to be on the premises somewhere between here and the cottage."

"I can help you look. And I'll ask around—maybe one of the guests picked it up and put it aside somewhere."

"Thanks. I've got a meeting to go to right now, but if you

find it while we're gone, could you tie it to the doorhandle at the cottage?" Simon requested.

"Sure." Meg softly touched the top of Cody's head, telling him, "Don't worry, we'll find it soon."

Simon started to walk toward the porch but Cody went limp, allowing himself to dangle from his father's arm. "I don't want to go. I want to find my blankie," he whisper-wailed.

Simon gently lowered him all the way to the floor and then released his hand. Squatting beside him, he said in a firm voice, "Cody, I *promise* you that as soon as we get back, we'll look for your blankie. But Daddy has a very important meeting to go to. If you don't get up and come with me right now, I'm going to be late."

During the momentary stalemate that followed, Meg felt emotionally torn. On one hand, she could tell that Simon was at his wits' end. Even though she had a hunch that his "very important meeting" was probably with the land developer, she took no glee in seeing him so stressed out. On the other hand, finding Cody's blankie was just as important to the little boy as the meeting was to Simon—maybe even more important.

"C'mon, up you go. On your feet," Simon urged his son. He stood up, but the boy just lay there, shielding his face and crying so hard Meg was afraid he'd hyperventilate. His meltdown might have been melodramatic, but it broke her heart to see him so despondent and she struggled to keep from scooping him up in her arms.

"Cody, I'm waiting," Simon repeated, to no effect.

"Can he stay here with me while you go to your meeting?" Meg whispered into Simon's ear. "Abigail can stay, too. We'll keep looking for Cody's blankie."

Relief washed over Simon's face, but he weakly objected, "I don't want him to disturb your guests."

In a voice loud enough for Cody to hear, Meg announced, "If you let Cody stay with me, he'll stop crying in a minute or two, because he can't help me look for his blankie if he has tears in his eyes. You go ahead to your meeting. I'll sit here on the floor with him until he's ready to start our search."

Simon reached down and touched his son's shoulder. "What do you say, Cody? Do you want to stay here with Meg and Abigail while I go to my meeting?"

Without uncovering his face, the little boy nodded, and by the time Simon had left and Abigail skipped into the room, Cody was sitting up and his sobs had faded into sporadic hiccups. Meg handed him a tissue to dry his eyes.

"He's going to need, like, five more for his nose," instructed his sister, looking on. "And you have to hold them for him so he can blow it, but be careful. Daddy says he's like a spouting whale."

Biting her lip to keep from laughing, Meg followed Abigail's sage advice. But when the little girl suggested they go outside to finish searching the yard for the blankie, Meg led the children to the window to show them that there was nothing blue on the ground between the inn and the cottage.

"We should go check the clothes in our laundry basket again," Abigail proposed instead. "Sometimes they stick together."

I doubt Simon would want me rummaging through his clothing—or even going inside the cottage without his permission, thought Meg.

Stalling, she suggested, "As long as we're already here at the inn, let's search the laundry room again, first. Maybe the blankie dropped between the washer and dryer when your daddy was transferring the clothes from the machines."

Meg didn't know who was more dismayed—her or Cody— when they didn't find the blankie there. She reluctantly agreed that Abigail should recheck the laundry basket at the cottage, while she and Cody searched beneath the pines in their yard.

"But before we go next door, I want to post a few signs here so if any guests see the blankie, they'll bring it to me right away."

"Can you write that if somebody finds it they get an award?" mumbled Cody, surprising Meg with his long sentence.

"A *re*ward?" she asked and he nodded. "How much money do you want to give them?"

"He doesn't have any," said Abigail. "But you could write that he'll give whoever finds it a hug and a kiss."

"No kiss," her brother whispered, wiping his mouth with the back of his hand in distaste.

"Okay, just a hug," Abigail allowed as Meg led them into the kitchen to make the posters.

There was something sticky on the table, so before laying the paper down, she went back to the laundry room to grab a rag from the rag bag. She reached in and when she saw what she'd pulled out, she shouted, "Cody! Abigail! Come here, quick! Quick!"

The children charged pell-mell into the room, with three adult guests close on their heels. "Is everything okay?" one of them asked.

"Everything's *fantastic*—look what I found!" She exuberantly held up the long blue strip of fabric as if it were a string of diamonds, and then dropped it into Cody's outstretched hands.

When Simon returned, Meg and Abigail were sitting in the Adirondack chairs, eating grape ice pops that Meg had taken from the box Ruby kept in the freezer for Chloe's children. Cody, who knew he wasn't allowed to eat an ice pop while wearing his blankie, decided not to have one, and he was running in wide circles on the back lawn, the material flapping against his back like a long blue tail.

"You found it!" his father exclaimed as he approached.

"*Meg* found it," Abigail corrected him.

"Three cheers for Meg." Simon raised a fist in the air before lowering himself into the empty chair beside her. "Where was it?"

"In a linen bag in the laundry room."

"She means the *rag bag*," interjected Abigail again.

Meg winked at Simon. "I was trying to be diplomatic."

He threw back his head and cracked up. It was the first time Meg had ever heard him laugh like that and since her comment hadn't been that funny, she assumed he was laughing with relief and elation that his son's blanket had been found.

"I wonder how it got there," he mused.

"Since it wasn't wet, Abigail and I figured out that you must have dropped it at some point after you took it out of the drier. Ava probably saw it on the floor and put it into the rag bag by accident. She's never met Cody, so she wouldn't have known what it was."

"Aha, that makes sense. Come to think of it, I chatted with Ava for a few minutes, to make sure she was done with the machines before I used them. She must have seen it sometime after I left. Good detective work."

They chatted for a few more minutes before Simon slapped his thighs and said to his children, "Okay, we'd better give Meg some peace and quiet." Twisting sideways, he looked into her eyes. "Thanks so much. You saved my skin. If there's ever anything I can do for you, anything at all, just let me know. I owe you big time."

Good, then will you reconsider selling the inn to a developer? The words were on the tip of Meg's tongue, but she replied, "It was no problem. Once the drama died down, we had fun hanging out together."

"Stop running in circles! You're making me dizzy and it's time to leave," Abigail bellowed at her brother. "Don't forget to say thank you to Meg!"

As Simon and Abigail stood up, Cody zoomed around the group one more time before coming to a halt right in front of where Meg was sitting. He leaned forward and wrapped his arms around her legs in a jarringly tight hug. Still embracing her, he lifted her head to meet her eyes and whispered, "Thank you, Meg."

She was about to tell him he was welcome but he dipped his head again and gave her bare kneecap a loud, wet *swack*, and then he took off across the yard toward the cottage.

It was, by far, one of the most memorable kisses Meg had ever received.

NINE

Ack, now I'm a mess, Meg complained to herself as she wound the garden hose around its reel.

Her great-aunt finally felt ready for a video chat, so Meg had intended to head into town where she could get a strong cell phone signal. But just as she was about to leave, a guest reported that he'd spilled his beverage on the patio, and it was attracting bees. Because Chloe had already left for the day, it was up to Meg to wash the viscous puddle from the tiles. In the process, she'd somehow sprayed her blouse and skirt, too.

She had wanted to look fresh and pulled-together for the video call. *If Aunt Ruby sees me this bedraggled, she might worry about the state of the inn, too*, she thought. *I'd better hurry upstairs and change into a sundress.*

But when Meg went back inside, another guest was waiting in the porch to speak to her. "We were very disappointed that all six of us couldn't lounge in the Adirondack chairs to watch the sunset last evening," the elderly woman said, referencing her companions who vacationed at the inn together every year. "It's one of our favorite Misty Point traditions. With my bad hip, I can't make it all the way out to the beach, which is why we depend on the convenience of taking a seat on the lawn."

"Oh, no, I'm so sorry," Meg apologized. "I asked the lawn crew to bring the chairs from the garage, but they must have forgotten again. I'm heading into town right now, but I'll be sure to put the chairs out in plenty of time for you to enjoy the sunset this evening."

I guess this means I won't be able to go to the museum to check out the nautical display after my phone call, thought Meg as she headed down the hall. Following her visit to the museum, she'd planned to enjoy an early supper at her favorite harborside restaurant, Arthur's Lobster & Clam Bar. Meg had really been looking forward to getting away from the inn for a while, and she was disappointed she'd have to cancel her plans. *I suppose I could come back to the inn after I talk to Aunt Ruby, put the Adirondack chairs out, and then return to Port Newcomb to go to the museum...*

But realistically, she knew that once she returned to the inn, she wouldn't want to face summer traffic again, especially not during most families' dinner hour, when the tourists swarmed the streets on their way to the numerous restaurants near the harbor.

As she headed upstairs to her bedroom, she was struck by a solution: she'd ask Simon if he'd take the chairs out for her. After all, he'd offered to help her, and the inn, in any way he could. She spun around—there was no time to change her clothes—and dashed outside. *I hope he's not at the beach with the kids*, she thought as she jogged across the back lawn.

She'd almost reached the pines when the cottage door popped opened and Chloe flounced outside, followed a moment later by Simon. For some reason, Meg was so surprised to see them emerge from the cottage together—where were their children?—that her first impulse was to turn and flee, but she knew she'd look foolish.

"Hi." She raised her hand in a half-hearted, waist-high wave.

"Hey, Meg. Simon was just giving me a tour of his castle." Chloe's lipsticked smile was radiant and her hair shimmered in the sunlight. When did she have time to curl it like that? That wasn't how it looked earlier when she'd been working. She must have been giving Meg the once-over, too, because she asked, "What happened to your clothes?"

Meg pinched the front of her blouse and wiggled the fabric up and down, trying to dry it. "A guest spilled his drink."

Simon's eyes went wide. "On *you*?"

"No, on the patio. I had to hose it down and I guess I got in my own way," she explained, feeling increasingly conspicuous.

From the other side of the cottage, three children's voices called, "Not it!" A fourth child yelled, "No fair—I don't want to be it again!" Meg figured they must have been playing tag or hide 'n' seek.

"I'm headed into town," she continued, addressing Simon. "I need to be in range for a video call with my great-aunt, and I'm running late, so I was wondering if I could ask you for a favor."

"Sure," he replied.

Yet after she told him about the guest's request, he twisted his mouth to one side, hesitating. Had he made time-sensitive plans with Chloe for the afternoon? Meg began to backpedal, saying, "If I'm disrupting something—"

But Simon didn't let her finish. "It's not a problem. I'll take care of it right away."

"Thanks a bunch," she replied with a grateful smile.

I wonder if Chloe muscled her way into the cottage or if Simon voluntarily offered to give her a tour, Meg thought as she drove into town. *It seems strange that he'd invite her in, considering I haven't even made it to the doorstep and I know him and the children a lot better than she does.*

Not that it was a competition, but it did make her suspect that Simon was as interested in Chloe as she was in him. *Why wouldn't he be? After all, she's very friendly, energetic, pretty, and she's a terrific mom—something I might never be...*

In an uncanny coincidence, her phone rang at that very moment: it was Josh. During the past few weeks, they'd been texting each other, and he'd left her a couple of voice mails, but since Meg usually could only receive and send messages when she was in town, their communication was sporadic, which was what she preferred. She didn't want either of them to redevelop an emotional attachment to the other, because she knew it would ultimately end in heartache. Again.

But there was something about knowing that Chloe and Simon were spending an afternoon together with their children that made Meg feel overwhelmingly lonely. And she rationalized that even though she and Josh wouldn't ever get together again romantically, there was no reason they couldn't be friends in the present.

Meg hit the green button on the display on the console of her car. "Hi, Josh. Perfect timing," she said in a sing-song voice.

"Uh-oh. What's wrong?"

"Wrong? Why do you think something's wrong?"

"Whenever you sound that chipper, it's usually because something's going wrong but you're trying to hide it. That's your everything-is-fine-here voice."

Meg laughed. "Am I that transparent?"

"No. I just know you that well. So what are you upset about?"

"Nothing. Not about anything that's important, anyway. I'm actually very happy because I'm heading into town for a video chat with my aunt. It'll be the first time we've seen each other since she left."

"That's terrific."

"Yes, it is. But let's not talk all about me this time. I want to hear what's new in *your* life."

As Meg drove, they chatted casually, mostly about Josh's job, although he also mentioned that his brother, Patrick, was dating a spectator he'd met at the last baseball game he and his brother had attended together.

"Did she have a friend for you?" teased Meg, honestly hoping he'd say yes.

"Nah. In fact, Patrick insisted on giving her a ride home and he made me sit in the back seat. In my own car!" Josh griped. "Talk about feeling like a third wheel."

Meg burst out laughing, and by the time she arrived in town, she'd forgotten all about Chloe and Simon and she didn't have to fake an upbeat tone when she said goodbye to Josh.

"I've gotta go, but I'm really glad you caught me." Then, so there'd be no question about her feelings, she added. "And I'm glad we can be friends, even if we don't have a future together as a couple."

"So am I." As if to prove he'd gotten the point, he signed off by saying, "Talk to ya later, *friend.*"

When Ruby's face came up on her phone's display, Meg nearly burst into tears of joy—both because she was thrilled to see her again, and because her great-aunt appeared so much stronger than she had on the morning she'd left Dune Island.

Although there was still moderate drooping on one side of her face, someone had apparently washed and styled Ruby's hair, and she was sitting upright in what appeared to be a very comfy armchair. She could even give two- and three-word answers instead of solely relying on gestures to communicate. Witnessing these improvements first-hand reinforced what Linda had been telling Meg all along: Ruby was receiving excellent care.

She asked her great-aunt a few yes-or-no questions, and briefly summarized how things were going at the inn. But knowing how much Ruby relished a good story, Meg spent most of the phone call regaling her with the anecdote of Cody's lost blankie. When she repeated Abigail's comments and described how Cody had rewarded her with a hug and kiss, Ruby seemed as tickled as Meg had been.

She laid a hand over her heart and made a one-word comment. Ruby had difficulty modulating her volume, and on her first try, the word was unintelligible. But then she repeated it and Meg understood. Sweet. Ruby was saying the word *sweet*.

"Yes, Simon's children are very sweet," she agreed fondly. "They're precious."

The nautical exhibit at Dune Island's small museum in Port Newcomb primarily featured information, photos, and items relating to ships and sailors, with a secondary focus on navigation. While Meg appreciated learning about nearby shipwrecks, antique compasses, and contemporary sonar equipment, she was most fascinated by the Fresnel lens displayed under a glass enclosure in the center of the room. Elaborate and beautiful, the lens was once billed as the brightest light in the world, and credited with saving an untold number of sailor's lives.

So Meg's trip to the museum was well worth the effort. But she was disappointed, although not surprised, that she hadn't discovered anything that provided insight about Ruby's clue.

Five words. The lighthouse holds the key, she thought as she left the museum. *How in the world am I going to figure out Aunt Ruby's entire story if all I have for a hint is a five-word sentence?*

It wasn't until later, when she was lying awake in bed, that Meg realized her great-aunt had left her with much more than a five-word clue; everything she'd said right before her stroke might also be helpful in figuring out her secret. *It would be just like her to give me a prologue to her story*, she thought, chuckling.

For the next several minutes, she struggled to recall exactly what Ruby had said before her speech went slurry. *She wanted Simon to hear her story because it indirectly involved his grand mother, Sarah. And she said she thought the secret might change Simon's mind about selling the property.*

No, that wasn't quite right; Meg had directly asked if her great-aunt's secret would change Simon's mind, but that's not how Ruby had originally phrased it. Hadn't she used one of her odd, formal expressions? *Oh, I remember it now! Aunt Ruby told me, "What I have to say could have a significant bearing on his life."*

It was a fine but important distinction. Ruby's exact wording almost made it seem as if what she was going to share was so important that once he heard it, Simon wouldn't have any choice *except* to change his mind. Granted, Ruby had always firmly believed that any good story had the potential to change a person's life. However, it occurred to Meg that it was possible her great-aunt's secret might effectively *force* Simon to abandon his plans.

But what did she know that would prevent him from selling the property? If Bradley's living trust named Simon as his beneficiary, then nothing Ruby said would change his right to do whatever he wanted to do with his inheritance. Unless... unless whatever secret Ruby had planned to share indicated that Simon *wasn't* the legal heir of the property.

Even as she tried to laugh off the idea, a shiver fluttered up Meg's spine. What if that's *exactly* what her great-aunt had intended to share? Meg recognized that it wasn't exactly Ruby's style, especially since her great-aunt initially had resigned herself to accepting Simon's plans. But perhaps after thinking over how detrimental a resort would be to Misty Point, as well as to the inn's business, Ruby had reluctantly changed her mind. Maybe that's why she'd seemed so conflicted, as if she'd been stalling?

But if Aunt Ruby was going to prove that the property didn't belong to Simon, she wouldn't just tell a story. She'd have to present concrete evidence—which may have been what her story was leading up to. But once she began to lose her speech, she skipped ahead to give me the most important piece of informa-tion, reasoned Meg, recalling her great-aunt's urgency to get the words out. *So maybe I should be looking for a physical key, not a figurative one, after all. A key that unlocks a diary or a drawer or a safe box of documents.*

It was unlikely that her great-aunt would've hidden such an important key in the lighthouse, though. For one thing, she didn't have easy access to its interior. And even if she had gone inside the lighthouse during a tour, it seemed that she'd be too concerned the keepers from the Lighthouse Society would have eventually found anything she'd left behind, no matter how well she'd hidden it.

What about outside *the lighthouse? Did she bury the key in a chest beneath the sand nearby?* The idea was so far-fetched that Meg giggled to herself. *Now I'm really letting my imagination run wild. I can't picture Aunt Ruby digging a hole in the sand, not even when she was much younger and in better health.*

Meg tried to remember the last time she and her great-aunt had walked to the lighthouse together. It must have been some time last summer, since Ruby hadn't been well enough to make the trek this past spring. Fortunately, she was content to admire the view from the living room window, which according to her, framed the scenery like a painting. A masterpiece.

Meg jolted upright in bed. A painting! Didn't people hide important documents within the frames of paintings and photos? *Aunt Ruby has a painting of the lighthouse hanging in the den. It's the one that guest who was an artist gave her as a gift about five years ago*, she remembered. *I bet there's something hidden behind it.*

She still didn't know whether her great-aunt had been speaking literally or figuratively about the lighthouse holding the key. But Meg figured that an actual key would be flat enough to fit behind a framed painting. On the other hand, if Ruby had been speaking figuratively, it was also possible that the lighthouse painting held key documents that would prevent Simon from selling his land.

Either way, Meg was so eager to find out that she was tempted to hop right out of bed, take the painting down from the wall, and disassemble the frame right then. But she knew she'd need special tools from the toolbox and she was concerned she'd wake the guests searching for it. So she lay back down facing the window, and counted the white flashes from the lighthouse until she could no longer keep her eyes open.

TEN

"I need to ask you something that might seem like an odd request," Alice began. "So feel free to say no."

Holding the cordless phone between her ear and her shoulder, Meg tightened the screw of a spring clip on the back of Ruby's lighthouse painting. To her great disappointment, after removing the back panel of the frame, she'd found nothing inside except the canvas itself. Feeling foolish because she'd been so sure her hunch about a key or document was right, she was hurrying to put the frame together again and rehang it on the wall when Alice called.

"Ask away," she said.

"Our book club's next meeting is scheduled for Wednesday. For one reason or another, none of the other members is able or willing to host it. I'd offer to hold it at my house, but my husband's painting the kitchen and TV room, and we've got furniture everywhere. So I wanted to know if we could hold it at the inn, even though Ruby won't be present? We'll sit outside or on the porch—wherever we won't be in the guests' way."

Knowing how her great-aunt would have answered, Meg

didn't hesitate. "Of course you can hold it here. That's no problem."

"Thank you. Everyone will be very pleased to hear that. We already postponed it once after Ruby went into the hospital and one of our members is supposed to bake a special dessert that she's been perfecting for weeks—don't ask—so she'd be crushed if we had to reschedule again."

Meg chuckled. "You must be talking about Joan's Black Forest gateau?"

"How did you know?"

"My great-aunt mentioned some of the members had differing opinions about reading the cookbook-slash-memoir that Joan chose."

"That's putting it mildly. Lucky for Ruby, she doesn't have to be here for round two of the controversy," Alice wryly remarked.

"Well, maybe everyone will have their mouths full of cake, so they won't be able to argue with each other."

Meg was only teasing, but Alice quickly said, "Don't worry, we'll behave ourselves, no loud arguments... And speaking of good behavior, do you mind if I bring my two grands? They'll play on the back lawn, where they won't be underfoot. I know I'm biased, but they're terrific children."

"I'm sure they are. And you don't even have to ask—they're welcome to come to the inn with you any time." Suddenly, Meg was struck by an idea. "Isn't one of your grandchildren a girl, about six or seven?"

"Yes, Charlotte's seven, and my grandson Chase is five."

Meg excitedly explained that Abigail would be delighted to meet another girl her age. "Both of Simon's children are very well behaved, too. Maybe Charlotte and Chase will want to play one of the inn's lawn games with them while your club is meeting?"

"They'd love that, and I can keep an eye on them from the

window or from the patio, so Simon won't feel obligated to supervise." Alice lowered her voice. "Just between us, I've got to ask if the rumors are true. Do you know if he's really going to sell his Misty Point property to a developer?"

Not if I can help it, Meg silently responded. "Yes, that's my understanding—but his children don't know anything about the deal, so when you meet him, please don't mention it in front of Cody and Abigail."

"I won't say a word—even though I feel like giving him an earful," Alice promised. "How did Ruby take the news?"

"Well, you know what she's like. She was very gracious to him, but I think deep down she was disappointed." Even though she trusted her great-aunt's friend to keep their conversation confidential, Meg saw no reason to mention that Ruby had hoped Simon would change his mind.

"Who can blame her? Misty Point won't be the same after a resort goes up. And the inn's her bread and butter, which I imagine she needs now more than ever. She told me this spring that her insurance didn't cover all her hospital expenses when she had the respiratory virus. I can only imagine that she's going to be hit with another big bill this time around, too."

I didn't realize that Aunt Ruby had to pay for a part of her hospitalization expenses this spring. I just assumed her insurance covered all her costs, Meg fretted after they ended their call. So, despite feeling discouraged about the lighthouse painting, she resolved to try even harder to find the figurative or literal key that would unlock the meaning behind her great-aunt's clue.

Until she began her search, Meg had never noticed just how *much* lighthouse paraphernalia her great-aunt had accumulated over the years. These included lighthouse mugs, plates, and a serving spoon with a lighthouse for a handle. Meg also found lighthouse wall hooks, calendars, shower curtains, and decorative pillows.

Instead of downsizing the bookcases, maybe I should've been getting rid of some of these knickknacks, Meg griped to herself. *I could gather them all in one room and post a sign that says,* MISTY POINT LIGHTHOUSE SOUVENIR SHOP. *The guests and tour participants could browse at their leisure.*

It was an exaggeration, but only a slight one. The more lighthouses she found, the more she seemed to notice. It was easier to eliminate some of these items as hiding places than others. For instance, it was obvious that the lighthouse coasters were simply lighthouse coasters. But when she discovered an opened but nearly full box of one hundred Misty Point Lighthouse holiday cards in the desk in the den, Meg couldn't be satisfied until she'd checked them individually to be sure there wasn't a relevant piece of information jotted inside one of them. Even as she was opening each card and then flipping it over to scan the back, she realized she was getting carried away, but she couldn't leave any stone—or card—unturned.

Her search was hindered by two obstacles. First, she didn't want the guests to catch her examining some lighthouse trinket or another in one of the common areas and ask what she was doing. Secondly, she couldn't comb through the guests' rooms until they'd checked out. Even then, she had to act quickly, before Chloe or Ava came in to vacuum or change the bedsheets.

Meg recognized that it was highly improbable that her great-aunt would conceal documents or a key in a guest room for the same reasons she doubted that Ruby would tuck them away in Misty Point Lighthouse. So a part of her felt ridiculous, launching a search of the entire inn. However, a bigger part of her felt it was necessary to get to the bottom of what Ruby had intended to say and Meg wanted to examine every potential hiding place in each room.

So on Wednesday afternoon, shortly after Chloe had left for the day but before the new guests checked in, Meg popped into Room 3 to do a visual sweep of the décor. Her eye was immediately drawn to the large wall mirror that was bordered by a silver lighthouse-shaped frame. She crept across the room to examine it more closely. The flat, metal frame was unremarkable, but Meg thought, *Maybe there's a key taped to the back of it.*

She tried to remove the mirror from the wall, but she quickly discovered the heavy frame was suspended from a thick loop of wire that seemed to have become snagged on the hook. Pressing her cheek to the wall, she lifted the edge of the frame to peek behind it. *Whoever wound that wire around the hook must have wanted to be very sure the mirror wasn't going to come crashing down from the wall.*

A realization came to her in a flash: the mirror was obscuring something important, like a wall safe or a secret compartment! Meg stood squarely in front of the frame and yanked on it so forcefully that when it broke free of the wall, she fell backward onto the bed. For a moment she just lay there, holding the mirror at arms' length above her face, and blinking at her stunned reflection.

"Meg? Are you upstairs?" a woman's voice softly called from the direction of the staircase.

"I'll be right down." She scrambled to her feet. Noticing there was nothing on the wall—no safe, no secret compartment—except a small hole where she'd pulled the hook and wall anchor from the plaster, she scanned the room for a place to stash the mirror. But it was too late; Alice stuck her head in the door. Meg had spoken to Simon about the play date for the kids earlier in the week, but since then, she'd been so intent on her search that she'd completely forgotten that the book club was meeting at the inn today.

"Sorry, I didn't mean to disturb you. I just wanted to let you know I've arrived and so have a few others. We'll be meeting on the patio, since no one else is out there. Simon came over to introduce himself to me and we agreed we'd let the kids play halfway between the cottage and the inn, so we can both keep an eye on them. They took that big wooden tic-tac-toe game out of the shed."

Feeling conspicuous about the large mirror she was holding, Meg plastered a wide grin on her face. "Great."

Alice tilted her head. "You need a hand? That looks heavy."

"No, thanks." Meg set the mirror down on the bed without explanation. Trying to keep Alice from noticing the hole in the wall, she shepherded her toward the door. "I meant to set out some teacups and dessert dishes for you to use, but I lost track of time. Let's go downstairs and I'll get you all set up."

"That's okay, I know my way around Ruby's kitchen. We've decided to wait to have dessert until after our discussion. Everyone would love it if you'd join us. No pressure, if you don't have the time, but they're hoping you'll give them an update on Ruby. We've invited Simon, too. We're going to motion him over in about an hour and a half."

"I'd love to join everyone for gateau," agreed Meg, brushing off her flustered feelings. *An hour and a half should give me plenty of time to rehang the mirror. but I'd better remember to shut the door or else the next time it might be a guest who walks in on me, and it won't look good if I'm reassembling the inn's furnishings!*

After forty-five minutes of rifling through the toolbox and searching the shelves in the garage for a suitable wall anchor to replace the one she'd ruined pulling the mirror off the wall, Meg was still empty-handed. She regretted not going to the hardware store from the start.

If I go now and traffic's bad, I might not return in time to replace the mirror before the new guests arrive. And I won't be able to have cake with Aunt Ruby's book club and Simon. As she bent down to examine the lowest tier of shelves, she felt increasingly desperate, as well as frustrated with herself. *Lately it seems like I'm always looking for something, but I keep spinning in circles and getting nowhere. It makes me wonder if all this searching is even worth the effort.*

But as soon as she hoisted an old coffee canister onto the workbench, she knew she'd struck gold. Prying off the lid, she discovered an assortment of nails, screws, nuts, and bolts, which she carefully poured into an empty paint tray. Sifting through them, she found at least half a dozen wall anchors. That discovery alone would have satisfied her, but as she was pouring the remaining fasteners and nails back into the rusty tin, something caught her eye.

She dumped the canister's contents into the paint tray again to make sure she'd seen what she thought she'd seen. Yes, there it was: a dirty, rusted key. She plucked it off the top of the bed of nails and screws, wiped it on the hem of her shirt, and then peered at it. Slightly smaller than a door key, it didn't bear any distinguishing marks or have a unique shape.

To Meg, it looked like an ordinary padlock or cabinet key, and she recognized that it was highly probable her great-aunt wasn't even aware that the key was in the canister, or what it unlocked. Furthermore, although the label of the coffee tin had peeled off and Meg supposed it was possible it might have once depicted a lighthouse, its only markings now were caused by rust. So there was no reason to believe that Ruby was referring to this container when she'd said, "The lighthouse holds the key."

Still, Meg couldn't dismiss even a minuscule possibility that Ruby had purposely hidden the key in the garage, where the guests wouldn't stumble upon it. She slipped it into her pocket and hurried back inside the inn.

After rehanging the mirror, she stood back to make sure it wasn't crooked. *Looks perfect,* she silently told her reflection. *But I can't say the same thing about my hair. And what's that mark on my shirt?*

Meg gathered the tools, straightened the duvet, and darted down the hall to change her clothes and brush her hair before heading downstairs for cake. As she stepped onto the porch, she could hear Betty's high-pitched voice carrying from the patio through the open window.

"Why would he leave a house like this to someone who wasn't even related to him?" she was saying.

Stunned, Meg froze in her tracks. She couldn't have heard correctly. Betty must have been discussing a book, and not speculating about why Gordon had bequeathed his house to Ruby.

"Don't be ridiculous," scoffed a man. Meg wasn't sure who it was, but it sounded like Henry.

"I'm *not,*" Betty insisted. "Think about it. Ruby was adopted. She was twenty-some years younger than Gordon, who'd been a bachelor until he was in his forties. Not to mention, he was also a novelist, so—"

Someone broke in, asking, "What does being a novelist have to do with anything?"

Betty snickered, as if the answer should've been obvious. "We all know what kind of lifestyles those creative types lead."

"That's a stereotype," another person objected.

"Maybe, maybe not. But if you ask me, all the evidence points to the same conclusion," Betty asserted. "Ruby was Gordon's love child and that's why he left his house to her, and why most of the land was awarded to Sarah's son, Bradley."

Meg's mouth dropped open and her face blazed with heat. Her impulse was to rush outside and tell Betty off for having the nerve to sit there on Ruby's patio and spread utterly ridiculous rumors about her. But she was so astounded that her feet seemed to be cemented to the floor. Fortunately, the other club members dismissed Betty's drivel.

"You've been reading too much crime fiction," one woman remarked.

"Or too many tabloids," said Henry, making several people laugh. But his voice was stern when he cautioned, "I hope you're not going to repeat your ludicrous theory to Simon."

"It's *not* ludicrous. But give me a little credit, Henry. Of course I have no intention of mentioning it to him." Betty sounded insulted. "Although I doubt it would come as a surprise. My gut tells me he already knows. It's probably the reason his father never came around here, and now it's the reason Simon's selling the property to a developer instead of keeping it for himself."

"Really? Your gut told you that?" someone ridiculed. "My gut only talks to me when it's hungry. And right now, it's saying, 'What's taking Joan so long to bring out that cake, anyway?'"

Everyone cracked up and as their laughter subsided, Meg heard footsteps behind her. She turned to see Alice coming from the kitchen with a tray of dessert plates and utensils, followed by Joan, who was carefully balancing a covered cake stand.

"Oh, there you are, Meg, just in time," said Alice. "Joan's dessert isn't really suitable for the children but I forgot to bring a snack for them. Do you have graham crackers or a piece of fruit they could have?"

"I've got ice pops. I'll go get them." Meg ducked into the kitchen and tugged open the freezer door, but instead of retrieving the frozen treats, she closed her eyes, allowing the icy draft to cool her flaming cheeks.

What is Betty's problem anyway? Why doesn't she accept the fact that Gordon left Aunt Ruby his house because she was good friends with him and Sarah? Is she jealous because Aunt Ruby

*lives in such a gorgeous location? Or is it that she simply refuses
to believe that people who aren't related can be so close?*

As tempted as Meg was to march outside and directly
confront Betty about her gossiping, she knew she'd only embar-
rass herself and make everyone else uncomfortable in the
process. Besides, she doubted anything she'd say would change
Betty's opinion or prevent her from spreading rumors in the
future.

Simon was just sitting down as Meg descended the porch stairs
to the patio, but when he saw her, he popped back up and
pulled out the chair next to him for her. His warm, genuine
smile was the perfect antidote to Betty's catty gossip, and Meg
reflexively relaxed her shoulders.

She greeted him and everyone else, but before taking a seat,
she started toward the children, calling, "I have something for
you."

The boys flew barefoot across the yard, plucked their ice
pops from Meg's hand, and raced back to the tic-tac-toe game,
but the girls stopped so Abigail could introduce her to
Charlotte.

"Now I have *three* friends who are girls," Abigail excitedly
told Meg.

"Three?" asked Meg, wondering who the third one was.

"Yes. Charlotte, Maddie, and you," she replied, before the
pair skipped back across the lawn and Meg joined the adults at
the table.

As she slid into the chair next to Simon, she caught a hint
of aftershave, and she glanced at his smooth cheeks and
jawline. Instead of the dark green tee he'd been wearing when
she'd spotted him outside the cottage earlier that day, he had
on a short-sleeved button-down Oxford. Meg had already
thought it was kind of him to agree to join the book club for

dessert, and now she was utterly charmed that he'd made an effort to dress up for the occasion, even though his shirt was rather wrinkled.

Joan's elaborately decorated, cherry-topped Black Forest gateau tasted even more decadent than it looked, and for several minutes, it was all anyone talked about. But after the compliments died down, someone asked how Ruby was doing. Meg told them about her progress, and then the conversation took another turn, when Henry addressed Simon.

"There are a lot of rumors circulating in town, but I like to get my information straight from the horse's mouth."

Uh-oh, here it comes, thought Meg facetiously. *Simon's not going to know what hit him...*

Henry proceeded to drill him about his plans to sell his property, and several other people chimed in, too. If Simon had ever believed that the development of his land was a private matter, the book club members swiftly disavowed him of that notion. They clearly felt their long-time status as residents gave them the right to weigh in with their opinions about what happened anywhere on the island, including on Simon's property.

"A resort is going to wreak havoc on Misty Point's fragile ecosystem," Henry said.

"That's part of the reason I'm here," responded Simon. "I want to be sure the developer has a vision for sustainability that aligns with mine before I finalize the deal."

"Another sustainable *eyesore*—just what this island needs," Alice muttered under her breath, but Simon heard her.

"Aesthetics are highly subjective, but again, my goal is to steer the developer and potential architects toward an attractive design that's symbiotic with the setting," he replied.

"You're sweating the small stuff," someone else told Alice. "Who cares what the resort looks like? This project is going to create a lot of jobs on Dune Island, both during the construction phase and the operational phase. The extra business will be terrific for our economy."

"Not if the developer brings in an off-island building crew," Henry pointed out. "It wouldn't be the first time that's happened after a developer promised to hire locally."

On and on the discussion went. Although a couple of the members were in favor of the resort, almost everyone else was opposed to it for the same reasons Meg was. She couldn't have asked for better support if she herself had scripted their arguments, and she almost felt sorry for Simon to be the object of their impassioned objections. But to his credit, he held his own; his responses were cordial and considerate, yet decisive.

Meg wasn't the only one who noticed how composed and congenial he'd remained under the pressure of their interrogation, which was a stark contrast to his behavior when Meg herself had previously tried to suggest he sell to someone who wasn't a developer. After everyone else had left, and Joan, Alice, and Meg were washing the dishes, Joan remarked, "I have to hand it to Simon. I know how intimidating it is to try to defend a decision in front of our book club. I admire the way he managed to be warm and open, without backing down."

"Yes, he seems like a great guy," agreed Alice. "I almost wish he weren't so nice. Then I wouldn't feel guilty about being angry at him for what he's doing to Misty Point and to Ruby's business."

Her sentiment expressed exactly how Meg felt about Simon and his family. *I was smitten with his children from the start, but Simon is a lot more likeable now than when we first met,* she thought later that night as she peered out Ruby's bedroom window toward the cottage. Yet she knew she couldn't allow her affection for the trio to interfere with her efforts to try to convince Simon not to develop his land.

He's charging ahead with his plans, regardless of how anyone else feels about it, so I've got to push forward with my plans, too.

Even if it's over-the-top and I feel silly doing it, tomorrow, I'll try to figure out what the key I found unlocks, she decided later that evening as she got ready for bed.

However, Meg didn't feel very hopeful that her search would result in a helpful outcome. *Maybe I should just casually ask Aunt Ruby a yes-or-no question, like, "Did you know there was a key in the canister of nails in the garage?" If she says no, then I'll know right away it's a dead end.*

But what if her great-aunt said yes? Meg didn't want to frustrate her with a guessing game about what the key unlocked. Nor did she want to upset her by bringing up what Ruby had said was a delicate topic—especially not in front of Linda or the rehab center staff, who were usually present to assist with Ruby's phone calls.

I might get lucky like I did with Cody's blankie, and discover right away that it unlocks something completely unrelated, like one of the toolboxes, she thought. *I wonder if it's too big to be a diary key?*

Not that she'd ever dream of reading anything of Ruby's without permission, but Meg's curiosity about whether her great-aunt had once kept a diary got the better of her. She quickly scanned Ruby's bookcases. Nope, no diary among the published books.

I should've read more mysteries, she said to herself when she glimpsed the books Gordon had written. *Then it might be a lot easier for me to figure out what lock the key fits into or what Aunt Ruby's clue about the lighthouse means...*

Since she didn't feel sleepy yet, Meg randomly selected one of his novels and brought it to bed to read. She flipped open the cover, pausing when she spotted his full name on the title page: Gordon R. Sheffield.

It's a good thing Betty doesn't know that R. is his middle initial, thought Meg. *Knowing her, she'd claim it stands for Rueben, and she'd insist that Aunt Ruby was named after him.*

Yet as much as Meg wanted to completely reject Betty's notion that Gordon was Ruby's father, she briefly allowed herself to consider the possibility she was right. *Theoretically, if Aunt Ruby was his daughter, I suppose that might be the reason she seemed so uncomfortable when she started to tell me the story about her past. And I guess it could also explain why Bradley never visited Dune Island—he might have been bitter about her inheriting the land, because he felt he was more entitled to it than she was.*

But Ruby had told Meg that the secret she'd wanted to share involved Sarah, and Meg couldn't make any connection between Betty's theory and Sarah. It wasn't as if Gordon could have fathered Ruby while he was married to Sarah because Ruby had been born long before they'd wed. Not to mention, Meg couldn't imagine her great-aunt lying so convincingly about the nature of her relationship with Gordon for all these years, either.

Henry was right, Meg concluded, putting the possibility to rest. *Betty's fabrication sounds like something you'd only read in the tabloids.*

ELEVEN

"You look tired. Did those college students keep you awake last night?" Chloe asked Meg.

"No. They've actually been a lot quieter than the two middle-aged couples who just left this morning. I'm tired because I stayed up late reading."

When Meg first started one of Gordon's mysteries on the evening of the book club meeting, she'd remembered why she hadn't read all eight of them when she was younger. The mystery was well-structured, and it contained several plot twists she hadn't seen coming, but she thought his narrative style was so dry it bordered on academic writing, and Meg hadn't really connect with the main characters. However, since she hadn't been able to sleep anyway, she'd decided to keep reading, and by the time she'd reached the midway mark, she couldn't put the book down until she'd found out how it ended.

The following evening, she'd moved on to his next book, reading it straight through. Over the course of several days, she'd devoured two more. In the wee hours of last night, she'd finished the fifth of the eight mysteries that Gordon had authored. Which was why, even though it was almost 1:00 and she hardly ever drank coffee after noon, she was pouring herself a third cup.

"Did you hear me?" asked Chloe.

"Sorry, my brain's still waking up. What did you say?"

"Do you care if I bring the kiddos to work with me the day after tomorrow? They'll probably spend most of the time outside playing with Simon's children."

"You can bring them with you whenever you want. You don't need to ask."

"Good. That'll save me the hassle of running back to my mom's to pick them up after I'm done here." Chloe wiped a coffee ring from the countertop and then wrung out the cloth in the sink. "If the weather's nice, Simon and I are going to take our kids for a picnic and a hike at the bird sanctuary and wildlife preserve. And if it's rainy, we're going to the cranberry museum."

"That sounds like fun," Meg insipidly replied. She couldn't put a finger on why it bothered her that Chloe, Simon, and the children were getting together again. It wasn't as if she thought Chloe was being disloyal to Ruby by cozying up to Simon. And Meg was genuinely glad that Chloe had a daughter who got along so well with Abigail.

Maybe I'm envious because almost the only social interactions I have are with guests, she realized. *Or maybe I'm just irritable because I'm overly tired.*

Aware that nothing could wake her up as quickly as a cool, refreshing swim, Meg drained her coffee into the sink, changed into her swimsuit, and headed out to the beach. When she reached the tip of the peninsula, she peered to the left, where the three college students Chloe had mentioned were sunbathing. Meg waved before turning to walk along the vacant stretch of beach to her right.

After about one hundred yards, she dropped her sandals and beach towel, shed her gauzy cover-up, and made a beeline for the water. It was so chilly that her skin prickled, but Meg barely broke her stride, stopping only when she was rib-deep in the mild swells. She turned to face the beach, held her arms out to her sides, and fell backward, as if collapsing onto a bed.

Ah, yes, that hits the spot, she thought as the water closed over her face and shoulders, and as soon as she surfaced, Meg felt as if her day had begun anew.

She languidly paddled parallel with the shoreline for almost the entire length of the sandy neck of land, and back again. Still not ready to get out, she rolled onto her back and floated, peering at the thin layer of diaphanous clouds veiling the baby-blue sky as the soothing undulations rocked her from side to side.

Just as she'd done countless times since discovering the key in the coffee tin, Meg pondered what door, box, or compartment it might open. She'd already tested it in the locks on the shed, the glass panels of Ruby's breakfront in the formal dining room, all three of the toolboxes, several dresser and desk drawers, and even the trunk of Ruby's car. It hadn't fit in any of them and she hadn't noticed any more locks she could try in the inn or on the grounds.

Is it possible it fits the cottage door lock? she wondered. *Or maybe it unlocks something* inside *the cottage, something Gordon might have left behind in the loft or closet? Didn't old typewriter cases used to have locks on them?* Aware she was grasping at straws, Meg took one last underwater plunge and then shuffled up the beach to where she'd left her towel. After spreading it neatly over the warm sand, she stretched out on her stomach, allowing the sun to dry her hair and skin.

Her dip in the Sound must not have been as rejuvenating as it had first felt because Meg fell asleep within minutes. The next thing she knew, she was woken by a whirring sensation near her ear and shoulder.

Pesky seagull! Annoyed that one of the notorious birds had invaded her space, she leaped to her feet before she had her bearings and she nearly toppled over sideways. As she regained her balance, Meg realized it wasn't a seagull that had disturbed her rest; it was Cody scudding by. He tore partway down the beach before looping back past her, and then toward Abigail, who was tossing a beach ball into the air and catching it again as she skipped over the sand. Simon trailed closely behind.

"Hi, Meg. Ooh, I like your swimsuit. It's purple like mine." Abigail didn't wait for a response before asking, "See my beach ball? We're going to play *keep away* in the water. Do you want to play with us?"

"I, um, uh…" stammered Meg, still discombobulated.

"Look who's here, Daddy," Abigail announced when Simon reached them. "She's got a purple swimsuit, too."

"Yes, she does. Hi, Meg." He met her eyes as she returned his greeting.

"But Dad, you're not even looking at her swimsuit. See?" Abigail gently touched the fabric on the side of Meg's hip. "It's sporty and beautiful, just like mine. Meg says that's a winning combination."

Simon's gaze flitted over Meg's torso. "Yup, it sure is," he said with a sheepish expression, as if he were apologizing because his daughter had insisted that he check Meg out.

Meg found that she didn't mind. "Thank you," she replied, confidently returning his smile.

"She's going to play *keep away* with us in the water, right Meg?" Abigail asked as Cody jumped to a halt inches away from them, spraying sand.

"Right," Meg impulsively declared. "Girls against boys."

"We accept the challenge." Simon prompted his son, "But

you know the rules, Cody. No blankie in the water. I'm going to take off my shirt, too."

As Simon peeled it off and extended his arms to lift the fabric above his head, Meg couldn't help noticing that Chloe was right; his biceps were *impressive*. Her observation was interrupted when Abigail slipped a sweaty palm into hers.

"Let's hold hands and run straight in without stopping," the little girl suggested.

Simon remained on the beach with Cody, but no amount of coaxing would convince him to shed his blankie. His father refused to budge on the issue, too. Because he only permitted Cody to go into ankle-deep water while wearing his blankie, the rest of them occasionally switched partners to compensate for the boy's disadvantage.

Abigail, Simon, and Meg splashed and shouted and tossed the ball until they were waterlogged, hoarse, and exhausted, and by then, even Cody's energy had fizzled.

"I'm hungry," he panted after downing half a bottle of water Simon produced from one of the canvas bags.

"Me, too. Can I have some grapes?" asked Abigail. "Or pretzels?"

Simon rooted around in each of the bags and then admitted, "I must have forgotten them at the cottage. We should go back anyway. We've had enough sun for one afternoon."

"Aww, Dad. Already?" objected Abigail, and Meg silently echoed her sentiment.

I haven't had this much fun since I got to Dune Island, she thought, as she dried her goose-fleshed arms with a towel.

Ordinarily, she might have found it somewhat pitiful that playing *keep away* was the highlight of her summer so far. But Meg knew that it was a comparative assessment; she'd been so consumed with worrying about Ruby's health and her business, and obsessing over her mysterious statement, that even a tiny bit of frivolity seemed like a blast. Also, there was no underestimating the effects of the endorphin release triggered by laughter, exercise, and fresh ocean air. Regardless of the reason for her bubbly mood, Meg wished her time with Simon and the kids wouldn't end yet.

"We can come back tonight to watch the sunset," he said, draping the children's damp towels around his neck.

"Will you come, too, Meg?" asked Abigail.

Meg stole a sidelong look at Simon, but she couldn't read his reaction to his daughter's invitation. "Sure, I'll meet you at the lighthouse benches, unless something comes up at the inn."

Cody and Abigail tromped ahead of Simon and Meg, who made small talk about Ruby's progress, the guests, and the children. She avoided mentioning his discussion with the book club members—Meg didn't want to spoil their carefree mood by making any reference to his plans for the property—but she inquired about his mother, which he seemed to appreciate.

"I spoke to my aunt yesterday and she said my mom's doctor just started her on a new medication. It's too early to tell if it'll be effective in slowing the progression of the dementia, but she's tolerating the drug well, so that's encouraging."

"Hey!" Abigail interrupted him. Walking backward, she pointed to the lighthouse behind him and Meg. "How did all those people get there?"

Meg glanced over her shoulder. "They traveled through the water from Benjamin's Harbor on something called a pontoon boat. It's sort of like a little ferry."

Abigail stopped walking. "Why are they on our beach?"

Meg understood the little girl's territorialism perfectly, but her father corrected her. "It's not *our* beach. We don't own it. Misty Point Beach is open to the public."

"Those people are here because they're going on a tour of the inside of the lighthouse," explained Meg.

"Can anybody ride on the pontoon boat and go in the lighthouse?"

"Yes, if they sign up, first," Meg answered the little girl.

Abigail stopped walking. Pressing her palms together, she wheedled Simon, "Then can *we* ride on the pontoon boat and go on a tour of the lighthouse, Daddy? Please?"

"No. Those visitors come by pontoon boat because that's the only way they can get to Misty Point. We're already here. We don't need to ride on a pontoon boat." Simon's swift and resolute response surprised Meg. Was he nervous about taking Cody and Abigail on a boat, the way some people felt about taking their children on a plane?

"Then can we walk back and get in line to go inside?"

"No. Like Meg said, you have to sign up, first."

Cody, who'd been distracted by a dragonfly, was trotting across the meadow, but Abigal persisted. "Can we go inside the lighthouse on some other day?"

"We'll see."

"But I've never been inside a lighthouse before," she whined. "I really want to go."

"Abigail, I said we'll see," Simon barked at her. "Now stop asking me about it and run up ahead and tell your brother to rinse his feet in the foot pail before he goes inside the cottage."

As Abigail turned around, she muttered under her breath, "Why don't *you* run up ahead and tell him?"

On one hand, Meg was startled by her impertinent response, but on the other hand, she fully empathized with the little girl. Not because her dad wouldn't give her a firm answer about touring the lighthouse, but because his expectations of her to look after Cody seemed unreasonable.

She's only six. It's sweet if she helps once in a while, but she shouldn't have to be her brother's keeper all the time. That's too much responsibility, thought Meg. Yet as upset as she felt on Abigail's behalf, she recognized she had no business commenting on Simon's parenting, so she clammed up the rest of the way across the meadow.

They'd almost reached the fork in the path when Simon came to a stop and broke the silence. "Thanks for hanging out with us. It was a really nice way to spend the afternoon... until I ruined it by snapping at my daughter."

When he reached up and rubbed his brow, Meg noticed that his expression had crumpled into a look of utter dejection. Her heart welling with compassion, she touched his elbow. "She'll forget all about it in five minutes."

"Yeah, but I won't." He shook his head in disgust. "Anyway, that's my problem to deal with, but thanks again."

Meg grinned. "Honestly, it was the most fun I've had in a long time."

Simon rolled his eyes as if he didn't believe her. "Then you really need to get out more. Don't you have a..." Whatever he was about to say, he seemed to change his mind mid-sentence. "...A social group here in Hope Haven?"

"Sure—you've met them. My aunt's book club, remember?" she joked.

"They'd be kinda hard to forget," he replied with a laugh.

Meg took advantage of the moment of levity to make a suggestion. "I didn't want to mention this in front of Abigail, but if it's okay with you, I could bring her on a tour of the lighthouse. I've been planning to go when I get the chance, anyway. We'd need to pre-register if we were going on the boat, but walk-ups for the tour are welcome, and admission to the lighthouse is free. I'd invite you and Cody to come with us, too, but I'm afraid he wouldn't be allowed in."

Simon cocked his head. "Because he's so active?"

"No!" Meg chortled. "Because he's too young. Actually, too short. There's a height requirement to climb the spiral staircase and the ladder to the lantern room."

"Oh." Simon hesitated. "Well, I know Abigail would love to go with you..."

"And I'd love to take her. The next tour will be a week from today. I think it'll be in the morning, but I'll have to check. It all depends on the weather and the tides, since they affect when the boat can dock at Misty Point." Meg paused before imitating Abigail's pleading tone, "So can she come with me? Pleeease, Simon? She's never been in a lighthouse before..."

He gave her a lopsided grin. "Okay, sure. It's a date."

TWELVE

I'm no closer to figuring out what Aunt Ruby meant now than I was a month ago! Meg lamented as she forced the key into the lock of the breakfront in the dining room. It wasn't surprising that it didn't fit; she'd already tested it there on three previous occasions, with no luck. *Oh, great, now it's stuck!*

"What are you doing?" someone asked.

Meg twisted her neck to see Chloe standing behind her, holding the cordless phone. She'd changed out of the khaki capris and white top she'd been wearing earlier; now she was dressed in a camo print V-neck T-shirt, frayed denim short-shorts, and hiking boots. *That's right, she's going to the bird sanctuary with Simon and his children today,* Meg remembered.

She kept her response vague. "I was trying to see if this lock works, but the key got stuck."

"Why do you need to lock it?" Chloe gave her a funny look. "Are you afraid someone's going to steal Ruby's china?"

"No, it's not that. I just... Never mind, it's a long story."

"Whatever." She held out the phone. "It's for you."

"Thanks. Have fun on your hike," Meg called cheerfully, but Chloe walked away without responding. Jiggling the key with one hand and holding the phone to her ear with the other, Meg greeted the caller. "The Inn at Misty Point, this is Meg speaking. How may I help you?"

"The house at Chestnut Drive, this is your mother speaking. How may *I* help *you*?" countered her mom with a chuckle. "Did I catch you at a bad time?"

"No, I'm glad you called. I'm just frustrated because I got a key stuck in a lock." Meg pulled harder but it didn't come loose.

"Here's what you need to do," her mother advised. "Press on the cylinder with one finger to hold it into place, and then quickly pull the key straight toward you."

Meg set down the phone and followed her mother's instructions; the key slid out on the first try. She picked up the phone again. "Worked like a charm! Where did you learn to do that?"

Her mom laughed. "Let's just say I was a bit of a snoop when I was a girl."

"That's funny—but I haven't been snooping," Meg quickly assured her mom. "Not exactly."

She carried the phone upstairs to her bedroom where she'd have more privacy. Until now, Meg had been reluctant to confide in her mom about Ruby's situation, but she was beginning to feel desperate. Figuring her mother might be able to provide additional insight that would aid in her search, Meg told her about Simon's intentions to sell his property to a developer, and she repeated the perplexing phrase Ruby had uttered before her stroke. Meg also expressed how deeply concerned she was about the inn going out of business, and how fervently she wished she could find a way to persuade Simon to reconsider his plans.

"I think deciphering Aunt Ruby's secret is my best chance at convincing him not to develop the land, but I keep hitting dead ends," she complained. "I've found one key, but it wasn't contained within a lighthouse. And I've found lots of lighthouses, but none of them held a key. At this point, I'm not even sure if I should be looking for a figurative or a literal key. I feel like I'm going out of my mind trying to crack the code of what Aunt Ruby meant."

Her mother was quiet a moment before gently suggesting, "Have you considered that what Ruby said was simply some kind of precursor or a reaction to the stroke? Sometimes when people are confused or afraid or in pain, they say things that they don't necessarily mean."

"That possibility has run through my mind. But there's too much at stake for me to dismiss what she said as simply some kind of emotional or physiological phenomenon," said Meg. "The problem is, if I question her about it, she might become frustrated trying to communicate what she meant."

"Yes, she's going through enough already. Right now, she only needs to concentrate on regaining her strength and abilities," her mother agreed.

"Did Dad ever tell you anything unusual about her life? Something that might help me with my search?"

"Unusual? Not really. He wasn't that close to her—*you're* probably closer to her than anyone else in her family was or is, except for perhaps her cousin, Linda. Have you spoken to her about this?"

"Mm, I've considered it, but I don't know her well enough to feel comfortable doing that. The only reason I confided in you about all this is because, well, you're my mom and I trust that you won't repeat a word of it to anyone else."

"Of course I won't. Not even to your brother."

Meg was quiet, contemplating whether to tell her mother about Betty's theory that Gordon had fathered Ruby. But the notion was just too absurd. Instead, she repeated, "Are you sure Dad never mentioned anything unusual about Aunt Ruby's life that might help with my search? Anything at all, no matter how trivial or farfetched it might seem?"

Her mother hedged, "Well, I did hear *something*, but it

didn't come from your father. Honestly, it might not even be true, and you know how I feel about gossiping..."

"Mom, this is really important. Whatever it is, I need to know. I promise I'll never let on to Aunt Ruby that you mentioned it."

"Are you sure you want to hear it, even if it's upsetting?"

Meg swallowed and sat down on the bed. Did Betty's gossip have a hint of truth in it after all? Clutching a pillow to her stomach, she said, "Yes, I'm sure."

After releasing a heavy breath, her mother began, "Well, you're too young to remember, but your father's family used to get together every year for a big, extended family reunion. They were such a clannish bunch, especially his aunts." There was a note of disapproval in her voice. "Anyway, I overheard one of the uncles who'd married into the family talking about how your dad's uncle Alan—that was Ruby's husband—had been a heavy drinker, and he'd had a gambling problem, too."

"Really? I can't imagine Aunt Ruby marrying someone like that."

"She was only seventeen when she met him, and he was just a year or two older. Maybe Alan changed after they got married. Or maybe she simply made a poor decision. I imagine that being passed around from one foster home to another before she was finally adopted may have taken a toll on her self-confidence. And how she felt about herself might have played a role in her choice of a husband."

Meg was still skeptical. "Yeah, but Aunt Ruby only ever said good things about him. Like that he was such a skilled machinist, and that he could fix anything around the house, too. Furniture, appliances, doors... I just don't believe she'd lie about what kind of man her husband was."

"I wouldn't say she was *lying*, Meg. I think she was emphasizing the positive. Like I said, the women on your father's side of the family were very tight, very protective. Alan was the only boy in a family of five girls, and they doted on him. Maybe Ruby felt like she had to sing his praises, too," suggested her mother. "Besides, things were different back then. People didn't openly discuss alcoholism or gambling problems. Even now, there's often a lot of shame or secrecy surrounding family members' addictions."

What her mother was saying made sense, especially when Meg considered Ruby's tendency to overlook what she called "little foibles" or "minor character flaws" that weren't always so little or minor. It saddened Meg to imagine that Ruby had no one to confide in about her husband's alcoholism and gambling addiction. *She must have felt so alone...*

"What else..." Meg asked, her voice catching. She began again, "What else did you hear about Aunt Ruby's husband?"

"Supposedly, he could be very controlling and that's why Ruby never worked—he didn't want her to have her own source of income. Alan also had quite a temper. He managed to hide it from his sisters, but his brother-in-law worked with him. They'd hang out together after their shift ended, playing poker with a few other guys. His brother-in-law said Ruby's husband was a sore loser—and that he lost often. When a game didn't go his way, he took out his anger by smashing whatever was handy. Beer bottles, bar tables, TVs, you get the idea."

A sickening thought crossed Meg's mind. "Did he ever..." She couldn't bring herself to finish the question, but her mother understood what she was asking.

"No, there wasn't any mention of Alan ever hurting Ruby physically, although supposedly when he was drinking, he had a cruel, foul mouth and he made a sport of belittling her. According to his brother-in-law, Alan also trashed almost every apartment he and Ruby lived in. That's why they had to move so often—the neighbors would complain about the ruckus, and the landlords would evict them."

Suddenly, Meg recalled how Ruby had once described

her first summer on Dune Island. "I couldn't believe I had the privilege of spending eight weeks at Misty Point in the company of my closest friends," she'd raved. "The house was so big and peaceful, with the majestic blue ocean right outside the door, and shelves upon shelves of books right inside it. The setting was my idea of paradise. And whiling away entire afternoons, with nothing louder than the sound of the surf in the background, felt like an escape within an escape."

An escape within an escape. Meg had always understood Ruby's phrase to mean that reading while vacationing was doubly enjoyable, a way to escape both in body and in mind. Meg had never given much thought to *why* or *what* her great-aunt had been escaping, other than the noisy bustle of city life. But now Meg wondered if Alan's addictions had become so unbearable by the summer of 1978 that she'd had to get away from him.

"Aunt Ruby told me that Alan didn't mind when she left to stay on Dune Island for the summer because he was always working late anyway," Meg said. "I wonder if that was true."

"He may have been *out* late, but according to his brother-in-law, he wasn't *working*," her mother answered. "He said Alan's gambling addiction was raging out of control that summer and he went through a massive losing streak—not just from poker games and lottery tickets, either. He bet on sports and horses, too. He owed a bookie so much money that two henchmen came to his apartment and gave Alan a black eye and a bloody nose as a threat of what would happen if he didn't pay up on time."

"Too bad, so sad," said Meg, unable to muster sympathy for the man who'd reportedly made life miserable for her mild, easy-going great-aunt. "Did he learn his lesson?"

"Well, he was pretty rattled. After his brother-in-law paid off the bookie for him, Alan went running scared. He and Ruby moved out of their apartment. He quit gambling, switched jobs, and broke all ties with his former acquaintances."

I always wondered why Aunt Ruby didn't stay in touch with Gordon and Sarah, thought Meg. *Alan must not have wanted anyone to know where they were.*

"The following winter, Ruby's adoptive father died and she inherited enough money so that they could purchase a home of their own in a nice suburb outside the city. It seemed as if they were living the American dream until a few years later, when he was out walking the dog one evening and, as you know, he was killed in a hit-and-run accident." Her mother hesitated before adding, "But Alan's brother-in-law claimed it *wasn't* an accident. It was intentional."

Meg gasped, genuinely horrified. Ruby's husband may have been a jerk and an addict, but he hadn't deserved *that*. "Why would anyone intentionally run him down? Hadn't he stopped gambling and paid back his debt by then?"

"He must have started up again, because after he died, Ruby discovered he'd taken out a second mortgage on their house, which he'd probably been using to pay off another bookie. Or *bookies*," she answered.

"Wow. That's some story. Do you think it's true?"

"Considering Ruby's life in retrospect, all the pieces fit, but the story is still just hearsay," Meg's mother replied. "The one thing I do know for certain is that if Ruby hadn't inherited the house at Misty Point, she would've been homeless, as well as bankrupt, because by all counts, she was on the brink of foreclosure. Gordon Sheffield wasn't just her benefactor—he was a lifesaver."

"I'm glad he was so generous to her," agreed Meg. "But if it's true, it's maddening that Aunt Ruby lost her house because of her husband's gambling debts."

"Yes, it seems very unfair, but sometimes that's the way life goes... and it's the way *marriage* goes," her mother said, with a sigh. "Listen, honey, I think it's admirable that you want to help your great-aunt. But regardless of what Simon does with his property, bear in mind that Ruby's getting older. She's long past retirement age. It might be time for her to sell the inn."

"Sell the inn?" squawked Meg. "No way. Aunt Ruby would never want to do that, not even if it goes out of business. She loves it here. Besides, if a developer builds a resort right next door, she wouldn't be able to list the inn for a fraction of what it's worth."

"Maybe not, but she'd still receive more than enough money to purchase a new home somewhere else on Dune Island," suggested Meg's mother.

"She doesn't want to live somewhere else on Dune Island, Mom. Misty Point is her *home*."

"If she can't afford the upkeep and taxes, or if she physically can't manage to live in such a big place on her own any longer, moving might be her only choice."

Their conversation turned to lighter topics, but Meg could barely concentrate. After they'd said goodbye and hung up, she gazed vacantly at the window. A smattering of droplets dotted the pane, and the thought ran through her mind, *I hope the rain doesn't ruin the hike for the children.*

Flopping backward onto the bed, Meg squeezed her eyes shut and contemplated what her mother had just told her about her great-aunt's past. After spending so much time with Ruby over the years, it felt strange to learn that there was so much of her past and her life that she had chosen to keep private, so much pain Ruby had experienced that Meg had never been aware of. *Poor Aunt Ruby. I wonder if it's true that Alan had a gambling problem. And if he did, was that the secret she wanted to share with Simon and me?*

Meg doubted it. *If she was too embarrassed or ashamed to tell any of her relatives about Alan's addiction when he was alive, it seems unlikely she'd tell an outsider about it now. Espe-*

cially since Alan died before Aunt Ruby inherited the property, so it's not as if his gambling was somehow connected to her inheritance, she deduced. *Besides, Aunt Ruby said the secret indirectly involved Sarah, but she never mentioned Alan.*

Meg had a hunch that like most people, her great-aunt had harbored more than one secret during her lifetime. But regardless of whether her mother's story was related to the one Ruby had wanted to tell, Meg felt more determined than ever to make sense of her great-aunt's riddle, and hopefully, to prevent Simon from developing his property.

Aunt Ruby didn't have any choice about being passed around from home to home when she was a girl. And she didn't have any choice about losing her first home as an adult, either, she thought. *So I've got to find a way to keep her from losing this one, too.*

THIRTEEN

The skies were clear and the sun was bright on the morning of the lighthouse tour, but Meg's eyelids were at half-mast.

Shortly after 1:00 a.m. the previous evening, the lighthouse-shaped mirror she'd rehung in Room 3 came crashing down from the wall. Meg had still been awake—she was reading Gordon's sixth mystery—but the rest of the inn's occupants had been jarred from sleep by the sound of shattering glass.

Understandably, they'd been alarmed by the experience, especially the room's occupants. They'd pointed out that it was a good thing they'd been in bed when the mirror fell, otherwise it might have landed on their feet or sprayed glass on their lower legs.

Fortunately, the inn wasn't full, so Meg had helped transfer their belongings to a vacant room, promising to refund the entirety of their three-night stay. She'd compensate them from her own pocket, since it was her fault the mirror had fallen and she knew her great-aunt didn't have contingency funds to cover this kind of mishap.

The guests had begrudgingly accepted her offer, but after everyone went back to bed, Meg had lain awake for hours, wracked with guilt for putting the guests in danger and worrying that they'd give the inn a bad review online. She'd finally drifted off around 6:30, but since she hadn't set an alarm, she'd slept until after nine.

Now she wouldn't be able to have a cup of coffee before going to the cottage to pick up Abigail; she barely had enough time to get dressed. Because Simon had suggested meeting them on the beach for a swim after the tour, Meg pulled on her swimsuit before putting on her T-shirt and shorts. She quickly washed her face, brushed her hair, and applied sunscreen. At the last second, she slipped the key she'd found in the garage into her pocket before jogging down the stairs and toward the porch.

She was halfway down the hall, when Chloe popped out of the laundry room, stopping her. "What happened in Room 3? It looks like it was struck by a hurricane in there."

Meg hurriedly explained that the mirror had fallen, adding, "I swept but I didn't want to vacuum in the middle of the night, so there still might be random shards of glass on the floor. I'm going on a lighthouse tour this morning, but just leave the mess for me. I'll take care of it when I get back, no hurry. We've got other vacancies so we don't need to put anyone in that room tonight."

"You also might want to think about covering up that jagged hole in the wall with a new picture or something before anyone books the room. It looks terrible," advised Chloe. "I wonder why it fell. My cousin hung it up for Ruby when she hired him to paint the bedrooms a couple years ago and he's usually a perfectionist about his work. I'll have to chew him out."

"No, don't do that. It wasn't his fault, it was mine. I, uh, noticed the mirror was crooked so I tried to straighten it, and I somehow ended up yanking it off the wall," Meg fibbed. "I guess I didn't do a very good job of putting it back up."

"Obviously." Chloe's face puckered with a scowl. "Next

time you see something that isn't up to your standards, could you please tell me and I'll fix it myself? It'll save me a lot of time and work."

"Sure, I'm sorry," Meg apologized, her guilt flaring again. "But really, leave the mess in Room 3 for me and I'll deal with it when I get back."

Chloe turned and ducked into the laundry room, muttering something else that Meg couldn't hear. She felt bad that she'd implied Chloe's housekeeping hadn't lived up to her standards, and as she hurried through the yard toward the cottage, she thought, *In chasing after Ruby's secret, I seem to be creating more problems than I'm solving.*

But when Meg saw Abigail swinging her legs in a purple portable outdoor chair beside her father, who was relaxing in a zero gravity recliner next to their cottage, all the tension melted from Meg's shoulders.

"Good morning, everybody," she greeted them, with a wave at Cody as he peeked out at her from behind a tree trunk, just like the first day she met him.

"Hello," said Simon.

"Hi, Meg. I like your shorts. I'm wearing sneakers, see? Daddy said they'd be better than my sandals for climbing up the stairs inside the lighthouse," she explained, dancing from toe to toe in front of Meg. "Why are you bringing your purse? I don't have one. Should I bring my bookbag instead?"

The little girl started toward the cottage but Meg stopped her. "It's not a purse, Abigail. It's a binoculars case—I thought we could take turns looking through the binoculars from the top of the lighthouse."

"You hear that, Cody?" Abigail yelled to her brother. "We're going to use binoculars from the top of the lighthouse! I bet we'll be able to see lots of great white shark fins from way up there."

"I was thinking more along the lines of looking at ships or

birds, or if we're really lucky, we'll spot a whale," Meg said, smiling at Simon. With thick stubble on his chin and jawline, and dark shadows beneath his eyes, he looked wiped out. "Late night?" she asked.

"Early morning," he answered. "Abigail was so excited she had us all awake before first light."

"There's a pot of coffee brewing at the inn," Meg offered.

"Thanks, but I already drank my max for today. My max for tomorrow, too." He squinted at her. "You look like you could use a cup though?"

She was going to tell him about the mirror falling off the wall in the middle of the night, but Abigail pleaded, "Can we go now?"

"Sure," agreed Meg. She squinted at Simon. "So, I guess we'll see you boys on the beach?"

"We'll be there in about an hour. Have fun."

"We will." Abigail threw her arms around his neck and gave him a big kiss on the cheek. Then she yelled, "Bye, Cody! Be a good boy for Daddy!"

The little girl slipped her hand into Meg's and she chatted all the way across the meadow to the lighthouse, where the tour group was clustered outside the door. Lou, the guide, welcomed them with a wave and a nod.

He'd already begun his presentation, which included information about the lighthouse's history and the story of the keeper's house burning down. He also provided facts about the structure, the lens, the keeper's duties, and the lighthouse society. Meg was surprised by how many tidbits she'd retained from childhood, and equally *un*surprised that nothing the guide said seemed to have any connection to Ruby's clue.

At the end of his speech, Lou asked if anyone had questions, and Abigail's hand shot up.

"When is somebody going to paint the bottom?" she asked.

Lou cupped his ear. "I'm sorry... what do you mean, 'paint the bottom'?"

Abigail pointed at the lighthouse. "It's only half red."

A few people broke out in friendly chuckles, but Lou said, "This young lady is asking a very smart question. Those of you who've seen the various lighthouses around the island—or around the world—have noticed that they're painted different colors..."

He continued, explaining that the lighthouse's shape, color, size, and flash pattern were all unique characteristics that were designed to assist mariners in identifying them and in navigating the waters.

"For example, Misty Point Lighthouse is partly red and partly white because the bright red color helps it to stand out in foggy conditions. It also distinguishes it from its sister, Sea Gull Light, which is completely white, with a black top," Lou said. "But I can understand why an observant youngster like this girl here might think we ran out of paint."

Again, the people around them chuckled, and Abigail tipped her head back to beam proudly at Meg. After Lou fielded the remaining questions, he opened the lighthouse door —Meg noticed it was secured with a keypad, not a traditional lock—and led the group inside. Only eight people were allowed to enter at a time, and since Meg and Abigail were the last to arrive, they waited for everyone else to take their turns, first.

As they were standing there, the pontoon operator wearing a nametag that read *Bill* gave Abigail a bumper sticker with a picture of the lighthouse on it. She thanked him and then excitedly showed it to Meg, saying, "I want to keep this, but I think I'll give it to Cody because he didn't get to come with us."

"Who's Cody?" asked Bill.

"He's my brother. Daddy said he's too little to go on the stairs. He's only this tall." She indicated his height with her hand.

"In that case, I have the perfect sticker for him, so you don't have to give yours away."

He handed it to her, and Abigail slowly sounded out the words that were printed around a sketch of the lighthouse. "I went-ed—no, I *wanted* to see the lighthouse, but I... What's that word?" she asked Meg.

"Mist."

"I mist it?" Abigail sounded confused.

"It's a joke, because it's misty near a lighthouse," explained Meg. "But it also means somebody *missed* being able to see it."

"Ohh, I get it. I wanted to see the lighthouse, but I *mist* it," repeated Abigail. "That's a good one."

Her giggling was so infectious that everyone around her laughed, too. And one of the older ladies remarked to Meg, "Your daughter is darling."

It was an understandable mistake, but for a split second, Meg was tongue-tied, unsure how to respond. She didn't want Abigail to feel like she was trying to take her mother's place, but neither did she want her to feel rejected if Meg pointed out the stranger's error too quickly. So she said, "I'd love to have a daughter like Abigail, but she belongs to someone else."

To her embarrassment, Meg's eyes unexpectedly welled with tears at the accuracy of her own sentiment. *Of all the times I shouldn't have forgotten to wear sunglasses...*

"Oh, I'm sorry," the flustered woman rushed to apologize. "It's just that you both have the same beautiful shade of red hair, so I assumed you were mother and daughter."

"Mommy's hair was light brown like my brother's," Abigail sweetly informed her. "Meg's is kinda like mine, but she doesn't have curls that go *boing* when she jumps, like this."

Abigail demonstrated by hopping on one foot, to the amusement of the elderly woman and everyone else within earshot. Meg laughed, too, and her momentary tearfulness instantly lifted. She quickly became engaged in chatting with the tourists, who were fascinated when they realized that she had ambled over from the inn. As she described the serenity of vacationing on Misty Point, Meg thought, *Maybe this conversation will help drum up some business for Aunt Ruby next year.*

When it was their turn to go inside, Abigail counted aloud every one of the fifty-nine steps on their ascent. Although she wasn't tall enough to see out any of the three full-sized windows along the way, to her delight, there was a step stool in front of one of the porthole-shaped windows on the watch deck.

As she climbed up and peered out, Lou asked her, "Do you know why this is called the watch deck?"

"Because it's where the lighthouse keeper watched for whales and sharks?" Abigail guessed.

"Close. It's where he stood watch at night, making sure the lantern stayed lit. He also watched for storms and shipwrecks or other emergencies. See that door? It's sealed shut now so visitors won't try to use it, but the keeper could step out onto the gallery and circle the lighthouse whenever he needed to take a really good look around." With a twinkle in his eye, Lou added, "And you're right, during daylight hours, he probably saw plenty of whales and maybe even an occasional shark, too."

Next, the old man nimbly led the way up the steel, secured ladder to the lantern deck. Meg instructed Abigail to go next, so she could follow closely behind the child to make sure she didn't lose her footing.

"Wow, you can see forever from here," Abigail marveled about the glass-enclosed tower. Inching her way past the two rotating lenses on a platform in the center of the room, she circled the perimeter, naming what she saw, just as she'd done from the window in Ruby's living room. "Look, the trees by our cottage look like broccoli, don't they? And there's the inn. And the ocean. And *more* ocean..."

When Meg showed her how to focus the binoculars, she was thrilled to spy a fishing boat to the south, and a dog running along a beach in northern Benjamin's Manor. Listening to her innocent exclamations of discovery, Meg felt like she herself were seeing the seascape from that vantage point for the first time, too.

She was so absorbed in sharing Abigail's experience that she nearly forgot to investigate the interior of the lighthouse for a connection to Ruby's clue. But it was virtually devoid of any furnishings or décor that could have served as a hiding place for a key. Meg surreptitiously peeked into a utility closet and ran her hand under the railing on her way back down to the base, but she didn't discover anything except a few sticky spider webs.

By the time she, Abigail, and Lou stepped out into the bright sunshine, the other participants were boarding the pontoon boat, and Meg noticed that Simon and Cody had just about reached the lighthouse. The little boy broke into a run toward a flock of seagulls that had gathered down the beach.

Abigail charged after him. "Cody, wait! I have something for you!"

"Thanks so much for the tour," Meg said to Lou. "I always enjoy listening to you talk about what life used to be like for the keepers... and of course, the view from the lantern room is enthralling, too."

"That it is," he replied, securing the door before he turned to her, a dour expression on his face. "Too bad some numbskull is going to ruin it by building a resort here. Can you believe it?"

Although she completely agreed with his sentiment about the view, Meg inwardly winced at Lou's use of the word "numbskull." Hoping Simon wasn't close enough yet to hear that part of his comment, she diplomatically replied, "It's going to be a huge change, that's for sure."

"You mean it's going to be a huge *mistake*," declared Lou. "There are scores of beautiful beaches in Hope Haven, but what makes this one so special is that the land is virtually untouched. When people visit Misty Point, they feel like they're stepping back in time. They get to experience what Dune Island was like before it was overrun by dime-a-dozen hotels, golf courses, and other tourist traps. I can appreciate that visitors to the area need lodging, but building a resort here is going to wreck the very quality about Misty Point that makes it so unique—namely, its seclusion."

Out of the corner of her eye, Meg could see Simon loitering a few yards away on the northern side of the lighthouse. Was that because his position allowed him to keep an eye on the children? Or was he hesitant to come forward to meet Lou because he could hear Meg's conversation with him? She had no intention of making Simon uncomfortable by drawing him into their spirited conversation, yet she also refused to soften her stance on the issue just for his sake.

"I couldn't agree with you more, Lou," she said. "I've always cherished the tranquility at Misty Point, and I was crushed when I heard about the plans to build a resort."

"Yeah, the members of the lighthouse society are crushed, too. For the past forty years, we've dedicated ourselves to serving as keepers, taking care of the grounds, and educating the public because we value the history of the lighthouse and we want to preserve the environmental integrity of Misty Point. We'd like to stop the resort from going up, but what can we do? We don't have the funds to put a bid in for the land, and a petition isn't going to accomplish anything, either." He huffed and wiped the sweat from his brow. "The way things are going, I wouldn't be surprised if someone suggests turning Misty Point into a theme park and the lighthouse into a B&B. They'll charge five grand per night so wealthy people can add 'sleeping in a lighthouse' to their bucket lists."

Meg chuckled. "I sure hope it doesn't come to *that*!"

"Stranger things have happened," said Lou, jiggling the coins in his pocket. "Anyway, I'd better set sail. Nice talking to you, Meg. Greet Ruby for me—and tell her we're still hopeful that something will prevent that monstrosity from being built in her back yard."

I'm still hopeful, too, thought Meg. "I'll do that. Thanks again, Lou."

He sauntered toward the pontoon and Meg ambled over to Simon, who held out a covered, insulated cup. "I brought you coffee—it's from the inn."

"Aw, that was thoughtful," said Meg, relieved that he either hadn't heard her conversation with the tour guide or that he wasn't defensive about it. As they walked toward the children, she mentioned why she'd been so tired earlier that morning.

"If you want, I can hang the replacement mirror or painting for you, to make sure it'll stay up," he offered.

"Really?" Again, Meg was grateful for his thoughtfulness. "I'd appreciate that. So would my guests."

"No problem. *I* really appreciate you taking Abigail on the tour," he replied as his daughter and son came running up to them, waving the stickers from Lou.

"Look what the lighthouse man gave us, Daddy," Abigail said. "Can you put them in the bag so they don't get lost?"

"Sure. What did you think of being inside the lighthouse?"

"It was *cool*. 'Cept it isn't really a house, there aren't even any bedrooms or bathrooms in there, only super-twisty stairs. Fifty-nine, I counted. And at the top, you can see all the way to Timbuktu. That's what the lighthouse man said. And he said I asked a smart question about the outside being half-red and half-white. Did you know it's like that on purpose?" Abigail didn't wait for Simon to respond to her long-winded reply before announcing, "I'm hot. Let's go swimming."

Like Meg, she'd worn her swimsuit beneath her clothes, which she immediately began to cast off, and then she scuffed down to the edge of the water. Watching her, Cody fiddled with the blue fabric knotted around his torso.

"What do you say, son? You want to come swimming with us today?" asked his father.

To Meg's surprise, Cody shrugged and then nodded. Simon helped him untie his blankie from his chest, and Meg squelched a giggle when she noticed that the little boy had a thick, pale stripe across his back, where the sun hadn't tanned his skin.

Oh, no, I forgot my towel, she realized, but she wasn't going to let that stop her from taking a swim, especially since Cody was finally shedding his blankie to go in, too.

Meg didn't want to crowd him, so she waded out to Abigail and showed her how to do the "mermaid kick," while Simon tried to coax his son farther into the water. Yet even though the waves were negligible, the water was nippy, and when it splashed onto Cody's bare belly, he turned and hightailed it to drier ground. He immediately wound his blankie around his chest again.

Simon waded out to where Meg was standing. While Abigal dived underwater, he subtly gestured toward Cody on the beach. "Look at him. It's like he thinks his blankie is a life preserver, but really it's a tether. It's holding him back. Sometimes I wonder if I should accidentally-on-purpose get rid of it, to help him realize he's just fine without it."

Even though Simon hadn't asked a direct question, Meg waited until Abigail took another dive and then she tentatively suggested, "I don't think you need to get rid of it for him. I think he's going to abandon it pretty soon. He's got to warm up to the idea on his own, first. And I think that's what he was doing just now. He's making progress."

Simon wrinkled his forehead. "You really think so?"

"Yes, I'm sure of it," she confirmed, staring into his glimmery green eyes.

Abigail suddenly popped up between them, spraying them both. "What are you two talking about?"

"Grown-up stuff," said Simon.

But to Meg, it was more like they'd been talking about *parent* stuff, and she felt highly complimented that he'd seemed to value her input even though she herself didn't have children.

When they got out of the water, Simon insisted she use his towel to dry off, and then he spread it out and they sat side-by-side on it. "Cody and I made PB&Js for everyone. Fine dining at its best," he said, distributing the sandwiches.

They hungrily devoured them, even though it wasn't quite noon yet. Then Cody asked if they'd help him build a sandcastle, and after that, Meg and Abigail went for another dip, while Simon and Cody took a jaunt to the marsh to look for fiddler crabs.

As the foursome finally strolled back across the meadow together, they crossed paths with three guests approaching from the opposite direction.

One of them asked, "Did you have a nice time at the beach?"

"We had a *great* time," exclaimed Abigail, which was exactly how Meg felt, too.

If only it hadn't been for my conversation with Lou about the resort, it would've been absolutely perfect. The single misgiving drifted across her mind like a stray cloud across an otherwise sunny sky, but she decided to ignore it.

"It was wonderful," she told the guests. "I hope you enjoy it as much as we did."

FOURTEEN

A couple days after the lighthouse tour, Meg went into the garage to search the storage bins of her great-aunt's extra kitchen items. She remembered packing away a collection of decorative plates that might make a pretty substitute for the lighthouse mirror that had fallen off the wall in Room 3. As she was looking for them, she literally stumbled upon the lock that matched the key she'd found weeks ago in the coffee canister.

More accurately, she stumbled *into* the old bicycle she rode as a teenager. When she tried to roll it out of her way, Meg noticed its wheel was fixed in place with a heavy-duty steel cable and padlock. *Who'd want to steal this old thing, anyway?* she thought, laughing to herself as she withdrew the key from her pocket. Even if the key fit into the padlock, she figured the damp ocean air would have rusted the lock shut, but it clicked open on her first attempt at turning it.

Until that moment, she'd been so frustrated about *not* finding the lock that she wasn't prepared for how disappointed she'd feel if she found it and discovered it obviously had nothing to do with her great-aunt's clue.

As long as I was searching, I still had hope. But now I just feel like I've wasted a lot of time for nothing, and I'm right back where I started. Even though she knew there was a vast difference between finding a match between the key and lock, and finding a match between herself and a potential spouse, Meg complained to herself, *This reminds me of how I've felt after virtually every breakup I've experienced in the past ten years.*

But there was no time to wallow: Simon had spackled the hole in the wall the previous afternoon and he'd be arriving soon to hang the plates for her. So Meg gave herself a pep talk. *The key was a red herring, but now that I've eliminated it as a possibility, I'm that much closer to finding the* real *key to Aunt Ruby's secret.*

Hopefully, once she found it, she'd also be that much closer to stopping the "monstrosity"—as Lou the tour guide had referred to the resort—from being built in front of the lighthouse.

Meg clicked the padlock shut with the key still inserted in it, and she lifted the bike out of her way. As she surveyed the bins, it occurred to her that even though time seemed to be rushing forward, it simultaneously felt as if it had been years since she'd downsized her great-aunt's kitchen and bookcases.

I had such high hopes for our summer together, she thought, feeling melancholy again. *I never imagined I'd be staying here without Aunt Ruby...*

She had to unwrap the newspaper from several dishes before locating the stack she wanted. A different sea creature was depicted in navy blue on each of the six white porcelain plates, and the effect was simple, but tasteful. She rewrapped the set, carefully carried it to the inn and placed it on the kitchen table, before hurrying upstairs to shower.

But when she reached her bedroom, she glanced out the window and spotted Simon, Cody, and Abigail traipsing across the back lawn toward the inn. *Already? He can't be coming here already!* Pulling a brush through her hair, Meg caught a glimpse of her flushed cheeks in the mirror. Why was she so flustered? It wasn't as if she didn't see Simon at least every other day.

She hustled downstairs to greet him and the children, but Chloe had beat her to it. Meg heard her voice carrying from the porch, "Hey there! I didn't know my favorite little friends were stopping in today. I didn't expect to see you until tomorrow, when we go to the boardwalk with Maddie and Sonny while your daddy's at his meeting in town."

Another meeting? Dismayed, Meg tucked this information in the back of her mind, set a smile on her face, and hurried down the hall to say hello to Simon, Abigail, and Cody. She gave the children each a cherry-flavored ice pop, and Simon sent them outside to eat them on the patio.

Meanwhile, Chloe took it upon herself to unwrap the decorative plates Meg had left on the kitchen table. "I can take Simon upstairs and show him where to hang these," she volunteered.

Meg recognized that Chloe may have intended to be helpful, but she was a little surprised by her take-charge attitude. "That's all right. I don't want to disrupt your work. Besides, I'd like to hang them a certain way."

Chloe rolled her eyes. "Last time you wanted to hang a mirror 'a certain way,' you made a hole in the wall. Don't you think you'd be better off leaving it to the professionals this time around?" She laughed, as if she were joking, but Meg felt embarrassed by her dig.

"I think she meant she has a certain aesthetic in mind; right, Meg?" Simon's tactful interjection made her feel even more chagrined; it was as if she needed him to defend her.

"Right," she said, squeezing past Chloe to gather the plates.

As Meg headed upstairs, Simon popped outside to remind the children to stay in the back yard where he could watch them from the window. To Meg's annoyance, when he entered Room 3, Chloe was right behind him.

"Oh, yeah, those plates will look great in here. They're the perfect color," he said. "If you point out where you think you want them, Chloe and I can hold them against the wall so you can stand back and get a visual."

"There are six plates, but you two only have four hands, so it'll be easier to spread them out on the bed."

"No, don't! I just laundered that duvet," Chloe protested.

Meg didn't know why Chloe was being so picky, but she dug in her heels and countered, "I washed the plates before I wrapped them in newspaper, so they're perfectly clean. But if the duvet gets dusty or rumpled, I'll take care of it." She spread the plates across the bed, shuffling and re-shuffling their order, but she couldn't settle on an arrangement.

After a while, Simon asked, "Can I make a suggestion?"

"Sure."

"The plates are all the same size, so you might want to break up the symmetry by doing something like this..." He repositioned them and Meg immediately recognized what he meant.

"Yes, you're right," she agreed. "But I think we should switch this starfish with the seahorse. There! Perfect. Thanks for the suggestion."

"Yeah, that looks nice," Chloe agreed, placing a hand on Simon's arm and gazing coquettishly up at him from beneath her lashes. "Have you always had an eye for beauty?"

Meg practically snorted with disbelief that Chloe would say something so ridiculous and shamelessly self-referential, but Simon answered earnestly, "Nah, I can't take credit for that. My wife was an interior designer, so some of her good taste must have rubbed off on me."

"She taught you well," Chloe enthused, before turning to Meg. "You don't need to stick around. My shift is over, so I'll help Simon in here. We've got to talk about the playdate plans for tomorrow, and other stuff that wouldn't interest you since you don't have kids."

Meg was so ticked off at Chloe's statement that she could hardly utter, "All right, well, thanks for your help, Simon."

"Happy to do it," he said.

Chloe gave her a triumphant smile. "See you tomorrow."

Meg flew down the hall and into her bedroom. Although she felt like slamming the door hard enough to knock the rest of the mirrors off *all* the walls, she wouldn't give Chloe the satisfaction. Too angry to remain within hearing distance of the younger woman's voice, Meg scooped her car keys from the nightstand and padded downstairs and out the porch door.

"Are you going some place, Meg?" asked Abigail, her hands and face cherry-red with ice pop juice. Cody was worming through the grass on his belly, apparently trying to sneak up on a bunny. Even from halfway across the yard, Meg could see that his face was stained red, too.

"Yes. I have to run an errand."

"But we didn't even get to talk to you," the little girl complained.

Although she felt a tiny prick of guilt, Meg recognized that she was in no mood to talk to *anyone*, and she didn't want to end up being cross with the children. "We'll see each other again soon."

"Can we go inside and wash our hands? My fingers are sticking together, look."

Meg's first impulse was to take Abigail and Cody into the inn and help them clean their hands and faces. But on second thought, she reasoned, *Why should I help them while Chloe is upstairs flirting with their father? After all, this is a job for someone who's a parent, and as she made a point of announcing, I don't have any kids.*

"Sure, that's a good idea," she said, beckoning Cody.

Instead of standing up to run, the boy rolled all the way across the lawn. Coming to a rest at her feet, he smiled up at her. There were blades of grass sprouting from his sticky cheeks like green whiskers, and he had grass and pine needles in his hair and on his blankie, too.

"You can wash your hands and faces in the bathroom upstairs," Meg instructed as she led the children down the hall. "Your daddy and Chloe will help you. They're in the room at the top of the staircase. I'll stand here and wait to be sure you find them."

A moment after Abigail and Cody disappeared into Room 3, she heard Chloe exclaim, "What are you two doing up here? I hope this doesn't mean I'm going to find a trail of handprints on the railing or the walls!"

Although it may have been immature, Meg smirked as she tiptoed out of the inn.

Meg rarely left Misty Point for the purpose of walking or swimming on another beach, but when she did, she went to Driftwood Hollow. Located on the "ocean side" of the island— meaning, it faced the open Atlantic—the beach boasted long, wide sandbars and rolling, moderate-sized waves, which made it the perfect place for bodyboarders and beginning surfers to hone their skills.

But what she appreciated most about Driftwood Hollow Beach today was that it was virtually deserted, because its so-called parking lot was a small square of sandy dirt with only enough room for four or five vehicles. She pulled up beside an SUV with a "Seas the Day on Dune Island" sticker on its back bumper, got out, and strode quickly along the path that cut through the thick wild rose shrubs and over the low dune.

The surf was more tumultuous than usual, much like Meg's thoughts. *What am I so upset about anyway?*

The obvious answer was that Chloe had struck a nerve— had pierced her *heart*, actually—when she'd drawn attention to the fact that Meg wasn't a parent. But that was only one of the many layers of emotion that were washing over her.

She recognized that she sorely missed her great-aunt. Missed her breezy, gentle ways, and their light-hearted conversations. Meg was also frustrated that she couldn't figure out Ruby's clue, and she was consumed with concern about her great-aunt's future. Stressed out from managing the inn alone, she vacillated between wishing the guests would all just go away, and worrying whenever there was a vacancy.

However, the longer she walked, the less burdened she felt; it was almost as if she left a little of her distress behind each time her feet slapped against the wet sand. And as she circled back to the dune where she'd begun her hike, she found herself half laughing, half cringing about the "trick" she'd played on Chloe by sending the children upstairs with dirty hands to interrupt her and Simon.

Why would I try to cause trouble like that? she mused. *Am I envious because Chloe is getting along so well with Simon and his children?*

Meg knew that wasn't the case; on the contrary, she genuinely felt like the more people who enjoyed being with Simon's children, the better. *I'm glad Maddie and Sonny are so fond of Abigail and Cody. Playing together benefits all of them.*

But how did she feel about Chloe's friendship—or whatever her relationship was—with Simon? Meg didn't think she was necessarily *jealous* that the two of them were spending so much time together. After all, Simon didn't know many other people on the island, and they both had children around the same age, so it was only natural that they'd hang out during their kids' playdates.

Yes, it was clear that Chloe was interested in going out with him, but Meg couldn't gauge the nature of Simon's interest in her. *He didn't seem to mind when she flirted and touched his arm in the bedroom.* Not that Meg would expect him to flinch and pull away, but he didn't seem at all surprised or uncomfortable with the gesture, which made Meg think it wasn't the first time Chloe had been physically demonstrative toward him.

She realized if she wanted to confirm whether they were seeing each other, she should just ask Chloe directly. But it really wasn't any of Meg's business, and she'd feel embarrassed if Chloe responded by saying something like, "Why do you want to know?"

Opening her car door to let the heat escape, Meg posed that uncomfortable question to herself. *Why do I want to know? It's not as if I want to date him... is it?*

She had undeniably felt a bond with Simon when they'd hung out on the beach after the lighthouse tour. But it wasn't a romantic connection; they'd bonded because of his children. And although Simon had been very attentive to her, Meg suspected that was only because he was grateful that she'd taken Abigail on the tour. Likewise, the feelings she'd had toward him weren't because she was attracted to Simon, in particular; it was because she was attracted to the *idea* of him. To what he represented as a family man, the father of young children, a devoted husband.

Nah, I don't want to date Simon—I want to date the kind of guy he represents, she rationalized. *Minus the part about him putting Aunt Ruby out of business!*

As she slid into the driver's seat, Meg suddenly recalled that Chloe had mentioned she was taking the children to the arcade the following day, while Simon was at a meeting in town. Because it seemed unlikely he had other business on the island, Meg assumed the purpose of Simon's meeting was related to the upcoming sale of his property.

It sounds like he's getting all his ducks in a row. I need to line up mine, too, instead of wasting any more time wondering about whether Chloe and Simon are going out, or analyzing my connection with him, either, she resolved, as she reversed the car's direction and headed back to the inn.

FIFTEEN

The only weather that made guests more disgruntled than a midsummer heat wave was a midsummer rainy streak. Personally, Meg considered the rain to be a pleasant change from the brilliant sunshine, a welcome excuse to laze around the inn reading after the work was done. But she understood why the vacationers felt so antsy, especially after several days of nonstop precipitation ranging from dripping drizzle to drenching downpours.

During sunny weather, the guests were either at the beach or sightseeing for such long stretches throughout the day that the inn often had felt empty. But when it rained, everyone seemed to be tripping over each other as they left and returned, heading back and forth to town.

On the fifth day of what was forecasted to be a seven-day rainy period, Meg decided she'd take what she considered to be a drastic action and bake a lemon pound cake for the guests. *Everyone appreciates a homemade dessert. I just need to pick up a few ingredients, first.*

Meg was so pleased for an excuse to get away from the inn that she didn't mind at all that the heavy traffic crept along at a snail's pace, or that the line at the cash register at the market moved even slower.

On the way home, she tried to phone her mother for a chat, but her mom didn't answer, so she pressed Josh's number on the console display, since he'd left her a couple of messages.

"Hey, Meg. How are things in paradise?" he asked.

"It's hardly paradise." Meg told him about the rain and the litany of guest complaints. She ended by saying, "I wish I were unflappable like my great-aunt, but my patience with everyone's bellyaching—including my own—is starting to wear thin."

Josh chuckled. "Sounds like you need a break. Have you done anything for fun lately?"

Meg didn't want to tell him that she'd had a blast playing with Simon and his children on the beach the previous week. So she cracked, "Fun? What's that?"

He started to say something but her phone dropped the call mid-sentence. Meg tried to call him back, but she was too far from town and she couldn't get a signal. A few minutes later she pulled into the parking area by the inn and was surprised to see a champagne-colored sports car she didn't recognize parked in the smoothly paved area reserved for people with disabilities.

That's odd—those plates are from Massachusetts. The guest who reserved the accessible room for tonight is coming from Maine, she recalled. *And he said he wouldn't be arriving until almost 9:00.*

Even though she made a dash for the inn, Meg was soaked by the time she got inside. Slipping off her sandals, she followed the sound of a cough to the den, where a man in a dripping jacket was standing with his back turned.

"Hello," she said brightly. "I'm Meg—"

He held up one finger, silencing her. She hadn't realized until then that he was talking on the inn's cordless phone. As she backed out of the room to give him privacy, she heard him say, "Listen, I gotta run. Yep. Okay, bye."

Meg took a step forward and began again. "Sorry about that. I didn't realize you were on a call."

"I'm done now. Here you go." He handed the phone to Meg and then strode toward the exit.

He's leaving just because I accidentally interrupted his phone call? Even though Meg thought that was an extreme reaction, she knew the inn couldn't afford to lose any business. "Do you need a hand with your luggage?" she asked, hoping if she was helpful enough he'd change his mind about staying.

"Luggage?" A look of realization dawned on his face. "I'm not *lodging* here. I was visiting the guy next door, Simon. Trying to, anyway, but I didn't see his car in the lot, so I popped in here to use the landline. I couldn't get a signal on my phone and I needed to make an urgent call. Don't worry, I asked, first. The proprietor said it was fine."

"Oh, really?" Meg raised her eyebrows. *He must have spoken to Chloe and gotten the impression she owned the inn.*

"Yeah, *really*," he echoed in a mocking tone. "Why, what's the problem?"

"There's no problem, you're welcome to use the phone, especially for an urgent call. But I noticed that your car didn't have a disability placard or plates and you parked in the accessible area."

"Busted. But like I just told you, I only popped in here for a sec." He eyeballed her dripping hair and clothes before adding, "And it's pouring cats and dogs, as you're obviously aware, so I needed to park close to the door."

Undaunted, Meg coolly replied, "And like *I* just told *you*, even though you're not a guest at the inn, you're welcome to use the parking lot while you're visiting Simon. But as *you're* obviously aware, the accessible space is reserved for people with disabilities. So if you park there in the future, even for a *sec*, your car will be towed."

"Not an issue, I won't be returning." With a sneer he muttered, "Not until we pave a separate parking lot, anyway."

As she watched him swagger out the door, Meg wondered if he was the developer or one of the architects working with Simon. *Either way, what an awesome sign of things to come*, she thought sardonically.

Heading toward the kitchen, she glanced into the living room and noticed several children's books on the floor. Because none of the current guests had brought children with them, Meg assumed Maddie and Sonny had been reading them. *Usually Chloe's so careful to make sure they pick up after themselves and put everything back where they found it*, she thought. *But she has a couple days off, so she must have been in a hurry to leave—not that I blame her.*

Then it occurred to Meg that this wasn't an oversight; it was possible that Chloe had deliberately permitted Maddie and Sonny to leave the books on the floor. Maybe it was payback for the ice pop prints that she'd had to clean off the staircase railing after Meg had sent Cody and Abigail upstairs with gummy hands. *I suppose I deserve it*, she silently admitted.

When she crouched to slide the books onto the built-in shelf beneath the window seat, something caught her eye: a painted ceramic bookend shaped like a lighthouse. *I forgot all about this!* Meg thought excitedly.

The kitschy statuette had been a birthday gift her brother had given Ruby when he was a child, and it doubled as a piggy bank. *It must have slipped my mind I moved this here from the den when I relocated the children's books*, Meg realized. Because the shelf was at a child's eye level, it made sense that she hadn't noticed the bookend during her search for lighthouse-themed decorations.

As she plucked it from the shelf, she heard something rattle inside. Tipping it upside down, she expected to find a rubber plug she could remove to empty the lighthouse replica of its contents. But the only opening on the lighthouse was the slot for inserting coins near the tip.

Meg up-righted the bookend and shook it again. It was clear from the sound that there was only one object inside it, but she couldn't determine whether it was a coin, a key, or something else. She tipped the lighthouse upside down again and shook it harder, and then gentler, expecting the object inside to slip from the slot. When that didn't work, she held the bookend overhead and shone her phone's flashlight into it, hoping she could see what was inside. She couldn't.

After several more minutes of trying and failing to jiggle the item free from the bookend, Meg thought, *Looks like I'm just going to have to break it open.*

Yet instead of going to the garage to get a hammer from the toolbox, Meg plopped down on the window seat. The bookend couldn't have cost more than five dollars, but she was aware that it had special sentimental value for Ruby, since it had been a gift from her great-nephew. But surely if she had to choose between keeping the statuette intact or keeping the inn, Ruby would want her great-niece to break the bookend, wouldn't she?

Meg slowly bounced the ceramic lighthouse in the air, weighing its heft. *What if the only thing inside is a quarter or a nickel and then I've ruined her keepsake for nothing?* she worried. *What if this is a repeat of the mirror-hanging episode, and I break something else for no reason? I'd better keep trying to jiggle it out.*

She replaced the books on the shelf, leaning them against one end of the bookcase. After putting her groceries away in the kitchen, she brought the ceramic lighthouse upstairs and left it in her bedroom, where she could deal with it when she had more time and patience.

. . .

Two days later, the sun coyly peeked out from behind the clouds and then it disappeared again, but that was all the encouragement Meg needed. She grabbed her towel and book and hiked out to the deserted beach where she could read in peace. Lying on the towel on her stomach, she cracked open Gordon's seventh mystery novel, which was titled, *The Wife of Oscar Claiborne*.

Maybe his style had grown on her, or perhaps it was because the protagonist was a female, but Meg couldn't read this book fast enough. The narrator's voice seemed much warmer and wittier than in his other books, and she was immediately drawn into the story. However, the overcast sky created a bright, white glare, and even though Meg was wearing sunglasses, she frequently had to stop reading to close her eyes. She'd lower her head for three to five minutes, and then dive back into the book again.

It was during one of these visual breaks that she dozed off. Ironically, she woke to Simon's hushed voice admonishing his children not to wake her. "Abigail, shh—and Cody, watch where you're jumping. You're going to disturb Meg. She's asleep."

"No, I'm not. Hi, everyone." Meg shifted into a sitting position and immediately noticed Abigail's face was red and she was sobbing. "Abigail, honey, what's wrong?"

The little girl dropped the fishing net and pail she'd been carrying, plonked onto her bottom next to Meg and tattled, "We had to leave our playdate with Charlotte and Chase early because of Cody!" She pointed an accusing finger at her brother, who obliviously continued to hop on one foot down to the water's edge. "He ruined *every*thing!"

"Aww." Without choosing sides or asking for details, Meg wrapped an arm around Abigail's shoulder and pulled her close. "I'm sorry your afternoon didn't turn out the way you hoped it would."

"It *would* have turned out the way I wanted if only Cody didn't—" the little girl started to say, but her father cut her off.

"Abigail, Meg doesn't want to hear about your argument with your brother," he told her. "I'm sure she came to the beach to enjoy some peace and quiet, and that's what I want to do, too. You said you were going to try to catch minnows, but if you've changed your mind, then maybe we should all go back to the cottage and have a nap. So, which would you like to do?"

Abigail wiped her eyes with the back of her arm. "Catch minnows," she sniveled.

Before the little girl got to her feet, Meg stroked her curls away from her ear and said just loud enough so Simon would hear and know that she wasn't contradicting him or interfering with his instructions, "I've got a little brother, too. Some other time I'll tell you about a big fight we had and what Ms. Ruby told us to get us to make up."

Abigail nodded, just a hint of a smile dawning on her freckled face. Then she picked up her net and pail, and waddled down to the water's edge, where her brother hopped over to her, splashing as he approached.

"Cody, I've told you to give your sister some space!" warned Simon.

"It's okay, Dad," shouted Abigail. "He's scaring the minnows and they're coming right toward me."

Simon pushed his hair off his forehead—it was getting so long—and apologized, "Sorry about all that."

"No need to be. Like I said, I have a younger brother. Arguments come with the territory of being a sibling." She patted the ground. "You want to join me?"

Simon didn't sit as much as he collapsed onto the sand beside her. He looked so out-of-sorts that Meg was tempted to wrap her arm around him, too, just as she'd done to Abigail. She had intended to tell him about the man who'd been looking for him at the inn, but this didn't seem like the right moment.

"Rough day?" she asked.

"I wish it were only a rough day. It seems like the three of us have been at each other's throats for the past week."

"Sounds like you've got a case of cabin fever," Meg suggested. "Thanks to the miserable weather, it's been going around at the inn, too. We're all climbing the walls—and we've got a *lot* more room than you do at the cottage, so I can only imagine what it's like for your family."

"That's why I thought it would be helpful for the kids to get out and spend time with some children besides Maddie and Sonny for a while, but... well, let's just say that we'll be lucky if Alice ever allows Chase and Charlotte to play with my kids again."

"I doubt that's true. Alice might be a doting grandmother, but I'm sure she recognizes that her grands aren't exactly perfect, either."

"Charlotte and Chase might not be perfect, but they're much better behaved and better adjusted than my kids are. I don't know what I'm doing wrong..."

"*Wrong?* I think you're doing a fantastic job raising them."

"If I'm doing a fantastic job, I'd hate to see what failure looks like," he ruefully replied. "One of my kids has an emotional attachment to a rag and he refuses to talk. The other one acts like she's a middle-aged micromanager who won't *stop* talking or bossing her brother around."

His exaggerated assessment of his children would have made Meg laugh if he weren't so dejected. "You're being too hard on them, Simon," she said gently, touching his arm. "And too hard on *yourself.*"

But he was inconsolable. "I just don't know how to help them grow. I've tried everything. Time-outs. Rewards. Ignoring the issue... I've read all the parenting books and I've asked other parents for advice. I don't know what else to do. When we get back home, I think I might take them to a child therapist.

Maybe an expert will be able to offer some insights and strategies."

"I suppose professional counseling might be helpful," Meg said thoughtfully, even though she questioned whether that was necessary. "On the other hand, can I just point out some of the amazingly positive qualities your children have going for them? They're bright and imaginative and most of the time, they get along better than a lot of siblings do. They're also polite and helpful and kindhearted. Obviously, I'm no expert, but I think that some of their, uh, *quirks* might just be normal developmental phases."

"So you really think they'll outgrow them one day?"

"Yes, but I hope they don't outgrow them too soon." Meg playfully elbowed him. "I know you're concerned about your children, but I happen to love their unique personalities."

"So do I—most of the time." A grin crinkled the skin around Simon's eyes and mouth. "Anyway, thanks for listening to me."

"Sure. There's just one other thing I'd like to suggest?"

"Go ahead."

"Maybe *you're* the one who needs to get out and be with some other people. Other adults, I mean. Without your children." Meg couldn't quite believe she was prompting him to go out with Chloe, but it really did seem like he could benefit from it, and she knew Chloe would be thrilled. "Maybe take a few hours to see some of the sights you haven't visited already? Or spend a night on the town?"

Even before she'd finished her sentence, Simon exclaimed, "That's a *great* idea."

A little taken aback by how overtly enthusiastic he was about going out with Chloe alone, Meg completed her suggestion, saying, "If you let me know ahead of time, I'd be happy to watch Cody and Abigail for you, either at the cottage or at the inn. We're not booked up for most of the summer, so if you end up staying out late, they could always crash in one of the vacant rooms. If Chloe can't find a sitter, I'd even watch Maddie and Sonny, too."

Simon's brows narrowed. "Thanks, I'll keep that in mind. Whatcha reading?"

He changed the subject so abruptly that Meg wondered if her offer had offended him. Didn't he want her to watch the children at the inn for some reason? She was so confused by the sudden shift in topics that instead of answering his question aloud, she picked up the book that was lying face-down beside her and flipped it over to show him the title.

"Oh, yeah," he said knowingly. "I think that one is Gordon's best."

Meg's eyebrows shot up. "You've read Gordon's books?"

"All eight of them, yeah."

She was fascinated by this piece of information. "Did your dad keep copies of his books in his personal library, too?"

"Pfft," scoffed Simon, as if the notion was laughable. "Even if my father ever had a personal library—which he didn't—he wouldn't have included Gordon's mysteries in it."

"Why not? Didn't he like the genre?"

"Er, it was more that he didn't like Gordon."

It was obvious from the way Simon's ears were turning red that he was embarrassed. Meg figured he'd probably blurted out more than he'd intended to disclose. But now that he'd mentioned Bradley's relationship with Gordon, her curiosity was piqued and she figured it was fair to prod.

"They didn't get along?"

"Uh, not really." Simon was quiet a moment, before explaining, "My dad was a teenager when Gordon married Sarah. I think he resented that Gordon had replaced his 'real' father in his mother's life."

Interesting. Is that part of the reason why Bradley didn't claim his inheritance? Meg wondered, but she knew better than to pry any more than she already had. "So if you didn't get the books from your dad, where did you get them? My aunt Ruby said they've been out of print for a while."

"I found them in a box, along with some of my grandmother Sarah's other possessions, when I was preparing my mom's house for sale. My guess is that my dad probably inherited the stuff from his mother decades ago, and he didn't want it, but he felt too guilty to throw it out," Simon hypothesized. "So after he put everything in the attic, he forgot all about it."

That's consistent with how Bradley acted about the estate at Misty Point, too. He just ignored it, as if it didn't exist, Meg silently observed. "But *you* were interested in Gordon's books?"

Simon shrugged. "They were a good distraction from everything else that was going on in my life at that time. Especially the one you're reading now. That was his best seller, you know."

"No, I didn't. My great-aunt never mentioned it."

"I wouldn't have known, either, but there was a clipping from a newspaper interview in the copy I found in the attic. Apparently, he wrote that book the first summer he stayed on Dune Island." Simon rapped on the book with his knuckle. "He said it came easily to him—must've been the inspiring setting, because the story is *really* good. It had a twist I never saw coming."

Meg covered her ears. "Don't tell me any more—I just started reading it."

"Then I'll leave you alone so you can continue. I've got two minnows to catch." He pointed to his children, who'd been sloshing through the shallows together and now had wandered about twenty yards down the beach.

Watching Simon amble toward them, Meg mulled over what he'd said about his father and Gordon, as well as his sudden change in attitude after she'd offered to babysit the children at the inn. Were the two things related somehow?

Maybe his father was so resentful of Gordon that he made Simon promise that neither he nor his children would ever stay at the inn, just like he himself had always refused Aunt Ruby's invitations, Meg guessed.

Yet she couldn't quite believe that was true. Even if Bradley had resented Gordon when he was in high school, surely he'd grown out of it by the time he became an adult? *Whatever reason he had for disregarding his inheritance, it had to be something a lot more significant than saltwater or a teenage grudge,* Meg thought. *Too bad I can't just ask Simon to level with me about it.*

But she'd already dropped hints about the subject; once, on the evening Ruby had hosted his family for dinner, and a second time, when Meg had delivered peach pie to him at the cottage. On both occasions, he'd seemed very cagey, immediately clamming up the moment she'd expressed curiosity about why his father had never returned to Dune Island.

So she wasn't going to risk alienating Simon by asking him about it a third time. Not yet, anyway. In a while, he might open up a little more. Or maybe if they kept having these chats, she'd be able to gather enough information to figure it out for herself.

Who knows, Bradley's reasons for disregarding his inheritance might be irrelevant if I unravel Aunt Ruby's clue, first, especially if it proves the property legally belongs to her anyway, Meg thought. *Or at least I might be able to give Simon additional information to consider before selling his land.*

For the rest of the afternoon, however, she intended to focus on a different mystery. Meg rolled onto her stomach, flipped open Gordon's book, and continued reading from where she'd left off.

SIXTEEN

"How was I supposed to know he was going to park in the accessible space?" retorted Chloe when she returned to work and Meg repeated the conversation she'd had with Simon's visitor.

"I'm not *blaming* you, Chloe. I'm *supporting* you," Meg said, surprised that she sounded so offended. "I told Ava about him, too. And I only mentioned what he did to emphasize that you have the authority to require anyone who inappropriately uses that space to move. We need to keep that spot available for people who truly need it."

"No kidding. This isn't my first summer working here, you know." She mumbled something beneath her breath that sounded like, "But I'm glad it's going to be my last."

Was I being overbearing? Meg wondered as Chloe went into the kitchen and began banging pots and pans in the sink. She truly hadn't meant to be; on the contrary, she'd actually expected Chloe to laugh at her imitation of the man's entitled behavior. Meg recognized that she should probably go into the kitchen and have a heart-to-heart talk with Chloe to find out if something else was bothering her. But frankly, she was tired, and she didn't have the patience to indulge pan-banging and surly attitudes.

The previous evening, Meg had stayed up past 1:00 reading until she'd finished the seventh mystery that Gordon had written, *The Wife of Oscar Claiborne*. She wholly agreed with Simon; it was better than any of his previous books, the final twist was a shocker, and Meg loved the narrative voice. But the book had been so suspenseful that even after she'd turned the final page, she hadn't been able to sleep. So she'd spent another hour trying to shake the object from the ceramic lighthouse bookend, with no luck.

Now, bleary-eyed and irritable, she retreated to her room. *Maybe a nice hot shower will put me in a better frame of mind,* she thought as she began to make her bed.

The instant she flung back the rumpled duvet to straighten the sheet, Meg remembered she'd fallen asleep with the bookend beside her. It went sailing across the room, hit the wall, and fractured into jagged chunks that smashed into smaller splinters when they landed on the floor. The shiny item that had been inside the lighthouse skidded under the bed.

Before Meg could retrieve it, she heard footsteps clomping up the stairs, as well as down the hallway, followed by rapping on her door. Cringing, she opened it to see Chloe with two guests standing behind her.

"What did you break now?" asked Chloe.

At the same time, one of the guests inquired, "Are you okay?"

"I'm fine, thank you for checking though. Something, uh, fell off the bed."

Stealing a glance over Meg's shoulder, Chloe said, "Sounded more like you *threw* it against the wall."

"No, of course I didn't throw anything. It was an accident." Meg smiled weakly at the guests. "I'm very sorry if I frightened or disturbed you."

"It's okay, but you can understand why we needed to check."

"Yes, of course, and I appreciate it." She smiled again and they returned to their room down the hall, but Chloe shot her a disparaging look.

"I don't remember anything like this ever happening when Ruby was in charge," she muttered, before turning back toward the stairs. "And it definitely never happened *twice*."

More than a little mortified, Meg softly closed the door and dropped to her knees to recapture the object that had come to rest beneath the bed. She stretched her arm as far as she could and blindly danced her fingers over the dusty floor until she touched the cool, flat metal disc. *Not the right shape for a key, but too large to be a coin.* She slid it toward her, picked it up, and examined it beneath a ray of sunlight streaming across the hardwood floor.

On one side was an engraving of a bearded man wearing an eye patch. On the other side, the pun PIRATE'S ARR-CADE was superimposed across an engraving of two curved, criss-crossed swords. Meg immediately recognized the token from the popular arcade on the boardwalk in Lucinda's Hamlet. It was her brother's favorite hangout when he was a kid, but she was certain that Ruby had never stepped foot inside the tourist attraction.

Anyone could've deposited the token into the bookend. It could've been Maddie or Sonny, or a child of a guest, or even Meg's brother, almost thirty years ago. All she knew for sure was that it had absolutely nothing to do with Ruby's clue.

Meg was so discouraged that as soon as she stood up, she sunk back onto the unmade bed. She'd spent over a month trying to figure out what her great-aunt had meant, and what did she have to show for it? She'd shattered a mirror, broken a bookend, disturbed the guests, and upset Chloe. Meanwhile, every day Simon was getting closer and closer to finalizing the deal with the developer—as the recent visit from the smarmy, accessible-parking-space-hogging guy had indicated.

I'm running out of time, she realized as she stared at the ceiling. *Which means I'm running out of options. The only way I can tell Simon whatever secret Aunt Ruby wanted me to share with him is if I know what that secret is, first. And unfortunately, the only way I'm going to learn that secret is by talking to her about it again.*

Meg dreaded upsetting or frustrating her great-aunt by bringing up the subject, but she dreaded even more what would happen if she didn't.

Amazingly, it was Ruby, not Meg, who initiated the conversation about the secret. The next time they connected for a video call, Linda was at a hair appointment. The nursing assistant had set up the technology and then left the room, so that they could enjoy a brief, private chat.

After Meg inquired about how her great-aunt had been feeling and told her about some of the happenings at the inn, Ruby excitedly asked Meg a question. However, Meg couldn't understand it, so Ruby had to repeat herself several times until Meg realized one of the words she'd said was "lighthouse."

"Did I see the lighthouse?" guessed Meg. Ruby said no and asked a different question, so Meg guessed again. "Something about the sea?"

"No-oo." Ruby coughed several times, cleared her throat, and then distinctly enunciated, "Se-cret. Se-cret."

"Did I discover your secret?" she ventured to ask, and her great-aunt enthusiastically signaled a thumbs-up and said the word *yes*.

On one hand, Meg was relieved to confirm what she'd suspected all along; Ruby indeed had been cognizant of what she was saying when she'd uttered the mysterious phrase. On the other hand, knowing she was about to let her down, Meg could hardly bear to witness her great-aunt's hopeful excitement.

Hanging her head, she confessed, "I'm sorry, Aunt Ruby. I've been trying so hard to figure out what you meant when you told me that the lighthouse holds the key. I've looked everywhere for it, but I'm at a loss. Is the key I'm looking for a literal key?"

"No-oo. Book. Book."

"I should be looking for a book?" Meg was thrilled when Ruby indicated *yes*. "Which book? Is it one of the mysteries Gordon wrote?"

"No. Liiight-house," she painstakingly enunciated.

"The book is in the lighthouse?"

"No." Ruby erupted into a coughing fit as the nursing assistant re-entered the room.

"Can we just have a few more minutes, please?" Meg asked. "My great-aunt's trying to tell me something important and I can't quite understand it."

"I'm sorry, but I need to bring her to physical therapy now. I can schedule another call later, if you'd like?"

Before Meg could answer, Ruby made a loud, harsh sound. "Wff. Wff." At first, she thought her great-aunt was coughing again, but then she realized she was emphatically saying a word. She asked Ruby to repeat it, but she still couldn't understand her.

The nursing assistant chimed in. "Are you saying wolf?" she asked.

Ruby signaled yes. Looking into the camera, she said to Meg, "Read. Light. House. Wolf."

"Oh, I get it!" Meg couldn't believe she'd been so dense. "You want me to read *To the Lighthouse* by Virginia Woolf, right?"

Ruby gave her a big thumbs-up and reiterated, "Se-cret."

"I understand, Aunt Ruby, and I'll read it right away!" she promised.

Meg was so ecstatic to finally understand what her great-aunt had meant by "the lighthouse," that she downloaded the book and read the first three chapters before she'd even left the parking lot.

Meg recalled that when she'd read *To the Lighthouse* as a college student taking an English Lit class, she'd thoroughly enjoyed Woolf's elegant, descriptive prose and sharp wit. But this time, Meg couldn't fully appreciate either the writing style or the story because she kept questioning whether every other paragraph was a clue to her great-aunt's secret.

She highlighted so many passages and added so many annotations on her e-reader that by the time she'd finished reading it, Meg felt as if she herself had written a book. Yet despite all her notetaking—and even after she'd scrutinized the entire book a second time—she didn't feel any closer to a revelation than before she'd begun reading.

So when Simon asked her if she'd mind watching the children so he wouldn't have to take them with him to a meeting in Boston later in the week, she jumped at the chance. Even though she assumed he was meeting with the developer, which meant that Meg was indirectly making it more convenient for him to sell his property, she welcomed the opportunity to think about something other than Woolf's novel.

"What time do you need to leave?" she asked, glancing toward the back lawn where Cody and Abigail were turning somersaults.

"A little before noon. But, uh, before you give me a definite yes, I need to mention that I might be gone until around eight p.m."

"No problem."

"Are you sure?" He looked dubious. "I know it's a huge ask but I've already thought of something I can do to return the favor."

"You don't need to do anything for me," she said, even though she was curious to know what he had in mind.

"It's not actually for you, it's more for Ruby," he explained. "I haven't seen all the rooms in the inn, but it seems like she might benefit from a few additional safety accessories. Nothing major, just things like grip bars in the bathrooms, maybe a ramp instead of stairs leading to the sunken den. If she agrees to it, I can install them so they'll be ready for her when she returns."

Meg was touched by his thoughtfulness. "That's very kind of you to offer, but it's not necessary for you to pay me back with favors. I'm happy to watch Cody and Abigail for the day—and I'm honored that you asked me. I promise I'll take very good care of them."

"I know you will. I don't usually leave them with anyone for more than an hour or two, but you really have a way with them, especially with Abigail. She doesn't have any women in her life who connect with her quite the way you do, not even Beth's sisters," he said. "You'll make a great mom someday—if you want to be one, I mean."

Meg didn't respond because she heard a floorboard creak in the hallway. Was a guest hesitant to enter the room because they were talking? Simon must have heard the sound, too; he glanced toward the doorway and then he rubbed his hands together.

"Anyway, I'd better go outside and put an end to the tumbling act before Abigail and Cody get sick to their stomachs. Thanks again."

As soon as he left, Meg peeked around the corner of the entryway and saw Chloe duck into the laundry room. Was she the one Meg had heard in the hall? She went to ask if Chloe needed her help with something.

"Why would I need your help? I'm perfectly capable of handling the workload around here. Ruby never micromanages me."

"Whoa, I'm not trying to micromanage you. I heard someone in the hallway when I was talking to Simon, so I thought you might be waiting to speak to me, that's all."

"You mean you thought I was spying on you." She snickered, pulling a handful of fluffy white towels from the dryer and depositing them on the large flat table beside it. "As if I don't have anything better to do with my time than watch you two flirting with each other."

Is that why she's been so snarly to me lately—she thinks I'm interested in Simon? Even though it wasn't any of Chloe's business what they'd been discussing, Meg explained, "We weren't *flirting* with each other. Simon dropped in to ask me to babysit for Cody and Abigail."

"Your mouths might have been saying one thing, but your body language was saying something else. Not that I care." She snapped a towel in the air, shaking out a wrinkle, and then expertly laid it flat on the table and folded it in three quick movements.

Her body language is saying the opposite of her mouth, too, thought Meg. In a low voice, she remarked, "Listen, Chloe, it seems like I've offended you somehow—not just now, but on a couple other occasions lately. That's not my intention at all, so can we talk about whatever it is I'm doing that upsets you?"

"I'm *not* upset. I'm *busy*," she replied brusquely, her back turned.

"All right, I'll get out of your way then. But if you change your mind and want to talk, let me know."

As she turned and went upstairs to peruse *To the Lighthouse* again, Meg felt surprisingly calm. Not even Chloe's peevish mood could ruin the compliment she'd received from Simon.

You'll make a great mom someday, he'd said, which was so much better than the other remarks she'd heard regarding her so-called maternal instincts. Like, *it's too bad you never had children.* Or, *you're so good with kids, I'm surprised you don't have any of your own.* Although she recognized the remarks hadn't been intended to insult her, Meg resented the implication that her opportunity for motherhood was in the past.

Simon, on the other hand, had said that one little hopeful word that had always buoyed Meg: *someday.* And on top of that, he'd said them with as much hope and certainty as if he'd been talking to a twenty-year-old, instead of to someone twice that age.

SEVENTEEN

Thunderstorms were forecast for the afternoon Simon went to Boston, so Meg offered to watch the children at the inn instead of at the cottage.

"You might want to send their pajamas and toothbrushes with them," she suggested to him. "Just in case you're later than you expect. Like I said, if they get tired, we'll have a vacant room tomorrow evening. It only has one bed, but it's king-sized, so they'll have plenty of space to stretch out."

Meg also invited Chloe to bring Maddie and Sonny to work so they could play with Cody and Abigail.

"I'll have to think about it," said Chloe. She wasn't quite as irascible as she'd been the previous day, but her tone was still frosty, so Meg had to subdue a smile when she added, "My kids have been so grouchy lately that I wouldn't want their bad attitudes to affect everyone else."

"I'm sure the children will get along just fine. It's supposed to rain all day, so I have some crafts planned that they might enjoy."

Meg intended to help the children make hanging mobiles with painted shells and small pieces of driftwood. But as it turned out, Abigail showed up with a bookbag full of games and a suitcase stuffed with toy animals, as well as her and Cody's pajamas and toothbrushes.

"Looks like she's moving in," Meg joked quietly to Simon as his daughter unzipped her suitcase and showed Meg, Maddie, and Sonny its contents.

"You should've seen how much more she was going to bring until I instituted a two-bag limit," he whispered.

Abigail broke away from the group to hug her father. "You'd better go now, Dad, or you'll miss the ferry."

"All right, I can take a hint." He squatted down and kissed her cheek. "Can I have a hug from you, too, Cody?"

The little boy flew into his father's arms with such force he nearly knocked him over. He buried his face in Simon's neck for so long that Meg worried he was crying, and he wasn't going to let him leave. But just as suddenly, he let go and said, "Bye, Daddy. I love you."

The amazing thing was, he said it at a normal volume. His voice was astonishingly deep for such a wisp of a child, but maybe it only sounded froggy from underuse. Meg caught Simon's expression and he seemed as surprised as she was that Cody appeared to be outgrowing one of his "quirks" already.

He echoed his son's sentiment, replying, "I love you, too, Cody. Have fun and I'll see you soon."

After Meg served lunch, Chloe resumed working and the four children spent the afternoon constructing an elaborate, multi-room zoo with Abigail's toy animals. It stretched from the den to the living room. Since none of the other guests were downstairs, Meg didn't mind if the kids spread out, especially since they were playing so harmoniously.

It occurred to her that perhaps, like Simon, Chloe was also feeling the stress of being a single parent. So after the young housekeeper's shift was over, Meg told her that Sonny and Maddie could stay at the inn for a couple more hours, if Chloe had errands to run or things she wanted to do on her own. It was an offer that pleased everyone, including Meg, who relished teaching the children how to make the hanging mobiles after they'd grown tired of being zookeepers.

Chloe returned to pick up Sonny and Maddie shortly before it was time for Meg to start supper. She enlisted Abigail and Cody's help in preparing homemade mac 'n' cheese, and even though it had an oddly gummy texture, Abigail declared it to be the best mac 'n' cheese she'd ever tasted in her entire life. Cody, however, stirred his around on his plate without lifting the fork to his mouth.

"If you don't like it, Cody, I can make a sandwich for you," Meg offered.

Her mouth full, Abigail mumbled, "He likes it, but his tummy hurts because he's scared of those black clouds." She pointed at the window before asking her brother, "You want to go under the table like we did last time we ate here, Cody?"

He nodded, his hair flopping so low over his eyes that Meg was surprised he could even *see* the foreboding sky.

"I have another idea that might help you feel more comfortable," she suggested. "My aunt Ruby taught it to me when I was a little older than you are."

"Were you afraid of thunderstorms, too?" asked Abigail.

"No, but I was afraid of... other things happening." She lowered her voice to confide, "Sometimes, I still am."

Cody jerked his head backward to peer at her from beneath his bangs. "You *are?*" he whispered.

"Yes, sometimes. But when I was a little girl, Ms. Ruby told me if I was scared or very upset about something I couldn't change, I should put all my brainpower into reading a book. She said it would take my mind off whatever was bothering me, and she was right." As she repeated Ruby's advice, it occurred to Meg that her great-aunt had practiced this coping technique from the time she herself was a child, too.

"But Cody can't read and I can only read little and medium words, not the really big ones."

"That's okay. *I'll* read to you," said Meg as the landline rang. "You can each choose two books from the bookcase. I bet once we start reading, you'll forget all about the storm and by the time we finish the books, it'll be over."

As the children raced into the living room, Meg plucked the landline from its cradle. It was Simon, calling to say he couldn't board a return ferry until almost midnight. "I didn't know I needed a reservation for my car, so there's no space left until the last crossing of the evening."

"Oh, no! I didn't realize you weren't aware of how difficult it is to get to Dune Island during peak travel season, or I would've mentioned it. But that's fine. Like I said, Abigail and Cody can sack out on the king bed in Room 4. I'll hang out in there and read until you get back, so they won't be frightened if they wake up in a strange place," said Meg. "You might as well crash with them when you return, too. It'll be less disruptive than waking them up in the middle of the night. I'll even make pancakes for breakfast."

"You don't have to do that—although the kids would love it if you did. Honestly, I'd love, too. We haven't had pancakes for breakfast since, well... it was another lifetime ago." He cleared his throat and asked to speak to Abigail.

Meg could tell by her expression and comments that the little girl was thrilled when Simon told her they'd be staying at the inn overnight and having pancakes for breakfast. But after Abigail handed the phone to her brother, Cody's eyes brimmed with tears. The woebegone little boy didn't say anything into the mouthpiece; he just shook his head or nodded while his father spoke, until a flash of lightning sent him diving beneath a pillow on the sofa.

Meg picked up the phone he'd dropped and discreetly told

Simon, "I think Cody's done talking. There's a little T-storm passing through."

"Uh-oh." Simon groaned. "Now I *really* owe you one."

"Promises, promises," Meg teased lightly. *But if you insist on doing me a favor, there* is *something I'd like to discuss with you,* she thought as she disconnected the call.

She settled onto the sofa, allowing Cody to burrow his face against her legs and cover his head with a pillow, while Abigail turned the pages for her. By the time they were halfway through the second book, the storm had subsided enough that Cody was occasionally lifting the pillow to peek at the illustrations—and Meg realized she'd been so distracted by the children that for once she'd barely thought of Virginia Woolf or her lighthouse novel.

She had just begun to read the third book they'd selected, when she heard someone enter the inn from the front door. *Usually, people only come in that way if it's their first time visiting the inn,* she thought. *But we don't have any new arrivals checking in today.*

A deep voice down the hall called, "Hello?"

Because she was sandwiched between Cody and Abigail, Meg couldn't rise to see who it was, but a second later, the man stepped into the room. In the dim light, it took a moment for her to register who it was.

"*Josh?*" she uttered, managing to untangle herself from the children's limbs and stand up. "What are *you* doing here?"

"Good to see you, Meg. You look fantastic." He gave her a peck on the cheek, but she was too shocked to return his greeting.

"Are you Meg's brother?" Abigail asked. "The one who had a big fight with her when she was little but then you made up?"

"No, I'm her *fiancé* who had a big fight with her but then we made up," Josh answered, laughing. "Right, Meg?"

"Right." Even though she thought it was completely inappropriate for him to tell anyone he'd just met—*especially* a child—about their history, Meg didn't want Abigail to get the idea that she was holding a grudge against him. However, assuming the child knew what a *fiancé* was, she couldn't allow her to think that they were still engaged, either. So she introduced him, saying, "Abigail and Cody, this is Josh, he's an old friend from where I live in New Jersey. And Josh, these are my new neighbors, Abigail and Cody. They're spending the summer on Dune Island."

Cody was still clutching a pillow over his head, and he didn't emerge to greet Josh, but Abigail beamed at him. "We live in the little house in the back yard by the pine trees, but tonight we get to sleep at the inn because Daddy had to go to Boston."

"That sounds... cozy," said Josh, raising an eyebrow at Meg.

"Abigail, could you please read the rest of the book to your brother? I'm going to talk to Josh alone for a minute." Meg leaned down and whispered into her ear, telling her she could make up the story, if she couldn't pronounce the words.

As she led Josh into the kitchen, he asked, "What's up with the leash?"

"What leash?"

"The long blue thing tied around that boy's chest. Is he pretending he's a dog or something?"

"I told you his name is Cody, and it's not a leash, it's... never mind. The more pressing question is what's up with *you* coming here out of the blue?"

Josh looked quite pleased with himself. "I'm here to take you out."

"You're *what*?"

"The other day on the phone you sounded really stressed, which can't be good for your health. You said you haven't had any fun. So I'm here to take you out."

Meg's mouth fell open. "You're not serious!" she exclaimed,

and Josh scowled. Clearly, he was offended, but had he honestly expected her to be delighted by his unannounced arrival? He knew she was a planner; that kind of gesture wouldn't even have gone over well with her when they were together. But now that they'd broken up, it seemed incredibly presumptuous.

She tried to see the gesture from his perspective. "I appreciate that you were concerned about me, but as I told you, I was feeling agitated, or like the walls were closing in, because we were having a rainy streak. It was only a fleeting emotion." She shook her head, realizing that once again, Josh had given too much weight to her momentary carping. "Besides, I don't understand why you'd hop a plane—"

He cut in to clarify, "I didn't hop a plane. I drove here."

So this wasn't just an impulse? He was on the road for over three hundred miles, and it never occurred to him that this was a dumb idea and he should turn around? Meg repeated, "Either way, I don't understand why you didn't discuss visiting me before you made the trip."

His ears turned red and he admitted, "I didn't *just* come here because you sounded bummed out the other night. I also came because I have something kind of serious to discuss with you and I wanted to say it in person. I was afraid if I asked you if I could come, you'd tell me not to."

You got that right. Meg couldn't imagine what he wanted to say to her, but he suddenly appeared so anguished that her stomach dropped. "What's wrong? Are your parents okay? Did something happen to Patrick? Or with your job?"

"Everyone in my family is fine, and this isn't about my job." He glanced at the doorway. "But it's also not something I want to blurt out right now. Or right here. Can you call a sitter for the kids? I'll take you out and tell you over dinner."

"No," Meg refused. "Cody and Abigail's father left them in my care, not a sitter's, and I've already eaten." *Besides, even if something's troubling you that you need to discuss, you can't just show up here unannounced and expect me to change my plans at the snap of a finger*, she thought.

"That's okay," he said, as if she needed consolation. "I knew that trying to get you to be spontaneous would be a long shot. Are you free tomorrow morning?"

Ignoring the gibe about how unspontaneous she was, Meg answered, "As long as nothing comes up with the guests, I'll be free after ten thirty or eleven." She figured that would allow her plenty of time to make breakfast for Simon and the children. She pointedly added, "I'll give you the number for the landline, so you can call, first."

"Why would I call? Aren't I going to stay here?"

"*Here?* We don't have any vacancies, Josh." Meg supposed that technically, he could sleep on the sofa bed in the den, but she was too annoyed by his assumption to make the offer. "I can recommend accommodations in the area, but most of them require reservations, too. Especially at this time of year."

"You should see your face." Josh laughed, his mood brightening again. "I was only kidding about staying here. I don't have *that* much nerve, Meg. Besides, you know me, I'm a golf resort guy, not a quaint-little-inn kind of person. I've booked a suite at The Manor—apparently, there was a last-minute cancellation, so I even got a discount. See? Sometimes it pays to be impulsive."

After he left, Meg finished reading to the children. By then, the storm had completely passed, so Cody felt comfortable playing a board game at the kitchen table. Then Meg guided them as they brushed their teeth and put on their PJs. Three minutes after she tucked them into the bed upstairs, Cody had fallen asleep, but his sister happily chatted away for almost another hour. Meg sat at the foot of the bed, occasionally making comments, but she was distracted by thoughts of Josh.

Long after Abigail drifted off, Meg wondered what was so important that Josh had come all this way to discuss with her.

He said everyone in his family was fine... But he didn't say anything about himself. Could it be that he's *the one who's seriously ill?* she worried. It still seemed odd that he'd come all the way to Dune Island to tell her, but Meg figured, *Maybe because I've been so upset about Aunt Ruby's stroke, he wanted to gently break the news about his own health condition.*

She was so concerned that she would have used the inn phone to call him to ask, but she had left it downstairs where it wouldn't disturb the children if it happened to ring after hours. And since it was nearly midnight, she decided, *If I go get it and Abigail and Cody wake up to find me gone, they might get scared. They're my priority right now, not Josh. Whatever he's going to tell me will have to wait until tomorrow.*

Determined not to allow her concern for Josh to ruin her morning, Meg hummed as she ladled homemade buttermilk pancake mixture onto the electric griddle. Simon, Abigail, and Cody sat at the table nearby, respectively sipping coffee and orange juice.

"Me and Cody helped Meg make mac 'n' cheese last night. It was super-yummy," Abigail told her father. "What did you have for supper?"

"I got a takeout salad from the grocery store."

"Aww, that's too bad," Abigail sympathized, making Simon and Meg chuckle.

"Yeah, I missed out, but now I get to eat pancakes. They smell delicious, just like your grandmother used to make, don't they?" he asked his children.

"Yes." Abigail told Meg, "Grandma used to make me an A pancake and she made Cody a C pancake. Can you guess why?"

"Hmm, let me think." Meg tapped her chin. "Is that because A stands for *amazing* and C stands for *courageous*?"

"Noo." Cody audibly informed her, "It's because A stands for Abigail and C stands for Cody."

"Hey, Daddy, did you hear that? Cody can talk out loud *and* he can spell!" Abigail got up from her chair to give her brother a congratulatory hug. "Good boy, Cody!" she exclaimed, almost as if he were her well-trained pet.

Hiding a grin behind his coffee mug, Simon winked at Meg as she brought the platter of pancakes to the table and took a seat opposite him. But she couldn't have concealed her smile even if she'd tried.

"Why are you laughing, Meg?" asked Abigail.

"Because I'm so happy to be eating breakfast with you," she said, placing three small pancakes on the little girl's plate.

"Yeah. Too bad we can't live in the inn. Then we could eat breakfast here with you every day and I could make supper with you every night."

"Abigail, it's a special treat to be here this morning," Simon said softly. "Meg has been very generous already, so let's not get greedy."

"I'm not being greedy. I said I'd help her," reasoned Abigail.

"What would we eat for lunch?" Cody wanted to know.

"Daddy could make sandwiches."

"At our little house? Won't he live here with us?" Cody looked alarmed. "I don't want to live here without Daddy."

"Of course he'll live here with us," his sister reassured him. "After he marries Meg. Then she'll be our stepmother, but not the mean kind, like in *Cinderella*. She'll be—"

"Abigail," Simon sharply cut her off. "It's not polite to talk with your mouth full."

"Oops, I forgot," she said with her mouth full.

Simon's cheeks were flushed as he caught Meg's attention and apologetically rolled his eyes. She'd thought Abigail's proposed scenario was heartwarming, but she understood why Simon wouldn't want the children to get ideas about an ongoing relationship with her, when they'd be parting ways at the end of the summer. And she knew *she* shouldn't entertain any ideas like that, either.

So she gave him a casual shrug and mouthed, "It's fine."

Josh showed up early at 10:00, just as Meg finished cleaning and putting away the breakfast dishes. He was disappointed that she'd already eaten because he'd wanted to take her out to brunch.

How was I supposed to know that? she thought, trying not to feel annoyed. *And even if he'd told me, I wouldn't have changed my plans. But* not *because I'm not spontaneous—because I'd already made a commitment to Simon and the children.*

She offered to make him pancakes, which he sullenly refused. *Maybe he's nervous about whatever it is he's going to discuss with me.* Meg suggested they walk out to the lighthouse, where they'd have more privacy.

Josh frowned when she pointed out the bench was still damp from the rain, but since he didn't want to remove his shoes and socks to walk along the beach instead, he sat down beside her. They were quiet for several minutes, watching a speedboat slice through the water on its way to the harbor, a long, white plume in its wake.

Finally, he shifted to face her and cleared his throat. "By now, you've probably guessed what it is I want to talk to you about."

"Yes, I think I know." Trying to make the subject easier for him to discuss, she solemnly questioned, "Are you ill?"

"Ill?" An amused smirk crept over his lips. "I should've seen that coming. It's classic Meg—leaping to a gloom-and-doom conclusion."

"I don't appreciate you ridiculing me, Josh," Meg hotly informed him. "I was up half the night concerned about you."

"I'm *not* ridiculing you, I promise. I love how worried you get. It shows you care." He placed a hand on her knee but she pushed it away.

"Then what's so important that you'd come all the way here to discuss it?"

"*We* are." He licked his lips, suddenly straight-faced again. "I came here to discuss *us*."

"*Us?*" she echoed incredulously. "There is no *us*. Not anymore."

"There *should* be. We were great together and we still are," he insisted. "Think about it. You've never stayed this close to anyone after a breakup, and neither have I. That's because we've got this enduring connection, no matter what. It's because no one knows you as well as I do, and vice versa. I love you, Meg, and I still want to spend the rest of my life with you. If that means having kids, then I'm willing to have—or adopt— them with you."

Meg's eyes filled. She could see how earnest he was being, so vulnerable yet so misguided. "Josh, I still care about you deeply," she began. "I'm very grateful for how supportive you've been while I've been dealing with my aunt's stroke and every- thing here. And I'd like to continue a platonic relationship with you—as *friends*—but we don't have a future together as a married couple. Or as a couple, period."

"Didn't you hear what I just said? I've changed my mind. I'll agree to have children. If that's what it'll take for you to be my wife, then let's have a whole brood of them!"

Flabbergasted, Meg laughed. "We're talking about human beings, Josh, not a litter of puppies. And it's not a transaction. You can't *buy* my love."

"I'm not trying to *buy* anything! I'm trying to show you that I'm willing to make a sacrifice for you. I'm willing to give up what *I* want for what *you* want. Isn't that what love is all about —making sacrifices for other people?"

On the surface, his motivation may have sounded altruistic, but Meg pointed out, "You wouldn't be giving up what you wanted so I could have what I want. You'd be giving up what you wanted so you could have *me*."

"If we both end up happy, what difference would it make?"

"We *wouldn't* end up happy. And the difference would be that our children would have a father who never truly *wanted* them." A tear dripped down Meg's cheek as she thought, *And I'd rather give up any hope of ever having children than to intentionally put them through that.*

To his credit, Josh didn't deny that she was right or try to pretend he really *did* want children. He stared out at the ocean, and they sat in silence for several long minutes. Meg noticed the sky was streaked with a vapor trail of a plane, its passengers already far from here and she wished she could be far from here, too.

Still peering toward the horizon, Josh shook his head. "I don't understand why you're so bent on having children."

No, you don't *understand*, Meg realized. *You say you know me so well—and it's true that you know things* about *me. You know about my behaviors and my personality. But that's not the same as* understanding *me. It's not the same as understanding what's in my heart.*

When she didn't answer, Josh turned and leaned toward her with tears in his eyes. "I just don't get it," he repeated. "You mean the world to me. You and me as husband and wife, that's all the family I need. Aren't I enough for you, Meg-aret?"

Digging her fingernails into her palms, she willed herself not to weep for him. Two or three months ago, Meg might have responded differently. But after nearly half a year—and after such a tumultuous yet meaningful summer on Dune Island— she had completely worked through her grief about their breakup. While she valued Josh's continued friendship, she no longer had any romantic feelings toward him.

She answered carefully, "I don't think it's a matter of you not being enough for me, Josh. I think it's a matter of us not being right for each other."

To her surprise, he lurched back and snickered. "I knew it. You're already seeing someone. It's the divorcee, isn't it?"

"*Who?*"

"The guy who's staying in the cottage with his weird kids."

Annoyed, Meg quickly set him straight. "For your information, Simon's not a divorcee, he's a widower. And his children are very sweet."

"Yeah, it's obvious that you've fallen for them, too. A ready-made family, how convenient. You might want to think twice about getting together with a grieving husband, though. I know you, and you'll get your heart involved, but for him, it might just be a rebound relationship. Or free childcare." Josh stood up and stormed off, calling over his shoulder, "Good luck with that."

EIGHTEEN

When Chloe had alleged that Meg was flirting with Simon, Meg had taken it with a grain of salt. After all, Chloe herself was interested in him, so it was possible she was projecting her feelings onto Meg, or imagining competition for Simon's affection when there wasn't any. Likewise, when Josh claimed it was obvious that Meg had fallen for Simon, she easily dismissed it, since Josh had never even seen her interact with him.

But he *had* seen her interact with his children, and Meg couldn't deny that she had, in a sense, fallen for *them*. They'd grown attached to her, too. And considering Abigail's wish, however fanciful it may have been, to live in the inn with her as their stepmother, Meg decided it would be better for everyone if she put some distance between her and Simon's family.

She tried to take her great-aunt's advice and immerse herself in reading, as a distraction from the things that were troubling her—including Josh's ill-timed proposal that had turned so cruel and sour. However, after being completely captivated by the seventh book Gordon had written, Meg found that his eighth and final book fell flat, and it just didn't hold her attention.

Her time with Simon and his family had in itself been a distraction from Ruby's secret, whatever it might be, and from her latest "lighthouse" research. Maybe it was time to get back to that? But reading *To the Lighthouse* made her feel worse instead of better, since it made her think about the upcoming sale of Simon's land.

Meg dreaded telling Ruby she'd read the book several times and she still couldn't figure out which part of it was related to her great-aunt's secret. So she'd postponed calling her for days as she compiled a list of yes-and-no questions she could pose, based on passages or characters in the book she figured might be significant.

However, before she had completed the list, Meg received a call from Ruby's cousin, Linda.

"Hi, hon. First off, don't be alarmed that you're hearing from me," she said, but her reassurance had the opposite effect on Meg. "I hesitated to call because I know you're so busy managing everything at the inn. But I promised I'd let you know if there were any changes in Ruby's health, no matter how minor."

"I'm glad you called, but what's wrong with Aunt Ruby?"

"She's had a little cough for a while now, which the staff thought was seasonal allergies—and that still might be all it is. But more recently, there's been a respiratory virus going around in Ruby's wing of the rehab center..."

"She already contracted that virus in the spring, so isn't she immune?"

"Unfortunately, it's a different strain, I think? I'm not too savvy about medical jargon, but the staff offered to discuss her health and care plan in detail with you if that would be helpful. The long and short of it is that last night she came down with a low-grade fever. And she's been fatigued, too, although it's diffi-cult to say if that's from all the exercise and physical therapy she's been getting or because her immune system is trying to fight off the virus."

Even after Linda repeatedly reassured her that Ruby's symptoms were mild, Meg's anxious heart was thrumming in her ears. She asked Linda to take the phone to Ruby so she could hear her great-aunt's voice and say a few encouraging words to her.

"She dozed off just before I left the room," Linda said. "But if you'd like, I can try to wake her."

"No, that's okay, she needs her rest. Would you give her my love and tell her I'll call soon?"

"Yes, I will. In the meantime, try to rest assured that she's in good hands here, just like Ruby rests assured that the inn is in good hands with you there," Linda reminded Meg, as she'd done on so many other occasions.

But after they'd hung up, Meg brooded, *Aunt Ruby is counting on me, and I feel like I'm letting her down. She's probably disappointed that I haven't called to tell her I've figured out her secret.*

Now what? Meg couldn't very well drill her great-aunt about lines or passages from *To the Lighthouse*, if Ruby was potentially battling a virus, in addition to recovering from a stroke. *The last thing she needs is to have to expend her precious energy playing guessing games with me.*

Deciding that she'd just have to try harder to figure out the connection between Woolf's book and her great-aunt's secret, Meg reluctantly retrieved her e-reader and began reading *To the Lighthouse* again.

The opening of the novel included a description of six-year-old James Ramsay's intense resentment of his father. The reason for the little boy's fierce ill will was that he'd keenly hoped to visit the lighthouse on a nearby island, but his father predicted that inclement weather would prevent them from making the trip.

James's extreme emotional response reminds me of Bradley's bitterness toward Gordon, Meg thought, her mind drifting to what Simon had told her about his dad. While she could understand why the young character in the book had felt so upset, she thought that Bradley's abiding disdain for Gordon seemed over-the-top.

It's hard to believe that Bradley never got over his resentment toward his stepfather. Especially because Aunt Ruby always said Gordon was completely devoted to caring for Sarah when she had cancer. Even if Bradley initially resented Gordon for replacing his father, it seems like when he got older he would've felt relieved or grateful that his mother had married such a kind and loving man...

The more Meg thought about it, the more she suspected that there must have been a deeper reason for Bradley's dislike of his stepfather—just as there must have been a deeper reason why he never returned to Misty Point.

Once again, Betty's theory ran through her mind. *There's no way that Gordon was Ruby's father,* she thought. Yet even as she resisted the idea, a niggling doubt still kept Meg from rejecting it altogether. She recognized that eliminating the possibility—like she'd done with the key from the coffee canister—would allow her to focus on more plausible explanations.

However, even if Ruby were in terrific health, Meg couldn't imagine asking her such a ludicrous question about Gordon, and she especially didn't want to mention it now that Ruby was ill.

I guess I'll have to talk to Simon about it, she decided. *Who knows, maybe he'll think Betty's theory is so laughable that he'll end up telling me the* real *reason his dad didn't like Gordon, and why he never returned to Dune Island.*

Meg anticipated the conversation would be awkward, and if the past was any indicator, Simon wouldn't be open to discussing his father with her. But the way Meg saw it, she didn't have any other option. *Besides, he said he owes me a favor, so I'm going to take him at his word and ask him to do the one thing that would help me the most.*

The following evening at twilight, when she saw Simon sitting alone outside the cottage in his zero gravity chair, Meg traipsed through the back yard to speak to him.

"Hi, Meg." He rose from his seat as she approached, a courtesy Meg had always found charming in men. "How are you doing?"

"All right, thanks. Do you have a few minutes to chat?"

"Sure." He motioned for her to have a seat in Abigail's chair beside him. "We haven't seen you around for a few days. I was starting to worry that watching Cody and Abigail the other evening had taken a toll on you."

"No, not at all! I loved every minute of it," Meg exclaimed. "I've just been busy and, honestly, a little preoccupied. I don't know if Abigail mentioned it to you, but my ex-fiancé showed up here unexpectedly that night. We had a long talk the next day, which was... difficult."

"Ugh." Giving her a sympathetic look she could barely see in the waning light, Simon asked, "Did his presence open up old wounds?"

"It's more like it dashed hopes—his, not mine. It's good to have closure, but it was still painful for both of us," she said. "Thanks for asking."

They were silent a while, listening to the fading strains of birdsong and watching the beam of the lighthouse grow brighter against the darkening sky. Then Meg told Simon about Ruby's fever and the virus circulating at the rehab center.

"I'm sorry to hear that. Sounds like the staff is being vigilant, though," he comforted her.

"You're right, but her recovery has been such a long, hard

road already. I hope she doesn't have to deal with another full-blown respiratory virus." Meg paused. It would be manipulative to play on Simon's sympathy for Ruby, yet this was the perfect segue for delving into the topic she'd come to discuss with him. She forged ahead. "You know, the evening my great-aunt had the stroke, she had just begun telling me a story—a secret—that she'd never told anyone. But she felt it was very important to share it with me, and she intended to share it with you later, too."

"Me?" He leaned forward. "What was the story about?"

Encouraged that Simon was curious, Meg continued, "I don't know, because I had to call the ambulance before she could tell it to me, although she mentioned it indirectly involved your grandmother Sarah."

"Hmm." Crossing his arms, he pushed himself back against the chair again. Why did it seem that whenever Sarah, Gordon, or Bradley were mentioned, Simon withdrew from the conversation?

Meg pressed on, hurrying before he shut down altogether. "I got the sense that what she wanted to say was upsetting for her to admit, but it was vital that she shared it with us. She even brought up the subject on the phone the other day, although her communication abilities are very limited. I've been trying to piece together parts of her past, regarding the inn and her relationship with Gordon and Sarah, but I'm not having much luck."

Meg paused again, reluctant to give voice to Betty's farfetched idea. Rather than planting the possibility in Simon's head if he wasn't already aware of it, she decided to ask him what *he* may have heard. "I'm very frustrated that I couldn't understand what my great-aunt was trying to tell me, and I think she's very frustrated, too. I hate to twist your arm, but it would mean the world to me if you could share whether your dad ever told you he'd heard rumors—no matter how preposterous they may seem—about my great-aunt. Or about the reason why Gordon supposedly gave her the house."

Simon was quiet for a long moment and when he did speak, he evasively hemmed and hawed. "Not exactly. He didn't mention any rumors."

"Then what *did* he mention?" pushed Meg. When he shrugged and remained silent, she pleaded, "I'd really like to hear it, Simon, no matter what it is. Chances are, I've already heard the same thing from someone else, anyway."

Simon gave a sigh. He was clearly reluctant, but Meg appreciated that he carried on. "My dad said that he, um, he suspected that, uh, Gordon and Ruby's relationship was closer than they let on. I mean, no one told him that, but personally, he felt he had reason to believe that they were, uh..." Simon seemed almost embarrassed to finish the sentence, so Meg finished it for him.

"Father and daughter," she said.

At the same moment, Simon mumbled, "Having an affair."

"What?" she yapped. "An *affair*? Are you kidding me?"

"I'm sorry. I'm really sorry, so sorry," he babbled. "I thought that's what you were asking me. I didn't know anyone ever thought they were father and daughter."

"Yeah, that's obvious," said Meg sarcastically, reeling from Simon's claim. "What in the world makes you think they were having an affair?"

"I didn't say *I* thought it. I said my dad did."

"But *why*?" she snapped. "*Why* did he think that?"

Simon leaned forward, his elbows on his knees, and raked a hand through his hair before sitting up straight again. "Listen, I shouldn't have said anything—and I never would have, if you hadn't asked me about it, so please, try to forget I ever opened my big mouth."

"No way!" exclaimed Meg. "I'm sorry, Simon, I know I pushed you—but I can't simply forget about what you just said.

For my aunt Ruby's sake, I deserve an explanation of why your father would tell you something like that."

"But it's not going to serve any purpose."

Meg wouldn't back down. "I want to know," she emphatically repeated.

Simon rubbed his forehead and gave a loud huff of resignation. "Okay, fine. But remember, this is my father's account of what happened. I'm only the messenger," he cautioned her. "My dad told me that during the summer of 1978—the first year Sarah and Gordon came here—he was traveling in Europe with some of his college pals. But he was concerned about his mother's health, and he flew back to the U.S. for her birthday. He wanted to surprise her, so he didn't let anyone know he was coming. He caught the last ferry of the evening from Hyannis, planning to hitchhike or take a cab to Misty Point. He didn't know the island was so sparsely populated and there wasn't any evening public transportation back then, so, long story short, he ended up walking."

He's stalling, thought Meg, when Simon paused and glanced toward the cottage door, as if maybe he'd heard one of the children. She impatiently prompted him, "Keep going."

"It was past one a.m. when my father arrived here. The house was dark, and he thought everyone was asleep but then he noticed a light on in the cottage, where his mother had told him Gordon liked to work on his books. He was about to go greet him when a young woman came out of the cottage and hurried toward the house."

Meg swallowed. "My aunt Ruby?"

"Yes, that's who he thought it was."

"But he wasn't *positive* it was her?"

"Not at first, no. Like I said, it was dark, and he'd only met Ruby briefly in passing at the apartment in Pittsburgh. But he was aware that she was staying at Misty Point to take care of Sarah, so he put two and two together."

Simon slapped at an insect on his calf, and then meticulously wiped his palm and fingers with the hem of his T-shirt. He obviously dreaded saying what happened next, and Meg dreaded hearing it, too. She waited in silence for him to begin again.

"My father hid in the den until Ruby tiptoed upstairs to her bedroom. Then he went to confront Gordon, who admitted it was Ruby who'd been in the cottage, but he denied there was anything illicit going on between him and your great-aunt. He said she knew he was working late on his book, so she'd just popped in to ask if he wanted coffee."

"That sounds plausible to me," asserted Meg.

"Yeah, but according to my father, Gordon acted so nervous and strangely that my dad suspected he was lying. He said something to the effect of, 'If you're telling the truth, then if I go ask Ruby why she was out here with you, she'll say the same thing you just said. And you won't care if I tell my mother that I saw Ruby coming out of the cottage in the middle of the night, either.'"

Meg briefly squeezed her eyes shut, anticipating Simon's response to her next question. Then she opened them and asked, "How did Gordon respond?"

"He begged my father not to say anything to Sarah or Ruby —even though Gordon still swore that it wasn't what it looked like, and there wasn't anything going on between him and your great-aunt. He pleaded with my father to take his word for it, but my father didn't believe he was telling the truth. Keep in mind, my dad wasn't even twenty yet, and he didn't get along with his stepfather anyway. So when he came to the island to surprise his mother and he saw what he saw..."

"Did your father ever tell Sarah what he suspected?"

"No, he didn't. He claimed he was afraid it would literally kill her."

"What about my great-aunt? Did he ever confront her?"

"No. He was so disgusted by—" Simon abruptly stopped talking, but it was too late; Meg had gotten the gist. "He told me he hardly spoke to her the entire weekend and he never saw her again after that."

"That's too bad, because if he had gotten to know her at all, he might have discovered she wasn't the kind of woman he thought she was," Meg retorted, unable to hold her tongue any longer. "I realize it was a long time ago, and people change, but I know my great-aunt's character."

Even if I don't know everything about her, she thought. *She might not have told me what her husband was really like, or the difficulties his gambling addiction created. But keeping her own pain private is completely different from hiding a secret about having an affair with Gordon and betraying Sarah.*

"I can't imagine her ever having an affair with a married man," she insisted aloud. "*Especially* not with the husband of someone she considered a close friend, *especially* not when she was her friends' guest, and *especially* not when her friend was going through cancer treatment. That's just not in her nature. My aunt Ruby was devoted to *caring* for Sarah when she was at her most vulnerable—she never would've hurt her like that."

"I'm sorry that I've upset you, Meg," Simon said softly. "But you insisted I tell you my father's version of events."

He was right. Meg had pulled it out of him. But that didn't change how she felt about the revelation. "Like you said, your dad was only a college student at the time, and most people aren't very mature at that age," Meg pointed out. "You've mentioned that he resented Gordon for replacing his biological father in Sarah's life. If your dad was still holding a grudge against Gordon, it could have affected how he perceived whatever happened that summer."

"That's possible, I guess, although if that were the case, it seems like he eventually would've outgrown his grudge, but he never did. Even after Gordon died, my father was still so angry that he chose to forfeit the opportunity to vacation at one of the most beautiful places in the world, rather than to acknowledge a gift from his stepfather. And he was certain that the fact that Gordon left the summer house to Ruby proved that they'd been having an affair."

"To me, that only proves what my great-aunt has always claimed is true—Gordon left the house to her because he was so grateful that she'd taken care of Sarah when she had cancer," argued Meg. Simon fidgeted, as if he were hiding something, so she prodded, "What is it you're not telling me?"

He sighed and then admitted, "My father didn't think it was believable that Gordon would have given Ruby such a big gift simply because she helped care for Sarah for one summer."

It sounds like Bradley never even spent any time with Aunt Ruby, and he never saw first-hand how much she helped Sarah, Meg thought sadly. *Which is why he couldn't understand Gordon's gratitude and generosity toward Aunt Ruby.*

Instead of sharing that thought, she asked Simon, "Do you believe your father's account of what happened between Gordon and my great-aunt?"

"I don't think I should comment on something that occurred before I was even born."

"I'll take that as a *yes*. You *do* believe they had an affair."

"Hey—don't put words in my mouth," Simon sharply objected. "I honestly don't know what to think. I find it hard to believe that my father could walk away from his inheritance for no good reason. He was very, *very* angry about what he thought happened here. So do I think *he* earnestly believed Gordon and Ruby were having an affair? Yes, absolutely. But that's not the same thing as saying *I* believe it, too."

Meg simply looked back at him, hardly able to see his expression in the pale light. She understood that Simon himself couldn't have ever really been sure about what had happened. But knowing her great-aunt, and remembering the way she spoke about Gordon and Sarah with such fondness, Meg was absolutely certain that what Bradley believed was impossible.

Simon tilted his chin toward the sky and massaged the nape of his neck for a moment. Then he dropped his hands and turned toward her. "I've never had a compelling reason to doubt my father's account of what happened that summer. But now that I've met Ruby, well, she doesn't seem like the kind of person who would... do what my father suspected her of doing. I mean, if she'd had an affair with Gordon, I'd expect her to be ashamed or embarrassed to meet me, because I'm Sarah's grandson. But that wasn't the impression I got of her at all. So, yeah, it does make me wonder if my father's perspective was skewed. I just don't think it matters anymore."

His own reasons for doubting Bradley's account were almost exactly the same as Meg's. It simply didn't align with Ruby's character: even though the alleged affair had been decades ago, Ruby couldn't have changed who she fundamentally was. "My great-aunt's reputation matters to *her*," said Meg. "And it matters to *me*."

"Yes, of course it does," he hurriedly acknowledged. "I only meant that my father's gone now, and so are Sarah and Gordon. So it's not as if anyone can set the record straight with any of them."

But Meg had another thought. "What about setting the record straight with *you*? Because if you decided you don't want to own property next to my great-aunt just because of some fabrication your father told you, then—"

Simon broke in, saying, "My father's opinion had no bearing on my decision to sell the property."

"Are you sure about that?" challenged Meg. "You may feel more sympathetic toward my aunt Ruby now because she's had a stroke, or because you've gotten to know me. But really, you seemed very cold when you first met her." She had never wanted to bring this up with Simon previously, and she'd always assumed his initial aloofness was because of his inten-sion to sell the property. But now, she knew that Simon had been thinking the worst of her aunt. "You hardly even glanced her way or acknowledged the memories she shared about Sarah and Gordon. And when I brought you the peach pie she'd made, you acted as if I were handing you a rotten fish—"

"Meg, that's not—" he interrupted again, but suddenly all the pieces seemed to be clicking into place, and she spoke over him.

"Why else would you have acted that way when you'd barely met her, unless you'd been influenced by your father's disparaging opinion of her and Gordon?" Meg clapped her hands on top of her head when another possibility occurred to her. "Is that why you decided not to keep your property before you'd even visited Dune Island? Was your father so vindictive that he convinced you to sell it to a developer because he knew a resort would put my great-aunt out of business and—"

"No!" Simon barked so loudly that she expected the chil-dren to wake up and come running outside at any second. "My father and I had hardly said ten words to each other since he divorced my mother and married someone half his age. So his opinion had nothing to do with the reason I'm selling the prop-erty to a developer. As I've already told you, I made that deci-sion based purely on financial reasons—not that I should have to explain myself to you."

His vehemence surprised Meg and she realized that in her desire to defend Ruby, she'd overstepped her boundaries. "That's true, you don't need to explain yourself to me," she quietly acknowledged. Their conversation had taken so many bad turns that she didn't know how to get it back on the right track again and she felt too emotionally depleted to try. Standing up, she said, "I'd better get back to the inn. Good night, Simon."

He hopped to his feet, too. "Listen, Meg, I can't emphasize

enough how sorry I am that I... put my foot in my mouth like that."

"No need to apologize again. Or at all. I asked you to share whatever your father had told you, and that's exactly what you did." She turned and hurried through the dark toward the inn.

Usually, Meg allowed the flash of the lighthouse and the sound of the sea to lull her to sleep, but tonight, she felt like retreating into a shell, and she drew all the shades before she crawled into bed.

It's unfair that Bradley refused to believe Gordon when he insisted he wasn't having an affair with Aunt Ruby, she brooded. *There could've been a dozen reasons why she was in the cottage late at night. Like, maybe she had a private matter to discuss with Gordon. She may have been worried about Sarah's health, and she didn't want Sarah to know. Or maybe Gordon was the one who was worried, and Aunt Ruby was listening to his concerns. It might have even been that Aunt Ruby was confiding in Gordon about her husband's gambling addiction...*

Although Meg had no way of knowing exactly what her great-aunt's reason was for a late-night meeting with Gordon, she was certain it was completely innocent. *I thought Betty's theory about why she inherited the house was absurd, but Bradley's speculation is even more outrageous.*

It was also offensive. Even though Meg recognized that she'd pressured Simon into telling her what Bradley had said, she was finding it difficult to separate the message from the messenger.

And as she pulled the sheet up to her ears, it occurred to Meg that after hoping for weeks that Simon would tell her the real reason why Bradley hadn't ever returned to Dune Island, now that she finally knew what it was, she just wished she could unhear it.

NINETEEN

Jolted awake by a knock on her door, Meg momentarily couldn't figure out where she was. The clock read: 10:39. She hadn't dozed off until sunrise, but she was surprised she'd slept in so late.

"Just a minute." She hopped out of bed and pulled on her bathrobe before opening the door.

"Sorry for disturbing your beauty sleep," said Chloe, holding out the cordless phone. "But it's Ruby's cousin, so I figured you'd want to talk to her."

"Thanks." Meg took the phone, hardly taking the time to close the door before breathlessly asking, "Linda? Is something wrong with Aunt Ruby?"

"She's okay now, but her fever spiked overnight, and this morning she had trouble breathing. She was just transported to the hospital," answered Linda. "Her nurse is here with me, and I'm going to let her talk to you so she can answer all your questions."

The nurse assured Meg that although Ruby was receiving supplemental oxygen, her condition was stable. "However, her chest X-rays indicate she has pneumonia. Given her recent health history, we want to keep her in the hospital until her *sats* —her oxygen saturation—comes up a bit."

"How long will that be?"

"It's difficult to say. A day or two, it might be longer."

"But if she's in the hospital, isn't that going to set her back in regard to her rehab from the stroke?"

"It might, a little. But clearing up her lungs is our priority right now. We need to keep her off a ventilator."

Meg gulped. "A ventilator is a possibility?"

"It's a possibility, but as I said, we're going to do everything we can to avoid that."

After the nurse had answered the rest of her questions, Meg spoke briefly to Linda again. "How serious do you think Aunt Ruby's condition is? Should I come to Pennsylvania?"

"Oh, honey, I don't think that's necessary. You wouldn't be able to do anything here that the doctors and nurses and I can't do for her. But you're the only one there who can manage the inn."

"I could ask her friend, Alice, if she'd take over for me for a few days," said Meg, even though she realized it might be a challenge for Alice to simultaneously look after her grandchildren.

"Well, it's up to you, of course. Ruby's sleeping, but when she wakes, I can try to ask her what she thinks about the idea, if you'd like me to?"

"Please don't do that," Meg said. "I already know her answer. She'd say she wants me to stay here and enjoy walking on the beach."

"Well, then, that's what I'd suggest you should do for now, too," Linda encouraged her. "At least wait to see how she's doing in a few days."

"All right," Meg reluctantly agreed. "But if she gets worse, no matter what time of day or night it is, you'll call me, won't you?"

"Of course. And regardless of any changes in her condition,

I'll call you every afternoon and every evening with an update. So don't panic when you see my name on the caller ID."

"I won't—but only because Aunt Ruby doesn't have caller ID," Meg replied with a feeble chuckle.

Yet almost as soon as she hung up, tears spilled from her eyes and ran down her cheeks. Meg dropped backward onto the bed. *Poor Aunt Ruby*, she cried to herself. *First, the respiratory virus, then the stroke, and now this. She's been fighting so hard to recover, but how much more can she endure?*

Meg rolled onto her side and waffled about whether she should go visit her great-aunt now, despite what Linda had said. *She kept assuring me that Aunt Ruby was in excellent care at the rehab center but look what happened there.* Rationally, she recognized that it wasn't the center's fault that Ruby was ill; she could've contracted pneumonia anywhere. But she wished her great-aunt weren't so far away; then the decision whether to visit her or not would be a no-brainer.

Too distraught to get out of bed, Meg must have lain there half an hour, mentally reviewing the pros and cons of going to Pennsylvania to visit Ruby, when a timid tapping on the door interrupted her fretting.

Go away. Meg figured if a guest needed something, they could ask Chloe for it. She was quiet, and the person left, but half an hour later, someone knocked again.

"Meg? It's me, Chloe. Can I come in?"

She groaned and sat up, "Yeah."

Chloe entered, carrying a tray of coffee and toast with raspberry jam. "You never stay in your room this long, so I thought you might need caffeine."

The small gesture was so sweet and so unexpected coming from Chloe that Meg burst into tears. Chloe carefully set the tray on the nightstand, sat down beside Meg, and wrapped her arm around her. "What's wrong? Is it Ruby?"

Meg nodded into Chloe's shoulder, but she was weeping

too hard to speak. Mostly, she was crying because of the uncertainty of her great-aunt's health, but she was also weeping over the uncertainty of Ruby's business, and because of the hurtful conversation she'd had with Simon the previous day. All the pent-up stress came pouring out. Chloe patiently rubbed her arm, letting her cry her eyes dry.

Then she reached for the coffee and handed it to Meg. "It might be cold by now."

After taking a few sips, Meg said as factually as she could, "My aunt Ruby was hospitalized last night. She has pneumonia and she's receiving oxygen because her oxygen levels were low, and she was having trouble breathing."

"Is that all?" Chloe exclaimed. "From the way you were crying, I thought she'd passed on!"

Meg jerked back in surprise at Chloe's frankness, nearly spilling her coffee. "I'm sorry if I alarmed you... but I'm just so worried. If Aunt Ruby's oxygen drops too low, they're going to have to put her on a ventilator."

"But she's *not* on a ventilator right now and she's in the hospital, which is the best place for her because they'll monitor her 24/7." Chloe picked up the plate of toast and offered Meg a slice before taking a piece for herself. "Besides, a ventilator isn't a death sentence, you know. My great-grandma needed to be put on a ventilator when she was ninety-two, and she made a complete recovery. Lived to be ninety-eight."

"That's impressive," said Meg. "But my great-aunt is still recovering from her stroke, as well as a virus, so her immune system is already maxed out."

"Yeah, but you know Ruby. She's a very strong person. It might not seem that way because half the time she's in la-la land, but she's a lot tougher than she appears," said Chloe, munching the crust of her toast. "She'd have to be tough to run this inn by herself all these years."

On the surface, her description of Ruby wasn't entirely flattering, yet Meg realized that Chloe had accurately captured her character. However, there was one thing she'd gotten wrong. "She hasn't run the inn all by herself. She's had help from groundskeepers and housekeepers, including you. I can't tell you how many times she's mentioned that she didn't think she could keep the inn running if it weren't for you helping her in her 'dotage,' as she puts it."

"That's true," Chloe unabashedly agreed. "I mean, she's strong enough to recover from pneumonia and a stroke, but I think she's ready to retire as an innkeeper. Sometimes, I get the feeling she's been keeping the inn open just so I'll have a summer job. That's one of the reasons I'm glad there's a resort going up next door. It'll probably put Ruby out of business, so it'll force her into retirement, which might be the best thing for her."

"She can't *afford* to retire and shut down the inn, not if she's going to continue living at Misty Point," objected Meg.

Chloe shrugged. "She might have to move." She stood up. "I've got two more rooms to clean before I leave. Can you bring that tray down when you're done?"

"Yes. Thanks for checking in on me, Chloe."

"No problem." With one hand on the doorknob and her back turned, she added, "I know Ruby's your great-aunt, but she's very special to me, too... Could you tell her I hope she's better soon? And that I'm trying to keep everything in tiptop shape here at the inn, but I miss her. A *lot*."

"Sure." Now Meg understood why Chloe may have been so irritable lately; she was trying to do Ruby proud—and she'd felt as if Meg had kept interfering, either by making messes, or by taking over.

After Chloe left the room, Meg walked over to open the shades, but the light was so bright she quickly closed them again. *I don't have it in me to face a sunny day*, she thought, climbing back into bed. She couldn't face reading *To the Light-*

house again, either, and she didn't want to think about the myriad of worries swirling in her mind. All she wanted to do was shut her eyes and go back to sleep.

For the next few days, Meg barely managed to greet the new guests and say goodbye to the departing ones, and to generally tidy the common areas each evening. But otherwise, she kept a low profile around the inn. She didn't go to the beach, either, since she didn't want to bump into Simon and the children. Mostly, she hung out in her bedroom as she waited for Linda's updates. Each time she called, she said that while Ruby's condition hadn't worsened, it hadn't improved, either.

Maybe Chloe's right. Maybe it's time for Aunt Ruby to retire, she thought, recalling that her mother had made a similar suggestion before Ruby had been hospitalized. At the time, Meg hadn't been willing to consider the possibility. But now that Ruby had suffered another setback, Meg had to accept the likelihood that her great-aunt might not be able to return to her innkeeping duties; she might not even be able to live alone after she completed rehab. Yet Meg refused to give up the hope that Ruby could continue to reside in her beloved Misty Point home.

Aunt Ruby's insurance might cover a visiting nurse. And Linda mentioned she's been very lonely, so maybe she'd be willing to stay here to help Aunt Ruby in the fall, like she did last spring, she schemed. *Next summer, I could take another sabbatical and return to run the business again. That might generate enough income to pay down her debt so she doesn't have to sell the inn.*

But how many guests would choose to vacation at the inn when there was a construction site right next door, or eventually, a bigger, more luxurious resort blocking the view of the water and the lighthouse? It always came back to that question, and Meg knew that stopping Simon from going through with the sale was the only chance the inn had for turning a profit in the future.

So she resumed perusing the pages of *To the Lighthouse* on her e-reader, making additional notes about how the book might be related to her great-aunt's secret. Even though she couldn't eliminate or confirm any of her hunches with Ruby yet, reviewing the book gave her a sense of purpose; it helped her feel as if there was still hope.

I suppose I should ask Simon when he intends to finalize the sale, she thought. Yet even a glimpse of him heading out to the beach with the children reminded her of their last conversation, which had soured her on speaking to him again.

One afternoon while fluffing the window seat cushions in the living room, she saw him crossing the back lawn toward the inn, carrying a basket of laundry. Cody raced ahead of him, while Abigail lagged behind, lugging a jug of detergent. Meg hastily retreated upstairs. She didn't come back down until hours later, when she was certain they'd completed washing and drying their clothes.

She felt very guilty avoiding the children, an emotion that was intensified when she discovered an envelope on the kitchen table with her name written across it in crayon. It contained a drawing of two red-headed figures—one had straight hair, the other had ringlets—standing in front of the ocean. They were holding hands and wearing purple swimsuits. In case there was any question about who they were, Abigail had written her and Meg's names beneath them.

Aw, she even included freckles on her face and my chest, she noticed.

Cody's drawing was an indiscernible scribble of blue and yellow, which was probably meant to depict the sea and sun. But it reminded Meg more of what the little boy himself looked like when he was running in his cape. Until she saw the children's drawings, she hadn't realized quite how much she missed them.

There was also a note from Simon. It read:

Hi Meg,

I was very sorry to hear from Chloe that Ruby is in the hospital. And I'm very sorry about other things, too.

If there's anything I can do, just let me know. I'd really like to talk when you're up to it.

Thinking of you,

Simon

She supposed it was a kind note, but as Meg secured the children's drawings to the fridge with magnets, she thought, *I'm still not ready to speak to him. Maybe tomorrow...*

"There's some guy downstairs who wants to see you," Chloe announced when she came into Meg's bedroom shortly before noon the following day.

Meg was lying on the bed, curled around her e-reader. "An early guest?"

"No. He said his name is Hunter."

Meg winced when she remembered who he was. "Fantastic, just what I need. I can't believe he showed up on my doorstep."

"You know him?"

"He's the grandson of one of Ruby's friends, Betty Moore. At the beginning of the summer, she wanted to set me up with him, even though I told her I wasn't interested. I thought by now she had let it drop."

"That would explain the bouquet."

"You're not serious!"

"Yep. Hydrangeas," Chloe said. "You should at least meet him. He's kinda cute in a nerdy way and he seems nice."

"Now you sound like Betty." Suddenly, Meg was struck with an idea. "Are you still interested in Simon?"

"Nah, I've been over him for a while. He may have trimmed down his love handles since he first got here, but he's too old for me, and too tightly wound." Chloe imitated Simon's rigid posture. "It's like, guy, just *relax*, would you?"

"He's got a lot on his mind," Meg said defensively, bridling at Chloe's "love handles" comment, too. She clearly hadn't meant the term as a compliment. Simon might not have had six-pack abs, but there was something reassuringly strong about his body. Something that made a person feel safe in his presence...

Chloe arched an eyebrow at her and Meg brought herself back into the moment.

"I knew it!" Chloe gloated. "*You're* the one who's interested in Simon."

Ignoring her, Meg started toward the door. "I'll go talk to Hunter, but only so I can send him away."

"Wait! If you don't want him, send him *my* way," Chloe protested, making Meg laugh. It was exactly how she antici-pated the outspoken housekeeper would respond.

She followed Meg downstairs, where Hunter was standing in the living room, holding such a big bouquet of hydrangeas that Meg could only see half of his face. Even so, it was enough to realize he was at least twelve years younger than she was. He might even have been younger than Chloe. *Did Betty expect me to date him or to raise him?* she thought incredulously.

"My grandmother asked me to bring you these from her yard. She thought they'd look nice in the inn," Hunter said awkwardly after introductions had been made. "You're going to need about a dozen vases, though."

Sensing that Betty had pushed him into visiting and that he

wasn't too happy about it, either, Meg felt relieved. She gathered the flowers into her arms. "Please tell her I said thank you. Can I get you a cup of coffee?"

"No, thanks." He glanced in the direction of the door. "I was just dropping these off for my grandmother. I can't stay."

He probably decided in a split second that I'm way too old for him, just like I think he's too young for me, thought Meg, fighting a smile. "Do you really have to go already? Since you came all this way, you should take a walk out to the beach. It's gorgeous. I'm sure Chloe would be happy to show you around while I finish cleaning, wouldn't you, Chloe?"

Hunter didn't attempt to hide his delight. "That would be great!"

Chloe quizzically tipped her head at Meg. "Are you sure you've got everything covered here?"

"Yes." Meg peeked over the mountain of hydrangeas she was cradling. "Take your time."

TWENTY

Shortly after suppertime, Linda called to report that Ruby's temperature had been climbing. Even more alarming was that her oxygen saturation level had been dipping lower, and her medical team indicated that if it didn't come up, she'd have to be intubated.

After their call ended, Meg's chest was so tight that she felt like if she didn't go for a walk on the beach, she herself might need supplemental oxygen to help her breathe. So, even though it was drizzly and there was too much cloud cover to watch the sun setting, she tromped out toward the lighthouse.

Relieved that she didn't see anyone else on the shoreline, Meg paced from one end of Misty Point Beach to the other, and back again. *All this time, I've been worried about what would happen to Aunt Ruby's inn, or whether she'd be able to keep her home, even if she lost her business. But now, the only thing I care about is whether she'll make it through the week*, she realized. *That does it. I'm going to Pennsylvania tomorrow to visit her.*

She hurried across the meadow, so intent on her plan to call Alice to ask if she'd manage the inn for a few days that she didn't notice Simon was sitting outside his cottage.

"Meg," he called in a hushed voice. It was just light enough for her to see him get up from his chair and wave.

She had no choice but to stop and say hello. When she was near enough that she didn't have to raise her voice to be heard, she said as casually as she could, "Hey, Simon. How are you?"

"All right. It's good to see you. I've been thinking about you a lot." He quickly added, "And about Ruby. How is she?"

Already emotional, Meg knew if she discussed her great-aunt's health in any detail, she'd break down in tears, so she simply replied, "She's had her ups and downs, but the doctors are monitoring her closely. Thanks for asking."

"Sure. I'm glad she's getting good care."

Meg quickly changed the subject. "Thanks for the note, too. I loved the drawings Cody and Abigail made for me."

Simon didn't seem to hear. "Can you sit down for a couple of minutes? There's something I want to talk to you about."

"Well..." Meg wanted to call Alice before it got too late.

"Please? It's important." Even in the near-dark, he appeared stiff-spined and uptight, just as Chloe had imitated.

Her heart softening, she asked, "What's up?"

"I've, uh, I've told you the reason my father never returned to Dune Island, but now I'd like to tell you the reason why I'm selling the property to a developer. I mean, it's true that I'm selling it for the money, but there's more to it than that."

A couple weeks ago, Meg would've been dying of curiosity to hear more, but now she just felt wearied by the topic. "Like you said, you don't owe me an explanation. It's none of my business and honestly, in the grand scheme of life, it doesn't matter to me as much as it once did."

"But I want to explain." He placed a hand on her forearm, urging her to stay. So she took Abigail's seat and Simon lowered himself into his chair beside her.

"Okay, I'm listening," she said, hoping he'd get straight to the point so she could go make her phone call.

"I was injured in the collision that took Beth's life," he began, which was not at all what Meg was expecting him to say. She reflexively shifted toward him, but it was too dark to see his eyes. "We were pulling into an intersection—my wife had a green light—and out of nowhere, a truck slammed into her side of the car. The coroner said the driver experienced a heart attack at the wheel, which is probably why he didn't see us or couldn't stop. He died, as well."

"How awful," Meg murmured.

"Yeah, it was, for everyone involved... Anyway, like I said, I was injured—my back and shoulder were messed up so bad it took almost a year of physical therapy before I could work again. In the meantime, I had outstanding funeral and medical bills to pay, in addition to our living expenses..."

Meg reached over and touched his arm. "I'm so sorry you went through that, but really, Simon, you don't need to go on."

He kept talking anyway, so she drew back and listened intently. "The other driver was uninsured, and the payment I received for the claim I filed with my own insurance company was a pittance. Somehow, I managed to scrape by, but two months after I started working again, I reinjured my back. Even after almost another year of physical therapy, I can only handle small projects, and I can't climb a ladder or carry anything heavier than about twenty pounds. Abigail's been in school, but I've had to take Cody with me whenever I work, since childcare is so expensive."

"Mm, I'm sure it is, especially in Hickory Falls," Meg sympathized.

"Yeah, I've considered moving somewhere cheaper, but I can't do that to Abigail and Cody. They've already had so much upheaval in their lives, so many traumatic changes—not only did their mother die, but the only grandmother they ever knew moved across the country."

"I can't even imagine what that's been like for them—for all of you," Meg sympathized. "But they're so fortunate they have you as their dad."

"I'm not so sure about that, but thanks for saying so," said Simon with an embarrassed chuckle. "After the accident, they had to adjust to my being in chronic pain. Or at least Abigail has had to adjust. I don't think Cody even remembers what I was like before my injury. I can't tell you how often I wish I could pick him up and carry him on my shoulders, like I used to do with Abigail."

Suddenly, Meg saw so many things about Simon in a new light. His rigid posture. His slight but frequent scowl. The way he was constantly fidgeting or shifting in his seat. *It's all because he's been in pain,* she thought, and almost instantly she was struck by a second realization.

"You moved the Adirondack chairs from the garage for me! Why didn't you tell me you couldn't lift anything that heavy?"

"I didn't want to have to explain about my injury," he admitted. "Besides, I was so grateful that you watched my children and searched for Cody's blanket while I was in town, even though you probably guessed that I was meeting with the developer. I figured if you made that sacrifice for me, the least I could do was move a few chairs for you."

"But you could've hurt yourself."

"I was careful. I took my time. The only thing I injured was my ego."

"What do you mean?"

"I had an audience, three elderly ladies, watching me from the patio. They must have wondered why such a big guy kept stopping to rest. They probably thought I was in terrible shape. By the time I carried the third chair out to the lawn, I think they were ready to come and help me," he said, making Meg chuckle.

But their levity was short-lived, as Simon continued, "Trust me, I calculate the risk of everything I do. I'm overly cautious about avoiding any activities that might result in another injury, because a physical setback would affect my livelihood, too. Which would be enough of a challenge if I was flat broke, but I'm in debt up to my eyeballs and I'm on the brink of losing our house. The children don't know this, and it's not something I'd normally share, but one of the main reasons we're staying on Dune Island for three months is that I leased our house in Hickory Falls for the summer to someone who needed temporary housing while their home is being renovated."

Both surprised by the extent of his financial problems, and touched that he'd confided in her about them, Meg said, "That was resourceful of you."

"Yeah, I guess. Honestly, I kind of hate the idea of someone else's family replacing us in our house, but I was desperate, and they were willing to pay my asking price. I think I told you my wife was an interior designer? That's how we met. I was custom building a staircase for someone who was also her client. Anyway, she designed the interior of our house, too. It's gorgeous, looks like it should be featured in a magazine."

"Sounds like she was very talented."

"Yes, she was. But what I love most about the house is that it's our *home*." His voice wavered as he explained, "It feels like it's been the only constant thing in my children's lives for the past two years. They need that kind of stability, but financially, I can't keep the house unless I sell this property to the developer."

Meg nodded slowly. "I understand. And I'm sorry that I've misjudged you. I was wrong about your motives."

"But you weren't wrong about my behavior. I wasn't very friendly to Ruby when I first met her," he admitted. "That was partly because I was nervous about telling her I planned to sell the property. But mostly, I was ashamed that my father had been such a jerk—that he'd treated her as if she didn't exist—the last time *he'd* been in the inn. I was worried Ruby might feel the same way about me as I figured she felt toward him. You know, guilt by association."

"It's not in her nature to prejudge people—*I'm* the one who has that tendency," Meg quipped. "Besides, I don't think she bears any ill will toward your father, and I know for a fact she was excited about welcoming you to Misty Point. That's why she hosted your family for dinner, and it's why she invited you to stay at the inn whenever there was a vacancy. She was so fond of Gordon and your grandmother, and she hoped to connect with you, too. Now that I think about it, I realize it's probably why she insisted I tell you that she'd made the peach pie using Sarah's recipe... It was her subtle way of saying, 'Your grandmother and I go way back.' It was like she wanted to show you that she cared about Sarah, so by extension, she cares about you, too."

"It was a very nice gesture, and the pie was terrific," Simon acknowledged. "I'm sorry I didn't receive it well, but it stirred up an old memory."

Meg was surprised; she thought that Sarah had passed away when Simon was only a toddler. "You remember your grandmother making peach pie?"

"I don't remember her making it, but I remember *eating* it," he replied. "It's probably my earliest memory. I was about Cody's age at the time, and we were sitting in the Adirondack chairs over there—"

"On the back lawn?" interrupted Meg. "But-but I thought your dad never returned to Dune Island after that first summer."

"He didn't. My mother brought me here on her own," he explained. "When I was much older, she told me she'd had a huge fight about it with my dad, because he refused to step foot on Misty Point. But eventually, he gave in and let us go without him."

"That's so cool that you can remember coming here as a child."

"Well, I only remember bits and pieces. Most of it's like a dream, but I do have a very vivid memory of sitting on my grandmother's lap in an Adirondack chair, eating peach pie. My mother told me later how concerned she was that I'd hurt my grandma's legs—her cancer had recurred, so she was awfully frail by then, and I was built a lot like Abigail. But my grandmother insisted she was fine." Simon made a sound that wasn't quite a laugh. "When I finished eating my pie, I leaned back and fell asleep in her arms—I remember that part because she smelled like cinnamon and lemon."

"Aw," uttered Meg, touched by his recollection of snuggling with his dying grandmother. "Do you remember anything else about being at Misty Point?"

"Just that Gordon took me to the beach one evening at sunset. My mother said he was trying to help tire me out before bedtime and even though I was wearing my pajamas, which I wasn't supposed to get wet, he let me wade into the marsh with him to look for fiddler crabs. It was dark by the time we started back to the house, and I was so tired that he carried me on his shoulders. When we passed the lighthouse, he told me if I reached up high enough, I might be able to touch the beam of light as it circled around."

"Oh, that's so sweet," Meg cooed. In a more serious voice, she said, "I appreciate you sharing your memories and your current situation with me, and I promise I won't repeat anything you've told me."

"I know, I trust you. And I want you to trust me, too, Meg," he solemnly replied. "It's important to me that you believe my decision to sell the property to a developer had absolutely nothing to do with how my father felt about Gordon or Ruby."

"I do believe you, Simon."

"Thank you." He rubbed his neck again. "I still regret that

the sale is going to affect Ruby so much. I've honestly tried my best to do whatever I could to minimize the negative impact it'll have on her business."

"She appreciates that, and so do I." After a thoughtful pause to reflect on everything he'd just shared with her, Meg earnestly declared, "If my aunt Ruby knew the whole story behind your decision, she'd agree with me when I say that I'm *very* glad that selling the property will allow you, Abigail, and Cody to remain in your home in Hickory Falls."

"You are?" Simon's voice rose with disbelief. "Even though the resort most likely will be detrimental to the inn's business? And it'll detract from Misty Point's seclusion?"

"Yes," she answered, reassuring herself as much as him. "Like you said, your children have already had to deal with major upheaval in their lives. Now it's time for everyone here to cope with a few changes. The islanders are a resilient bunch, and that includes my aunt. I am, too," she answered, reassuring herself as much as him. "Don't worry, it may take a while, but we'll adjust." Even as she spoke, Meg felt as if a weight was lifting from her shoulders. It was kind of a relief to put her worries to one side and begin to accept the new reality.

"You don't know how much that means to me," he said. "When Ruby's feeling better again, will you tell her why I decided it was necessary to sell my property?"

"Sure," agreed Meg. But she was thinking, *I just hope Aunt Ruby does feel better again.* She stood up and said, "I should get back to the inn, so I guess I'll say good night."

"Night, Meg," Simon said softly.

She phoned Alice as soon as she entered the kitchen, but her call went straight to voice mail, so Meg left a message and then carried the phone to her bedroom with her. It was only 10:00, but after the emotional conversation she'd just had with Simon, she felt too wiped out to pack her suitcase. *I'll be more efficient in the morning, after I've had some sleep.*

Yet once she was in bed, Meg lay awake for hours, contemplating what Simon had told her, worrying about her great-aunt, and watching the lighthouse pulse and flash in the distance. *White light. Pause. White light. Pause.* Again and again, as rhythmic as a heartbeat.

TWENTY-ONE

Meg was packed and ready to leave for Pennsylvania by 8:30, but Alice still hadn't returned her call. *I'll wait until 9:00 before I try her again*, she thought.

Because Chloe hadn't arrived at the inn for work yet, Meg decided in the meantime, she'd clean up the mess several inconsiderate guests had left in the kitchen. She had just finished wiping bacon grease from the surface of the stove and she was about to wash the frying pan when the phone rang.

Although she suspected it was Alice, she answered with her customary greeting. "The Inn at Misty Point, this is—"

"Meg, it's me," the woman interrupted, and it took a moment for her to realize the caller was Linda, not Alice.

The urgency in her voice made Meg feel woozy, and she grabbed the countertop for support. She licked her lips, afraid to ask. "Is Aunt Ruby..."

"Yes, she's doing better! Her oxygen level improved overnight and the new medication must be working, because her fever broke, too. Can you believe it?"

"No, I can't. I can't believe it," Meg uttered, shocked. Tears of relief sprang to her eyes. She dropped into a chair, and then she immediately popped back up again, unable to contain her joy. "That is *fantastic* news!"

She paced the room as Linda told her how optimistic the doctors were after Ruby's dramatic improvement. They'd indicated that as she continued to recover, they'd start weaning her off the supplemental oxygen, to see how she tolerated breathing without it. "That's the first step, and it may take some time, but if she continues in this direction, she'll be able to return to the rehab center soon."

"I really can't believe it," Meg repeated for a third time. "I was so worried that I was planning to drive down there today, in case... you know, in case it was time to say goodbye."

"I don't think you need to make the trip," Linda assured her. "Especially not now."

"I'd still love to visit just for the sake of seeing Aunt Ruby in person again. But I haven't heard back from her friend Alice about whether she can cover for me at the inn, so let me find out if she's available, first."

When Meg phoned Alice a second time, the older woman said, "I just noticed I had a message from you. I'm sorry I missed you last evening, but I've got two sick children on my hands."

That settles that, thought Meg. There was no way Alice could leave her grandkids if they were ill, nor could she bring them to the inn. Meg didn't bother to mention why she had called Alice the previous evening. Instead, after inquiring about Charlotte and Chase, she gave Alice a brief account of Ruby's health setback and her recent hospitalization. "But I'm thrilled to report that last night she took a significant turn for the better."

"Doesn't that just figure? There's nothing Ruby appreciates more than a skillfully executed plot twist," said Alice, chuckling, and Meg laughed, too.

When Chloe arrived, she was equally pleased to hear Meg's

update. "I told you Ruby was tough," she said with a smirk. "Now, can I have the kitchen to myself?"

"I don't mind finishing up in here."

"Seriously, Meg, get out of the kitchen," Chloe reiterated. "You just heard great news, so stop moping around here. Go out to lunch or to the shops or something. Summer's almost over. You should go have a little fun."

So Meg did the only thing she really wanted to do, which was to take a walk to the beach.

"Hi, Meg," called Abigail. She dropped her pail and net and ran toward Meg, her curls springing with each footfall. When she reached her, the little girl threw her arms around Meg's stomach and grinned up at her; she was missing another tooth. "I haven't seen you in, like, a hundred days."

Meg patted the child's head. "I know, it's been an awful long time. Thank you for the beautiful drawing of us at the beach."

"You're welcome. Wanna go swimming with me?"

"Sure, in a few minutes. Let me say hello to your dad and Cody, first."

"They got their hair cut this morning and Cody cried," Abigail tattled as her father and brother approached.

"I did not. I had sand in my eyes," Cody argued, his voice at a normal speaking volume.

"There's no sand at a Barbara shop," Abigail contradicted.

"There's no *Barbara* at a barber shop either," Simon told his daughter, smiling at Meg. "Just a guy named Ron."

"Well, Ron did a great job. You both look very handsome. It's nice to be able to see your eyes." Meg noticed that while Simon's haircut made him appear more boyish, Cody's made him appear a little older. How was it possible that the child had grown taller since the last time she'd seen him? "Abigail and I are going to take a swim. Are you guys coming, too?"

"I want to catch minnows," said Cody.

His sister reminded him, "You have to take your blankie off first, or the ends will get wet."

In a voice louder than Meg had ever heard him use, Cody yelled, "Stop telling me what to do!"

"Then stop *needing* me to tell you what to do," Abigail shouted back.

Their exchange perfectly summarized their relationship dynamic, and Meg had to stifle a giggle, but Simon instructed them to lower their voices. "You're going to scare away the minnows—and Meg."

But she thought their argument was a sign of growth. Besides, she was so happy to be in their company again that it would take a lot more than a little noise to scare her away.

The weather was gorgeous for the rest of the week, and Meg fell into a pattern of walking along the beach in the late morning. Right around the time she'd finish her stroll, Simon and the children would show up and join her for a swim or a game of water *keep away*. They'd all take a break from the sunshine and go indoors for lunch, and then they'd meet up again in the late afternoon for a lawn game or another dip.

Twice, they were joined by Chloe, Maddie, and Sonny, as well as Hunter, who seemed to be hitting it off well with Chloe's family. Meg liked him, too, and she had to admit, his pushy grandmother had been right about him; he truly was a "sweetie."

One particularly hot afternoon, as Simon, Meg, and Abigail dropped their towels on the sand and headed straight for the water, Cody whined, "I want to come with you, Dad."

His father patiently unknotted Cody's blankie, took his

hand, and waded into the shallows, where Meg and Abigail, who were also holding hands, waited for them. Cody reached up and grasped Meg's free hand, and the foursome continued moving toward the horizon, step by step.

"It's like we're a human chain," said Abigail.

Or it's like we're a family, Meg thought longingly.

When the water reached Cody's chest, he dropped Meg's hand and tugged on the leg of his father's swim trunks. "Pick me up, Daddy. I want to go in deep with you."

"You know I can't pick you up, son." Simon explained to Meg, "I wrenched my shoulder the other night. So I've got to be extra careful this week or I'll wind up needing physical therapy while I'm here on the island."

"*I* can carry you into deeper water, Cody," Meg offered. To her delight—and to Abigail's dismay—he extended his arms for Meg to pick him up. She released Abigail's hand and lifted Cody to her hip, and slowly advanced until the water was up to her ribs.

"Don't let me go." He wrapped his arms around her neck like a tree frog clasping a twig.

"I won't," she promised, touched that he trusted her to keep him safe.

"Can you see any fish or crabs?"

"We might be in too deep to spot them, since they're usually near the bottom and the water's a little cloudy today. But let's look." She slowly strolled parallel with the beach as Cody hung his head sideways, peering at the ocean floor. After about fifty yards, she turned and headed back toward where Simon and Abigail were making a game out of talking to each other underwater.

When they reached them, Cody told Meg, "Let's go again. Faster!"

To his glee, she took long, bounding strides in the opposite direction. Cody let go of her neck with one hand and leaned over to feel the water streaming through his fingers.

"Faster!" he demanded. So Meg increased her speed until they reached their turn-around spot and he said, "Do it again."

They repeated this pattern several times until Meg finally told him, "Hold on, Cody. I've got to catch my breath." As she slowly paced in a wide arc, he leaned against her chest, his head tucked beneath her chin, the salty scent of his fine, flyaway hair tickling her nose.

"I hear your heart," he told her.

"I'm sure you do. Is it saying, 'I'm tired, I'm tired'?"

"No." He was quiet a moment, listening. "It's saying, 'I'm happy, I'm happy.'"

"You've got that right," said Meg and kissed the top of his head, trying not to think about how fleeting this happiness might be. Soon Simon's family would be leaving the island; it would be her last summer here with them, and depending on what happened with her great-aunt and the inn, it could be Meg's last summer at Misty Point, too.

A few days later, Ruby was discharged from the hospital. When Meg met up with Simon's family on the beach and told him the news, he spontaneously enveloped her in an enthusiastic bear hug. Just as she'd imagined it would be, his embrace was powerful yet soft, and she reveled in the warmth of his sun-kissed arms and chest.

"I never thought I'd be so happy that my great-aunt's back in a rehab center," she marveled after he let her go. "I guess that's the difference a couple of weeks can make. It's all relative."

"Returning to rehab is definitely progress," Simon acknowl-edged. "But how does Ruby feel about being back there?"

"Linda said she was thrilled to check out of the hospital, but I haven't chatted with my Aunt Ruby yet," she answered.

If she were being brutally honest, Meg would have confessed that she'd almost felt relieved that it hadn't worked out for her to speak to her great-aunt while she'd been in the hospital. Ruby had been sleeping more hours than she'd been awake, so it was less disruptive if Meg communicated with her through Linda, and vice versa.

However, Meg realized that soon she'd need to talk to Ruby one-on-one, so she could explain Simon's situation to her. And although she dreaded it, she also needed to confess that she'd read *To the Lighthouse* several times, but she still didn't have a clue about how it was related to her great-aunt's past.

Not that there was necessarily a pressing reason anymore for Ruby to share her secret with Simon in the next few weeks. Meg anticipated that once she explained to her great-aunt why it was imperative for him to sell his property to a developer, Ruby would be very sympathetic, and she most likely would drop her attempt to change his mind.

And while Meg herself was still burning with curiosity about her great-aunt's secret, she had to admit that it was a relief not to think about Virginia Woolf's book every waking minute of the day. Instead of reading *To the Lighthouse*, Meg relished actually *going* to the lighthouse, especially when Simon and his children went there, too.

She told him, "I'm going to wait until my great-aunt settles into her room and gets used to the regimen again. Then I'll schedule a video call with her, and I'll share what you asked me to tell her."

As they were speaking, Cody galloped from the shallows where he'd been stalking minnows with Abigail. Unknotting his blankie, he asked Meg, "Can you carry me into the deep water?"

"Give Meg a chance to go swimming by herself before you latch on to her like a barnacle," Simon told his son.

"That's okay. I don't mind." In fact, Meg loved it.

However, today when they reached the waist-deep water, Cody insisted she let go of him. "I want to swim to Daddy," he announced, pointing to his father who was ten or twelve feet to their right.

"Okay. I'll hold you under your stomach, and you kick your arms and legs."

"No. Don't hold me. Let go," he insisted, trying to wriggle free of her grasp.

Meg felt panicked. She was planning to teach him to swim step-by-step, the way she'd been taught. *He hasn't even learned to put his face in the water and blow bubbles yet*, she thought. "Your head might go under water if I don't hold you up," she warned him.

"It's all right," Simon said, stretching out his arms. "I'll grab him if that happens."

That was all the encouragement Cody needed to hear. Without warning, he flung himself out of Meg's grasp and thrashed his way through the water until he'd reached Simon. His father squatted low, allowing him to stand on his knees.

"Way to go, son!"

But it was his sister's praise he wanted. "Abigail!" he shouted. "Did you see me? I swimmed!"

She stopped skimming the water with her net and looked up. "I missed it. Do it again."

So he cast himself toward Meg with wide-open eyes and a huge smile, battering the water so ferociously that he drenched them both.

"Good job, Cody!" Abigail called, tossing her net onto shore and charging forward. "Now swim to me!"

Simon, Meg, and Abigail spread out in triangle formation and for the next half hour, Cody swam from point to point, grinning the entire time. Finally, Meg suggested to Simon, "I think we should take a little rest. If Cody swallows any more water, he might get a tummy ache."

"I don't have a tummy ache," he protested.

"Good, we want to keep it that way," his father said. "Especially because we're going to the boardwalk for supper later on."

"Can Meg come with us as our special guest?" asked Abigail.

Knowing how tight Simon's budget was and feeling embarrassed that his daughter had put him on the spot, Meg started to object, "You don't have to..."

But Simon said, "Abigail took the words right out of my mouth. Will you join us as our special guest? We need you there to help us celebrate Cody learning how to swim... and to celebrate Ruby's recovery."

"In that case, I'd love to," she agreed.

That evening, after devouring their fish 'n' chips as greedily as a flock of ravenous seagulls, and then strolling along the boardwalk savoring chocolate-cranberry ice-cream cones from Bleeckers, the foursome returned to Misty Point to watch the sunset together. Since guests were already using the Adirondack chairs on the back lawn, and the kids were too tired to hike to the beach, Simon suggested they watch it from the cottage.

"Let's go put your PJs on and brush your teeth, first," he told his children. "Meg can relax out here."

"You can sit in my chair," offered Abigail.

"No, I want her to sit in *my* chair," argued Cody. "She taught *me* how to swim, not *you*."

His sister wouldn't give in. "I said it first, and my chair is purple. Meg likes purple a lot more than blue."

"Hey, guys, let's not argue or else when we come back out, Meg might not be here."

That's okay, she thought as they disappeared into the cottage. *It's nice to feel so popular.*

She wound up sitting in the purple chair, while Cody and Abigail squished together in his blue one. They were barely able to keep their eyes open, and the moment after the sun slid below the horizon, Simon instructed his children to say good night to Meg. She received a hug and a kiss from each of them, as well.

She was about to stand up and head toward the inn, but Simon said, "I'll be out in a few minutes, okay?" So she settled back into her chair, happy their evening together wasn't ending yet.

When Simon returned, he remarked, "They were both asleep before their heads hit their pillows."

Noticing how slowly he lowered himself into his chair, Meg asked, "Are you in pain?"

"My back hurts a little," he admitted, rubbing his shoulder.

"Would a massage help?"

She half expected him to decline the offer but instead he replied, "That would be great, thanks."

Meg rose and stood behind him. Touching his shoulders, she said, "Tell me if anything I'm doing hurts, okay?"

As she began to work the tight knots from his muscles, she heard voices across the back lawn. It was still light enough for her to see that the guests who'd been watching the sunset in the Adirondack chairs were returning to the inn. Could they see her, as well, or was it too dark beneath the cover of the pine trees? Meg felt slightly self-conscious, although she wasn't sure why. *I'm only giving Simon a back rub because he's injured*, she tried to tell herself.

Yet as she kneaded his brawny shoulders and his tension seemed to melt beneath her fingertips, Meg found herself thinking about how amazing his embrace had felt earlier that afternoon. *This is the first time I've admitted to myself how attracted I am to him,* she realized, She had to fight the impulse to drape her arms over him and whisper into his ear, "Thank you for sharing the best day I've had all summer, maybe even all year..."

No sooner had the whim occurred to her, than she remembered Josh's cynical remark, "A ready-made family, how convenient."

Is that all this is? Do I only feel attracted to Simon because he's Abigail's and Cody's father and I like them so much? she asked herself.

"Are your hands cramping up?" Simon's question made her realize she'd stopped massaging him and had rested her palms flat against his shoulder blades.

"No, but my fingers are getting a little tired." She smoothed his shirt and gave him a platonic pat on the back before circling around in front of him. "I'm getting a little tired, too. And I should probably get back to the inn to make sure there aren't any messages from Linda."

"Oh, okay." He sounded disappointed but he stood up. "Thanks for the massage—it felt great. And thanks for helping Cody reach such a huge milestone. If you hadn't spent so much time lugging him around and helping him acclimate to the deeper water, there's no way he would've been ready to swim this summer. This is a day he'll never forget, and neither will I."

Meg had barely parted her lips to reply when he leaned in and kissed her on the corner of her mouth. Surprised, she faltered backward, a wave of heat coursing from her chest to her face. "You're... you're welcome. And thanks for including me in your celebration. G'night, Simon."

What was that, *anyway? A misplaced peck on the cheek? A friendly expression of gratitude?* she wondered as she scampered toward the inn. Or had the kiss meant more than that? Had it been a romantic gesture?

Meg hurried into the kitchen to check the phone for

messages. There weren't any, so she removed her sandals and tiptoed down the hall, slinking past the living room without the guests noticing her. She hastily retreated upstairs to sit in Ruby's rocking chair by the window. As the lighthouse beam swooped through the sky, she tried to make sense of her feelings about Simon.

Maybe Josh was right. Maybe if Simon didn't have children, I wouldn't be interested in him, she thought. After all, hadn't Meg essentially been claiming the same thing for weeks? Hadn't she told herself that she didn't like *Simon,* she liked the *idea* of him, as a father and a family man?

But that was before he'd opened up about his financial situation, and about why he'd acted so strangely around her great-aunt. *I was in denial about my feelings for him because I was conflicted about being attracted to someone who was putting Aunt Ruby out of business,* she finally admitted to herself.

However, now she had a much better understanding of the kind of person Simon truly was. And yes, part of his appeal was that he was a devoted dad to his darling children, but that was only one reason on a very long list of reasons of why she was attracted to him. The more she reflected on those qualities, the more confident Meg felt that if Simon didn't already have a son and daughter—as difficult as that was to picture—she'd still like him every bit as much as she did now.

But did he reciprocate her feelings? Reflecting on his awkward kiss, she couldn't quite gauge the nature of his affection. And while part of Meg hoped Simon was romantically interested in her, once again Josh's comments plagued her thoughts. It wasn't that she believed Simon would deliberately use her as a babysitter or for a rebound relationship. But she wondered if subconsciously he might be attracted to her because she was kind to his children, or because she was a temporary distraction from his loneliness for Beth?

The more she obsessed over it, the more her doubt and

confusion grew, until she felt like pulling out her hair. *I am so fed up with assumptions and guesses and hints and hypotheses! And I'm sick of trying to read between the lines and solve unsolvable mysteries*, she vented to herself. *Why does everything have to be so complicated? Can't I just get a simple, straightforward answer to anything?*

The next second, it dawned on Meg that of course she could get a simple, straightforward answer; but first, she'd have to ask a simple, straightforward question.

She didn't even stop to put on her sandals before tearing out of the inn and across the back yard. Nearing the cottage, she noticed a shadowy figure growing taller; Simon was rising from his chair. "Meg?" he questioned in a hushed voice.

"Yes, it's me—ow, ow, ow." She had stepped on a pine cone and she groaned as she hopped forward on one foot, nearly crashing into him. He caught her by the shoulders to steady her.

"Are you all right?" he asked. "Is Ruby okay?"

"I'm fine. She's fine. We're both fine. But there's something I need to know," she answered, panting. "Why did you kiss me tonight?"

"What?" When he uttered the word, Meg could feel Simon's breath on her cheek. Her eyes were adjusting to the darkness, and as his features came into focus, she saw he was looking intently at her, obviously confused.

"I mean, was it just a good night kiss between two friends, or were you kissing me as a way of saying thank you because you were grateful I helped Cody learn to swim, or—"

"No," Simon interrupted, his answer firm and unwavering, just like his stance. "I kissed you because I'm attracted to you, Meg. I *like* you."

Although he probably thought he'd been crystal clear, she had a follow-up question. "But *why* do you like me? I mean, is it just because I'm, you know..." Suddenly embarrassed about calling attention to the fact that she got along so well with his children, Meg let her sentence trail off.

Simon finished it for her. "So pretty?"

She could feel her cheeks flaming. "No—but thank you. I was going to say because I'm... *here*, and I happen to have been spending time with your children. Maybe you're only interested in me because I'm wild about Cody and Abigail."

"Who and who?" Simon asked, lifting his hand to fiddle with a lock of Meg's hair.

"C'mon, I'm serious."

He sighed. "That *isn't* why I'm interested in you. I mean, obviously it would be a dealbreaker if you were mean to my kids. But the fact that you're so sweet to them isn't the only reason I like you," he insisted. "Case in point—Chloe's nice to Abigail and Cody, too. But even when you tried to push us together earlier this summer, and you offered to take care of the children so I could get away from the cottage, I wasn't interested in going out with her."

Oh, so that's *why he acted so strange that day!* Meg thought, remembering how he'd seemed excited about her idea at first, but then he'd quickly dropped the subject. Was it possible that Simon initially had thought that Meg was suggesting he should go sightseeing with *her*, instead of with Chloe?

"I could list a dozen qualities I like about you that have nothing to do with how you interact with my children. But the bottom line is, from what I know of you, I like you for who you *are*. And I want to get to know you even better." Simon continued, "But it's a two-way street. I never would've considered this possibility until you brought it up, but I wouldn't want *you* to start seeing *me* just because you click so well with Abigail and Cody... That's not what's happening, is it?"

Meg admitted, "Honestly, I wondered about that, too."

"Wow, tell me how you really feel," Simon said, with a playful little laugh.

"I didn't finish. I wondered about that, too, because Abigail and Cody *did* win me over a lot quicker than you did—"

"Again, *ouch*."

"But the more I got to know you, the more I started to like you, Simon," she said sincerely. "As adorable as Cody and Abigail are, they aren't the reason I want to date you. After all, I've met lots of single dads with adorable children. Yet here I am, still single."

"Lucky for me." He moved toward her, but she pulled back.

"Wait, there's something else I need to know." She had to be sure there weren't any assumptions or miscommunications between them, like there had been between her and Josh. "Have you considered whether you might only be interested in me because... because you're lonely for Beth?"

"You mean you're worried that I'm dating you on the rebound?" Simon bluntly asked.

"That's not the way I would've put it, but yes."

"Maybe I shouldn't admit this, but you're two women too late for that."

"*Two?*" she echoed. "I don't know if that makes me feel better or worse."

"Third time's the charm," he teased, inching forward. "*You're* the charm, Meg. And I'd really like to kiss you again before sunrise, which is when Cody and Abigail wake up."

Oh, no, I forgot about Cody and Abigail—will we need to tell them that we're seeing each other, or are they too young to under-stand? Simon only lives a little over an hour from me in Delaware, so there's no reason we can't keep dating after the summer ends, but maybe we should wait to see how it goes before we mention anything to the children?

Even as her mind whirled with concerns, Meg was aware that she was overthinking. She was looking too far ahead, worry-ing, planning for what came next. But then Simon cupped her face, leaning closer, and the only thing on her mind in that moment was the warm fullness of his lips softly touching hers.

TWENTY-TWO

Ever since learning to swim, if that's what Cody's wild splashing motions could be called, the little boy abandoned his blankie. Meg could only guess whether that was because he spent so much time in the water that it became too much of a hassle to tie and re-tie the blankie or because he no longer felt the emotional need for it. In either case, Simon was delighted, and so was Abigail.

"Did you notice something different about my brother?" she whispered, her breath hot against Meg's ear. Before Meg could answer, the little girl pointed out, "He's not wearing his blankie. But Daddy said not to draw attention to it, so pretend you don't know, okay? It's our secret."

"Sure," she whispered back, admiring Abigail's newfound self-restraint.

Meg herself was having difficulty containing the secret *she* shared with Simon. Their unspoken agreement was that they didn't openly express physical affection in front of the children. Instead, they waited until Cody and Abigail were tucked into bed before stealing fervent kisses outside the cottage, or sitting in the dark and holding hands as they stargazed and watched the lighthouse's revolving ray. It reminded Meg of being a teenager, in the best possible way, and their shared secrecy enhanced the romance of their relationship.

However, she felt less delighted about *Ruby's* secret. Although Meg had given up meticulously analyzing every line in *To the Lighthouse* she'd resumed leafing through the book for a plausible connection between the novel and her great-aunt's past.

It wasn't that Meg kept searching for the link because she still hoped to stop Simon from building the resort; she'd genuinely meant it when she'd told him that she understood and supported his decision. She'd even made peace with the probability that Ruby would need to sell her home. Considering her great-aunt's condition, Meg recognized that retirement and relocation might well be in her best interest, which was the top priority. But she kept trying to figure out the secret anyway because she hated admitting defeat, especially when Ruby was counting on her.

Yet as much as she regretted disappointing her great-aunt by confessing she'd failed to solve the riddle, Meg missed Ruby so much that she couldn't postpone a video chat any longer. She scheduled the call for a time when Linda wasn't there, so they could speak privately.

"Hi, Aunt Ruby!" she exclaimed when she saw her great-aunt's face on the phone screen. Meg was amazed by the noticeable improvement in the tautness of Ruby's right cheek and eyebrow. "I'm sorry you were so ill, but you look terrific now! How do you feel?"

"Good. You... look... great... too," her aunt said slowly but very distinctly, returning the compliment.

Meg was aware that recovery from a stroke happened in spurts and stops, and that patients with Ruby's type of aphasia often omitted prepositions and other small words from their sentences. But she was elated about the overall improvement in

Ruby's speech and appearance, especially because she'd had a reduced therapy schedule at the hospital. *All this time I've been so worried about her, but she seems stronger now than she did before she got pneumonia.*

Her great-aunt was pleased to hear updates about the inn, as well as greetings that Meg passed along from Alice, Chloe, Ava, and a few of the long-time guests. But she was especially delighted by the brief tales Meg told about Simon, Abigail, and Cody.

"Simon. Fell. Love," she remarked, and for a moment, Meg thought her great-aunt meant he'd fallen in love with *her*. But then Ruby shook an *I-told-you-so* finger in the air and Meg remembered she'd been hopeful that Simon would fall in love with Misty Point and change his mind about selling his inheritance.

She sighed and said, "Yes, all three of them have fallen in love with Dune Island. Unfortunately, Simon still intends to sell the property." She was about to launch into the account of his injury and financial challenges, as well as his concern about his children, but Ruby became visibly distressed, waving her hand to interrupt Meg.

"Did... you... tell... Simon... secret?" she slowly asked.

Meg apologized, "No, I'm sorry. I tried my best to figure out how *To the Lighthouse* is related to your past, or to the property at Misty Point, but I couldn't."

Again, Ruby wagged a finger, and even though her face was still partially paralyzed, there was no mistaking the stern look she gave Meg. "You... didn't... read... book."

A little offended that her great-aunt didn't believe her, Meg assured her, "I *did* read it, Aunt Ruby, at least half a dozen times. I even took notes. I jotted down questions and high-lighted some passages in my e-reader, but—"

"No!" barked Ruby, waving her hand. "No. No. No."

"Okay, we don't have to discuss it now," Meg agreed,

concerned about how quickly her great-aunt had become agitated. They'd been talking for half an hour, which was much longer than their calls usually lasted. Maybe Ruby was getting tired? Regretting that she'd agitated her, Meg said, "I'll read it again and we can talk about it during our next phone call if you'd like."

"No," snapped Ruby, demonstratively aggravated. Why hadn't the nursing assistant returned yet to check on her? She repeated, "Read... my... lighthouse. Read... my... lighthouse."

That's what I just said I'd do, and it seemed to upset her, thought Meg. But she would've agreed to anything to allay her great-aunt's frustration, so she enthusiastically agreed, "Okay, I will, I promise."

"Good. Good," Ruby repeated. "Share... secret... Simon."

"I will. I'll share your secret with Simon," she readily agreed. *Assuming I can figure out what it is.*

Relieved that Ruby seemed contented at last, Meg made small talk for a few more minutes until the nursing assistant returned.

"It's going to be a busy weekend at the inn—we've got a full house," Meg told her great-aunt, hoping that with more time, she might have a breakthrough about Ruby's secret. "But I'll touch base with Linda soon to set up a video call for next week, okay?"

"Thank you." Ruby gave her a big thumbs-up. "Love... you."

"I love you, too, Aunt Ruby," Meg replied. *I just don't understand you...*

As she drove back to the inn, it occurred to her that she'd been so distracted by Ruby's sudden change in mood that she hadn't ended up telling her great-aunt about Simon's situation. And unless Ruby's secret was that she had a legal right to stop him from selling the property—which Meg had grown to recognize was highly unlikely—then it wouldn't "have a significant bearing on his life," like her great-aunt had hoped.

But a promise was a promise, so Meg resolved to reread *To the Lighthouse* one more time. *Even though her secret won't change Simon's mind, if sharing it with him is important to Aunt Ruby, then it's still important to me*, she thought.

The following day was Maddie and Sonny's birthday, so Chloe took time off to get ready for their party, which included a suppertime cookout. Simon and his children were invited, and Meg was, too, but she couldn't attend because she had too many new guests arriving, plus she was covering Chloe's cleaning duties. So, she'd promised to meet Simon at the cottage after the children were in bed and the final guest had checked in.

It took almost until 5:30 before Meg had finished the house-keeping and greeting new guests, and could steal a few minutes to herself to eat a sandwich on the porch.

I wish I could've gone to the cookout with Simon and the children, she thought, glancing toward their cottage. Every moment with them became more precious as time slipped by. This coming Tuesday, while Meg watched the kids, Simon was going to Boston for a final meeting with the developer to authorize the sale. A week after that, he'd return to Delaware with Cody and Abigal, and a few days later, Meg would have to go back to New Jersey. How could it be that her "entire summer" on Dune Island was already coming to an end?

I should find out when the rehab staff estimates Aunt Ruby will be discharged, she planned. *And I need to talk to Linda about whether she's willing to come to Hope Haven and stay with her this autumn, or if we should make other arrangements for her care...*

Feeling melancholy, Meg finished eating her sandwich and then went upstairs to shower. Afterward, she put on her bathrobe and peeked out the side window at the parking lot to check for new guests. Because she didn't see any vehicles that hadn't been there earlier, she decided she might as well peruse *To the Lighthouse* again while she was waiting.

Ack. I left my e-reader in the car. Meg was too hot to blow dry her hair, yet she didn't want to go outside looking the way she did, in case she bumped into any new arrivals in the parking lot. *I'm sure Aunt Ruby wouldn't mind if I borrowed her copy, just this once.*

Scanning the bookcase beside the bed, she spotted her great-aunt's leather-covered Bible, two picture books she'd saved from childhood, and several signed editions, but Woolf's novel wasn't on the shelves. Next, Meg checked the bookcase closer to the window. At first, she couldn't locate it there, either, but it was a slim volume, so she searched again, touching each book's spine with her finger to be sure she didn't overlook it.

Oh, here it is. She slid the hardcover edition toward her and settled into the rocking chair. From this vantage point, she noticed that Simon and the children still weren't home. Not that she expected them to return early, but selfishly she wished she could see Abigail and Cody before they went to bed.

As soon as she opened the cover of *To the Lighthouse* Meg noticed something about it didn't feel right. The book fanned apart unevenly, and when she flattened down the first four or five pages, she found a neat, shallow rectangle carved into the remaining pages, which were glued to the back cover. Inside the hollow space was an envelope with Ruby's full name, Ruby Jane Berton, written across it.

What in the world...? It took a moment for Meg to process that what she was holding was a homemade book safe, a hiding place for valuables. *This must be it—this must be what Aunt Ruby meant by, 'The lighthouse holds the key'! Whatever is inside this envelope is the key to her secret!*

In a flash, she understood why her great-aunt hadn't believed that she'd read *To the Lighthouse*, and why Ruby had become so aggravated when Meg mentioned highlighting passages of Woolf's book on her e-reader. *She'd wanted me to read* her *print copy, not my digital version!*

The next instant, she was struck by another epiphany. *No wonder Aunt Ruby was so adamant about not downsizing her personal library—she must've been concerned I'd accidentally throw this envelope out...*

After weeks and weeks of searching, Meg was so astonished by her accidental discovery that she spent several moments just staring at the envelope before sliding it from its hiding place. As certain as she was that Ruby wanted her to look inside it and to share the contents with Simon, her fingers trembled as she hesitantly lifted the flap and pulled out a single sheet of paper.

She unfolded the yellowed stationery and saw the words, *From the Desk of Gordon R. Sheffield* embossed across the top of the page. Typed below them was the date, November 14, 1986, and the rest of the text was also typed instead of handwritten.

Even though the paper looked more like a professional memo than a personal letter, and even though her great-aunt had given her permission, Meg felt uneasy about reading it— almost as if she were eavesdropping. But she took a deep breath and started to move her eyes over the first lines.

TWENTY-THREE

Dear Ruby, the letter began.

> *If you are reading this, it means I am reunited with my beloved Sarah, so please don't shed any tears for me!*
>
> *By now, my attorney has explained that I am leaving you the summer house and a small parcel of land at Misty Point. It's what Sarah would have wanted. She wholeheartedly believed that she wouldn't have recovered from the ravaging effects of her cancer treatments, were it not for your care and companionship, along with the life-affirming beauty of Dune Island.*

Meg stopped reading to revel in a moment of smugness. She would love to show this letter to Betty, Bradley, and anyone else who doubted what her great-aunt had always claimed about Gordon's motivation for giving her the house.

She read on:

> *Sarah's fondest dream was for her son to experience happiness and healing at Misty Point, too. Bradley wasn't physically ill,*

but Sarah recognized that his anger and bitterness were like an insidious disease affecting every aspect of his life. She always hoped that spending time at the oceanside with his loving family would be the cure for what ailed him.

Although that didn't happen during her lifetime—nor has it happened yet—Bradley once allowed his son, Simon, to visit Misty Point shortly before Sarah's death.

Upon seeing Simon's name, Meg smiled, but she thought, *Aunt Ruby never let on that she knew Simon had come to Dune Island when he was a child. Is that because she didn't want to explain that she'd found out about his visit through Gordon's letter?*

She continued:

We all treasured our week together, and after Simon and his mother left, Sarah wandered off to sit in an Adirondack chair on the back lawn. I expected she was weeping because she knew she had seen her grandson for the last time.

But when I joined her, she was gazing toward the lighthouse with a rapturous expression on her face. I asked what was on her mind and she said, "I can still picture Simon meandering back home through the meadow... and I can imagine my great-grandchildren meandering through it one day, too."

Meg's eyes welled as she read Sarah's quote. *I'm so glad Simon's mother insisted on bringing him to Dune Island, even though his father didn't want him to come here.*

Blinking, she picked up where she left off:

Therefore, it is in honor of my wife's memory that I have bequeathed Bradley most of the property at Misty Point, as well as "The Writing Pad." He's lawfully entitled to build a full-sized summer home on the land, but my Trust prohibits him from selling any part of the estate. (Rather, that option will be passed to Simon upon his father's death.)

Again, Meg paused, but this time it was to chuckle. Gordon's stilted writing style and word choice reminded her of why it had taken a while for her to warm to his novels. *I feel like I'm reading a legal doc instead of a letter to an old friend*, she thought.

Despite Gordon's diction, Meg admired his commitment to honoring his wife's memory by leaving his stepson the property, even though Bradley had been such a jerk to him.

She resumed reading:

By giving Bradley the land abutting yours, I'm afraid I've put you in an untenable position. I feel compelled to warn you— although you're so perceptive you probably sensed it—that the night Bradley arrived at Misty Point, he saw you coming out of the cottage, and he completely misconstrued the nature of our relationship.

Oh, no! Meg groaned and lowered the letter to her lap. *Aunt Ruby never indicated she was aware that Bradley thought she was having an affair with Gordon! Not that I blame her—it must have been so hurtful and humiliating to know he had such a low opinion of her... I just can't understand why she kept inviting Bradley to be her guest at the inn. If someone had accused me of something like that, I wouldn't want to be within a hundred miles of them!*

She lifted the letter again.

Of course, I denied there was anything illicit going on between us, but I refused to tell him the real reason you were there.

Squinting in the sunlight, Meg peeked down at the tiny

abode in the far corner of the yard. *I'll bet it's like I thought—the real reason Aunt Ruby went to the cottage was because she needed to talk privately with Gordon about Sarah's health or Alan's gambling problem.*

Meg refocused her attention on the letter to see if she was right.

> *By that point in his life, Bradley was already so spiteful toward me that I was concerned he'd disclose our secret to my publisher. As a result, you and I would have faced dire financial and legal consequences.*

Uh-oh. Meg didn't like the sound of this. Why would Gordon be concerned about his publisher discovering their secret? And what did he mean by "legal consequences"? The only illegal writing-related activity Meg could imagine was plagiarism. She knew her great-aunt would never participate in anything like that, just as surely as she'd known Ruby would never have an affair with a married man. But was it possible that *Gordon* hadn't been as scrupulous as her great-aunt had led Meg to believe?

The next few sentences made her even more uneasy:

> *Furthermore, Sarah would have learned our secret, too, and the stress would have taken a toll on her health. (As you recall, that was my worst fear, even before the night Bradley saw you leaving the cottage.)*

Meg could hardly stand the suspense of not knowing what Gordon meant by "our secret." But she figured, *Since Ruby already knew what the secret was, I suppose there was no reason for Gordon to spell it out in this letter.*

Hoping she was mistaken, she couldn't read the rest of the page fast enough:

Rather than admitting what we were doing, I pleaded with Bradley to consider every word I'd ever spoken, and every deed I'd ever committed, as proof of my enduring faithfulness to his mother. He didn't believe me then, but there's still time for him to change his mind about the kind of person I was—and about the kind of person you are, too. (If Bradley ever visits Misty Point again, for Sarah's sake I humbly ask that you'll exercise the same graciousness toward him that you always demonstrated to her and me. He will need it.)

In light of Gordon's request, Ruby's invitations to host Bradley at the inn—as well as her hospitality toward Simon—made sense to Meg. Yes, her great-aunt's attitude was consistent with her character, but it was clear that she'd also acted out of respect for Gordon and Sarah's wishes.

When Meg flipped the paper over, she was disappointed to see the letter only contained two brief paragraphs before Gordon's signature line. *I guess this means he's not going to explicitly name whatever secret he shared with Aunt Ruby.*

But she'd guessed wrong. The very next line said:

Because we lost touch after the summer of 1978, I never properly thanked you for authoring The Wife of Oscar Claiborne, *when I was stymied with writer's block.*

"What?" yelped Meg, jumping to her feet. She could hardly believe her eyes, so she reread the sentence and confirmed it said what she'd thought it said: her great-aunt had written *The Wife of Oscar Claiborne*, the seventh book in Gordon's mystery series—and the book Meg herself had enjoyed so much.

"This is *huge*," she exclaimed aloud. Of all the secrets she'd speculated that Ruby may have been keeping, Meg never, ever would have guessed her great-aunt had written—and *published*—a mystery novel, and an excellent one, at that.

In hindsight, she could clearly see similarities between the protagonist's old-fashioned phrases and the figures of speech her great-aunt frequently used. *I always knew Aunt Ruby was a great storyteller*, she thought with admiration. *So I guess I shouldn't be surprised that she has such an engaging narrative voice as a writer, too.*

Meg was so blown away by her great-aunt's achievement that she almost forgot to finish reading the remainder of the letter.

Gordon had written:

Not only did you prevent me from violating my publishing contract, losing my advance, and being evicted from our apartment, but the book's enormous success later allowed me to pay off Sarah's medical bills, as well as to purchase the house at Misty Point.

So, it is with my deepest appreciation that I bequeath our home to you now; you deserve it, Ruby, and so much more. May you experience as much joy at Misty Point as Sarah and I did.

Gratefully yours,

Gordon

"Wow," Meg uttered, deeply touched by the mutually caring, respectful, and appreciative relationship Ruby shared with Sarah and Gordon.

Considering her great-aunt's talent, she was impressed by Ruby's humility and her dedication to keeping such a juicy secret for decades. Meg herself felt like running through the inn proclaiming, "My great-aunt wrote a bestselling novel!"

She couldn't do that, of course. She couldn't even tell Simon, since he wasn't back from the party yet. *No wonder Aunt Ruby asked me to share her secret with him—she must have suspected Bradley told Simon that she'd had an affair with Gordon. And she might have been concerned that's why Simon didn't want to keep his inheritance,* she thought as she perused the letter a second time. *I can understand why she'd want to clear her name, but I hope she isn't under any illusion that once he reads this, he'll change his mind about selling the property.*

Her exuberance waning a little, Meg decided to call Ruby and tell her how impressed she was by the amazing book she'd written. She also intended to gently break the news to her great-aunt that Simon's decision was strictly a financial matter—it had nothing to do with Bradley's opinion of her and Gordon.

But as she was getting dressed to go downstairs, Meg heard the familiar crunch of tires against the shell driveway: the second group of guests had arrived. So she slid the letter into its envelope and set it on the nightstand. Later, she'd use the inn's photocopier to make a duplicate for Simon to read.

Aunt Ruby must trust him an awful lot to share her secret with him, she thought as she jogged downstairs to greet the new guests. *I may have had my doubts at the beginning, but now I trust him an awful lot, too.*

TWENTY-FOUR

An issue with a guest's bathroom sink kept Meg occupied until dusk. By then, she figured Simon had already returned to the cottage and put Cody and Abigail to bed, so she carefully folded the copy of Gordon's letter into thirds and slipped it into her back pocket. Then she hurried to where Simon was sitting beneath the pitch pines.

Leaning down, she kissed his cheek and whispered in his ear, "Hello, handsome. Am I ever glad to see you."

"Hey."

Because Simon barely acknowledged her greeting and he didn't return her kiss, Meg wondered if he was in pain. Had he reinjured his back? She settled into Abigail's chair and asked, "Is everything okay?"

"No, *nothing* is."

"Why, what happened?"

"*Islanders*, that's what happened." He shook his head in disgust. "You know, I was a good sport about it when Ruby's book club interrogated me about my plans for my inheritance. And I took it in stride when the lighthouse tour guide made those remarks about me building a monstrosity in Ruby's back yard, or when the local environmental society VP harangued me on the ferry all the way to Hyannis that day I went to Boston... But this time, they went too far."

"Oh, no, did someone at the party get on your case about your decision to sell the property?"

"They didn't get on *my* case, but Maddie and Sonny told the children that it's too bad that I'm selling their great-grandparents' cottage and that we have to go back to Delaware, because it means Abigail and Cody won't be able to come to their birthday party next year."

Meg winced. "Ugh. That must have been so upsetting—although I doubt Sonny and Maddie knew they were letting the cat out of the bag. They were probably just repeating something they'd overheard."

"No joke," Simon said, an edge of sarcasm in his voice. "I don't blame them—they're just kids. I blame the adults in their lives. Maddie and Sonny never should have overheard anyone talking about *my* decision in the first place. Can't anyone on this island mind their own business?"

Meg understood why Simon was upset, but she thought his comment was unfair. "Some of us are very discreet," she calmly reminded him. "And I think the reason the residents have been discussing the resort is because they care about what happens on the island. But you're right, like any other small, tight community, Hope Haven has its share of blabbermouths."

Simon folded his arms across his chest and jiggled his leg. "Yeah, well, one of those blabbermouths suggested—*in front of* Abigail and Cody—that since the kids seem to like it here I should consider relocating. Then someone else at the party jumped on the bandwagon. She went on and on about how carpenters are in high demand on Dune Island and the school system here is excellent. She told me I should sell our house in Hickory Falls and build a new one at Misty Point. Can you believe someone I hardly know thinks she has the right to pressure me like that?"

Yes, I can, because it sounds like what Chloe had suggested, before she lost interest in you, thought Meg. She agreed, "That's pretty gutsy, but she probably only meant to be helpful."

"Helpful? *Ha*. After she planted that idea in the kids' heads, it was all they could think about. When we got home and I told them that moving to Misty Point wasn't an option, Abigail cried so hard that she got sick to her stomach, and Cody went into total meltdown mode because he couldn't find his blankie again. He threw himself on the floor and now he's got an egg-sized lump on the back of his skull."

"Poor Abigail and Cody." Meg wished she could've been there to help Simon comfort them after the party.

He leaned forward and buried his face in his hands. "The last time I saw my daughter this devastated was when my mom moved to Arizona."

"That must have been so hard for her. And now she's probably upset about leaving her new friends." Meg stroked his back. "I know how happy she was about having a couple of girl playmates here."

"She's not just sad about leaving her friends. She's sad about leaving the beach and the cottage, too—and so is Cody." Simon dropped his hands and sat up straight again.

"Sounds like they've really fallen in love with Misty Point," she remarked, quoting her great-aunt's sentiment. Meg only meant it as a sympathetic reflection, but her words sparked an emphatic response from Simon.

"Of *course* they love it here. What's not to love? It's summer and we've been on vacation the entire time. But this isn't our real life. It isn't our real *home*," he snapped. "Our real home is in Hickory Falls—it's the house their mother decorated."

Even though she felt a little stung by how sharply he'd replied, Meg understood the reason for Simon's intense reaction. She herself had such a strong emotional attachment to her great-aunt's inn that she could imagine Simon's connection to his family's home—and all its associations with his wife—was even stronger. *His kids might not feel quite the same way, but they don't remember Beth as well as Simon does. And children tend to focus more on the moment, and on what's right in front of them, than on the past.*

Pushing aside her own feelings, she consoled him, "Once they return to your home, they'll see and experience everything they love about living there. They'll be so thrilled to be back in familiar surroundings they'll probably never want to leave again." *Which is too bad, because I'd love it if you all came back here,* Meg thought wistfully.

"I hope so, but right now they can't get past the idea of selling the house in Delaware and moving here. I explained that the cottage isn't winterized, but they said they don't care, they'll wear hats and mittens indoors, and that Cody can use his blankie as a scarf instead of as a... blankie," he said. The children's fantastical plan might have been amusing to Meg if only Simon wasn't so dejected.

He continued, "What did I expect? This is what happens when you spend the entire summer essentially camping in a two-room cottage, without any daily routine except beach-combing when the tide's out and swimming when it's in. I don't even know how I'm going to convince them to wear clothes and shoes instead of swimsuits and sandals again, much less make them adhere to a school and work schedule. And if they're this sad now, what's going to happen on the day we pack up and leave?"

"Most children are resilient, especially yours." Meg asserted, "It might take a little time, but they'll adjust."

"That's just it—they're going to have to go through another adjustment. My goal was to provide more stability in their lives, not more upheaval."

"I understand it's painful to see them so unhappy right now, but you *have* given them stability, Simon. The kind of stability they need most—your constant loving presence in their lives," she said encouragingly. "You've also given them a vacation they'll never forget."

"Some vacation. It's going to end in tears." He rubbed his temples in slow circles. "Makes me second-guess whether we ever should've come to Dune Island in the first place."

"For their sake, I'm glad you did. The very fact they don't want to leave shows what a wonderful time they've had," countered Meg. "And selfishly, I'm grateful you brought them here. Otherwise, I never would've met them—or you. And vice versa."

When she gave him an affectionate nudge, Simon stiffened and pulled away, which hurt her feelings, but not as much as what he said next.

"That's true, but unfortunately, I still wonder if coming to Misty Point was a mistake." Like a blow to the chest, his words took Meg's breath away. Oblivious, he kept talking. "I can see now the children are too vulnerable. They weren't ready for such a big change. It was too soon."

Fighting tears, Meg swallowed hard. "Is it..." She could barely bring herself to complete the question, but it was too important not to ask. "Is it possible that maybe *you're* the one who wasn't ready for such a big change? I don't mean coming here. I mean, is there some part of you that feels like getting involved with me was a mistake? That it was too soon?"

She wanted him to leap to his feet, clasp his hands over his heart and passionately deny it. During the silent pause that followed, the lighthouse flashed five times, which Meg knew meant twenty-five seconds had passed, but it seemed like forever before Simon answered her question.

"It-it's complicated," he stuttered. "I'm sorry, Meg."

"So am I." She stood up, slid the folded sheet of paper from her back pocket, and dropped it on Simon's lap. "I... had something I wanted to tell you. I finally figured out my great-aunt's secret, and I promised her I'd share it with you. It's all explained in this letter from Gordon."

Originally, she'd intended to say a lot more than that, but now Meg was on the brink of sobbing, so she turned and fled to the inn, allowing her great-aunt's secret to speak for itself.

Meg wasn't angry at Simon for continuing to mourn the loss of his wife. Nor was she angry at him for not wanting to sell their family's house in Hickory Falls. She wasn't angry that Simon wasn't ready to be in a romantic relationship, either.

She was angry that he hadn't *recognized* he wasn't ready, even after she'd specifically questioned him about it. And she was crushed that he'd proved Josh right: Meg *shouldn't* have gotten involved with a grieving widower because he ended up breaking her heart.

She lifted her phone from the nightstand. Her eyes were so swollen from crying she could barely read the time: 6:53 a.m. *I'd better go make coffee and unlock the doors for the day*, she thought.

A few minutes later, when she was in the kitchen eating toast, she heard the porch door bang shut. *Someone must have taken a walk out to the beach already.* Even though she didn't feel sociable, Meg went to say good morning to the guest.

But it was Cody who had come inside the inn. He was wearing his blankie around his bare chest, which was an understandable regression, considering yesterday's chaos. At least his voice was audible when he asked, "Is Abigail hiding in here?"

Assuming they'd been playing a game, Meg answered, "No. I just unlocked the doors a few minutes ago, and you're the only one I've heard come in. But let's take a look around." They padded down the hall calling Abigail's name softly so they wouldn't wake the guests. The little girl wasn't in the laundry room, the bathrooms, the living room, or the den. "I don't think she'd go upstairs. She must be near the cottage somewhere, maybe in the back?"

"No, I looked three times. And in our minivan, too."

"Hmm. Let's go around to the side of the inn to see if she's hiding beneath the hydrangea bushes."

As they stepped out of the porch, Simon came striding across the back lawn. His feet were bare, and he was wearing a white undershirt and what appeared to be pajama bottoms.

"Hello, Simon," Meg said stiffly when she reached the bottom stair.

"Meg." His greeting was equally rigid. "I want Abigail to come back to the cottage immediately."

"Right. I'll let her know as soon as we find her." Meg started toward the other side of the inn, but Simon pulled on her arm.

"Isn't she inside, hiding?"

She shook free of his grasp. "Obviously not, or we wouldn't still be searching for her. We're going to look beneath the hydrangea bushes."

Simon cupped his hands around his mouth and hollered in the direction of the side yard, "Abigail! Abigail!"

Meg was surprised he was being so inconsiderate. "Shh! You'll wake the guests."

"What do I care?" he snarled. "My daughter is missing!"

"Missing?" Meg's stomach dropped. "I thought she was playing hide 'n' seek with Cody."

"Nuh-uh," mumbled Cody, as his father took off around the corner of the inn. "She ran away when Daddy was sleeping. She's sad."

"Oh, dear," clucked Meg, although she felt a rush of relief to hear that Abigail's disappearance had been deliberate, and not the result of something more sinister, like an abduction. *That poor, willful little girl—she's probably either crying or pouting behind a tree somewhere.*

She and Cody hurried to catch up with Simon by the hydrangea bushes, but he was already coming back. Wild-eyed, he announced, "She wasn't there and she wasn't in the front yard, either. Where else could she be?" He didn't give Meg a chance to answer before stamping past her. "Abigail! Abigail!"

"Wait, Simon, please. Listen," Meg pleaded, so he came to a stop near the patio. As she talked, he ducked down to peer into a basement window. "Abigail couldn't have gone very far. If she's upset, she probably found a private place to cry. She might be afraid to come out because she thinks she's in trouble."

"She *is* in trouble—*big* trouble!" Simon barked, nearly knocking over his son as he jumped to an upright position.

Meg recognized that Simon was panicked because he couldn't find his daughter, but his behavior was counterproductive. She calmly suggested, "How about if Cody and I go inside and search the inn from top to bottom, while you check the cottage and parking lot again? The garage should be locked, but you might want to give it a try, too. Let's meet back here when you're done and if we haven't found her, we'll decide what to do next."

Simon rushed toward the parking area and Meg and Cody re-searched the first floor of the inn. This time, they checked the closets, too, and they even scoped out the basement before going upstairs to check the hall bathrooms on the second floor. There wasn't any trace of her.

Meg considered knocking on the guests' doors to ask if they'd seen Abigail from their bedroom windows. But she figured before disturbing them, she'd wait to find out if her father had found her.

When Meg and Cody came downstairs, Simon was pacing the living room, and his face fell when he saw the two of them.

"Are you sure you looked everywhere? Did you ask the guests if they've seen her?"

"Not yet, because—"

He interrupted, half demanding and half pleading, "You've *got* to go ask them."

"Okay, I'll start knocking on their doors," Meg agreed. "While I'm doing that, maybe you should go look on the beach again. She may have slipped out there while we've been searching the inn."

"The beach? I haven't checked the beach. Abigail knows the rules. She'd *never* go to the beach without an adult." Simon gestured toward the picture window. "Besides, if she were out there, I'd be able to see her."

"Not necessarily. Try these." Meg lifted the binoculars from the bookshelf and gave them to him. As Simon scanned the horizon, Meg crouched down to speak to Cody, "I need to tell the guests what Abigail looks like from a distance, in case they saw her from their windows. Do you remember what she was wearing?"

"Her purple sneakers that light up when she walks and her purple swimsuit." He paused and then added. "And a shirt with a starfish on it."

"Is her shirt purple, too?"

He woefully shook his head. "I don't know the name of that color."

"Did Abigail take anything with her?"

Cody shrugged and covered his face with his arm, giving Meg the impression he was being evasive.

"She's not out there," Simon cut in, lowering the binoculars. "Why are you talking to Cody instead of asking the guests if they've seen her?"

Meg ignored him and addressed his son in a firm but quiet voice. "Cody, this is very, very important. Before Abigail ran away, did she say where she was going?"

"I can't tell you," he squeaked. "Or she won't let me come and play with her."

Bending down, Simon pulled Cody's arm away from his face. "Cody Bradley Harris, I want you to take me to your sister right now."

"But I can't," he whined. "I don't know where she is."

"You just said you do—and I'll give you until the count of five to bring me to her." Simon started counting, but Meg recognized that Cody had answered truthfully. Abigail must have told him where she was going, but her brother hadn't understood where that place was.

"You know what, Cody? You don't have to bring us to Abigail. If you tell us the name of where she went, your daddy and I will know how to find her," she said gently. When he still didn't answer, Meg prompted again, "Where did she say she was going?"

He sniffed a few times and then he confessed, "To Timbuktu."

Exasperated, Simon dropped his son's arm. "Enough's enough." He warned Meg, "If you're too afraid to disturb the guests, then *I'll* go do it."

She stood up so fast she felt dizzy. "But... When we went on the lighthouse tour, Lou told Abigail we could see as far as Timbuktu from the lantern room." For the first time since hearing that Abigail was hiding, Meg herself felt too alarmed to worry about keeping Simon calm. "What if she thinks Timbuktu is another island? She wouldn't try to swim there, would she?"

Simon answered by dropping the binoculars and charging out of the inn. Cody followed, and then Meg, but she overtook them both halfway through the meadow, the sound of her footsteps and heartbeat drumming in her ears. Scanning the beach for any sign of the child's telltale hair, she shot straight past the lighthouse. *Abigail! Abigail!* She silently screamed. *Where are you?*

"There she is!" Cody shouted from behind her.

Meg glanced over her shoulder to see him pointing at the lighthouse. The little girl was sitting on the bench halfway around the curve, swinging her legs, her arms crossed over her chest and a small lavender suitcase standing upright near her feet.

"Abigail!" Meg gasped her name. She slowed and changed direction, giving the girl a gigantic wave, just as Simon caught up to Cody and spotted his daughter.

"Abigail Elizabeth Harris! What did I tell you about going to the beach without a grownup?" he thundered. "I want you to march yourself back to the cottage right this minute."

Cody rushed forward and grasped her suitcase handle to carry it for her, but she swatted him away. "Don't touch that, Cody. I'm not going to live with you and Daddy anymore. When the lighthouse man comes, I'm going on the pontoon boat far, far away."

Cody immediately burst into tears and wrapped his arms around his sister's legs. "Please don't go far, far away, Abigail. Please don't go to Timbuktu."

"No one's going anywhere except back to the cottage," Simon demanded, towering over both of them. But when he tried to take them in hand, Cody wouldn't let go of his sister's legs, and Abigail gripped the armrest.

She screamed. "I'm running away from you!"

"Don't go. Don't run away," wailed Cody.

Still panting from her sprint, Meg shuffled toward them and quietly suggested to Simon, "Do you mind if I rest a minute on this bench with Abigail, and you and Cody can rest a minute on the boys' bench, over there?"

Red-faced, with droplets of sweat on his upper lip, Simon

relented. "Yeah, okay. C'mon, Cody. Abigail's not going anywhere."

The little boy reluctantly allowed his father to lead him by the hand to the other bench, and Meg took a seat beside Abigail.

"I don't want to live with Daddy anymore," insisted the little girl, her lip thrust out. "He's being a big mean terrible daddy."

"From what I've seen, he's a wonderful daddy. What makes you say he's mean and terrible?"

"Because he doesn't want me to have any friends who are girls. Not Maddie or Charlotte or you," she answered, her voice quavering. "That's why he said we can't stay in the cottage even though it belongs to us. We have to go back to Hickory Falls and I *hate* living there."

Meg put her arm around the little girl's shoulders. "Why do you hate it?"

"Because the boys next door call me *Crabby Abbey* and they call my brother *Cootie*, not Cody. And because our house is big and echo-y." Tears bounced off her lashes as she blinked repeatedly. "And Grandma can't come to see us there anymore."

Meg's eyes filled, too, but she kept her voice even, acknowledging, "I understand why those things make you feel very sad. Sometimes, I feel like the inn is too big and echo-y without my aunt Ruby there."

"You do?"

"Yes. But I can think of something that would make you feel even sadder... And that would be if you ran away from your Daddy and Cody."

"I told Cody he could come with me," she sniveled. "But he wanted to stay and eat breakfast."

Meg supressed a laugh. "Whether your brother comes with you or not, if you ran far, far away, I know you'd miss your daddy so much you'd cry every single day. And so would he."

"No, he wouldn't. Daddy doesn't cry. Not ever. Not even

when his back hurts really, really, super bad," Abigail sincerely defended him. "He's very brave and strong."

"That's true. So maybe he wouldn't cry on the outside, but on the inside, he'd feel like crying like a baby all the time because he'd miss you so much." Meg was quiet, allowing her words to sink in, before suggesting, "Your daddy isn't making you go back to Hickory Falls because he doesn't want you to have girl friends, Abigail. He's taking you back there because it's where your school is and it's where he works—it's your home."

"But I want the *cottage* to be my home," she whined.

"I know you do." Sensing Abigail was less emotional, Meg switched to a firmer tone. "But your daddy is the grownup, so he needs to keep you safe, and healthy, and to protect you and to teach you things. *And* to make sure that whatever home he chooses is the best one for you and Cody. That's his job as your dad. Your job as his daughter is to listen to what he says... which means not running away when you're upset. And *definitely* not going to the beach without an adult."

"I *didn't* go to the beach without an adult," Abigail earnestly asserted. "I stopped when I got to the lighthouse."

"Right. But you still ran away and your dad was very worried about you." She discreetly gestured toward Simon and Cody, softly adding, "Look how sad you made your brother."

Abigail leaned forward to peek past Meg. "I don't want them to be sad."

"Then what do you think you can do about that?"

She scooted off the bench, loudly announcing, "Daddy and Cody, you don't have to worry or be sad anymore. I'm not going to run away ever again." She hurried over to them and Simon enveloped her in a hug. Cody wiggled his way into their embrace, too.

"Thank you," Simon mouthed to Meg, and she noticed that the children's very strong and brave father, who never, ever cried, had tears in his eyes.

TWENTY-FIVE

Meg deliberately called Linda when she knew Ruby was in physical therapy so she wouldn't have to speak directly to her great-aunt. As eager as she was to express her amazement about *The Wife of Oscar Claiborne*, she dreaded explaining why she didn't know how Simon had reacted to Gordon's letter. Nor could she bear to inform her great-aunt that he apparently was carrying through with his plans, regardless.

"Will you give her a very specific message?" Trying to be discreet, Meg requested, "Please tell her I finally read her copy of *To the Lighthouse*, and I shared it with Simon, too. I was very impressed and I'm looking forward to discussing it with her."

"Got it."

"Thanks. If you or a nursing assistant would set up the technology, I'd like to have a private video chat with her as soon as things slow down a little and I can get away from the inn. Does noon on Wednesday work?"

"No problem," agreed Linda. Then, before Meg could bring up the topic, she said, "I've given a lot of consideration to what will happen after Ruby's discharged. She won't be able to live on her own for a while, and she can't afford to move into an assisted living facility. Of course, she's chomping at the bit to get back to Misty Point. The lease on my apartment is coming up in a couple months, so I've decided to put my belongings in storage and stay with her until she's back on her feet again. She seems very pleased with the arrangement, and I think it'll work out nicely for both of us. It'll save me money on rent, and she needs me to help care for her and take her to appointments. We'll both enjoy each other's company."

"Oh, Linda, are you sure? Because that's *wonderful*," exclaimed Meg. "I've been so worried about what would happen when Aunt Ruby's discharged that I've considered asking the university to extend my leave so I could stay with her this fall. But I doubt they'd approve of that, and just between you and me, I really can't afford to take any more unpaid time off. It's such a relief to know you'll be living with Aunt Ruby for a while. I'll visit as often as I can on the weekends, so if you ever need a break, just let me know."

"Don't worry about that, sweetie. You've gone above and beyond for Ruby by taking care of the inn all summer, but you've got to focus on your own life now. I'm sure your friends and family and coworkers in Jersey are eager to have you back with them again."

"You're probably right," she acknowledged. But the truth was, aside from wanting to see her mom, her brother's family, and her closest friend, Meg had no compelling desire to return home. On the contrary, the very thought of going back to the university made her head hurt. How was she ever going to muster the enthusiasm required to help usher in a new class of students?

This was supposed to be my once-in-a-lifetime summer. I thought I'd return home rejuvenated and ready to date again, she brooded. *I'd say I'm right back where I started, but the truth is, I'm further away from feeling refreshed or ready to be in a rela-*

tionship now than I was in June. And Aunt Ruby's financial situation is worse off now than it was then, too.

Making matters seem even more futile was Meg's promise to her great-aunt that at the end of the season, she would reshelve all the books she'd stored in the garage. *Oh well*, she thought. *At least it'll keep me too busy to dwell on anything else.*

Yet as hard as she tried, Meg couldn't stop herself from wondering whether Simon had read Ruby's letter from Gordon and what, if anything, he'd thought about it. But she'd been avoiding him since Abigail had run away, and he clearly wasn't seeking her out, either. Which put her in an awkward position regarding her promise to watch the kids while he went to Boston to finalize the deal with the developer.

He hasn't even told me what time he's leaving yet, she thought. *But I'm not going to beg him for information. He'll let me know when he's ready. Or he can just bring Abigail and Cody to the inn at the last minute. I might not want to see* him, *but I can't wait to see the children again!*

On Tuesday as Meg was eating a late breakfast, Ava poked her head into the kitchen. "Hello."

"Hi, Ava. I'm surprised to see you here on your day off."

"I forgot my hoodie on the coat rack last week, and I figured I'd better grab it before I take Cody and Abigail on a hike across the meadow—it's kinda nippy today."

Meg froze with her spoon midway to her mouth. "You're taking Cody and Abigail to the beach?"

"No, not as far as the beach. Simon doesn't want them near the water without him there. We're just going to the lighthouse."

Meg set down her fork and clarified, "You mean you're taking care of them this afternoon?"

"Yeah. Simon has a meeting in Boston, so he asked me to

babysit. Not just for the afternoon, either—he'll be gone until eight or nine this evening," the young woman replied. "Which is great, 'cause I really need the extra cash."

"Mm, sounds like a win-win," Meg replied with a feeble smile. "I'm sure Cody and Abigail will have a lot of fun with you."

"I hope so! See you later."

Feeling too upset to eat, Meg covered her bowl of fruit and yogurt and placed it in the fridge. *I can't believe Simon changed his mind about me watching Cody and Abigail today. Just because we aren't seeing each other anymore doesn't mean he should cut me out of his children's lives!*

Trying to give him the benefit of the doubt, Meg supposed Simon might have assumed that after their last discussion, she no longer wanted to do any favors for him. *Still, he could've at least talked about it with me. But maybe it's better this way,* she rationalized. *Maybe it'll help Cody and Abigail get used to not being with me, so it won't be such a big adjustment for them when they return to Delaware...*

Suddenly faced with a free afternoon, Meg began to prepare the inn for autumn. But throwing herself into carrying bins of Ruby's books from the garage and reshelving them in the den was no distraction from her inescapable sense of loneliness.

Later that evening, Meg drove back to the inn after an unsatisfying trip to town. Shopping and eating dinner out had been another failed attempt to take her mind off her heartache. Now, even though it was nearly dark, she couldn't wait to get back to the inn to walk on the beach completely alone.

When she pulled into the parking area, Meg spotted Ava's car, but not Simon's. Had he failed to secure a reservation on the ferry again? *I wish he'd get stranded in Boston for the rest of the week*, she fantasized peevishly. *Then Abigail and Cody could stay with me at the inn.*

She hurried inside to change into warmer clothes and check to see if the guests needed anything, before scurrying down the porch steps. Using her phone to light the path, she trekked across the meadow. Yet even wearing a jacket, she felt too cold to continue all the way to the beach, so she stopped at the lighthouse and took a seat on the bench.

The surf was little more than a white curl, briefly made brighter by the twirling light overhead. Meg hugged her arms to her chest and closed her eyes as the breeze caressed her face. *Once the resort opens, it'll probably feel as crowded here as it does in town*, she mused. *But tonight, I'm glad I have it all to myself.*

The thought had barely crossed her mind when she heard approaching footsteps. Opening her eyes, she peered at the shadowy figure and immediately recognized his posture.

"Can I sit here?" Simon asked.

"It's all yours." She stood up. "I was just leaving."

"Wait, there's something I want to tell you."

"If it's that Ava was going to watch Abigail and Cody today, instead of me watching them like we'd planned, I already got the memo, thanks." She started to walk away, but he tugged her fingers.

"I can explain. Please, Meg?" he pleaded.

So she sat down and he did, too. Flattening her hands beneath her legs to warm them, she stared straight ahead at the water. "Okay, go ahead. Talk."

"I, uh, I read the letter Gordon wrote to Ruby," he began. "I was floored to find out she's the author of *The Wife of Oscar Claiborne*. It's an awesome book."

"Yes, it is."

"And I was blown away by how generous Ruby was to Gordon and Sarah." He chuckled nervously. "It's ironic, but I guess my father was right, in a way. Gordon didn't leave Ruby the house simply because she took care of my grandmother for one summer. He left it to her because she also saved his career and prevented them from being evicted."

"True, but the way I see it, your father was far more wrong than right about my great-aunt," Meg defensively retorted.

Simon immediately agreed. "That's for sure. I was only trying to emphasize how generous Ruby had been to my grandmother and Gordon. But yeah, my dad was *dead* wrong about what kind of person she was. He was wrong about Gordon, too." Out of the corner of her eye, she could see him shaking his head. "Sometimes, my father could be a real jerk, to be honest, and lately I've realized I'm becoming just like him."

Softening a little, Meg objected, "I think that's a stretch."

"No, it's true." Simon heaved a sigh. "I didn't even recognize it about myself until I read what Sarah said about my father's bitterness being like a disease. I've allowed the death of someone I love to negatively affect my life and my relationships, just like he did."

"You don't seem like you're someone who feels angry all the time."

"No, but I do feel guilty. And as my grandmother Sarah said, it's insidious. My guilt has been like this... this *undercurrent* that's affected some major areas of my life—and my children's lives," he confessed. "That's why I got so bent out of shape when someone at the party suggested I could sell our house in Delaware."

"It makes sense you wouldn't want to move from your home. Not only did Beth design the interior, but you must have so many family memories of being together there."

"On some level, yes, I do. But a bigger part of me kind of loathes that house, even more than Abigail apparently does," he said with a grim laugh.

"Why?"

"Where do I start? It cost far more than it's worth—and certainly more than we could afford. It's located in a gated community, which I resent on principle, and the neighbors are snobs. And even though the house is huge and Beth decorated it beautifully, the yard is the size of a postage stamp," he said. "Our house was the only major source of conflict between her and me. But she felt it was beneficial to live there to attract a certain level of clientele, so we bought it shortly before Abigail was born—and then we argued about it for the next four years."

Meg felt it would be intrusive to comment, so she remained silent.

After a pause, Simon continued, "Considering how I felt about the house, it seems like I would've been eager to move after Beth died. But I couldn't. I just felt too guilty, because I'd resented it so much when she was alive." He angled sideways to look directly at her. "That doesn't make much sense, does it?"

Meg nodded. "Actually, it kind of does."

"My guilt has also affected my relationship with you. I'm sorry I hurt you, Meg."

It took a while for her to answer, and she chose her words carefully. "I've never lost a spouse, so I can't imagine how excruciating that has been for you, especially because Beth was also the mother of your children." She focused her attention on her knees, trying to keep her voice steady. "And I'd never, ever ask you to *forget* about her. But I admit, I wish you had figured out that you weren't ready to start a new relationship before we got involved, even though I understand *why* you're not. Everyone grieves at a different pace. I'd never want to rush you through that process."

"I loved my wife with everything in me, and I'll always cherish the life we built together, and my memories of her... but I *am* ready to start a new relationship," Simon insisted, placing his hand on her shoulder. Meg could feel his warmth through the fabric of her jacket, and she half wished she could nestle against his chest, and he'd enfold her in a hearty, comforting embrace.

Instead, she said, "I'd like to believe you, Simon. It's just that I'm afraid your actions have shown how ambivalent you are."

"I'm sorry that's how I behaved the other day, and I don't blame you if you feel like you can't trust me again. But like I said, Gordon's letter made me realize I've been acting like my father. When really, I should be more like my son."

Meg didn't see the connection. "Like *Cody*?"

"Yup. That boy isn't even five years old yet, so if *he* can give up his security blanket—well, not counting a temporary relapse —then I figure, *I* can give up the things that are holding me back, too."

She chuckled. "No more tether?"

"No more tether," Simon echoed. "I'm breaking free of guilt. I'm giving up the house in Hickory Falls."

Meg couldn't tell if he was still speaking metaphorically. "What do you mean you're giving it up?"

"I'm selling it. We're moving here. I told the developer today the deal was off."

"You *didn't*!" Meg drew back and squinted at him. "Did you?"

"I sure did. And I've got two black eyes to prove it," Simon joked. "He was *not* happy with me, but I figure if I could survive the ire of Ruby's book club, I'll survive his reaction, too. I imagine a lot of Dune Islanders who were counting on the resort to boost the local economy or provide jobs aren't going to be happy with me, either. But at least in the short term, I'll be hiring local residents to help me build our new house as quickly as we can."

"But-but-but backing out of the sale is such a sudden change of plans," Meg stuttered. Not that she wasn't thrilled—it was exactly what she'd always hoped would happen—but she couldn't quite take it in. "You changed your mind all because of what you read in Gordon's letter?"

"Yeah, it was a huge part of what made me seriously reconsider going through with the sale. Like I said, my grandmother Sarah's observations about my father were very eye-opening about my own mindset and behavior. And when I read that it was essentially her dying wish for me to return to Dune Island with my children one day, it hit me right here." Simon patted his chest above his heart.

Aunt Ruby knew it would. I'll bet that's why she wanted Simon to read the letter for himself, Meg realized. *It wasn't only that she wanted him to know she'd never had an affair with Gordon. It was also because she sensed that reading Gordon's narrative—which included a direct quote from Sarah—would have a bigger impact on Simon than anything Ruby herself could tell him.*

His voice raspy, Simon added, "But the real clincher was when my daughter ran away and I thought... Well, let's just say, when your child disappears, even for thirty minutes, it puts everything else in perspective." He paused to clear his throat. "As you pointed out to Abigail, it's my job to choose whatever home is best for my children. So I'm choosing to make Misty Point our permanent home."

"Wow. That's absolutely fantastic. Do Abigail and Cody know about this yet?"

"Yes. That's why I asked Ava to watch them this afternoon. I knew the moment Abigail saw you, she'd spill the beans and I wanted to tell you for myself when I could talk to you alone about other things..." He tentatively asked, "Like if you'd consider being my girlfriend again?"

She felt her cheeks grow hot; at forty years old, she still blushed like a teenager to be asked to be someone's *girlfriend*. Given all he'd just shared, Meg no longer had any qualms that he was ambivalent, but she questioned, "You're aware I have to return to New Jersey in less than two weeks, aren't you?"

"Yeah, but the kids and I will need to travel back and forth between here and Delaware until I get everything squared away with selling the house in Hickory Falls, so we could meet up with you then. Maybe you'll come this way to visit Ruby on weekends when you can, too, and there's always next summer," he said, impressing Meg with his foresight and planning skills. "I know a long-distance relationship can be challenging, but I think we can make it work."

Inwardly smiling at his use of the word *relationship*, Meg answered, "I like the sound of that."

"Really?" Simon's grin shone in the dark. "You have no idea how happy I am that you're willing to give me another chance."

He leaned in and his mouth met hers in such a luscious, lingering kiss it made Meg shiver. So he bundled her in his arms, and as she snuggled against his chest, they watched the lighthouse brush its ivory ray across the water too many times to count.

Simon and Meg sat in her car behind the library, their heads only inches apart. Instead of using her phone, she'd brought her laptop with her and propped it up on the dashboard so her great-aunt could easily see them both during their video call.

Ruby was delighted that Simon had joined them. "You look well rested," she told him, as if he were the one who'd been recovering instead of her.

"Thanks, I am," he answered with a friendly chuckle. "That's what being a beach bum does for a person."

He asked about Ruby's health and progress, and then regaled her with an account of Abigail and Cody's latest antics. Meg was enchanted by his effortless rapport with Ruby, despite her great-aunt's communication difficulties: it was such a change from how detached he'd been when he first met her.

But Meg couldn't wait to get to the heart of the matter, and as soon as there was a break in their chitchat, she piped up, "Simon and I both read the letter from Gordon and we're so impressed that you wrote *The Wife of Oscar Claiborne*, Aunt Ruby."

"Yeah, it's an amazing book. I was hooked from the first page," Simon agreed.

Meg added, "I always knew how much you love to read, but I never suspected you were a writer, too."

"I'm not." Ruby held up a finger. "One book."

Meg translated what she meant, telling Simon, "Gordon used to quote the saying that everyone has at least one good book in them, one good story to tell. And I think she means that *The Wife of Oscar Claiborne* was the only book she had inside her, right, Aunt Ruby?"

"Right," she confirmed, nodding. "And Gordon helped me."

Meg didn't need to explain to Simon that Ruby was saying she was only able to write the book because Gordon helped her. While she accepted that modesty was a fundamental part of her great-aunt's character, Meg objected, "Gordon may have helped you write the book, but I recognized your voice throughout the story. You're so talented."

"Yes, you are," Simon enthusiastically agreed. "And you're extremely giving. My father wasn't able to fathom why Gordon was so generous to you, but you were the one who was unbelievably generous to Gordon and my grandmother."

"We were *friends*," Ruby firmly declared, and Meg knew what she meant was that the reason she had helped Sarah and Gordon, and they in turn had given her their summer home, was because they were close friends. And that's what close friends did for one another.

But Simon seemed to think Ruby was emphasizing that her

relationship with Gordon was solely platonic. "I know, and I'm so sorry about the accusation my father made," he apologized. "But I hope you believe that his opinion had nothing to do with why I wanted to sell the property to a developer."

Then he poured out his heart to Ruby, telling her all about his financial struggles, his concern for his children, and his guilt. As he spoke, Meg shifted sideways. Watching him interact with her great-aunt, she marveled at how vulnerable he was being, and from the way Ruby pressed her hand to her chest, it was clear that she was moved by Simon's openness, too.

After telling her his story, Simon turned the conversation to Ruby's letter again. "You kept your secret for all those years. Considering my father's behavior, it's amazing you'd feel comfortable enough to—"

Ruby waved to interrupt him and then she enunciated, "I trust you."

"Thank you. But still, I realize telling me was a huge risk and I'm overwhelmed and grateful that you'd share your secret with me."

"You needed it." Ruby's simple answer confirmed Meg's suspicion: her great-aunt had never intended to stop Simon from selling the property for her own sake, or for the sake of her business. Recognizing he was struggling, she'd wanted him to reconsider for his and the children's benefit, and she'd believed sharing Gordon's letter would persuade him to change his mind.

Meg noticed his Adam's apple bob up and down as he swallowed twice before speaking; obviously Simon felt emotional. "You're right, I did need to hear it."

He launched into an admission of how Gordon's letter—and Sarah's words—had profoundly affected him. Simon concluded by telling Ruby that he'd changed his mind about selling the property after all. "The only building being constructed on the land will be a house for Abigail, Cody, and me. We're going to become permanent, year-round Misty Point residents—and your new neighbors."

Ruby's mouth dropped open and she was speechless for so long that Meg might have been concerned something was wrong, except her eyes were shining. Finally, she exclaimed, "That's splendiferous!"

Not only did Meg share her great-aunt's delight about Simon's news, but she was thrilled that Ruby's vocabulary seemed to be returning to her.

Nothing about this summer went as planned, she reflected, blinking away joyful tears. *But* splendiferous *is the perfect word to describe how everything turned out.*

EPILOGUE

"The dinner Linda is making smells delicious." Meg plonked down on the sofa beside her great-aunt, who had just removed her earbuds and set aside her e-reader. Ever since Ruby's convalescence in the rehab facility, she'd become hooked on listening to audio books, and now she owned almost as many sets of headphones and earbuds as reading glasses. Meg added, "I can't wait to have a slice of the peach pie you and Abigail baked."

Even though Ruby had regained moderate use of her right arm and hand, she'd invited Abigail to the inn earlier that morning, a Saturday, to help roll the crust and prepare the filling. The little girl was delighted to learn her great-grandmother Sarah's recipe, and to be included in the "girls only" preparations for Meg's birthday festivities.

"You and Simon could have gone out alone," Ruby said. "Linda and I would have been glad to watch the children."

"Thanks, but I can't think of a better way to celebrate than by taking a walk to the lighthouse and then eating dinner here, just the six of us." Meg peered across the meadow toward the Cape-style house some one hundred yards beyond the cottage, reflecting on how dynamic the past six months had been for everyone.

Simon's house in Delaware had sold within four days of being put on the market. His family's new house at Misty Point wasn't habitable yet, but it had been a mild winter, so construction was scheduled to wrap up in the spring. Simon and the children had lived in the cottage until the weather turned cold in late October.

Ruby had wanted the trio to stay with her and Linda. She felt as if it was the least she could offer after he'd installed so many safety features in the inn, converted the den into a second accessible bedroom, and arranged for an upgrade to the Wi-Fi service. However, Simon was too concerned that Cody and Abigail's energy level wasn't conducive for Ruby's recuperation, and he'd rented an off-season condo in town for the winter. But he and the children frequently popped in to visit and to ask if he could be of assistance to the two older women.

Shortly after returning to New Jersey at the end of the summer, Meg had an epiphany about a way to help her great-aunt earn extra income during the off-season that wouldn't be too taxing for her or Linda. She had run the idea past Simon, first.

"What if Aunt Ruby rented out rooms to writers who need a quiet, inspirational setting?" she'd proposed. "I could organize all the details remotely, and Chloe might appreciate having year-round employment doing the housekeeping."

Simon thought the idea was brilliant, and he offered the use of the cottage during the warmer months, too. "It would be a great way to honor Gordon's memory."

From there, Meg's idea had gathered momentum, and with Ruby's approval, she'd created a program for writers' retreats and conferences at the inn throughout the off-season, aptly named, "The Writing Pad."

Quickly realizing that as the program grew, it would require a full-time director, Meg had arranged to resign from her position at the university in late January. She'd permanently moved to Dune Island just last week, so she could oversee the program when it launched in March, as well as manage the inn through the summer months.

I can't believe how much has changed since my last birthday, she thought, turning to catch a glimpse of her great-aunt, who was gazing toward the lighthouse.

"What are you thinking about, Aunt Ruby?" she asked.

"How happy Sarah would be that Simon and his children live here now," she replied. Although she spoke slower and used a simpler syntax, her speaking abilities had vastly improved since her stroke. "And Gordon would be happy there will be writers using the cottage again."

Meg smiled as she stood up to get her coat; she could hear car doors closing.

"Hi, everybody," she greeted Simon, Cody, and Abigail when she met them outside.

"Happy Birthday," they chorused.

"We have a surprise for you," Cody announced.

His sister elbowed him. "You're not supposed to tell. It's a secret, remember?"

"Oh, good, I love secrets," Meg said, with a facetious wink at Simon.

Because it was almost 5:00 and the sun set at 5:15, they strode briskly to the lighthouse. All four of them squeezed onto the same bench, snuggling together for warmth, as the sun frosted the puffy winter clouds with pastel pink, and then ducked beneath the horizon.

Although Meg would have liked to linger, savoring the beauty of the moment she'd been anticipating all day, Simon abruptly rose from the bench. Just as suddenly, his knee gave way and Meg's first thought was that his back was in spasm. But then Cody and Abigail imitated him, kneeling on one knee beside him in the sand. Was this a birthday game, part of the surprise?

They exchanged glances and Simon nodded. In unison, the trio enthusiastically exclaimed, "We love you very much, Meg, and there's something we want to ask you..."

Simon took her gloved hand in his. "Will you be my wife?"

"Will you be our stepmother?" Abigail and Cody asked simultaneously.

The last time Meg's heart had fluttered this fast, she'd been riding in the back of an ambulance. She dropped to her knees, too.

"Yes, I'll be your wife," she uttered, kissing Simon, first. "I love you."

Then she embraced Abigail and Cody, giddily telling them both, "I love both of you too, and I can't wait to be your stepmother—the nice kind, not like the one in *Cinderella*."

She laughed at her own joke, but Abigail frowned and urged her father, "Dad, what about the you-know-what?"

"I was so nervous I forgot!" He fumbled in his pocket, before producing a box, which he opened to reveal a square-cut diamond ring with an amethyst on each side. Its band was the same silver shade of the water behind him.

Meg's hands trembled so much that Simon had to help her remove her glove so he could slip it onto her finger. Holding her arm out in front of her, she peered at the ring, speechless, but Abigail piped up.

"The middle diamond is from Daddy, and the littler ones on the sides are from me and Cody, see?" she asked. "They're purple because that's your favorite color, and because it's your birthstone. Do you like it?"

"I *love* it," Meg answered the little girl, but she was looking into Simon's sparkling green eyes as she said it.

Clearly bored talking about jewelry, Cody hopped to his feet and announced that he was hungry. "Can we go to the inn and eat now?" he asked, not waiting for an answer before disappearing around the curve of the lighthouse.

"Yeah, c'mon," Abigail urged the adults, following her brother's lead. "I can't wait to show Ms. Ruby and Ms. Linda the ring we got for Meg. They're going to be so surprised."

"I doubt it. Ruby has always been able to read me like a book," Simon said wryly as he helped Meg to her feet. "I've been even happier than usual lately, so she probably suspects something's going on."

"Come to think of it, she did mention several times that if you and I preferred to go out alone this evening, she and Linda would watch the children. So, you're right, she might have had a hunch you were going to propose." Meg teased, "I wouldn't be surprised if right now the two of them are watching us from the picture window."

"In that case, we'd better not keep them in suspense about how you answered." He stepped into plain view of the inn, drew her toward him, and gave Meg an exaggeratedly exuberant kiss. Turning to face the window, he raised both hands overhead, making the thumbs-up sign and causing her to giggle.

Then Simon and his family—which soon would include Meg, too—meandered back across the meadow, just as Sarah had envisioned so many years ago.

A LETTER FROM KRISTIN

Dear reader,

I'm so pleased you chose to read *The Secret of Ruby's Lighthouse*—thank you! My hope is that you were completely absorbed in Meg's story.

If you did enjoy this book, and want to keep up to date with all my latest releases, just sign up at the following link. Your email address will never be shared and you can unsubscribe at any time.

www.bookouture.com/kristin-harper

Reader feedback is incredibly rewarding to me and it's crucial in helping new readers discover one of my books for the first time. So if you'd like to share what you enjoyed most about *The Secret of Ruby's Lighthouse*, I'd be very grateful if you could leave a short review.

In addition to sharing a review, you can also get in touch through my website, where you'll find my email address. It's such fun to hear from readers and I always try to reply as soon as possible.

I truly appreciate your feedback and reviews. And thanks again for reading *The Secret of Ruby's Lighthouse*!

Best wishes,

Kristin

www.kristinharperauthor.com

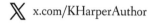 x.com/KHarperAuthor

ACKNOWLEDGMENTS

Thank you to my generous and loyal readers—your interest in this series is why I joyfully keep writing Dune Island novels! Thank you to my family and friends, for your enduring encouragement, support, and celebration throughout the entire process. And to Ellen, my editor, who never wavers in her enthusiastic helpfulness. She's one very talented member of a very talented team; a complete list of these publishing experts can be found on the following page. How fortunate am I to have such a formidable force of people committed to the quality and success of my books?! I'm beyond grateful.

PUBLISHING TEAM

Turning a manuscript into a book requires the efforts of many people. The publishing team at Bookouture would like to acknowledge everyone who contributed to this publication.

Commercial
Lauren Morrissette
Hannah Richmond
Imogen Allport

Data and analysis
Mark Alder
Mohamed Bussuri

Cover design
Emma Graves

Editorial
Ellen Gleeson
Nadia Michael

Copyeditor
Sally Partington

Proofreader
Elaini Caruso

Marketing
Alex Crow
Melanie Price
Occy Carr
Cíara Rosney
Martyna Młynarska

Operations and distribution
Marina Valles
Stephanie Straub
Joe Morris

Production
Hannah Snetsinger
Mandy Kullar
Jen Shannon
Ria Clare

Publicity
Kim Nash
Noelle Holten
Jess Readett
Sarah Hardy

Rights and contracts
Peta Nightingale
Richard King
Saidah Graham